A DREAMSCAPE WAF

PRICE OF VENGEANCE

KURT D. SPRINGS

Jessica
Adventure Awaits
Kurt D. Springs

Black Rose Writing | Texas

ISBN: 978-1-68513-362-7
LIBRARY OF CONGRESS CONTROL NUMBER: 2023943766
PUBLISHED BY BLACK ROSE WRITING
www.blackrosewriting.com

Printed in the United States of America
Suggested Retail Price (SRP) $22.95

Price of Vengeance is printed in Gentium Book Basic

*As a planet-friendly publisher, Black Rose Writing does its best to eliminate unnecessary waste to reduce paper usage and energy costs, while never compromising the reading experience. As a result, the final word count vs. page count may not meet common expectations.

PRAISE FOR
PRICE OF VENGEANCE

"From the cover to the opening pages, *Price of Vengeance* grabs the reader and takes them on a wild ride. Fasten your seat belts for this book."
    –S. J. Francis, author of *Shattered Lies*

"This action-adventure, military-science fiction, young adult novel is non-stop action from start to finish, interspersed with dreamscape and paranormal and romance sequences."
    –Charles Freedom Long, author of *Dancing with the Dead*

"Springs strikes an excellent balance between world creation and character development. He paints a vivid picture, while simultaneously developing and executing a strong plot."
    –Jessica Lauryn, #1 Bestselling Romance Author

This book is dedicated to the memory of my high school English teacher, Stanley M. Gorski (June 20, 1942–August 17, 2013). For over fifty years, students of Trinity High School in Manchester, New Hampshire, have learned to appreciate your words of wisdom on grammar, and your recitation of and commentary on William Shakespeare's Macbeth and on Beowulf. Rest in Peace, Mr. Groski.

PRICE
OF
VENGEANCE

New Olympia

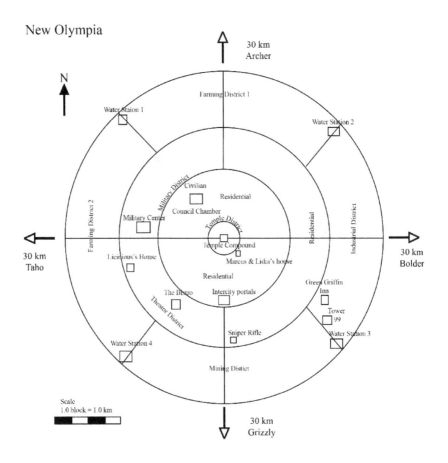

30 km
Archer

30 km
Taho

30 km
Bolder

30 km
Grizzly

N

Farming District 1

Water Station 1

Water Station 2

Civilian

Residential

Military District

Council Chamber

Military Center

Temple District

Temple Compound

Farming District 2

Licinious's House

Marcus & Lidia's house

Residential

Residential

Industrial District

The Bistro

Intercity portals

Green Griffin Inn

Theator District

Tower 99

Water Station 4

Sniper Rifle

Water Station 3

Mining District

Scale
1.0 block = 1.0 km

PROLOGUE

Lidia looked up as her husband entered the house.

"Marcus, what happened?" Then she saw the child in his arms. "Dear Creator! Is that—"

Marcus nodded. "Seámus and Deirdre are dead. We arrived just in time to save Liam."

The toddler whimpered and clung to him, still in shock.

"Mommy, Daddy?"

The two turned as their seven-year-old son, Randolf, enter the room. Randolf's eyes fell on the child. He looked confused.

"The bugs killed his parents, Randolf," Marcus explained. "Liam doesn't have anyone else to take care of him."

Randolf's face darkened, and he turned away. Lidia went to go after him.

"No, Lidia. It's as much a shock for him as it is for us."

"What about the other farmsteads?" Lidia asked.

"They seem okay for now," Marcus replied. "However, the pro-Founder's group still won't allow them into the city."

"The chitin will butcher them."

"I agree." Marcus sat down. "I sometimes wish I could just order the Council to do the right thing, but I've read history. When one person forces others to do what he thinks is right, democracies fall. The Council, however, has no say in who we adopt. At least we can save Liam."

Lidia took the child from Marcus. Tears came to her eyes. She looked up as she held the poor child to her. Standing at the door, Randolf frowned and left the room.

. . . . .

That night, Marcus and Lidia woke to the sound of Liam screaming in terror. Both leaped from their bed. The screams gave way to frightened whimpers as they raced down the hall. When they got to the boys' bedroom, Randolf was not in his bed. He had climbed into his old crib—which they had set up for the little one—and cradled Liam in his arms as the child clung to him.

Randolf looked up at his parents, his face full of concern. "I think he had a bad dream."

His parents looked relieved and, after a few moments, left them alone. Randolf glanced at Liam, who looked up at him with desperation in his eyes.

"Don't worry, Liam," Randolf whispered. "You're my little brother now. I'll take care of you."

CHAPTER 1

Twenty years later.
Liam strapped down his armor and slid a knife into his shoulder sheath. Around him, soldiers in the locker room donned armor and weapons. Some were heading to the interdimensional portals in the Military Center to prepare for transport to the city's defensive outposts. He considered his sniper rifle but decided to use the one at the outpost. Instead, he took his assault rifle—specialized enough to sharpshoot at medium range. After checking his ammo and power pack, he slung the rifle onto his back and slipped his pistol into its holster.

Liam heard familiar footfalls approaching the locker room and smiled.

"Hey, little brother!" Randolf began putting his gear into his locker, then cast a concerned look at Liam.

Other soldiers entered the locker room, having finished their tours at the outposts.

"Hi, Randolf." Liam strapped a larger blade to his thigh and straightened. He saw the expression on Randolf's face. "How are things at the outposts?"

"All quiet." Randolf frowned. "You volunteered for extra duty again?"

Liam sighed and nodded, looking up at Randolf. At two meters, Randolf stood a full head taller than Liam—like everyone else in the city. The handsomer of the two, Randolf had dirty blond hair and ice-blue eyes. He cut a fine figure, especially when he wore his dress uniform. Liam had a more gracile build—slim and lethally agile. He had dark brown, curly hair, but his eyes were gray. Their mother referred to them as steel-gray.

"I was hoping we could go into the plaza together this weekend." Randolf put his weapons in his locker. "Festival Day will be here soon. I hoped you would take part this year."

"You know I'm not comfortable with celebrations." Liam closed his locker. "I don't fit in, Randolf. You know that. People aren't comfortable with me. So, I guess it's mutual."

"You don't even try."

Liam did not want to argue. "I know what I'm good at, big brother. I can do my part to protect the city and keep the celebrants safe."

"Father—"

"Father understands." Liam turned back to his brother, reading the profound disappointment on his face. "Besides, if Councilor Licinious sees me, he'll make trouble."

Randolf clenched a fist. "Is that fool still talking about you?"

Liam suppressed a bitter laugh. "Which would be a relief. Usually, he's shouting about me." Liam scooped up his helmet and holstered his plasma blade. "I sometimes wonder if he'll ever accept the truth."

"Oh, I've been meaning to tell you. I met a priestess last month." Randolf stripped off his armor and stowed it in his locker. "We've been seeing quite a bit of each other. We are planning to meet again this evening—"

"Then you don't need me along." Liam grabbed his rucksack with a laugh.

"Actually," Randolf paused for a moment. "I do want you to meet her."

Liam stopped and gave his brother a thoughtful look. "This sounds serious. Have you introduced her to Mom and Dad?"

"I was thinking of telling them during Festival," Randolf replied. "Maybe she has a friend."

Liam shook his head. "I promised Jorge I'd cover for him so he can be with his family for Festival Day."

Randolf opened his mouth but shut it. Instead, he put his arm around Liam and squeezed his shoulder. "Take care, little brother." Liam turned and headed to the portal room for Taho sector.

Randolf watched Liam go. He stood staring after him, lost in thought.

"Problem, Lieutenant?"

Randolf turned with a start. "Sorry, Captain."

"Problem?"

"Just my brother." He grabbed the things he would need for his shower. "He knows those outposts better than his own bedroom at home."

Captain Targus nodded.

"I remember when Father first brought him home after his parents died," Randolf told him. "I was jealous at first. He was about two years old. That first night, we all had to rush to him because he started screaming. Afterward, I couldn't leave him. I guess I became his big brother that night."

"Can't get used to the fact he no longer needs protecting?" the captain asked.

Randolf gave a grim chuckle. "I guess he's grown up. I used to protect him when kids picked on him. He was always small. They used to wonder why he didn't blow away."

"What he lacks in size, he makes up for in agility," the captain noted, "and he's a lot stronger than people than people realize."

Randolf thought back to that incident in training when Licinious's son attacked Liam. Jochan did not live long enough to regret it. One more reason Liam brought out the worst in that old fool.

"Licinious has been calling him a threat ever since," Randolf thought out loud.

The captain looked up. "That matter with his son? The boy was a bully and not fit for military service. We made our views on the matter clear. While we wish Liam had just knocked him out, Jochan attacked when Liam was vulnerable—with an actual knife."

"Now Liam just hides at the outposts," Randolf slammed his locker closed. "When he should be..."

The captain nodded. "Like a light hidden under a basket."

"What's more, he's going to miss Festival. Again."

"I won't order him to stay here," the captain said. "It's his choice. If we try to force him, we could make things worse."

•   •   •   •   •

Liam stepped out of the portal. "Hi, Jorge."

Jorge looked back at his replacement.

"Hi, short stuff," he replied.

Liam knew Jorge well enough to know he meant no malice. A good-hearted man with the gift of laughter, Jorge was big, even by the standards of the Neo-Etruscans.

"Any trouble here at Taho?"

"Not a sign." Jorge put his binoculars away. "It seems as if the chitin have given up. Funny, we've had no sign of them in the past three years."

Liam switched his comm to the Military Center's headquarters. "Taho-331, on station at Taho number three outpost." He lifted his binoculars and did a quick scan. "Shield barrier force field between Taho and Archer functioning normally. Shield barrier force field between Taho and Grizzly functioning normally."

"Taho-331, HQ. Confirmed by Archer-077 and Grizzly-010. Barrier secure."

Liam switched back to local as they went into the outpost's locker room. He checked the ammunition locker and made sure everything was in order. "I wouldn't get my hopes up. They never leave. Once they get your scent, you can't escape—even in sleep."

"Still having nightmares after all these years." Jorge gave him a look of concern.

Liam looked at his friend and nodded. "At least Father taught me a trick to control my dreams."

They stepped back out onto the platform, and Liam did a quick check of the other four outposts of his sector. The engineers had constructed each against the cliff face with a semicircular wall around its portal and heavy weapon emplacement.

"Well," Jorge said, "I wish we still had aircraft capability. It would certainly give us a useful advantage."

"My father still wonders why we can't find what's generating that mysterious force field around the planet."

"How is Marcus?"

Liam was glad to change the subject. "He's doing well, considering the burden he carries as high councilor. How are Sharina and the kids?"

"Fine, all looking forward to Festival." Jorge looked at him. "You know, I have been lucky. For the past several years, you've taken my place when it's my turn to be on watch during a holiday. Sharina understands. Maybe I should take my watch this year, and you should celebrate Festival."

Liam smiled and shook his head. "Festival Day is a time for family, my friend. You have a wife and the twins. You should be with them."

"Just because you aren't married doesn't mean you don't have a family." Jorge shouldered his rucksack. "You've been a diligent soldier, Sergeant. Everyone who's worked with you knows you've a toughness that belies your size—brave and as ferocious as a bear-lizard. You work hard. You should play hard."

Jorge picked up his gear. "By the way, Sharina wants me to get you to join us for dinner. Justin and Sylvia want to meet their 'Uncle Liam.'"

Liam looked sharply at the man. "'Uncle?' What have you been telling those kids about me?"

"Only that you're one of the best." Jorge laughed. "If it weren't for you, they wouldn't have their daddy on holidays."

Jorge ducked through the portal, back to the city.

"Maybe I should request to stay out here permanently," Liam muttered to himself.

•   •   •   •   •

Randolf felt lucky to have met Teresina. The beautiful blonde was flirtatious and fun. She wore the robes of a priestess. Not full ceremonial attire, but garb that displayed her rank among the priestesses. This uniform also marked her as an empathic healer, should an emergency arise.

"Dinner before we go to the theater?" Randolf asked.

"Yes, I'd like that."

"I know a good bistro near here."

They held hands as they made their way through the crowded theater district until they reached the café and found a seat. Peter, the owner, came over to them.

"Good to see you again, Randolf," Peter called.

Teresina looked up at Randolf and smiled. Randolf felt a thrill go through him. Then he remembered Liam and felt troubled. He peered into a glass of water and tried to see his brother in it.

"Hey!" Teresina snapped her fingers.

Randolf looked up.

"You know, it's not polite to ignore your date." Teresina pretended to be cross. "Especially a priestess."

"I'm sorry." Randolf blushed. "I guess I am a little distracted."

Teresina's face softened with concern. "You want to talk about it?"

"It's my brother," Randolf replied. "Adopted brother, really. He is almost like a real brother to me."

"It sounds like you're very fond of him."

"Teresina!"

Both of them started at the greeting.

Two priestesses approached. "So, this is your soldier. We've been looking forward to meeting him."

Teresina gave Randolf an apologetic look. Randolf stood. Both priestesses were as attractive as Teresina. One wore the robes of a high priestess.

"Sorry to barge in. We decided to eat here and just saw you," the high priestess said.

Teresina gave them a sharp look. "Please join us. This is Randolf," she replied, trying to hide her annoyance. "Randolf, this is Kia," indicating the brunette before turning to her friend. "This is High Priestess Celinia."

Celinia had a slender frame and was not quite as tall as Teresina. She had a mane of red hair and eyes as green as emeralds.

"Randolf is worried about his brother. He was just about to tell me." Teresina gestured to her date.

Randolf gave her an uncomfortable look. She returned the stare, saying without words, "Trust me." Celinia picked up on the mood immediately. She took a seat and indicated Kia do the same as Randolf reclaimed his chair.

"Then, perhaps the Creator sent us here for a purpose other than embarrassing a friend on her date." Celinia's tone became official. "Please, start at the beginning."

Randolf grew uncomfortable with this turn of events but felt the need to talk. "I was just telling Teresina that while Liam is my adopted brother, I can't help thinking of him as my little brother."

"Liam is not a name of our people," Kia noted.

Randolf shook his head. "His family was part of the farmstead people who lived on the plains outside the city."

All three gave a visible shudder. The massacre of the farmstead folk over twenty years ago meant that the story was far from a happy one.

"My father—"

"High Councilor Marcus," Teresina supplied.

Randolf nodded. "He had dealings with them. I was very young. Sometimes, he used to bring me with him. They stood somewhat shorter than our people, but not stocky. Petite, I guess. I remember them as very kind, and the wife was a marvelous cook. Even my mother admired her ability."

Teresina smiled.

"They had a baby named Liam. I met him just after his birth. Being a typical five-year-old, I was curious but not impressed. He was too small to play with. Then, about two years later, Father received a call from them. He left right away. He came back with the baby. Chitin had attacked the farm. I didn't learn the details until I was older."

The three priestesses braced themselves. Chitin were a huge, colony insect that stood four to five feet tall and measured seven to eight feet long. They had formidable pincers, and when they reared up, they had sharp claws on their first pair of legs. They had appeared on the planet Etrusci forty-five years ago, and no one knew where they had come from. Then, forty years ago, they started attacking cities. Around the same time, aircraft began crashing on takeoff. By thirty years ago, they had abandoned all the other cities on the planet. New Olympia became the Neo-Etruscan's last bastion. The chitin decimated the planet's population. Those remaining had retreated to New Olympia.

"Father and some troops arrived to find the farm destroyed. While they killed the chitin, they were too late to save Liam's parents or the other farmhands. Father found Liam hidden in an outbuilding. After they buried the dead, Father brought Liam home. My parents adopted him legally. Since then, he's been my little brother."

They reached out and placed their hands on his. It comforted him.

"That night, he had a nightmare and woke up screaming. Any resentment I had of him intruding into my family died that night. How could I hold on to it? I appointed myself his protector."

"He couldn't ask for a better big brother." Kia smiled at him.

"He's always had trouble with nightmares. When he was older, Father taught him a trick for controlling his dreams. Liam doesn't wake up screaming anymore, but..." Randolf searched for words. "He became grim."

Celinia shook her head. "He will carry those emotional scars until the day he dies."

"I know," Randolf agreed. "Then he entered school. He was always a head shorter than everyone else his age and that marked him as different."

Teresina grimaced. "Children can be cruel, I know. Being his protector, you had something to say about it?"

Randolf gave a bitter laugh. "They sent me to the headmaster for fighting more times than I could count. Headmaster Metie understood but tried to impress on me that there were better ways. Father had a friend in the military—an expert at exotic fighting arts. When we were old enough, he offered to give us lessons. We both enjoyed those lessons. Liam took to it more quickly than I did. Once fully trained, I think he would have protected me from the bullies. The next time anyone tried to bully him was the last."

The three chuckled.

"You know Councilor Licinious?"

Celinia scowled. "Only too well. Ambitious and cunning, that one."

"He and Father's rivalry goes way back," Randolf noted. "He started trying to use Liam against Father. When Father took Liam in, he called Father a sentimental fool and said he should have left him to his own kind. Liam joined the military after I did. What he lacked in stature, he made up for in skill. Licinious's son joined too but wasn't cut out to be a soldier."

"Jochan was more like his mother than his father," Kia noted. "You know she died when he was quite young."

"I imagine Licinious influenced Jochan's views on the farmstead people," Celinia put in.

Randolf nodded. "I think his father pushed him into joining the military because of Liam."

"I heard about the incident," Celinia remarked. "It's my understanding that Jochan attacked a fellow soldier while that soldier held a hatch cover in place for Jochan to fasten. Jochan attacked him with a knife, cutting him across the ribs. The soldier used the cover as a shield, and it broke Jochan's neck."

"Licinious tried to have Liam charged with murder. Luckily, Jochan was fool enough to attack where we had surveillance, and the tribunal ruled it self-defense. He may have done it to please his father. Licinious is still trying to convince everyone that Liam is a 'dangerous foreigner.' He also throws around the term *misborn*. Liam never felt comfortable in crowds. Now he's a virtual hermit. He volunteers for the outposts whenever he can. He goes especially during holidays. Everyone he takes over for is grateful, but our parents want to see more of him."

"And so would you." Teresina squeezed his hand. "Do you think he's trying to find peace at the outposts? A peace he can't find here?"

Randolf nodded. "He doesn't wake up screaming anymore, but..."

"He lives his life with passion, but no joy." Celinia tapped her cheek. "I have a thought."

•   •   •   •   •

Once again, Liam raised his binoculars. He scanned across the plains to the wooded hills on the horizon. *How long ago since I lived on those plains? Twenty years? Or maybe twenty lifetimes.*

He checked the outposts on his flanks. On his right, Devon noticed him checking and waved. Micha, on his left, scanned the horizon with his binoculars. Liam dialed in his comm.

"Anything?"

"Nothing," Devon reported. "How about you, Micha?"

"I thought I saw something move."

Liam frowned and focused his binoculars to the area Micha electronically marked. "Stay sharp. If it's chitin, they won't advertise their presence. I am going to alert HQ."

"What? Because Micha—"

"We don't know what he saw," Liam interrupted. "We need to report anything peculiar."

"It may have been my imagination, Sergeant," Micha replied. "I am nearing the end of my shift."

"Noted." Liam lowered his binoculars. "Keep your eyes peeled."

Liam switched channels and used his personal designation. "HQ, Taho-331."

"What is it, Sergeant?" Captain Targus answered.

"Taho-333 says he saw something," Liam reported. "He concedes it might be nothing but sleepy eyes, but—"

"Logged it," the captain replied. "He might be right, but outposts in other sectors have reported movement. Let's hope it is just sleepy eyes."

"I am going to look through the sniper scope," Liam responded, "and will advise if we get contact."

Liam switched the comm back to local. "Anything?"

"Not so far."

He stepped into the locker room and went to the ammunition locker. This sniper rifle wasn't as good as his personal one, but it was here, and it worked. Liam checked the magazine, took some extra magazines, and checked the power pack—full charge. Cycling the magnetic coil, he returned to the edge of the outpost, opened the bipod, set the rifle up, and scanned the surrounding area.

"What are you doing?"

"The sniper rifle has better optics. It also has high velocity projectiles propelled by a magnetic coil—just in case."

He heard a quick laugh.

Liam scanned back to where Micha had marked movement and traced backwards toward the outposts. Then he spotted it. A surge of hatred and revulsion went through him. A large, straw-colored insectoid, camouflaged in the dry grass, slowly made its way toward them. In an instant, he took in its flat body, crouched to present a low profile, and its four antennae waving as it tested the air. He fired, and the creature collapsed.

He snapped on his comm to general broadcast. "Taho-331! Contact! Contact! Contact!"

He lined up another shot and fired. Another chitin stiffened and fell.

"What?" he heard Devon shout, then swear.

A burst of three shots came from Devon's position. "Taho-330! Contact! Contact! Contact!"

Micha's shots rang out. "Taho-333! Contact! Contact! Contact! We have a big bug problem!"

Taho-332 and Taho-329 both shouted contacts.

•   •   •   •   •

"So, my command will require Liam to attend." Celinia gave them an impish grin. "In full dress uniform, no less. Better still, even Councilor Licinious knows better than to make trouble for a high priestess's escort for Festival Day."

Randolf's spirits rose as he heard Celinia's idea. His brother would enjoy Festival this year despite himself.

Randolf started when an alert came over his comm. He checked the message, planning to ignore it. Then he froze, his blood going cold. Chitin were moving in on the Taho outposts.

"Randolf, what's...?" Teresina started as he leaped to his feet.

"I'm sorry. This is the one thing that could pull me away. Liam's sector is under attack."

Teresina's eyes opened in shock.

Celinia recovered first. "We'll come with you to the portals. You may need us."

Kia and Teresina nodded.

Peter approached with their tray. "I'll bag it up, Randolf. You can pick it up when you can. I hope Liam's okay. Tell him we miss his business."

"Thanks, Peter."

They rushed toward the ground transports.

"Interesting," Teresina noted. "For a hermit, many people seem to like your brother."

Randolf smiled. "I hope we can convince him." Randolf and the priestesses ran to the street and dialed in a local transport. The automated cab stopped in front of them, and they entered.

"Military Center," Randolf ordered. "Lieutenant Randolf, priority code Epsilon."

"Epsilon priority accepted," the voice on the computer responded. Soon, the transport moved onto the street. The other vehicles moved aside.

•　　•　　•　　•　　•

Randolf did not wait for the transport to stop before he leaped out and ran to the locker room. Teresina and the others would alert the support people to their presence. He threw on his armor and grabbed his weapons. Then he went to Liam's locker and grabbed his brother's sniper rifle. He slung his own assault rifle and dashed to Taho's portal room. Teresina waited for him.

She squeezed his arm. "Take care," she whispered, her lips brushing his cheek.

He joined his platoon at the portal.

"Checking clearance," Captain Targus called over the comm. Randolf waited with growing impatience. He knew if they opened on an overrun position, it could let chitin into the city. He also knew his brother could be dying—or worse.

"We've got an opening! Go! Go! Go!"

The portal opened, and the platoon dashed through.

•   •   •   •   •

Liam lined up his target and fired in rapid succession. The chitin knew the soldiers had spotted them and abandoned stealth. His chamber clicked empty, and he reloaded. The chitin advanced on the soldiers' positions. Not for the first time, Liam wished he had taken his own sniper rifle. It would be hand to claw soon.

"Forces are gathering," the captain called. "Hang tough."

Liam swept the field, using the scope on his rifle. He had time. So did Micha. With the chitin almost overrunning Devon, he lined up and fired on the closest and kept firing, hoping to buy his teammate some time, and his rescuers some space.

"Liam! Look out!"

Liam turned as a chitin leaped at him. He swung the sniper rifle and knocked it aside, recovered, aimed, and pulled the trigger. The chitin stopped moving. He could not bring the gun around fast enough. He dropped it as the next one jumped over the wall, grabbed the knife on his shoulder, and flung it in one clean motion. The blade imbedded itself in the creature's head. The chitin slumped to the ground as another attacked. It crouched between Liam and his assault rifle. He whipped out his pistol and fired three shots. This chitin collapsed, as did the next two, but more followed it.

The portal flared, and he heard, "Go! Go! Go!"

Shots rang out, and the chitin fell back.

Liam looked over his shoulder and almost cheered as his brother and thirty men charged through.

Randolf tossed Liam his own sniper rifle at a run.

"Good to see you, big brother!"

"I hope you left us some," Randolf quipped as he came up beside him.

More shots rang out as the platoon engaged the enemy.

"No worries there!"

"Taho-330's position is overrun!" Devon screamed. "Don't open the portal!"

Liam swore. "Permission to take a squad to clear Taho-330's position."

His brother hesitated, then nodded.

"Third squad!" Liam shouted, scooping up his assault rifle. "With me!"

Liam leaped the wall and headed to Devon's position. Knowing that third squad followed, he slung his sniper rifle over his shoulder and cycled his assault rifle as he ran.

Liam and Third Squad made their way across the ridge to the next outpost. Liam saw Devon fighting like a madman, plasma blade in one hand, dagger in the other. Then, out of the corner of his eye, Liam spotted four chitin closing on his own squad. He signaled to the man next to him. They turned and fired several bursts, and the chitin went down. Now he had time.

"Keep going!" he shouted.

He dropped the assault rifle and unslung his sniper rifle. He kneeled and aimed. It felt like an old friend. A gift from his father, he had fine-tuned every part of the weapon so every projectile would hit where he aimed.

Devon tried to keep five at bay. Liam aimed, fired, reset, and fired until he'd killed all five. Devon did not waste time resting. He grabbed a grenade, pulled the pin, and threw it toward the advancing bugs. The grenade wiped a hole in the line. The chitin trying to regroup bought him time and distance to grab his assault rifle and start firing.

Liam slung the sniper rifle and grabbed his assault rifle. A chitin crashed into him. Liam shoved his rifle into the bug as he fell backwards. He landed hard but could still fire. The bug collapsed, but others came up behind it. He kept firing and tried to struggle to his feet. Shots rang out, and he found he was clear. He looked back to his outpost and saw his brother flanked by sharpshooters, waving for him to get moving. Liam rolled to his feet and ran to catch up with his force.

He looked ahead. Third squad had reached Devon's position. They'd driven the chitin back.

"Taho-330's position is secure," came the call. "Send the reinforcements."

"On their way."

"We're getting heavy weapons set up," he heard Randolf shout. "Move, little brother!"

Liam ran as fast as he could, trying to catch up with his squad.

"Liam!"

A horde of chitin closed in on him. He dropped his assault rifle and shrugged off his sniper rifle. He grabbed his plasma blade and ignited it. Liam refocused his mind, and time around him slowed but had no effect on him. "Stepping out of time," his teacher had called it. He closed with the bugs, who were startled that he was now on top of them. The first went down in a blur. He rolled under a strike by a second, taking half its legs out. The third's head sailed from its shoulders. The fourth and fifth tried to flank him, but he slipped past them and killed the sixth. He dispatched the fifth with a backswing. The fourth died as time resumed its normal course. The remaining four found themselves out of position and scrambled to recover. He pulled his pistol and fired. One came at him. It went down with a blade of white-hot plasma through its thorax. He shot another just as a pincer closed on his arm. The armor kept his arm from being crushed. The chitin lifted him and flung him down the hill. Hard.

Liam saw stars but still struggled to get to his feet. A chitin landed on him, and its claw found the weak joint in his armor under the right shoulder. Liam screamed, grabbed his thigh dagger with his left hand, and shoved it into the bug's neck. The bug slumped over to the side. Liam tried to roll to his feet, but the last chitin closed the distance before he could bring the knife around to defend himself. A shot rang out. The chitin stiffened and fell.

"They're falling back," someone shouted. "They're falling back."

"Liam!"

Liam heard frantic footfalls coming for him. While unable to pick out his brother's, he felt Randolf's presence. Then he remembered no more.

•   •   •   •   •

Liam regained consciousness as he felt himself transitioning through the portal.

"Devon?" he gasped.

A familiar hand closed on his. "Devon's fine, little brother. He, third squad, and you bought time for the other platoon to come through."

Liam winced at the pain in his shoulder.

Strange hands touched his temples. The headache eased. Other hands moved to his wound. The pain dulled.

"How bad?" Randolf asked.

"Soft tissue damage," a female voice replied.

"And a concussion." Another female voice.

Liam opened his eyes. The swirl of faces slowed and stopped. Two beautiful women in priestesses' robes looked down at him.

"So," said the redhead, "you're Liam. Your brother told us about you."

Liam threw a withering look at Randolf, then dropped back to the stretcher. "I thought my brother had better manners. I hope it wasn't during dinner."

"Hadn't arrived yet." The blonde laughed. "I think he's feeling a little better."

Liam looked back at his brother.

"Liam, this is Teresina," Randolf gestured to the blonde. "The one I told you about earlier."

"And I am Celinia," the redhead finished. "Our friend Kia is helping with other injured. Your friend Devon, for one, though he just had some scrapes and bruises."

"Did we lose anyone?" Liam feared to hear the answer but had to face it.

Randolf's smile fell. "We lost four in our platoon—Samuel, Titus, Jamie, and Quinticus. We also lost Micha."

Liam felt his heart constrict.

"The platoon got through the portal, but the chitin still almost overran them." Randolf told him. "Micha died during a counterattack. It gave us time to use the heavy weapons."

Liam felt tears coming.

"I'm sorry, little brother," Randolf whispered.

"No!" Celinia pressed a finger between Liam's eyes. Her voice softened. "Not now. Grieve later. Sleep." The voice went lower still. Liam felt himself sinking into the arms of Morpheus.

"Teresina and I will get him to the Temple infirmary. His wounds will quickly heal."

"Thank you for everything." Randolf's voice seemed far away. "Attending Festival will do him a world of good."

"Huh?" Liam thought as consciousness sped away.

•   •   •   •   •

Licinious gave a shiver of fear. Anger boiled just under the fear. He traveled to meet with one of the most dangerous creatures he knew—a creature who could grant him substantial power or tear him to pieces without breaking a sweat. After the attack, he manipulated the schedule so his own people to be on station at Archer sector, allowing him to get out of the city unnoticed. Taking only two armed men with him, the walk to his ally's hiding place in the hills seemed interminable, and he wasn't as young as he used to be.

His escort nervously waited at the entrance as two chitin escorted him through the tunnel, deep into the hillside cavern. He had come here several times before but could never shake the feeling he was entering his execution chamber.

I told Azurius about the defenses. Will he be pleased? He just tested them. Pity the chitin didn't kill Marcus's adopted brat.

Licinious seethed just thinking about him. *They all think I hate the brat because he killed Jochan. While my son turned out to be a disappointment, I'm certainly not happy about it.* However, it wasn't the major reason. *That Finnian farm family was providing intelligence to Marcus. It could have disrupted our plans. When I arranged to have them killed, that misborn brat should have died with them.* He hated loose ends. *If Marcus had given the boy to another farm family, he'd be safely dead by now. If Liam ever discovers my role in his biological parents' deaths...* He suppressed a shudder as he entered the main chamber.

It's changed little since my last visit—comfortable, but with mismatched furnishings he scavenged. Licinious sniffed derisively. *Azurius doesn't seem to care about decor.*

"Well, Councilor," a voice spoke from the shadows, "we have tested the defenses. They seem impressive to me."

The voice seemed cheerful. It was deceptive. Licinious knew better than to drop his guard. "As previously discussed, the sabotage wouldn't be detectable."

A shadow detached itself from the darkness and came forward. The master of the chitin was not chitin himself. Licinious was familiar with the Gothowan race who looked human, but fine black scales covered their bodies. Azurius wore a military-style tunic with pants and boots. He kept a plasma blade on his belt, though Licinious did not understand why he would need the weapon. His eyes glowed with his mood—red at rest, green when amused, yellow when angry, and black. Licinious suppressed another shudder. At the time, he did not know black could glow. Though he'd only seen the results once, he never wanted to see it again.

Azurius sat down in a comfortable chair. Even in these sparse surroundings, he allowed himself a few luxuries.

"I saw the energy signatures showing the sabotage is in place," Azurius confirmed. "It will suffice. When the true attack comes, we will activate it remotely."

"What of that brat?" Licinious asked.

Azurius fixed him with a look. Green. He thought Licinious's fear was funny.

"Liam, the Finnian boy from the farm?" Azurius asked. "You do seem obsessed with him."

"He is a danger," Licinious presumed to warn him. "He looks small and weak, but—"

The glow turned to yellow. "Weak? You put too much importance on size. I know this Liam's race. They were an experiment—bred for war. I know what they can do. Liam is just beginning to feel his power. He has capabilities you can't begin to guess."

Licinious tried not to tremble—to show weakness.

Azurius continued, "I watched him today. Despite his youth, he's become a skilled fighter. I don't underestimate him. I also suggest you don't obsess over him. Obsession can be more dangerous than ignoring him."

Azurius gave his treacherous ally a bland look. "Allow me to paraphrase the ancient human Bard. If you prick them, do they not bleed? If you tickle them, do they not laugh? If you poison them, do they not die?" Azurius's eyes turned to an almost stern red. "And if you wrong them, do they not revenge?"

Licinious nodded and closed his eyes. Outwardly, he showed respect. Inwardly, he continued to seethe.

After a moment, he reported, "The Finnian always mans an outpost during Festival."

Azurius nodded. "Make sure he does this time. Watch carefully and mark to which post they assign him. We don't want any surprises. Make sure there are none."

"He will be there," Licinious assured him. "If it looks like he might alter his habit, I know how to bring him back."

"Very well." Azurius waved his hand in dismissal. Licinious departed to make his long walk back to the city.

•   •   •   •   •

After Licinious left, Azurius stood, stretched, and walked to the cavern's mouth. He glanced up at the setting sun. Looking around, he noticed much of the vegetation beginning to change color.

Interesting how seasons change on planets orbiting around yellow stars.

The old excitement before the beginning of a battle washed over him. This feeling recalled the opening of a play by that ancient (and his favorite) human playwright, William Shakespeare's *Henry V*.

Oh for a Muse of fire, that would ascend
The brightest heaven of invention:
A kingdom for a stage, princes to act,
And monarchs to behold the swelling scene!

•   •   •   •   •

Liam struck out at the chitin that killed his parents. He cut with his plasma blade again and again. Liam bared his teeth with fury. He would have used them as a weapon if he could. They all had to die. It still wasn't enough.

"It is enough, Liam," a voice cautioned in his dream. The chitin melted away. The burned-out home dissolved, replaced with a garden and a fountain.

Confused, Liam spun around to face the speaker. Celinia stood there. She smiled, and with her hand, bade him look.

"You can find more pleasant things to dream of." Her voice came again.

He looked. The beauty of the garden overwhelmed him. A mixture of wild and tame. More than just a pleasure garden. Oddly familiar.

The bushes rustled. Liam whirled; blade ready as a chitin burst forth.

"Enough!" The chitin vanished.

"I can see I will have trouble with you."

Celinia took his hand. He felt her pull and opened his eyes.

He lay in a bed in the Temple hospital. Celinia still held his hand.

"You've controlled your dreams to a point," she observed. "You're no longer helpless in your nightmares, but you still can't defeat them."

He looked at her. "Why?"

"Because you insist on keeping them nightmares," Celinia told him.

Her other hand closed around his hand.

"I know you will always carry the emotional scars of that day," she consoled him. "No child could forget something so horrible, but you don't have to let it have dominion over your life."

Liam looked puzzled. "I don't understand."

"With those words, you take the first steps on the path of wisdom." Celinia squeezed his hand. "Dreams are what we make them. Your parents' deaths hurt. It hurts so much you feel you will bleed to death because of it."

Liam nodded.

"When you were young, your nightmares were night terrors," she continued. "You would struggle against your tormentors until you awoke, still struggling."

"Waking my family in the process."

"They didn't mind comforting you, though they wanted a decent night's rest." She arched an eyebrow meaningfully.

"Father taught me to control my dreams," Liam remembered. "'Look at your hands and feel strength enter you. Then, you can defeat your opponent.'"

"And your family could sleep better," she agreed, "but you found you could now battle your tormentors, even torment them yourself. Make them pay for what they did."

He nodded again.

"That hunger is the trap, Liam," Celinia told him. "Vengeance is always a trap. You have trapped yourself in a dream that won't give you peace. Rather than fighting foes every night, why not just change the scene, banish the chitin, and have dreams you can enjoy?"

She touched between his eyes, and he fell back through the arms of sleep.

He was back in the garden. Celinia stood beside him. He heard the chitin rustling as if confused by the garden.

"Remember, this is your dream. I can help, but you are in control. They"—she pointed to the advancing horde—"are only a nuisance."

Liam turned to the horde, which now seemed completely confused.

"Get lost!" he ordered.

The chitin vanished like smoke on the wind. He could not even sense their presence.

"Where is this place?" Liam asked.

"Perhaps a place where your parents took you as a child," she suggested. "A place where you were once happy? You can explore it whenever you want."

He turned to her and froze in shock. Her priestly robe had vanished, replaced with a sheer, diaphanous gown which showed her shape. He became even more shocked and embarrassed to find himself robed in something similar. Like everyone else, she was taller than he. He realized where he was staring and looked away.

Her laughter rang like silver bells. "I am not without power over dreams. A brave warrior—yet so bashful." She reached out, and with her thumb and forefinger on his chin, turned his head to face her. "I find it remarkably charming."

"Umm." His eyes flashed downward.

"I don't mind," she whispered. "This is, after all, your dream. After so many bad dreams, you need a pleasant dream for a change."

With that, she drew his lips to hers. Her kiss woke something in him. Yet he feared he would treat her as a hungry man treated a steak. She sensed his concern as they separated.

"I understand. Let me lead."

He surrendered to her arms as they embraced.

●   ●   ●   ●   ●

Liam dozed the rest of the day. When awake, his thoughts turned to Celinia. He also grieved for his friend Micha. In the years since they started training, Micha proved methodical and brave. He died a soldier. Liam was slow to make friends, but when he did, the bond was strong. He did not even want to think about losing his brother.

A knock distracted him from his brooding. The door opened, and Jorge popped his head into the room. "Hi, short stuff."

Jorge pushed the door open, and Liam saw he had not come alone. Sharina and two children accompanied him—a pair of four-year-old twins, Justin and Sylvia.

"Uncle Liam!" The two charged forward before their parents could restrain them. The bed proved only a minor hindrance. They clambered up opposite sides, burrowed under the sheets, and snuggled under each arm, all without hurting his injured shoulder.

Their parents gave him an apologetic look.

"Well, I guess it's official." Jorge's wife sighed. "You're their Uncle Liam."

Much to his shock, it felt good. An innocence and love radiated from both. He detected plenty of mischief, but they restrained it for now.

"How's the arm?" Jorge asked.

"Much better," Liam replied.

"After Festival Day, you will come to have dinner with us." From the tone, Sharina did not sound like she had made a request.

Liam relented and nodded.

The door opened again. Celinia entered and stopped when she saw Liam was not alone.

"Oh."

Liam recovered his wits enough to make introductions. "High Priestess, this is my friend, Jorge; his wife Sharina; and their children, Justin and Sylvia. Everyone, High Priestess Celinia, daughter of Thomasia."

"Pleased to meet you." Jorge took her hand.

His wife also extended hers.

Celinia took each of their hands. "I'm glad you've come. I don't want my patient moping around without company."

"Children," Sharina admonished. "Manners."

"Hello," the two said in unison.

Then Justin announced, "This is our Uncle Liam."

Sylvia piped up, "Are you going to be our aunt?"

Liam almost choked. Jorge and Sharina turned crimson.

Celinia laughed that silvery laugh of hers. "That remains to be seen. It is as the Creator sends."

The children became solemn as they nodded, respectful of the high priestess's authority.

Celinia turned to the parents. "Are you related to High Councilor Marcus, or is Liam an adoptive uncle?"

"Adoptive, I guess," Jorge stammered.

"We love him," Sylvia announced.

Celinia smiled at the parents. "She certainly is forthright."

Sharina smiled back. "She is at that." She looked at the twins. "Come on, children. We need to get home. You will see Uncle Liam in a few days."

The children seemed reluctant but obeyed their mother. They each kissed him on the cheek and got off the bed. Liam felt sorry to let them go.

"I hope you weren't too embarrassed," Jorge apologized.

"Not at all," Celinia replied. "Children can sometimes see what adults don't. It has been a pleasure meeting you."

"Likewise."

Jorge closed the door behind them.

"Interesting," Celinia observed. "So beloved, and yet you still try to live at the outposts."

Liam had no answer for her.

She took a chair, pulled it next to him, and took his hand.

"You looked good with the children. You should have children around you."

"I—"

She pressed a finger to his lips. "I know what I saw, Sergeant. There is no point denying the truth."

Liam laid back and enjoyed the feel of her hand in his. "I wonder..."

Celinia cocked her head.

"Perhaps after my parents' death...," he started. "I don't make friends easy. The friends I make, I feel responsible for them."

Celinia smiled. "I would rather to think of you as a protector rather than a hermit."

"Perhaps that's why I switch with Jorge," Liam mused. "I don't want his family to think of the Festival, or any holiday, as the day their father died."

"I think you're finally looking for an answer," Celinia noted. "However, you are off this Festival Day. You need time to recover."

Liam looked at her. "I thought I'd be healed."

"The wound will be closed," she replied, "but healing will be more than physical. Jorge told your captain he would take his spot back."

"What!" Liam tried to jump out of bed.

Celinia restrained him. "Even if you didn't need more healing, you're still very weak."

"Don't you understand?" Liam demanded. "The chitin are on the move again. They may well strike at Festival. If Jorge—"

"He is a skilled warrior himself," Celinia countered. "He knows and accepts the risks. The Military Council will take extra precautions—full platoons at the outposts and all heavy weapons ready."

Defeated, he lay back in his bed.

"Besides, you will have another duty this Festival Day."

Liam looked at her.

"You will be an escort to a high priestess."

Liam stared at her in surprise. "You didn't have to do that."

"I wanted to." She smiled at him. "Your brother will escort Teresina. I think he's happy his brother will be there with him." She smiled impishly. "You might need to protect him from her."

Liam laughed. However, he still felt troubled.

•   •   •   •   •

Licinious looked up as his agent entered. "Yes, Colonel?"

"Sir, the High Priestess Celinia requested the person in question as her escort for the Festival," the man reported. "The sector captain approved."

Licinious grunted. Manipulating events had become more complicated than he thought. "The sector captain, Targus, is due for a promotion?"

"Yes, sir."

"Very well," Licinious decided. "Accelerate it. Move him to HQ front desk and give him the next three days off to celebrate during Festival."

With that part of the problem solved, he considered what to do next. Replacing Targus with his own man would put Liam on his guard, making him wary.

"Tell Major Thomia to rotate in for the Festival," Licinious ordered. "Then give him orders to recall the sergeant. They won't discover the deception until after Festival. By then, it will be too late."

"Major Thomia is highly skilled," the agent pointed out.

"Thus, they have no reason to doubt him, Colonel," Licinious replied. "His standing makes him perfect. He won't realize we have used him until there is nothing he can do to stop it."

Still, they needed to put Liam off his guard. "The orders should read the sergeant is familiar with the Taho sector outposts, and they'll need his skills. Also, Liam is up for promotion too. Accelerate his promotion and put him in charge of the sector. He will feel the full weight of responsibility when the sector falls."

"Very good."

"Also, time the orders for his recall for the last possible moment," Licinious commanded. "The less time anyone has to think, the better."

•   •   •   •   •

Festival Day arrived. Liam had seen Celinia several times since being released from her care. When away from her, she filled his mind.

Liam's parents and Randolf had gone out early that day. Councilors always met for a morning breakfast on the day of Festival. They left him alone with his thoughts.

When a knock at the front door disturbed his musings, Liam went to answer.

A man in uniform stood there. "Message from command, Sergeant." He handed a sealed envelope to Liam.

"Thank you."

Liam closed the door and opened the envelope.

From: Military Council
To: Sergeant Liam, Foster Son of Marcus
The Military Council has given orders to promote you to the rank of lieutenant, with all duties and privileges

commensurate with that rank. Due to your experience with the Taho sector, you are ordered to report to the Military Center for duty, which includes command of Taho Company's sector.

Contents of these orders are not to be discussed with anyone and are to be destroyed upon reading.

By order of the Military Council.

Liam read through the orders again to make sure he had not misinterpreted anything. He wondered about the secrecy but decided to get going. He wished he could contact Randolf to let him know. For once, he found himself looking forward to Festival Day, despite the itchy dress uniform. Celinia was going to be upset, but orders were orders.

He went back to his room and changed into fatigues. Then he caught a transport to the Military Center.

•   •   •   •   •

Liam saluted the officer at the front desk. He nodded and waved Liam through, picking up the comm, only to say: "He's here, sir."

Liam went to the locker room to armor himself. He finished strapping down his blades. This time, he would have his personal sniper rifle with him.

Major Thomia came into the locker room.

"Sorry to disrupt your plans, Lieutenant." The major removed the sergeant's stripes from Liam's shoulders and replaced them with lieutenant's insignia. "Congratulations. You've earned this."

"Thank you, sir," Liam replied. "What happened to Captain Targus?"

"Major Targus now," the major told him. "Off. They recalled me almost the same time they recalled you. I just wish you had time to share this promotion with your family before being thrown into the bear-lizard's den."

"A lot of people made plans."

"They may forgive us, in time." The major frowned. "This situation doesn't feel right. Any of it. Why sealed orders and secrecy for a holiday patrol?"

"I agree." Liam felt some relief that someone else sensed what he sensed. "I'll keep my comm on general and keep everyone alert. Permission to give Jorge the day off at least."

The major shook his head. "You'll need your full platoon. Orders. You'll take charge of the entire company at Taho."

Liam nodded in resignation. "I'd better get going then."

•   •   •   •   •

Liam stepped out onto the outpost platform.

"Company Commander on deck." Everyone came to attention.

Liam started but remembered the proper response. "As you were."

He walked up to Jorge as everyone returned to their duties.

"I'll never get used to that. Report."

Jorge shook his head. "Nothing so far. So much for our plans."

Liam sighed. "I normally feel better out here, but I can't shake the feeling that something's wrong."

Jorge nodded. "Neither can Major Thomia—nor me, for that matter."

"Stay close," Liam told him. "Whatever happens, I want to make sure I send you back to your family."

Jorge pulled closer. "Sorry, Lieutenant. You can't show favoritism."

Liam gave him a look of concern. Jorge was still a corporal. Yet, he had helped break in his share of officers.

Jorge softened his voice. "What you can do, if anything happens to me, is make sure they're okay. I understand if the worst happens, everything is up in the air. Just spare what you can to make sure they're taken care of."

Liam nodded.

"Movement!" someone shouted.

Liam raced to the embankment and swept the plains with the scope on his rifle. He spotted the chitin horde at once. "HQ, Taho Leader. Contact! Contact! Contact!"

Liam sighted his rifle and fired.

"It's a full-scale attack!"

Calls of contact rang out from the other Taho outposts.

"I am sounding full mobilization," the major's voice came over the comm.

"Heavy guns aren't firing," one soldier cried.

"Check the connections." Liam started shooting at will. "Fire as they come in range! We must hold until we're reinforced."

A man grabbed the other sniper rifle and began shooting.

•   •   •   •   •

Randolf waited at the Temple of the Creator. He felt annoyed with his brother and worried. It wasn't like him to be late.

"Where is Liam?" Celinia sounded irritated.

Randolf shook his head. "He should be here. He's not at home."

An alarm sounded. Then a general announcement came over the public system. "We are under attack! All fighting teams report to your portals!"

Randolf exchanged horrified looks with Celinia and Teresina. His comm chirped.

He activated it as the others gathered around him for news. "Yes?"

"Lieutenant," Major Thomia ordered, "I need you back here on the double. It looks like the chitin have organized a mass assault."

"Yes, sir," he replied. "Sir, my brother—"

"He's trying to hold the Taho outposts together. The heavy guns aren't working."

Randolf swore.

"I'll explain when you get here."

The comm went dead.

Randolf did not even address the priestesses. He just ran for the transports. Celinia did not hesitate. She followed, pulling Teresina with her.

•   •   •   •   •

Randolf rushed through his weapons and armor as Major Thomia walked into the locker room.

"Sir?"

"Lieutenant," the major began. "The short story is the captain got promoted, and I received orders to report to the Military Center. I had secure orders to promote Liam to lieutenant and recall him to take charge of Taho sector. With everyone at Festival, I had no one with whom I could confirm the orders. It didn't feel right. Now, I believe someone set this up. We have a traitor somewhere, but it doesn't make sense."

"I've got to get to my brother."

The major nodded, and they both rushed to the Taho portal room.

•   •   •   •   •

Liam had switched to his assault rifle when the proximity of the chitin made volume of fire more critical that precision. Jorge and several men struggled to get the heavy weapons back online.

"Sir!"

Liam looked back at Jorge.

"Sir, someone has sabotaged these weapons. If we keep poking, they'll—"

A tremendous explosion rocked the outpost, followed by a second and third. Liam shook off his shock and cursed under his breath. "This is Taho Leader. Hold off on the heavy weapons. Someone's rigged them to explode if you tamper with them."

Liam looked across the ridge. Where three of the five Taho outposts once stood lay smoking craters.

"Taho Leader," Major Thomia demanded. "What the hell is going on?"

"Sir, we've lost three outposts," Liam reported. "Someone has sabotaged the heavy weapons."

"We're getting ready to send reinforcements."

Liam started to thank him, then froze when he saw the chitin centered on his outpost. "Negative. Leave those portals shut."

"Lieutenant—"

Ten chitin made it to the barrier and leaped over the wall. Ten of Liam's men fell before the platoon managed to kill them all. The next wave would soon be on top of them with many more behind them.

"They're focusing on my position!" Liam called. "Without the heavy weapons, we need to fight in numbers. Which is what they want. They want us to open the portals."

"Liam, let us pull you out!"

Liam felt the pain in his brother's voice.

"Sorry, Randolf, there's no time. Look after Father."

He walked up to the portal and smashed the controls.

His remaining troops looked at him in shock.

"We're it!" Liam shouted. "Jorge, figure out how to make the heavy gun go bang on command. When we're about to be overrun—"

"I understand, sir." Jorge nodded with grim approval.

Liam returned to the embankment. His people set down a withering fire against the chitin, but the bugs kept coming.

The next wave surged forward, almost on top of them.

"Grenades!" Liam ordered.

Liam and his men hurled the grenades as the chitin closed with them. With the grenades gone, they returned to the assault weapons. Chitin overran the wall as the last of the ammunition ran out. Pistols and plasma blades became the order. By the time Liam and the survivors retreated to the dead portal, only five soldiers remained. Liam looked at Jorge, hidden in the heavy weapon's access bay. Liam nodded.

"It's been an honor, Lieutenant."

The heavy gun exploded, and Jorge vanished with it. The explosion slammed Liam and the others against the wall. Liam thought of Celinia as he lost consciousness.

CHAPTER 2

"Liam!" Randolf looked in horror as the portal went black. He turned. "We have one surviving portal. We can still get to him."

Major Thomia grabbed his arm. "Randolf! No! He knew he was as good as dead. He didn't want us to open the portal and let the chitin through."

"Major!" a portal tech yelled. "Someone jammed the controls on this portal. We can't close it from this side."

"Major, Taho-269," a voice called over the comm. "The chitin are converging on Taho Leader's position. We're going to support them."

Major Thomia swore under his breath. "Negative. Prepare to fall back to the city. Rig your heavy gun to explode and get out of there."

"Sir—"

"They're giving you cover, Taho-269," the major ordered. "Don't waste their sacrifice."

"Archer Leader!" came a call from the next sector. "Contact! Contact! Contact!"

Major Thomia swore again. He grabbed Randolf and shook him. "When Lieutenant Janus and his platoon come through the portal, destroy those controls. Shift everyone to the Archer portals. I'm promoting you to captain. Like it or not."

Major Thomia dashed off to HQ, the Military Center's primary control hub.

Teresina gave Randolf a quick embrace, then went to help the injured coming through the last Taho portal.

"This is Taho-269!" The comm crackled. "We're coming through." Then Randolf heard him whisper, "Creator, have mercy."

The base shook. A few minutes later, it shook again.

Breathless, Lieutenant Janus, Taho-269, came up to Randolf. "We destroyed Outpost Number Five."

Randolf looked at Janus's face. "Number Three?"

Janus shook his head and followed his men.

Randolf reached for his gear and found Celinia behind him, tears in her eyes.

"Oh, Randolf..."

He put an arm around her and held her.

"We have duties," he told her. "He won't thank us for dereliction."

She nodded and followed him.

Randolf skidded to a stop, and Celinia almost crashed into him.

"Captain!" Major Thomia called through the comm. "Stay there and wait for further orders."

"Yes, sir," Randolf checked his ammo status. "What's the status on Archer's heavy weapons?"

"Archer Leader had them checked when he heard about Taho's," the major replied. "The troops there found them sabotaged as well. They managed to get one online again before the chitin attacked. However, they didn't have time to fix the others."

"What's the condition of the rest of sectors?"

"Boulder and Grizzly are still quiet. I wonder why." The major's voice was grim.

"Could they be decoying us at Taho and Archer?" Randolf asked. "Drawing our strength away from one of those two sectors?"

"Which is why I want you in reserve," the major replied. "I would have expected the chitin to attack all sectors at once. I've held two companies in reserve, plus what's left of Taho. We may have to man the city's defenses. We built the outposts at a day's travel overland for a reason. I'm trying to get command to activate the city's militia. We're getting resistance from the Civil Council."

Randolf swore. "Sir, suggest that command activate the militia and apologize to the Council later."

Major Thomia grunted.

The ground shook again.

"Archer-177!" came a panicked call. "The chitin took out Archer Leader's heavy weapon! They've overrun Archer Leader's position! The chitin destroyed the heavy weapon! Look out for the portal!"

The portal flashed, and chitin burst into the room.

"They've breached Archer Three Portal!" Randolf shouted as gunfire erupted. "Shut it down."

"It won't shut down!" the tech shouted. "Someone sabotaged it too!"

The priestesses froze in shock.

"Go!" Randolf yelled. "Get back to the Temple!"

Celinia grabbed Teresina's hand, and they ran as chitin poured into the room.

"All sectors, Archer's portals are frozen open," the major announced. "Withdraw to the Military Center. Your portals may be sabotaged. Take them down any way you can."

Another explosion shook the building.

"Major, what's going on?"

Randolf received no answer.

"Major?" Randolf felt an icy fear creep up his spine.

The remains of Archer forced their way into the room. Everything was chaos.

Archer-177, a sergeant, made his way to Randolf. "Captain!" the man reported. "I have all my men through. We destroyed portal five's controls."

"Good," Randolf replied. "You're in charge here, Sergeant. Get what's left of Archer through and push the chitin out of the portal. HQ isn't answering. I'm taking a squad to check."

"Yes, sir! Good luck."

Randolf called his squad and ran down the hall. Approaching the stairs to HQ, they found debris at the bottom. Randolf and his men peered up the stairs through the smoke—then raced up. The explosion had ripped the door to HQ off its hinges. Randolf shoved it aside, and it fell with a crash. The scene that greeted them was something out of a nightmare. The blast had torn people apart. He could not even tell which body belonged to Major Thomia.

He started to give a command to look for survivors when a hail of bullets took down his troopers. The man behind him shoved him through the door before he died.

Randolf recovered and crouched inside the room. Careful to stay under cover, he peered out the doorway, over his dead men. A group of soldiers stood at the foot of the stairs; weapons drawn. Their leader was a colonel.

"Come out, Lieutenant," the colonel called. "Let's not prolong the inevitable."

"Why are you doing this?" Randolf shouted back.

The colonel laughed. "Just following orders, Lieutenant. Nothing personal."

"Your treason killed most of my friends." Randolf pulled a grenade, but kept it out of sight. "And my brother."

"Stop trying to play the hero, Lieutenant," the colonel replied. "You're trapped in there. Chitin are decimating your soldiers as we speak. Why postpone the inevitable?"

"Just tell me this first, Colonel. Who are you working for?"

"Can't you guess?"

"Licinious," Randolf snarled. "What can the bugs offer him? Besides being the guest of honor at some feast."

The colonel laughed. "You disappoint me, Lieutenant."

"It's Captain now."

"Oh, the late Major Thomia promoted you." The colonel sneered. "Pity you won't get the chance to enjoy it. But you're right. The chitin wouldn't normally have anything to offer. Then again, they rarely gather in hives of this magnitude. You must realize there is an intelligence behind it."

It hit Randolf with the force of a heavy weapon explosion. He cursed under his breath.

For over forty years, why hadn't we seen it?

"I am tired of waiting, Lieutenant."

Gunfire erupted, causing Randolf to crouch back.

"Captain!"

Randolf heard a familiar voice. He looked and saw the traitorous soldiers and colonel lay dead. The leader of Grizzly Sector stood at the bottom of the stairs.

"I heard the last part of it." Grizzly Leader looked on the bodies without pity. "I considered taking him alive but figured it would get too complicated. We can try him for treason later."

"Thank you, Captain...?"

"Simon, son of Laris and Hercna." With a wave of a finger, the captain sent a squad up the stairs to check for survivors. "We had to destroy our portal controls to shut them down. Boulder did the same. The chitin forced Archer out of their portal room. They could not shut down two of their portals. We have chitin between us and those portals."

"I need a link to the Council!" Randolf told him.

"Military comm links can't reach the Civil Council. It's on the civilian network. Let's check HQ."

They went into the room. One soldier looked at them and shook his head. No survivors. The explosion demolished the communications equipment.

Captain Simon looked around the room that once housed HQ. "I've worked with demolition. It looks like someone set high explosives along the perimeter of the room, likely when it was last upgraded. Someone planned this attack for a long time."

"Sir," another man spoke up sheepishly. "I know it's against regulations, but I have my personal communicator with me."

Randolf wanted to hug the man. "If you let me borrow it, I won't tell."

The man handed him his personal communicator. Randolf dialed in his father's code and sent as urgent.

"High Councilor Marcus," came the voice on the other end.

"Father, it's Randolf."

"Randolf!" The voice sounded relieved. "Is Liam okay?"

Randolf's throat closed as the grief came back.

"I'm sorry, Father." His voice came out hoarse around the lump in his throat. "He died defending his outpost."

"No." His father's voice cracked.

"Dad, listen!" Randolf had to push himself past his grief. "If Councilor Licinious is there, hold him. This is his doing."

"Wait a moment."

Randolf heard his father talking to someone.

"Randolf?"

"Yes, Father?"

"He's left the Council Chamber. I have ordered him taken into custody."

"Father, the chitin have breached the Archer portals," Randolf reported, "and I just found out that an intelligence controls them. We may have to fall back outside the Center. You need to activate the militia and get them here five minutes ago."

Randolf motioned Grizzly Leader to take his men back to the Archer portals. He followed them.

He heard his father swear. "I wondered why Licinious was blocking their activation. I hope we still have time."

"Father." Randolf wondered how he would keep this situation under control. "Licinious's people destroyed HQ. Everyone here is dead."

"Dear Creator," Marcus gasped.

"I need to get back." Randolf stopped to throttle down his grief again. "One more thing. If you catch Licinious, he's mine. I intend to blow his head off."

Randolf shut the communicator down without waiting for a reply.

•   •   •   •   •

The horde of chitin charged.

"Go!" Liam commanded.

The chitin wavered and vanished.

"Very good, Lieutenant," a deep voice commented. "You seem to have mastered part of it. Pity it's too late."

Liam whirled and saw a strange-looking humanoid standing amid the ruins of his family's home.

"I am Lord Azurius," the creature declared. "Allow me to commend you on your skill and courage. Those are traits I admire even in those who oppose me."

Liam remained silent, mostly because he did not know what to say.

The creature looked around the ruined homestead. "Ah, home. Even in ruins, one finds comfort in it."

"You're controlling the chitin?" Liam asked.

"I suspect you know my answer already," Azurius replied. "I suspect you also have guessed who betrayed your forces."

"Licinious." Liam clenched his fist.

Azurius became sympathetic. "Yes, I know. A vain, egotistical man. For the high councillorship of what is left of the city, he betrayed you. He's a skilled manipulator. Though I suspect it grated on him to give you your promotion just to make it work. A promotion you earned, by the way."

"Make what work?" Liam asked, careful to hide his feelings.

"To bring you out and place you on the battlefield, as I ordered."

Liam cocked an eyebrow. "You want me on the battlefield? Why?"

Azurius smiled. "I wanted to test you. Farmsteaders, as the Neo-Etruscans called them, are my enemies of old. I needed them neutralized, and Licinious was eager to help. You would have died too had not Marcus rescued you. Poor Licinious, he gets so obsessive about loose ends. You, however, intrigued me. Licinious is ambitious and clever—but weak. I need a stronger second to take charge."

Liam's eyes narrowed. "A stronger second?"

"The plan Licinious acts under requires much of the city's population to fall to the chitin. He intends to let them feast as an example. Incidentally, he will see to it that anyone you care about will die some truly painful deaths, just as he did for your parents, for no other reason than they were your foster parents' friends."

Again, Liam's fists clenched in anger. He turned and looked at the remains of his parents.

He felt Azurius step behind him. "I have a better plan. You can return from the dead and rally the defenses. I can pull the chitin back, and you will become a hero. You may save most of the population and your friends. Eventually, the high councillorship will pass to you. Slowly, you will turn the Neo-Etruscans into something I can use in my designs. You will become the general of my forces, second only to me."

Liam nodded. "Those who won't turn, no matter how subtly we manipulate things?"

"Regrettably, they will have to be put out of the way," Azurius replied as if reluctant. "But think of the greater good."

Liam laughed and rounded on Azurius. "Begone!"

He had the satisfaction of seeing the shocked look on Azurius's face before he vanished.

The conversation told him what he needed. Taking a chance, he recreated the feeling Celinia had used to bring him out of his dream.

•   •   •   •   •

Liam groaned. He did not think he was on death's door, but he knew the explosion left him badly injured. It hurt to breathe. He checked his armor's health monitor—dead. He had to guess: cracked ribs. Liam tried to roll to his feet. The chest pain increased. He rocked back to his knees, forced himself to straighten, and looked around the place he found himself. He lay in a room of burned-out electronics and machinery. The explosion must have thrown him through a breach in the dead portal's maintenance room.

He found his plasma blade a few feet away. His pistol laid just beyond it. He got up and picked up his plasma blade. It looked all right. Liam activated it to confirm it still worked and had a decent charge. Bending to pick up his pistol, he felt his ribs complain. The pistol had several rounds, and the power pack had a full charge. On his belt, he found he still had two magazines and an extra power pack. His helmet was nowhere to be seen.

Staggering to the opening, Liam saw the explosion of the heavy weapon had created a crater one story down. He scanned the area and saw no sign of life—human or chitin. Fortunately, the Neo-Etruscans had constructed the outposts on a slope. The crater seemed shallow enough at the other end. He found a short length of cable. Not much, but it would have to do. With great care, he lowered himself down to the ground from the opening. He dropped the last few feet and gasped as his ribs exploded with pain.

Liam looked for any sign of his sniper rifle. Finding a twisted and mangled mass that looked somewhat like it, he picked it up and saw part of the engraved plate on the stock. Liam thought he should feel sad at the loss. His foster father had given it to him when he had completed his sniper training, and it had been a constant companion ever since. He felt numb. After losing his platoon and friends, it seemed of little importance.

Clutching his side, he walked across the crater and climbed the embankment at the far end and viewed the battlefield. Chitin bodies lay strewn across the area. He looked back at the other outposts. The chitin had destroyed all five. He closed his eyes for a moment, then looked back toward the city. The force field barrier still shimmered behind the outposts.

It's a day's walk to the city. It might as well be on the other side of the planet.

He began walking south. *Perhaps I can get help at Grizzly sector.*

He stopped to try his comm, but the blast had damaged it. He tried to get water from his canteens but found both had ruptured.

Liam struggled along for hours. He continued walking, forcing himself to ignore the pain, thirst, and hunger.

Grief closed in on him. *How many friends did I lose? How many did I order to die?* Guilt followed grief. *They trusted me. I should have died with them.* His steps faltered as tears filled his eyes.

Jorge. Steady, friendly, funny Jorge. *How can I face Sharina, Justin, and Sylvia? I killed him. I might as well have shot Jorge myself.*

Then it was as if Jorge walked beside him.

Stop thinking that way, the presence seemed to scold. *You did what you could to give our people a fighting chance. You need to survive to help the survivors. Honor us by making sure it wasn't for nothing.*

Then he was alone again. He shook his head. Dream state? Mirage? Ghost?

He realized it did not matter. *It's the sort of thing Jorge would say.*

Liam took another step and fell to his knees. He tried to force himself to stand, knowing the danger of plains' predators and scavengers. He fell forward, unconscious before he hit the ground.

•　　•　　•　　•　　•

Liam felt consciousness returning. He lay on his back, and something supported his shoulders and head. He felt something pushed against his lips and water began dribbling into his parched mouth. Liam drank gratefully, raising his hand.

Caution, spoke a voice in his head. *No haste in drink.*

Liam opened his eyes and choked on the water he inhaled. He stared into the enormous face of a bear-lizard.

A furry, grayish-brown, hand-like paw removed a primitive waterskin from Liam's mouth.

Caution again. The creature sounded amused. *Good for drink. Not so good for breathe.*

The bear-lizard looked quizzically at him. Liam had never had an opportunity to see one this close before now. He never realized how big they were.

"You can talk," Liam gasped, still clearing the water from his lungs. "Telepathically at least."

No parts in mouth make your sounds, the creature replied. *Lucky find you. Felino eat.*

"What about you?" Liam asked.

The bear-lizard nodded sagely. *We not eat thinking creatures.*

"I didn't know," Liam replied.

Difficult to communicate except close range, the bear-lizard scratched an ear with his hind paw. *Assume things, no communication.*

"Is that the reason you're helping me," Liam asked, "to communicate?"

Good opportunity. Stand you?

"I think so." Liam sat up and realized they were at Grizzly sector. He blinked and looked at the outposts.

Is where you wanted? the creature asked.

"Yes," Liam confirmed, "but how...? Oh, right: telepathy."

Again, opportunity.

Liam winced as he forced himself to his feet. The bear-lizard stood on all fours and lent a shoulder to steady him. Liam leaned his head against the shoulder. Placing his hand through the shaggy fur, he felt a strap. The creature had, what appeared to be, a rawhide strip across his shoulder, crossing under his front legs, and secured by another strip around his waist. Looking closer, he noticed it seemed to have several pouches—a primitive utility belt.

Ribs hurt?

"Cracked in the explosion, I think," Liam replied. "I don't think I could move if I'd broken them."

The creature nodded as he tucked the waterskin away.

"Since no one has challenged us," Liam observed, "I'd say Grizzly Company abandoned the entire sector. That's not good. Come on."

He climbed to the outpost where Grizzly Leader would have been. The bear-lizard followed him.

"Portal's dead. The chitin must have broken through somewhere." He turned to his companion. "May I ask your name?"

Swift Hunter, the bear-lizard replied.

"Swift Hunter." Liam gave a slight bow. "A moment ago, I gave you a command, forgetting I have no authority over you. Please accept my apologies."

Understand. Swift Hunter gave a good-natured grin. *May lapse again. Will treat as suggestion.*

"You are a wise being. My name is Liam."

Pleasure.

They climbed the embankment and went to the locker room. He found spare water, rations, and a diagnostic kit. He went for the last first and plugged it into his armor.

"This device works with my armor," Liam explained. "It will tell me what's wrong with it and with me."

The creature nodded, looking over Liam's shoulder.

"My armor's internal diagnostics are cooked. I can only get it fixed at the factory."

Liam looked up, realizing his explanation might be outside of the creature's experience. The creature shook his head in dismissal.

I see your thoughts. They are enough.

All at once, Liam understood. "It isn't my words you understand."

The bear-lizard nodded. *Understand thought behind them. To speak, must think.*

Liam checked his own condition. He confirmed he had fractured three ribs and told the diagnostic to treat. He felt a slight tightening in his chest. It was like his ribs being taped. The pain reduced dramatically. He saw he suffered from dehydration.

"Now is a good time for a break." Liam glanced at his new friend. "Hungry?"

The bear-lizard licked his chops. *Tarpier?*

Liam laughed. "It's my favorite too."

Liam pulled out two faux beef stew rations, opened them, and handed one to Swift Hunter. He wondered what kind of animal real beef came from on Old Terra. The tarpier was the closest facsimile on this planet. Rations could not beat fresh and home cooked, but for someone starving, they were delicious. He took out a bottle of water and drank.

"It's amazing how wonderful water tastes when you're thirsty." He fell silent, thinking.

A plan you have? Swift Hunter asked. *Kill big bugs?*

Liam sighed. "I have to get into the city. I have important information for my people."

Bug master and plans.

"You know of Azurius?"

Swift Hunter nodded. *Have seen him a few times, coming out of hole. Bugs seem to respect him—or fear him.*

"Where did you see him?" Liam asked.

Hole in hillside. The creature shrugged. *A day's walk to north.*

Liam nodded. "If we locate an open portal and reach the armory, we can get fresh weapons."

You, the bear-lizard reminded him.

Liam nodded. "Forgive me again. I shouldn't have assumed. No, this is our fight."

He sat back and chewed his meal.

"Okay, Swift Hunter." Liam put his rations aside. "I'm going to think out loud, but feel free to express your opinion."

The creature nodded.

"I can get weapons," Liam continued. "My armor's more problematic. It's modular, but I'm smaller than most of the people. So, the military had my armor custom made. I might refit some modules, but the engineers built the automated diagnostics and treatment into the system."

He looked at the kit. "I'll have to use the mobile diagnostic kit, and the kit is heavy."

What have to do? Swift Hunter asked.

Liam checked the locker again. "It looks like they grabbed all the weapons and ammo. It means that when they left, they were expecting trouble. They didn't take the time to destroy everything, for which I'm grateful. Perhaps I can find something to carry rations and water in."

When they finished their meal, they scouted the other Grizzly outposts. All the portals were inoperable. He had nothing with which to carry supplies. Liam replaced his two ruptured canteens with fresh ones and looked longingly at the rations. He also discarded his damaged comm.

"I'll have to carry the diagnostic kit by hand. I think I can jury-rig a strap to use as a handle."

City? Swift Hunter asked. *Place where lots of two legs live?*

Liam shook his head. "I want to check the other sectors first. I need to locate the breach. The problem is, it's a day and a half's travel from one sector to the next until I find a live portal."

For you. I much faster. Half time. I get you there after nightfall.

"Even carrying my weight?"

Swift Hunter's lips curled in a smug grin.

Carried you here. Not notice weight.

"Swift Hunter. You've given me more hope than I had before. Shall we go?"

Swift Hunter lay down and let Liam climb onto his back.

Carry cubs this way. He stood up. *Lots heavier.*

•　　•　　•　　•　　•

Randolf looked around at the force he had surrounding the Military Center. He did not see Teresina, Kia, or Celinia, but he saw other priestesses and adherents helping the wounded. He hoped they would be all right. The personal communicator he had borrowed chirped again.

"Yes, Father?"

"Bad news," his father told him. "Licinious is nowhere to be found."

"Great," Randolf replied between clenched teeth. "I'll see your bad news and raise. The chitin have pushed us out of the Center.

We're trying to contain them. The militiamen have bolstered our numbers, but they're trickling in slowly."

"They want to protect their families." His father sounded bleak.

"I don't blame them," Randolf conceded, "but a few troops won't do much to save their families if they face a swarm."

More shots rang out as another group of chitin tried to probe their line.

"Look, Father." Randolf turned away so no one could hear him. "I doubt we can contain them in the Center. What's the next step?"

"Abandon the city?"

"If we can," he agreed. "The chitin won't think of it, but the intelligence behind them probably will, if it hasn't already. If we can get to one of the abandoned cities, we may be able to shift around and keep our enemy off balance. If we can't leave the city, we'll have to use the Temple compound as a rally point."

"Desecrate the Creator's Temple?"

Randolf sighed. "Under the circumstances, I think the Creator will understand. Perhaps She can provide a miracle."

"I'll talk to Arch Priestess Arria," Marcus promised. "You may be right. When I'm through here, I'll collect your mother and head to the Temple. It's only a block from home."

"I'll call if there's any change."

Randolf closed the link and found a familiar face.

"Lieutenant Janus," Randolf shouted. "I want five companies to fall back one hundred meters as a reserve. If we get hit hard, we'll need someone to help us push back, create a secondary hold line, or fade back and continue the fight. If we lose contact, rally on the Temple compound."

"Yes, sir!"

Captain Simon pounded up to him. "Just a few probes so far."

"I think they're going to try to break the line," Randolf guessed. "I put five companies in reserve one hundred meters back. If you lose contact, we rally at the Temple."

They heard a crack, like lightning. The city had lost power. Transports rolled to a stop. Soldiers and militia had to leap out and run to get to the battle lines.

"Licinious. So much for using the intercity portals to escape. They must be getting ready to surprise us."

"I liked them better as dumb animals that were predictable," Captain Simon complained.

"They still are. If we can neutralize the intelligence behind them, we stand a better chance." Randolf clicked his comm button. "Military comm still works, but I can't use the personal communication network without power."

"Do you think the loss of power means they've stopped coming through the portals?"

Randolf turned to him. "The Military Center has its own power supply, just like the Temple."

"Can we get to the Center's power generator and destroy it?"

Randolf shook his head. "Not with this mob of chitin between us and it. I think you'd better get back to your company. If the line breaks, get everyone you can to the Temple compound."

Simon nodded. "Good luck."

"You too."

Randolf open his comm on general. "They're getting ready to make a move. If the line collapses, the Temple is the rally point. Tell any civilians you find. Reserves, wait for orders to move."

He closed the link. Then, remembering something, he reopened it. "One more thing. Keep an eye out for Councilor Licinious. Remember, he's mine."

He turned to the Center just as the chitin charged. It looked as if they were emptying the building.

"Fire!"

The first waves fell, wavered, regrouped, and attacked again. Soon, the fighting devolved to hand-to-hand.

Randolf got ready to join the fray when the sergeant, Archer-177, stopped him. "No, sir!"

"Sergeant—!"

"You're one of the few officers left now, Captain," the sergeant insisted. "We can't afford to lose you. Get back with the reserves."

Randolf started to argue.

The sergeant shoved a pair of high-powered binoculars at him. "You'll need these to direct the battle."

Randolf pelted to the reserve line and turned. He hoped they would find a higher-ranking officer soon. The chitin pushed the front-line back. Forces in adjacent buildings started firing down on their foe. The chitin jostled each other to close with the humans.

Raising the binoculars to his eyes, Randolf wondered if he could press the line back. Then, scanning the battlefield, he saw it. A humanoid creature with black scales on his face. The chitin close to it gave it a wide berth as they tried to enter the fight. The creature's eyes seemed to glow red as it surveyed the battle.

Could this be the intelligence behind the chitin?

"Sharpshooters!" Randolf called. "Someone, take that thing down!"

Shots rang out from around the battlefield as he raised the binoculars again. Viciously, Randolf hoped they had killed it. The alien spun aside but remained on its feet. It spun away from the bullets again. Randolf knew where he'd seen this ability before. Liam had it. This creature could apparently step out of time, as Liam used to. Significant information, but what did it mean except that part of the setup was to get his brother out of the way? Without warning, a violent windstorm obscured the creature and knocked the chitin into the front line. Chitin died on the blades and by the bullets of the defenders, but defenders fell under the pincers and mandibles of the chitin.

The snipers could not see to fire. The dust cleared, and Randolf relocated the creature. He'd never seen black glow before. The line exploded, ripping chitin and human alike to pieces. Several snipers opened fire, but with no more success than before. The chitin had blown through, and Randolf could not hold them.

"Fall back to the rally point! Fall back to the rally point!"

His troopers executed a fighting withdrawal. The snipers continued to try to get the creature. The beast.

"Codex and Dragon Companies, plug that hole!" he shouted. "We have to keep this situation from becoming a rout."

The soldiers raced forward, preventing the chitin from exploiting the break in the line.

The creature struck again, this time striking a building upon which some snipers stood. It creaked and groaned and threatened to fall. The swaying building unnerved the snipers. They scrambled out of the building and retreated with the rest. Chitin poured out into the city.

Randolf stayed in position, peering through the binoculars, though the sergeant pulled on his arm. He watched the creature slump a little and go back under cover.

"Thought so."

"Come on, sir!" the sergeant yelled.

Randolf turned and followed. "He couldn't keep using those abilities for long. It requires a great expenditure of energy to do the things he does."

"Can we use that information?" the sergeant asked.

"We can use it. The real question is, will he give us the opportunity?"

•   •   •   •   •

Lidia looked up when Marcus entered the house. She'd heard the explosions and had been pacing in worry. The chitin had broken into the city.

Marcus came into the kitchen. He looked so much older than this morning.

"Marcus?"

"Liam's dead," he whispered.

Her mouth fell open, and she felt her heart falter. Grief seized hold of her. Marcus took her in his arms.

"He died defending his base," he told her. "According to Randolf, he destroyed the portal and destroyed his outpost rather than let the chitin get past."

Lidia wept bitterly for her youngest son.

"We need to get to the Temple," he whispered. "Come on, Lidia. He'd want us to be strong."

She pulled back and nodded. "Let me get my coat."

She made it partway down the hall when someone knocked on the front door.

"I'll get it," Marcus called.

She heard her husband open door.

Marcus said, "What—"

She heard the discharge of a pistol, a gasp, and the sound of a body hitting the floor. "Marcus?"

In a panic, she dashed to the entry to see her husband in a pool of blood. A man she did not recognize aimed as she turned to flee. The pistol fired again, striking her in the back. She died before she started to fall.

•　　•　　•　　•　　•

Night had fallen when Liam and Swift Hunter arrived at Boulder Sector. Liam admired the strength and grace of the creature he thought a dangerous predator.

Now? Swift Hunter asked.

"Let's go up there." Liam pointed.

They went to the nearest outpost. Liam slid off Swift Hunter's back and went to the portal. His shoulders slumped. It was dead, just like at Grizzly. Poking at the inactive controls, he realized he would not find a live one he could use. Frustrated, he entered the locker room and tried the door to the portal machinery space.

"It's locked, but I can force it open." Liam drew his plasma blade.

He adjusted the blade to a small, needle thin beam, cut open the lock, and the door popped open.

"Shelter," Liam noted. "Water and rations. Like the other sector."

He tossed a ration packet to Swift Hunter and got one for himself.

"Do you want me to refill your waterskin?" Liam asked.

Thank you, Swift Hunter replied, passing the skin.

Liam undid the stopper and refilled it from the water, then passed it back to the bear-lizard. Liam felt well hydrated now but tired from carrying the diagnostic kit. He checked himself one more time.

"Like before." Liam turned the device off. "It shows nothing new. Moreover, it can't further lessen the discomfort."

Leave behind, Swift Hunter suggested.

"I think you're right." Liam unplugged it and putting it aside. "I'll check the other four outposts."

His luminescent torch still worked, and they used it to scout the other outposts. As he feared, the portals no longer worked.

"More supplies," he noted in frustration, "but nothing to carry them in."

They returned to the first outpost.

Can smell danger, Swift Hunter told him. *Will wake if trouble.*

Liam removed his armor and cleaned it. Then he taped his cracked and bruised ribs with tape from the med kit. Risky, but he needed some decent rest outside his armor.

"Do you have a family?" Liam asked.

Mate, Great Heart. Visiting children now. Hatched four cubs. Grown now. Visit sometimes. You?

"My birth parents are dead. Marcus and Lidia adopted me when I was very young. I have a foster brother named Randolf. We're all very close."

Good. Mate?

"I spend too much time at the outposts." He smiled. "I met a girl just before the attack. She's beautiful and wise. She helped me through some problems."

Swift Hunter nodded. *Promising. Should have mate.*

Liam laughed. "You too? I think the Creator Herself has ordained every being in the universe to be my matchmaker. It wouldn't surprise me if Azurius started pushing me to get married."

Swift Hunter made a rumble that almost sounded like a chuckle. "I'm going to try to sleep. Do you need anything?"

Swift Hunter shook his head.

"Come in if you want. Especially if the weather gets bad."

Liam entered, retrieved a blanket from a medical kit, wrapped himself, and lay on the floor of the locker room. He found it difficult to get comfortable with his ribs, but finally, he drifted off.

* * * * *

Liam found himself in the garden again. He sent a mental wave to drive nightmares off. He wanted to explore this place. Perhaps it held clues to...what? A part of himself?

He walked to the fountain, remembering the time he spent here with Celinia. It had been only a dream, but it felt, smelled, and tasted real. He wondered if he could summon her presence.

"You can't summon her." The female voice had an odd accent. "She'd need to be with you when you went to sleep."

Liam spun to find the speaker but saw no one there. He walked in the direction he thought he heard the voice. It came from somewhere near a flowering bush. Liam pushed past the bush and came upon a man and a woman having a picnic with a small child.

"Mom? Dad?" he whispered, remembering their faces.

Seeming to hear him, the three looked up at him, then vanished.

"Don't go!"

"We are always here," a male voice replied.

He turned. Again, he saw nothing.

"Why can't I see you?"

"Close your eyes," the woman's voice said. "Relax, just let yourself go."

He did not know what she meant but tried to follow her instructions. He felt himself drifting away as if falling asleep within the dream.

"Very good, son." The man's voice held a hint of pride. "Your mind is quick."

He felt arms being wrapped around him.

"Open your eyes now, Liam, and you can see us," the woman told him.

He opened his eyes. He seemed a child again as before the chitin came. His mother held him. His father had his arms around them both.

"You can speak." His father smiled. "It's just that this form helps you to see us because you remember us this way. Later, it won't be necessary."

"How can this be?" Liam asked. "I mean you're..." He stopped, fearing to be rude.

"Yes." His mother nodded. "We're no longer part of this life, but we are here, in your dream. I don't know if I can explain properly."

"What I'm about to say isn't a perfect explanation, but it's as close as I can come," his father explained. "People who love us plant a bit of themselves in us. Into our souls, if you will. This is especially true of families. Though we died, we never left you. We were always right here." His father pointed to Liam's heart.

"I think I understand," Liam replied. "Like I heard Jorge admonishing me even though he'd died, as I traveled between outposts. It sounded just like him."

"Just like he would if he were still alive," his father agreed.

"You were hurt, dehydrated, and grief stricken," his mother told him. "Your defenses were down, and your despair called to him."

Liam looked around him. "What is this place?"

"We took you here for picnics, my love," his mother told him. "You used to like it here. So much to see and do. A world full of adventures."

His father chuckled. "Not to mention a fountain you found irresistible. One we had to pull you out of every couple of days."

"Usually by the scruff of the neck." His mother laughed.

"Marcus and his family have been very kind to me," Liam informed them. "Regardless of what anyone else said or did, they made me feel wanted."

His parents' faces fell. He reached out with a tiny hand to comfort them.

"They've been your family in every way that matters." His father spoke as though he never wanted Liam to forget that fact. "We are truly grateful. Because of them, you've grown into a fine young man. You are brave, strong, and loyal. We are so proud of you."

"But you were our son." Tears came to his mother's eyes. "We should have chased the night fears away. It is we who should have comforted you when you were hurt, to be there for the milestones. I would like to be there when you get married."

Liam started.

His father chuckled again. "Mothers are like that, son. Their child get married is the first step in providing them with grandchildren to spoil."

"She is beautiful," his mother observed. "She would be such a lovely bride."

"I suppose it isn't wise to dwell on marriage and children with Azurius on the move," his father warned her.

"Someone once told me," Liam said, "it's easy to find something worth dying for. Something worth living for is a much greater prize. Perhaps she is what keeps me going. If I do get married, I will bring her here to meet you."

His mother smiled at the thought.

"What can you tell me about Azurius?" he asked.

His father shook his head. "I wish we could tell you. If we were still alive, we could."

"We could have a friend talk to you," his mother added. "He is still alive, and we can get a message to him. He can help you."

"Yes, and he could teach you more about your abilities," his father agreed. "I'm afraid we can only give you a comforting presence and some fatherly or motherly advice. Tactical information is best left for other sources that are better placed. Keep coming to the garden. Jarek will find you."

Liam vanished from their arms. They found him standing before them, an armored warrior.

His mother smiled at him. "You are so handsome."

"I think your friends would prefer to see you in something like this," Liam's father added.

He felt his clothes shift. It looked like something his foster father would wear at a formal dinner.

"Oh!" His mother clapped her hands. "That's better. You will have all the lasses after you."

Liam looked at his image in the pool. He had to admit he looked good, but he focused and changed back into his armor. His mother looked disappointed.

"This is what I am," Liam told them. "It's what I'm good at."

His father nodded. "For now."

His mother kissed him. "Remember, Liam, we love you very much."

•   •   •   •   •

Randolf made it to the Temple compound. The chitin were on a general rampage. He had soldiers executing fighting withdrawals, trying to give the fleeing civilians cover.

Celinia and Teresina came as he leaned against the wall in exhaustion.

Celinia touched his should. "Arch Priestess Arria says you may use the Temple as a base of operation. She has gone to her chambers, praying for deliverance."

"Have any of the higher ranks arrived?" Randolf wanted to pass the reins of command to one of the Military Council.

Teresina and Celinia exchanged looks.

"I heard from one of the other officers that those they've seen have been assassinated," Celinia informed him. "Several councilors are missing, too."

Randolf felt his exhaustion leave as terror gripped him. "Mom, Dad?"

Celinia shook her head. "We haven't seen them."

He turned and ran for the gate.

"Randolf, wait!" Teresina shouted.

Desperate to get home, Randolf picked up his pace. She called to a nearby sergeant, Archer-177.

"Grab a squad and go with him," she commanded.

The sergeant called to his men as he ran after Randolf. Randolf heard nothing but the roar in his ears as he ran to his parents' house. The door stood open as he neared. A man in black stepped into the doorway and took aim. He managed to just dive to the side as a bullet sped past him. The man ducked back into the house as the squad returned fire. Randolf rolled to his feet and charged the door.

"Sir! No!"

He stopped short upon seeing his father's body.

"Licinious sends his greetings."

Randolf threw himself back out the door as the bullet grazed his armor. The assassin tried to follow and died in a hail of bullets. The squad had caught up.

"Are you all right, sir?"

Randolf nodded as a soldier help him up.

"Don't ever run off that way again, sir," the sergeant scolded. "It's hard enough to hold these boys together. It doesn't help when the officers act like they don't have any sense."

Randolf almost apologized but figured it would lead to another scolding. Three of the squad entered the house.

"You can go in when we've cleared the house," the sergeant told him.

"Thank you, Sergeant."

One soldier came back to the door. The sympathetic expression on his face said it all.

"It's all clear, sir, and I'm sorry."

He stepped aside to let Randolf enter. Randolf looked down at his father. The three soldiers went outside, touching his shoulder in sympathy as they passed.

"I should have been here," Randolf whispered.

"Don't think that way!" the sergeant snapped. Then whispered, "It's not your fault, sir. It's the fault of that traitor, his followers, and the beast who's controlling the chitin."

Randolf did not answer, knowing the sergeant did not expect one. Pulling away from his father, he went to his mother's body and kneeled beside the woman who had given birth to him. He picked up her hand and held it.

"Sir." The sergeant crouched beside him, a hand on his shoulder. "I know you want to grieve and don't care who sees, but you need to hold on to it a little longer. I'll send three men with you. We'll bring your parents' bodies back to the Temple."

Randolf nodded. With shaking hands, he unclasped the pendant of the Creator his mother always wore. He put it around his own neck and tucked it under his armor. Then he stood, unable to take his eyes off the violence done to one of the gentlest beings he had ever known.

"Licinious will pay for this, Mom." His voice shook. "I promise."

The sergeant took his arm and led him to the door. He indicated three men.

"Get the captain back to the Temple," he ordered. "Help him find a quiet place to get this out of his system. The rest of us will rig litters and bring the high councilor and his wife to the Temple. We'll also get this traitor back. His equipment may give us some information."

· · · · ·

Private Virgil and the others could not escape.

"Keep up your fire," the corporal yelled.

They had gotten cut off. Now the chitin had cornered them at Water Station Three. Virgil, the corporal, and two others were the only survivors.

"We've got to break out now!" the corporal yelled.

They made a desperate push forward. A chitin yanked one man off his feet. He screamed as the chitin drove its pincer into his chest. Virgil shot the creature off, but it was too late.

"Corporal, look out!"

Virgil turned. A chitin grabbed the corporal from behind. The man did not have time to scream. His head fell away from his body, becoming lost under the press of chitin. Virgil and the private stood back-to-back with plasma blades drawn. He heard the man scream as he cut down two chitin. Virgil turned to help when a searing pain came through his back. He looked down and saw a chitin's claw protruding from his chest. His vision going black, he realized it had his heart.

CHAPTER 3

Shadows lengthened. Randolf knew he was lucky he had the three soldiers with him. In the state he was in, he would have walked right past the Temple. As they guided him in, they found Teresina, Kia, and Celinia waiting for them. After a brief conversation, the three priestesses dismissed the soldiers and took charge of him.

Soon, he entered a room with a few captains, a few councilors, and Arch Priestess Arria. Celinia walked around the table and whispered in the arch priestess's ear. The arch priestess nodded.

"Captain Randolf, son of Marcus," the arch priestess began, "forgive us for demanding your presence now. We know you are grief stricken and exhausted to the point of collapsing. Unfortunately, we need to hold a council of war."

Randolf nodded, took several deep breaths, and tried to empty himself of emotion. Teresina guided him to a seat and pushed him into it.

"The traitor Licinious and his followers have been thorough." The arch priestess looked around the table. "Soldiers and militia have confirmed most of the Council are dead, save for those members here. None of our officers above the rank of captain have survived. Chitin run amuck in the city, with our soldiers trying to keep between them and our citizens. I don't think I need to impress upon you how dire the situation is."

"No, milady," Randolf replied.

Captain Simon spoke up. "Thank the Creator the chitin are less active at night."

"This will give us a chance to assess the situation," another captain agreed.

"You have observed the being who seems to command the forces arrayed against us." The arch priestess turned to Randolf.

"A strange figure," Randolf reported. "He appears almost human, save for the black scales. His eyes glow. When they glow black, then it seems he can unleash hell itself."

Worried glances went around the room.

"Also, he has an ability my old fighting instructor called stepping out of time," Randolf continued. "Very much like the ability my brother, Liam, had..." He choked back his grief. "It appears to give him superhuman speed, agility, and reflexes. However, like Liam, he can't use it indefinitely. It requires he expend energy. When he tires, he's like anyone else. Strong and fast, perhaps, but he can be killed."

"He's just exceedingly hard to kill," one officer remarked.

Randolf nodded. "He has to make a mistake, like use all of his energy before he can go into cover or put chitin between himself and his enemies."

"Or a sniper gets him lined up unaware," another man put in. "The question is, what can we do to stay alive until the opportunity presents itself?"

"We need to track down his agents in the city and eliminate them," Randolf added. "Licinious for one. So long as they remain active, they can make an arduous job almost impossible."

"I must also point out," one councilor said. "We don't know who those agents are. Licinious himself may not know all our enemy's agents. From what we've determined, they must have planned this attack for some time. Plenty of time to plant spies virtually anywhere. Among the poor people who are rushing to the Temple for safety, for instance. As you well know, we found them among the soldiers and officers who were supposed to defend us. Forgive me, Arch Priestess, but it's possible he even has agents in the clergy."

"I understand, Councilor," the arch priestess replied, "and I forgive your distrust. However, you know the Temple chooses priestesses for their abilities. I can sense each priestess. We have no traitors among us."

"We don't know the full extent of the powers arrayed against us," Randolf warned. "For every ability, there exists a counter ability. Ways to plant agents among you may exist, and that person is not even aware that they are an agent, but we must be cautious of such talk."

Randolf stood and made eye contact with each of those present, as his father taught him, to show he was in earnest.

"Spies are a significant danger. However, fear of spies can accomplish the same thing. We have no way of knowing who a spy is unless he makes a mistake. All we can do is take precautions. We can't check everyone, and it would be unwise to try. We don't want to spread paranoia."

The arch priestess's smile radiated a warmth that reminded Randolf of his mother.

"People say that High Councilor Marcus is dead," she declared in a firm voice. "I answer, 'That is a matter of opinion.' For a moment, I saw him standing before me."

Randolf sat back in surprise.

"I hereby confirm your field promotion to captain," the arch priestess continued. "Those of us remaining here have consulted together, and we agree. We request you take charge of coordinating the defenses of our city."

Randolf bowed his head. "I will do my poor best to live up to this honor."

Then she picked up a box, opened it, and motioned Randolf to approach. Randolf stood and came to her as she rose from her seat. She removed the battered lieutenant's rank decals from his shoulders and replaced them with the captain's insignia.

"May the Creator strengthen your arm." She made a sign of blessing.

Then the arch priestess addressed the others, "Regarding the possibility of traitors among those of us here, I will examine each of you."

She began with those nearest her. She cleared the councilors and then the officers. Randolf came forward last.

"We trust you, Captain Randolf," she told him in a low tone.

"I am honored by your trust, milady," he replied, "but I must lead by example."

She fell into her trance. He felt a warmth go through him. She stopped in surprise.

"You wear something under your armor."

"I..." then he remembered his mother's pendant. He took it out, unclasped it, and placed it in her hands.

She looked at it with a critical eye. "This was your mother's. I blessed it before your father gave it to her. She treasured it and never took it off. I wonder how Licinious managed to get a transmitter into it."

She closed her eyes and concentrated. The pendant glowed a moment and returned to normal.

Randolf looked at it with horror. "Milady..."

She held up her hand. "I know there is no treachery in you, Captain, and I have sent a stern warning to our enemy. Hopefully, it will give him pause. I picked out a name. Azurius. Fortunately, we discussed nothing I would say we needed to keep secret. It is safe to take it back."

Randolf hesitated.

The arch priestess regarded him. "The pendant is as innocent as your mother, Captain. I have purified it. I think you will wish to keep it."

Randolf relaxed and took it back.

"I dismiss you for now," the arch priestess announced. "Captains, you all have duties to perform. You will report directly to Captain Randolf. Teresina, Captain Randolf is exhausted to near dropping. Locate a room where he can rest and grieve. However, he must be ready to resume his duties in the morning."

She gave Teresina a meaningful look. Teresina bowed, took Randolf by the arm, and guided him out of the room.

Teresina led Randolf to a small chamber with a bed, where she helped him out of his armor and put it outside the door.

"Someone will come by to clean and repair it." She stood regarding him for a moment. "Oh, Randolf, I'm so sorry. This is more grief than anyone should bear."

Randolf sat on the bed, and tears streamed down his cheeks. Teresina took him in her arms and rocked him as he wept, clinging to her as if to a lifeline. Randolf had lost his father, his mother, men he had served with since he entered the military, and his brother. Fearing fate would rip her from him, too, he held her close. She rocked him, weeping with him.

Over time, his grief exhausted him. Sensing his weariness, Teresina pushed him back onto the pillow and touched him between the eyes.

"Sleep, my love," she whispered.

Randolf felt his conscious thought slip away. She tucked him in, kissed him, and slipped from the room.

•   •   •   •   •

Azurius had learned the importance of self-control long ago.

Darkness fell as Licinious had made his way to the Military Center for a prearranged meeting. Licinious approached him as if ready to flee at the first sign of Azurius's displeasure.

"Have any of your agents entered the Temple yet?" Azurius asked in a low voice.

"Not yet, Azurius," Licinious replied.

"Contact them and tell them to suspend the operation," Azurius ordered.

"What—"

"Don't argue with me!"

Licinious turned away and grabbed his communicator, which was on a secure system, independent from the military's comm system. Azurius used the time to help regain composure.

He opened his eyes and saw his reflection in a window. Slowly, a dull red replaced the blue glow in his eyes. It would not do for Licinious to see him worried. Azurius decided to be honest with himself. Shaken was a better word. First, the boy had thrown him out of his dream. Then he received a shock from the arch priestess.

Her telepathy is formidable! How did she short out the transmitter—and my receiver?

"Done."

Azurius turned to him. "I am disappointed in you, Licinious. Be grateful. Most people don't survive the experience."

He watched Licinious stiffen.

"I warned you about your obsession," Azurius went on. "Now, we have a problem. A minor one hopefully, but a problem nonetheless."

"I don't understand."

"You sent an assassin to kill High Councilor Marcus and his wife, Lidia."

"On your orders." Licinious's tone became defensive.

"You should not have had him wait for their son," Azurius told him. "Oh, your assassin might well have killed him, but the chances were remote he'd come with less than a squad. His soldiers killed the assassin. Now, they have his body in their hands, along with his communications devices and protocols. Their comm experts can detect our spies' communications. Now, we must assume our communications are being monitored. Since our only expert, the colonel, is dead, changing the protocols will be difficult."

Licinious remained quiet. Azurius knew he had decided not to press his luck. *Wisely.*

"We almost had a rare bit of good luck I didn't anticipate," Azurius continued. "The son claimed his mother's pendant, the one your agents got a listening device into, when she took it to the jewelers for repairs. It had been providing wonderful information. We almost had an ear in our enemies' inner council. The Emergency Council has placed Randolf in charge of their defenses."

Licinious had stiffened. "Almost?"

"They discovered the device and destroyed it." Azurius took a seat. "I could say your assassin put them on guard. They suspect we have more agents, though they aren't sure how many or where they're placed."

Azurius watched Licinious as his mind raced. *Let's twist the dagger a little more.*

"You, however, have an even bigger problem. What's more, I need to test you."

Licinious took an involuntary step back. "Test me?"

"Your failures are growing," Azurius told him, "and your weaknesses have become more apparent. I need to know you can overcome these weaknesses, perhaps turn them into strengths. In short, I need to know my second is worthy of my service."

"How must I prove myself, Azurius?" Licinious tried to hide his fear.

"Survive." Azurius glared at him. "The high councilor's son survived your attack. You killed his father, but I never ordered the death of his mother. Now, he will be looking for you with murder in his heart. You must figure out how to prevent him from killing you. Once I am sure of the arch priestess's powers and have forced the citizens of the city into the Temple compound, I will summon you."

I won't trouble him with the knowledge of the other son's survival.

Licinious turned without a word and left.

I expect he will start running once he's out of my sight. Azurius had an amusing vision of the two brothers battling for the right to wring the life out of the old fool. His eyes turned green, and he laughed out loud.

His thoughts turned to the foster brother. *That one intrigues me. Liam must have realized he can bar unwanted visitors from his dreams. Moreover, he did it in a way that left my head ringing.* Azurius waited until he sensed Licinious leave the building.

Then he tranced down. Azurius darted to his island off the southern continent and entered the corridor of his laboratory.

I am rather proud of this discovery.

He looked around the lab. *After the leaders in the Rebellion betrayed me, it was the perfect time to explore the potential of Etrusci. Step one: locate an uninhabited island. Then, over fifty-five years ago, build this laboratory complex. Then move in chitin starter nests.*

He smiled as he entered the control room. *The only way into this complex is through the dreamscape—a dream gate. For all her skill with dreams, I doubt even the arch priestess considered the possibility.*

First, he checked the controls of the chitin and then the planetary force field. *It won't do for outside help to spoil things now.* With everything in order, he sat down and contemplated.

Things are going according to plan. Not the plan Licinious thinks he knows about, nor the one I described to Liam. He had a far deeper plan. *Like the Finnian, the Neo-Etruscans have abilities their founders hadn't thought possible.* He remembered his conversations with the Neo-Etruscan/Utopian Founders. *Before we placed them in stasis, I realized they had no idea what they had truly created.*

Azurius stroked his chin. *These abilities, especially telepathy and the empathic power to heal, seem concentrated on certain females. These capabilities became the foundation for becoming a priestess. It cost me time to research these observations, but the conclusion's inescapable: the powers of the Finnian and Neo-Etruscans are linked.*

Azurius spun around in his chair. *Most people assumed the powers these two groups of genetically engineered people have are the unintended consequences of their founders' genetic tampering. They were on the right track, but it provides only part of the answer and doesn't go far enough.*

The major mystery is the speed with which these powers manifested themselves and the skill with which both use them. If I can extract the right genetic material from some of the more powerful priestesses, I might unravel the mystery. People with these powers could put the Rebellion back on top and restore me to my rightful place. I will need to do it under controlled conditions. Once I pacify New Olympia, the rest will be easy.

Liam provides another clue. When the boy's powers manifested themselves, I needed to research the appearance of the Finnians' abilities. Interestingly, with the Finnian, males and females can have these powers. Then came my epiphany: five hundred years ago, a delegation of Finnian, with a group of Terrans, visited Etrusci. With the five eugenics wars the Terrans had fought, they wanted to find out if there would be a sixth. Once satisfied the Neo-Etruscans had no interest in conquest, the Finnian and Terrans left. Shortly after, the Finnian abilities at stepping out of time and managing the dreamscape mushroomed. They became formidable almost overnight. It's the connection which has left me stymied. Is it something the Finnian picked up on Etrusci itself? Azurius shook his head. *I've worked in genetics all my life. If I have this planet under my control, I can explore this connection in greater detail.*

Liam was born on Etrusci and grew up with Neo-Etruscans. He's grown far more powerful than most Finnian. He just needs some additional training in how to use these abilities. Azurius smiled. *Liam will prove an excellent replacement for that fool, Licinious. He has a quick mind and is a fighter.* Azurius sighed. *I will eventually have to confront him in the real world. The big question: can the boy overcome his loyalty to the city? If he'd been an outcast at every turn, it would be easy.* Azurius had seen that he and his adoptive brother were extremely close. He could assume his foster parents had also been supportive. *The troops he commanded were loyal—and not just out of duty.*

Turning him will not be easy, Azurius mused, *but it will be worth it. Perhaps love could be his weakness. If I can stab his adoptive parents' murders into his heart and twist—perhaps he will lose control. Having lost control, he could start down a path and never get off it.*

Azurius paused for a moment. *Manipulating his emotions this way could be very delicate. If I go that far, Liam will lose nothing in killing me and taking my place. A worrying thought, but I can defeat the young Finnian if it comes to blows.*

Idly, Azurius wondered how Liam would gain entrance into the city. *The fastest course is through the portals, but I still have chitin coming through. Liam will have to contend with the city's defensive force field. The battle left him injured, and those injuries will hamper him. Other ways exist, but using them requires knowing those ways. I'm uncertain of all the ways with which one can gain entry into the city, but I know the places Liam will have to pass if he manages it.*

Azurius stood, went to the controls, selected a few observer-chitin, and had them burrow in strategic places and watch. *They will obey my orders to the letter. They will stay until they starve to death, which doesn't trouble me in the least.*

•   •   •   •   •

Liam had drifted into deep sleep after his trip to the garden. Waking up that morning, he felt his ribs throbbing. Swift Hunter had curled up by the door and was just waking up.

You dreamwalk.

Liam started. "How did you know?"

Mind make noise, Swift Hunter replied. *You have mind of dreamwalker. Like shaman.*

"Do you dreamwalk?" Liam asked, hoping to learn more.

Swift Hunter shook his head. *Not have that ability. Where you walk?*

"I found myself in a garden my birth parents took me to when I was a baby." Liam struggled to his feet. "I saw my parents. We talked. They said someone would come to help me learn more."

Swift Hunter nodded. *Among my people, powerful vision, see one's parents. Words will guide you with power.*

"Thank you, my friend. Again, you give me hope."

Liam put on his armor. "I have to check one last sector. I suspect there are open portals which the chitin are using to get into the city."

Dangerous.

"I don't ask you to go," Liam replied. "You have helped me immensely, but your life isn't mine to risk."

Swift Hunter reared onto his hind legs and enfolded Liam in a hug.

No need ask. You friend. Outside place of two legs, help as I can.

Liam returned the hug. "I seem destined to find friendship where it's least expected. Thank you, my friend. Let's have breakfast, then go to Archer sector."

Swift Hunter pushed him back and looked down at him.

We go with caution.

Liam nodded. "Always."

He used a diagnostic kit to reset his armor. Then he dismantled the one he'd carried from Grizzly sector.

What do? The bear-lizard asked.

"I need something to carry rations and extra water in," Liam explained, tossing a rations packet to Swift Hunter. "We should stop for breaks. I could sense even you were getting tired."

Swift Hunter nodded as he used a claw to open the packet. *Thanks.*

Liam placed several rations and some extra water in the casing. Hefting it by the straps, it felt much lighter than the original device.

"I'm going to prepare in case we need to return," he told Swift Hunter. "If I can get through, fine. If not, I need to return here and consider an alternative plan."

Liam placed everything he did not need back in the locker room.

Ready?

"Let's move." Liam climbed onto his friend's back.

•   •   •   •   •

Devon waved people on to the Temple.

"Keep moving!" He shouted. "Get to the Temple before the bugs cut you off!"

He went toward a woman who was hysterical with terror. Kia appeared, holding a small child. The woman raced to Kia, who pushed the child into the mother's arms.

"Bless you, Lady Priestess."

"Get to the Temple," Kia ordered.

The woman clutched her child and ran.

"You should go too," Devon warned. "The chitin are consolidating."

"We're almost finished," Kia replied. "We need to get all we can to the Temple compound."

A group of chitin appeared, and Devon fired several bursts.

He swore under his breath. "Let's go, Kia. We're standing out like sore thumbs. Everyone else has pulled back."

"But—"

Devon grabbed her hand and pulled her toward the retreat. When she saw they were alone and almost surrounded by chitin, Kia ran with him. Suddenly, they heard a cry from a side street. Kia pulled him to a stop.

"Kia!"

"Someone's in trouble." She headed for the sound.

Devon cursed and followed her. They came upon a group of men in black armor. One held his leg.

"Are you all right?" Kia asked.

In an instant, the men leveled weapons at them. Devon realized it was a trap and raised his own. A blow to the back of his head staggered him, and someone tore his weapon from his grip. Kia screamed as another blow drove him to his knees. Someone dragged him backward and lashed his arms to a light pole.

When his eyes cleared, he saw the traitors manhandling Kia.

"Leave her alone!" he yelled, struggling against his bonds.

Several men pushed Kia, face first, into a building wall with bruising force, knocking the wind out of her. Two men held her pinned.

"Well, well. Private...Devon, I believe."

A shadow detached itself and came into the light.

"You!" Devon tried to lunge for the traitor despite his bound hands.

Licinious laughed. "So, I see my man's little accident yielded some unexpected benefits."

Licinious ran his hand up Kia's thigh. Kia cried out and kicked back, almost hitting him in the groin.

Licinious struck her face. Devon tried to break free and get at him.

"You have fire in you, Lady Priestess Kia." Licinious leered at her.

"Leave her alone, traitor!" Devon shouted.

"My, you are brave for one who's helpless." Licinious stepped away from the girl and approached Devon. He squatted down and looked him in the eye. "This civilization is a corruption of what it should have been. They have corrupted even the Creator from the vision of the Founders."

"The Creator is God," Devon replied with conviction. "The Founders were mortals and fools."

Licinious lashed out, his fist catching Devon full in the face and slamming his head back against the pole.

"You speak of what you do not know," Licinious growled. "The 'Creator' was nothing more than a construct that the Founders used to keep their vision for our people until they returned. Now it has a life of its own. The arch priestesses have diluted it with a false morality and would have us mingle with the misborn. Even allowing a misborn to live among us."

Devon shook his bleeding head and laughed without humor. "If you mean Liam, he was fifty times the man the Founders were, and a hundred times the man you'll ever be."

Licinious lashed out again. Devon slumped, gathered himself, and stared at the traitor with all the insolence he could muster. Then the warrior spat into his face.

Licinious recoiled back and prepared to strike the defiant soldier again—then stopped. He stood and wiped his face.

"No one shows me that kind of disrespect," he snarled. "Your punishment will be to watch us punish her." He jerked his head back toward Kia.

Devon lunged against his bonds again. "No!"

Licinious turned and nodded to the waiting men.

. . . . .

Upon waking, Randolf found his armor where Teresina had said it would be. He put it on and headed into the main wing of the Temple.

The sergeant, Archer-177, who seemed to have appointed himself Randolf's aide and guardian, fell in beside him.

"The arch priestess has cleared a spot to use as a ready room," the sergeant informed him.

"Thank you," Randolf replied.

"Sir," the sergeant ventured. "I know you're new to all of this authority, and it's not my intention to be disrespectful, but when you thank someone junior to you, you should include his rank."

"Thank you, Sergeant."

"Better, sir," the sergeant replied.

"Just make sure we're alone when you feel the need to correct me."

"Of course, sir."

They came upon Celinia, Teresina, Captain Simon, and Lieutenant Janus talking. From the animated gestures, it looked like a problem. They stopped as Randolf and the sergeant approached.

"What's happened?" Randolf asked.

"Sir," Lieutenant Janus answered. "I recognize this may be a low priority, but we have two people missing."

"Who?" Randolf asked.

"Private Devon and Priestess Kia," Lieutenant Janus told him. "They were in the city, trying to cover the evacuation of civilians to the Temple compound. They didn't return last night, and we can't raise Devon's comm."

Randolf looked around the group. Teresina and Celinia looked frantic. Captain Simon and the sergeant looked grim. Lieutenant Janus looked worried but resolved.

"They were my friends too." Randolf straightened. "While I want to drop everything and tear the city apart looking for them, we can't afford the time. We have people out there still trying to make their way to safety, and an enemy bent on killing us."

They all nodded.

"Lieutenant, Captain," Randolf ordered. "Order the men to watch out for them. We can't go looking for them, but perhaps we'll get lucky and make contact."

"Yes, sir," they replied.

"Sir, I'm getting ready to take a platoon out," Lieutenant Janus offered. "No one has assigned me an area yet. I think I can push into where they were last seen. Stragglers may still be there, anyway."

Randolf looked at Captain Simon, who turned to the lieutenant.

"Very well, Lieutenant," Captain Simon told him, "but you heard what Captain Randolf said. A closer than cursory look, but no more. Clear?"

"Yes, sir," Lieutenant Janus replied.

He saluted and went to gather his men.

Randolf turned to the two priestesses. "You better report what happened to Arch Priestess Arria."

Celinia and Teresina nodded and left.

Captain Simon stepped next to Randolf. "I hope we're not giving them false hope. Chances are we won't find them."

"If they're still alive," Randolf replied, "I don't want to abandon them. Lieutenant Janus will find them if they're out there. Otherwise, he won't waste time."

Randolf turned to the captain. "I'll be in the ready room if anyone needs me."

"Yes, sir."

•   •   •   •   •

Swift Hunter did not set as rapid a pace as yesterday, but it was still much faster than Liam could set alone if he pushed. They stopped for frequent breaks.

Approaching Archer sector, Swift Hunter slowed.

Bugs ahead, he warned Liam.

"I think you're right." Liam rose a little and wished he had binoculars. "They've probably secured at least one portal to gain entry into the city. The last two sectors we scouted were in good condition. They wouldn't have abandoned them unless the chitin had gotten into the Military Center."

Swift Hunter paused his pace, glancing up at the man-made ridgeline.

Safer up there, the bear-lizard suggested. *Bugs not see us.*

"The terrain looks rough on that ridge," Liam told him. "Harder going. We set a faster pace down here. If you tried to keep this pace up there…"

Trip, the creature agreed. *Ribs bad enough without Liam breaking Swift Hunter's fall.*

Liam laughed. "Not to mention Liam's ribs."

The bear-lizard snickered. Liam appreciated his new friend's sense of humor. He found Swift Hunter amiable and wise, but shrewdly cautious.

"When we get closer," Liam decided, "we should slow down, anyway. We can move into the ridgeline then."

Keep pace, Swift Hunter agreed, *and be careful.*

Liam had Swift Hunter pause as the base came into view. He slid off the bear-lizard's back and drew his pistol.

"Let's get on the ridge now." Liam pointed to the ridgeline. "Can you move along it without attracting attention?"

The bear-lizard leveled a bland look at him.

Liam winced. "My mistake. Predator—stalking prey."

Swift Hunter nodded, and they climbed the ridge. They had several options open to them. None of them were attractive. They crouched lower as they got closer. They heard the chitin before they saw them. Without a word, the two lay on the ground. Inching forward, Liam felt his ribs complain the entire way. Finally, they peeked over the ridge above the Archer sector's outposts.

"Structurally, all five outposts seem intact," he whispered. "The central one there looks like they hit it hard."

He pointed to where Archer Leader's post would have been.

The explosion blackened the remains of the outpost, and the heavy weapon lay in ruins. It looked as if they used it to protect the sector for a time. Broken bits of armor and body parts littered the outposts. However, it was not as many as Liam had feared.

These two overrun. Swift Hunter pointed to the central outpost and the one to its left. *Rest abandoned, like other two bases.*

Liam tried to peek over the edge but retreated. "I can't see the condition of the portals."

Bugs concentrate on these two. Swift Hunter told him.

Liam saw he was right. A column of chitin traveled through the forest. The column split into two groups, each going into the two Archer outposts that must still have active portals.

"This means, with those two portals back to the city open, they're getting into the Military Center." Liam slumped with resignation. "It means there are chitin in the city. Azurius is there as well."

Liam turned and slid back down the embankment into a seated position. "I was afraid of this."

Swift Hunter sat on his haunches. *What now?*

"I could try to take down the portals and prevent anymore chitin from going in," Liam mused. "The problem is, I'd have to battle the chitin, which would alert Azurius to my presence. Even if I get to the portals, I doubt I can make good my escape before the chitin overwhelmed me."

Walk to city?

"It's a day's walk over open ground—if I were healthy. I wouldn't have to worry about the chitin. They're concentrating on their own way in, but other creatures prowl the plains."

Might meet hungry felino.

Liam looked toward the city. "The perimeter force fields are still active. Azurius hasn't bothered to take them down. I wonder why?"

Not worried about it? Swift Hunter suggested.

"They possess independent power sources, and I can't get to them from this side." Liam brooded for a moment. "Let's backtrack to Boulder sector. I have to think the situation through."

Liam took one more look at the Archer outposts.

"I notice weapons and equipment down there. The chitin must have carried the bodies away." Liam slid back down. "Swift Hunter, I'm going down between the two outer outposts and scout for weapons."

Swift Hunter looked down. *Dangerous. Take care. Will move to edge of outpost. Come if trouble.*

Liam nodded, backed away from their vantage point, and crept along the ridge. Once he had slid into position, he crawled along the wall of the number four outpost and slipped down. Crouching, he drew his pistol. Upon giving the area a quick scan, he saw pieces of armor and some belt cases. Creeping closer, he found a full set of power cells and ammunition magazines. After a brief search, he saw the chitin had smashed any actual weapons. After replenishing his own utility belt, Liam checked to make sure he was not in any chitin's line of sight. Then, crouching low, he crept to the number five outpost. Here he found a damaged assault rifle that looked like he could fix.

Look out! Boomed into his mind.

Liam turned to see a chitin looming above him. He threw himself backward as the creature struck. A claw glanced off Liam's armor, and he rolled to his feet, drawing his plasma blade. The creature charged. Liam stepped out of time and decapitated it. He saw others coming. Liam turned his head and saw Swift Hunter galloping toward him in seeming slow motion. Liam drew his pistol and kept firing until the bear-lizard had reached his side. Then he returned to normal time.

Swift Hunter roared, and with a swipe of his claws, shredded two chitin. Liam cut down one that tried to grab his friend, then gunned down two more who tried to flank them. Then they had a free space.

Get on!

Liam grabbed the bear-lizard's scruff and flung himself onto Swift Hunter's back, ignoring the pain from his ribs. Swift Hunter turned and dropped to all fours at a run. They sped away, leaving the chitin behind them. After a few kilometers, Swift Hunter slowed to a walk. Liam slid off his back, and Swift Hunter took his waterskin from its thong and took a long drink. Liam drank from his canteen.

Not smartest action, Swift Hunter commented. *Worth it?*

"I think so. I have a rifle now, and I think I can fix it. Whether it was smart..." Liam shrugged.

Go back now? Swift Hunter asked.

Liam nodded. The great predator put his waterskin away. Liam climbed on his back, and they trotted back to Boulder sector.

•   •   •   •   •

The trip back was uneventful. When they got back to Boulder sector, they both were sagging with exhaustion.

Rest edge on bank. Nice breeze.

Liam nodded. "I'll eat then fix the rifle. Want something?"

The creature nodded eagerly. Liam opened the door to the locker room and set down his prize. He handed a packet to Swift Hunter and took one for himself. Swift Hunter went to the edge of the outpost and lay down.

Liam ate, then got a tool kit and set the rifle on the base of the heavy weapon's platform. He removed the rifle's magazine and power pack and carefully removed the optics. Then Liam disassembled the coil and removed the barrel and trigger. He checked each piece with care.

Weapon usable?

Liam nodded. "The trigger needs a little lubrication—standard for my tool kit. The other pieces are in satisfactory condition. However, it has a damaged connection from the power pack to the coil."

Bad?

"Well," Liam replied, "without it, the coil can't generate a magnetic field to fire the gun."

Can fix? Swift Hunter asked.

"Difficult," Liam told him. "I have a cold soldering iron, but I don't have the right gauge of connector in my tool kit to reconnect the coil. I'll have to improvise."

He went into the locker area to see what he could scavenge. Liam's eyes fell on the pieces of the diagnostic kit he had disassembled. "The diagnostic kit has some connectors in it. I should be able to separate one of them from the rest. It's a heavier gauge, but it might work."

Liam took a small folding knife from his kit, sliced into the bundle with great care, and separated the connectors. He brought a connector back to his work area and soldered it in place. Now he needed to put the assault rifle back together. Reassembling the rifle, usually child's play for Liam, required more pressing, fitting, and backtracking, since the heavier gauge connector made for a tighter fit. Careful not to sever or strip the connection, Liam re-assembled the weapon. He inserted the power pack and loaded the magazine.

Swift Hunter watched curiously. *Fixed?*

"I intend to find out."

Hefting the weapon, Liam took it to the side of the outpost, picked out a stone at the rifle's maximum range and squeezed the trigger. The coil cycled, and the rock shattered with a loud crack. Liam grinned back at the bear-lizard, who had jumped at the sound.

"I guess it works."

Good, Swift Hunter grumped. *Now heart has to slow down.*

"Sorry," Liam replied, "but I feel a lot less naked now."

He picked up the parts and tools and put them away. Then he put everything back.

"I'm going to lie down myself, Swift Hunter," Liam said. "I'm going to dreamwalk."

Will keep watch, Swift Hunter assured him.

Liam found a reasonably comfortable spot, closed his eyes, and relaxed into his exhaustion. Soon he drifted off.

●   ●   ●   ●   ●

Liam found himself in the garden again. It seemed the chitin were not even going to bother annoying him this time. He walked to the bush where he had first seen his parents. The glade appeared empty. He wandered to the fountain, remembering what they had said about fishing him out of it. It seemed it still held an attraction for him.

"Liam?" a strange voice spoke behind him.

Liam spun and saw a black-scaled humanoid. At first, he thought it was Azurius but noticed the being had brown eyes that did not glow. With light brown hair, graying at the sides, he was dressed in a different uniform as well, in colors of gray and black. Liam saw he wore comfortable shoes instead of boots.

"Yes?" Liam asked suspiciously.

"I'm a friend of your parents, Seámus and Deirdre," the creature replied. "My name is Jarek. I am an ambassador for the Galactic Alliance. Your parents asked me to help you. I have certain obligations I owe your family."

Liam hesitated for a moment, then extended his hand. Jarek took the hand in a firm, friendly handshake.

"Azurius has attacked the city," Liam told him. "He's gotten past the defenses and now has an entire horde of chitin on the rampage through New Olympia."

Jarek grimaced in distaste. "Azurius. That explains a great deal."

"You knew my parents?"

Jarek gave Liam a warm smile and touched his arm.

"My people, the Gothowans, live almost ten times longer than a human," Jarek explained. "Hence, we tend to avoid forming close attachments with shorter-lived species. However, I considered your parents very close friends. They were kind people who loved the soil. They were also cunning warriors. I understand you inherited some of their skills from them."

Jarek sat at the edge of the fountain.

Liam became lost in thought. He did not know his parents had been warriors.

"Let's be comfortable, Liam." Jarek drew Liam's attention back to the conversation. "I'm afraid I have a lot to tell and teach you and little time. We may need several sessions. Azurius is a deadly foe, and I am doubtful of your ability to defeat him without this knowledge."

Jarek contemplated the fountain for a moment as Liam sat next to him.

"Let me start with your parents," Jarek decided. "Your parents, Deirdre and Seámus, were humans. However, they were also the product of an experimental program carried out by three Terran geneticists some six centuries ago. They worked on a planet in the Orion cluster to create, shall we say, super soldiers? Their purpose was conquest, beginning with Old Terra, then known as Earth. The genetic tampering had one interesting aspect. Over time, some individuals developed a strain of telepathic abilities, including dreamwalking. Some also developed the ability to step out of time—abilities known to some other species, including my own. The project ended centuries ago, and rather than try to exterminate them, the Earth government ceded to them some colonies in the Orion cluster. These people called themselves Finnian, after a group of warriors from the mythology of Old Terra. They trained as soldiers and maintained contact with Old Terra. Though everyone trained as warriors, they also studied for other professions. They've stood by the Terrans ever since. My people met up with humanity three centuries later."

Jarek paused, as if struggling to find words.

"I take it there was a problem," Liam coaxed.

Jarek nodded. "The Galactic Alliance, of which the Gothowans are members, was in the middle of a civil war, one which persists to this day. The Rebel faction just couldn't keep it private and inflicted it on Terran space. Azurius led that faction. We intervened and fought some horrendous battles. A heavy bombardment of Old Terra's sun caused intense solar flares. It made civilized life almost impossible. So, the Terrans evacuated to other planets they had colonized. The Finnian jumped into the thick of it. The war ebbed and flowed—lengthy periods of boredom followed by moments of terror. It seems this situation is always the way with war."

The alien paused a moment. "Now, another group of geneticists created another subspecies of humans at the same time as yours. The creators of this group were Utopianists. They sought a perfect society." Jarek threw him a wry smile. "As you know, there is no such thing. They made their creation to be beautiful and perfect, at least by their standards. However, they didn't plan on certain individuals developing strong telepathic and empathic abilities, especially females. These capabilities became the basis for their healing powers, almost unique in the galaxy. We can only guess why this happened. One theory suggests it was another unintended consequence of genetic tampering. The Utopian Founders chose this world as their cradle, eventually establishing their first city of Visul. From there, they spread out, creating new population centers which, over time, became the Neo-Etruscan's seven major urban centers. They adopted elements of the ancient religions of

Terra, and like many known civilizations today, centered the religion on a Creator. The Founders originally called the planet Utopia, but over time, your adoptive people called it Etrusci, after a culture from Terra's Classical Period."

"So, how did my parents end up here?" Liam asked.

"Our war seemed to wind down, and we had pushed Azurius's faction back," Jarek explained. "The Neo-Etruscans were wiser than their creators. After the Founders disappeared, the Neo-Etruscans abandoned the utopian vision in favor of something a *bit* more realistic. While they chose to be neutral and didn't take part in the war, your adoptive people kept in touch with us. Then, about forty-five years ago, they reported chitin making appearances. We became alarmed since chitin are a biological construct which Azurius created, and the Rebellion used. At first, the chitin acted as though no one controlled them—possibly an accidental infestation. Then, about forty years ago, they began moving against the cities. The Neo-Etruscans lacked experienced soldiers. So, they weren't prepared to defend themselves against the chitin and certainly not against any sentient beings. This lack of experience was one of the things we found worrying."

Liam nodded. "My foster father said that when the chitin attacks began, a force field appeared around the planet, which cut Etrusci off from outside aid and neutralized their air power."

"Yes," Jarek agreed. "I should have known it was Azurius's doing. Over time, the Neo-Etruscans had to abandon all of their major population centers. Originally, New Olympia was a rich mining town on the plains of the Central Continent. Its mineral resources were the reason the Alliance was eager to trade with Etrusci. Surviving refugees from the rest of the planet gathered in New Olympia because it proved to be the most defensible area. Your parents told me, when we could still communicate, the town sat on top a hill surrounded by a defensible plateau."

"I guess that defense is why my father laid the city out in a circular pattern," Liam observed.

"One of the reasons, yes. Before the force field came up, your parents were part of a group of commandos the Alliance sent to settle here and monitor the situation. They established observation posts around the cities under the cover of a series of farms. However, some Neo-Etruscan factions were prejudiced against non-indigenous humans. When the chitin attacked, they kept the Finnian out of it until it was almost too late. At last, the Neo-Etruscans didn't have a choice but to accept the Finnians' help. With the cities falling, the commandos withdrew to redeploy around the last refuge. The Finnian helped establish a defensive grid around New Olympia to keep the chitin away."

Liam nodded.

Jarek continued, "They contacted Marcus, your adoptive father, who kept them abreast of the situation in New Olympia. This intelligence was of immense help in their efforts to keep the chitin at bay while Marcus built and reinforced the city's defenses. Moreover, they provided the city with fresh food while the citizens created hydroponic gardens and genetically engineered some of the herd animals so they would be smaller and easier to handle within the confines of the city. I understand they even bio-engineered things like teas and coffee to grow in the hothouses. At first, New Olympia found itself overrun with refugees. Fortunately, the mining engineers, your foster father especially, proved to be capable civil engineers, too. Your foster father had to turn a small mining town into a well laid out, functioning city almost overnight. His people automated the mining operations and concentrated resources on defenses and then services. The Neo-Etruscans still had elements who disapproved of this arrangement. Then, about thirty years ago, we lost subspace contact with our people here. After Azurius put the force field in place, we could still communicate. Then I suspect he must have added a subspace barrier of some sort. The chitin moved with a purpose again and began picking off the farmsteads. Your parents were exemplary at moving in the dreamscape. We maintained contact for a few years, but things were desperate."

"I remember my father"—Liam corrected himself—"foster father, Marcus, telling us about what happened. He wanted to move the farmsteaders into the city. Our food production could take up the load by then. Councilor Licinious and his supporters blocked this move. At first, I thought it was simple prejudice. Now I know Licinious is working with Azurius. Azurius told me as much when he invaded my dream the other night."

Jarek's eyes opened in surprise. "He invaded your dream? How did you survive the encounter?"

"I threw him out."

Jarek looked impressed. "That's good news. You seem to possess more power than most of the Finnian, and that's saying something."

"I can also step out of time," Liam told him.

"This is very good," Jarek replied. "With my help, you may prevent a catastrophe. Well, to finish the story, one day, your parents were gone. The only thing remaining were their shades. They expressed their love for you and asked I help when I could. Last night, they placed a message in my dreams that you needed help. I watched the dreamscape, so I could see when you entered."

"Interesting," Liam noted. "I talked to my birth parents last night. Apparently, there are limits, but also some surprising abilities."

Jarek chuckled. "You'll find these abilities and limits won't seem to make a great deal of sense because there is a great deal about minds and souls we don't understand and probably never will. If we had the knowledge of the Creator, we'd probably see it has rules and flows logically."

Then, Jarek asked, "What time is it where you are?"

"Late afternoon," Liam replied.

"Let's not spend any more time here now. I've got things I need to do. Why don't you prepare for tonight, and we'll begin our first lessons when we meet again? Later tonight, then?"

Liam nodded in agreement. "Thank you, Jarek. I look forward to it."

Jarek chuckled. "You say that now. Until then."

Liam clasped his hand, then moved back to consciousness.

•   •   •   •   •

Liam opened his eyes and winced with pain as he got to his feet.

Ribs? asked Swift Hunter.

"Partly," Liam replied, grimacing. "After riding, I'm finding muscles I never knew I had, and they're connected to the ribs."

Swift Hunter nodded in sympathy. *Dreamwalk profitable?*

"Very," Liam replied. "I met the person my parents talked about. He gave me some background about what's happening."

Good. From spirit world?

"No," Liam told him. "He lives on another world. Tonight, he said he would start teaching me about my abilities."

Swift Hunter looked impressed. *Must be powerful shaman then. Good teacher.*

"My thoughts exactly," Liam agreed. "How much longer can you hang around?"

Two sleeps. Great Heart nearing home then.

"Okay," Liam replied. "I'm going to prepare for the tonight. I'm not sure how long what Jarek has to teach me will take. If it takes longer than you can stay, I'll get by."

Nights getting colder, Swift Hunter suggested. *Want fire?*

Liam nodded. "Good idea. However, I don't want to build one inside."

Build here. Night clear. Sleep outside.

"I still need to find a way into the city soon." Liam looked back to New Olympia. "While there's still a city to get into."

Swift Hunter nodded. *Will get wood.*

He moved off, down into the forest. Liam continued preparing his camp. He could use this room for storage. He went to the other four Boulder outposts and collected the rations and water. Swift Hunter returned soon.

Have cache, the bear-lizard explained as he set down a pile of wood.

The creature started selecting wood to start the fire. Then he brought out a kit of tinder and two rocks. With two strikes, the sparks caught, and the fire began to burn.

"You are very good." Liam felt amazed as he warmed his hands. "If I tried that method, I'd have taken all night."

You have other method? Swift Hunter asked in surprise.

"One could call it a modern method." Liam sat by the fire. "But I love watching a master in action, especially when it's old school."

What learn from shaman? Swift Hunter asked. Liam settled back to tell his tale.

•   •   •   •   •

After a late dinner with Swift Hunter, Liam lay back by the fire and let himself drift into a trancelike sleep. He found himself back at the fountain.

"Jarek?" he called.

After a few moments, Jarek appeared. "A lucky confluence. My attention wasn't required elsewhere, so I could come right away."

Liam nodded. "About that. Is there some way we can arrange to meet? We need to move fast."

"I know." Jarek's smile faded. "I've put an alarm here to tell me when you've come. It will let me know if you need me. You're worried about the city."

Liam looked down. "I hope my brother and parents are all right."

Jarek looked puzzled for a moment. "Ah, right, you have a foster family, including a brother."

"Randolf, son of High Councilor Marcus and Lidia. He's been my brother in all but blood," Liam said warmly.

Jarek sat at the fountain again. "I think we should start with the dreamscape."

"What is it exactly?" Liam asked.

"I believe your human ancestors once called it astral travel," Jarek replied. "However, the way its adherents presented it at the time, most people could not accept it as something real. It allows us to walk in our dreams and retain control over them. We move in the familiar and communicate with people who are within range and have dreamwalking capability. Also, we can talk to people we know have died. Their shades anyway."

Liam nodded.

Jarek added quickly. "I should warn you against bringing the shades of the dead back too often. It is said if you don't let go of the dead, they find it difficult to find peace."

"Someone helped me through some nightmares recently by accompanying me," Liam told him. "She was in the room with me. However, when Azurius burst in, I threw him out."

"Anyone with a certain amount of aptitude for dreamwalking can accompany you into your dream," Jarek replied. "Azurius and I can enter dreams over a distance. We must be familiar with the *feel* of the person before we can attempt it. Azurius must have observed you for some time. I could home in on something that felt like your birth parents. Once I was with you, and you accepted my presence, it became easier."

"So, my acceptance is important."

"Very," Jarek agreed. "Once you rejected Azurius, you barred him from your personal dreamscape."

"Is there any way I can use dreamwalking to see what's in the real world rather than just what is inside my head?"

"As a point of fact," Jarek replied, "yes. Some of us can reach out from inside ourselves and walk in a place between. You can scout a short distance from your body. Be careful, however, you can't bar Azurius from the dreamscape outside of yourself. If you meet him there, he could hurt you."

Liam nodded.

"Feel up to trying now?"

Again, Liam nodded.

"Where are you sleeping?"

"At an outpost."

"Excellent." Jarek clapped his hands together. "Return toward consciousness, like you were going to wake up, but stay in a trance."

Liam felt himself return.

"Very good," Jarek encouraged. "Now this part we call 'feeling the you inside you.'"

Under Jarek's guidance, Liam felt himself as distinct from his body.

"You want that part of you to stand without your body."

Liam stood and turned, seeing his still slumbering body. He found Jarek beside him.

"I feel like I am looking down on my corpse," he whispered.

"The first time usually does. Note the rise and fall of the chest. If that movement stops, then it's okay to worry."

Jarek looked around Boulder Sector. "Who's your furry friend?"

"A bear-lizard named Swift Hunter. They communicate telepathically."

"His mind seems limited to short range," Jarek noted, "but I think his kind have the potential for much more. I'll bet certain individuals are quite formidable. Those portals look dead. You're using the locker room as a camp?"

Liam nodded. "The chitin have destroyed most of the portals. I know the chitin are using two at Archer sector."

"Let's start there. Focus on a point about two kilometers out and up about forty degrees," Jarek instructed.

Liam looked at him. "Why so far away?"

"The closer we are," Jarek told him, "the easier it will be for Azurius to detect us. We approach with caution."

Liam nodded and concentrated. The shock of being in the air stunned him, and he started sinking. Jarek grabbed him.

"Careful!" Jarek warned. "You can hover. Believe it."

Liam stabilized himself and looked down.

"Forgive me, Liam. I should have explained this concept to you before we started. In this kind of existence, belief is critical. We can work on 'belief,' but I don't want you facing Azurius out here for that reason."

"I don't understand," Liam replied.

"If I were to take that pistol at your side and shoot you in the heart, what would happen?"

"I'd die," Liam stated.

Jarek nodded. "What would have killed you?"

"A bullet."

Jarek shook his head. "In this existence, your own mind would have killed you. You don't actually have that gun. The bullet is a phantom in this existence. It would kill you because you believe it would kill you."

"So, if I didn't believe it, I wouldn't die."

"Exactly," Jarek replied, "but not believing isn't as easy as it sounds. Most people would retain some doubt, and the slightest doubt could kill you. Even for my race, this skill takes years of training your mind, but it's never a sure thing."

Liam nodded again.

"You mentioned we could only travel a short distance from our bodies," Liam ventured. "What's the limit?"

Jarek smiled. "Relatively short, yes. It varies depending on a person's strength and experience, and certain things can block you, either by keeping you out or in. Your priestesses, for instance, maintain a defensive barrier around the Temple which prevents dreamwalkers from entering or leaving. The maximum I know of is a planet. If you gather some powerful dreamwalkers together, they could scout parts of the galaxy. I believe you are powerful enough for that kind of range."

"What about you?"

Jarek grinned. "I can extend my range using your body as a relay. You *boost* my signal."

"I see," Liam mused, "but how could you get to me in the first place?"

"When I first came to you," Jarek explained, "I was fully in the dreamscape. That means I was just communicating with you. Depending on strength and experience, that kind of communication can be almost unlimited. I came into your dreamscape and jumped off from your body."

Liam's eyes opened wide. "I bet that's a handy skill."

"Okay, let's move closer," Jarek advised.

They closed to within half a kilometer of the sector and watched chitin going through the two portals.

"When I was here before," Liam informed the Gothowan, "I considered trying to destroy those remaining portals, but I knew the chitin would be all over me before I could get anywhere."

"You'd need something like a rail launcher or a bayonet grenade to take them down from this side of the portal," Jarek noted. "Tossing a couple of grenades into the portal might destroy them, but their going off at the right distance would require a lot of luck. You were wise not to attempt it."

"If I had some explosives. I could place them above the portal and bring down the cliff face."

"Do you have training in explosives?" Jarek asked.

Liam shook his head. "I don't even have explosives."

"Let's not dwell on 'what ifs.'"

Jarek turned around and stopped. "Now that's interesting."

Liam tried to follow his gaze. "I don't see anything."

Jarek glanced at him. "It's very subtle. I just know what to look for. Let's see where it goes."

He grabbed Liam's arm, pulling him in a southerly direction.

CHAPTER 4

Lieutenant Janus had slipped into the residential area where Devon and Kia were last seen. Janus knew the score. He had little hope of a happy ending. The chitin converged on another area, masking his platoon's movements. Already, they had found some civilians in hiding and sent them on to the Temple compound.

"Sir," his sergeant called over the comm, "over here."

Lieutenant Janus followed the call to the source, with the rest of his men close behind. He saw the squad leader ahead waving to him. He stopped as he drew abreast of him. The sight that greeted him caused his heart to sink. Devon lay tied to a pole, and Kia lay out on the ground, her clothing cut away. Someone had cut their throats.

A man started forward, but Janus held him back.

"Sir?"

"This place is a crime scene, soldier." Lieutenant Janus spared the soldier a glance. "We take it in layers."

He scanned the area. "Chitin didn't kill them. Humans did. Get me a tricam."

A man brought him a three-dimensional camera.

Another man spoke up. "Sir, I'm from the militia and normally work in criminal investigation. I'm familiar with investigative procedures. Should I do the pictures?"

"Please." Lieutenant Janus passed the man the tricam. "We must be quick. Prepare to move the bodies back to the Temple compound should the chitin approach this position. Time permitting, we look for evidence. When you're done, I want you to supervise the removal of the bodies, to prevent the loss of evidence."

"Very good, sir."

"Sergeant," the lieutenant ordered. "I'm keeping a squad here to help. Take the platoon and finish the sweep. Report back here when you're done."

"Yes, Lieutenant," his sergeant replied. "I don't envy any of you."

The sergeant followed the rest of the platoon. Lieutenant Janus watched the man work with the camera. He knew his job. He worked his way through the scene, taking pictures from several angles, using his shoulder knife as a scale.

Once finished, he directed the gathering of the evidence and motioned Lieutenant Janus to him. "Sir, normally we'd have a priestess trained in forensics view the bodies *in situ*. Seeing how that isn't possible here, I took all the pictures I could. From what I can tell, someone assaulted her—brutally."

The man kneeled, and with a gloved hand, closed Kia's eyes.

•   •   •   •   •

Liam followed Jarek and realized they had traveled a significant distance over a short space of time. It surprised him when they reached the southern continent, which the people had abandoned long ago. They approached an island, and Liam started seeing faint traces of something.

"I see something now, Jarek. I just don't know what."

Jarek smiled at him in approval. "Think of it as a path Azurius has worn into the carpet of the dreamscape through constant travel back and forth. It's more complicated, but that explanation will do for now. I doubt Azurius expected anyone to get this far, or he'd have done a better job covering his tracks."

They hovered over the island.

Jarek gave a grim laugh. "One of Azurius's more brilliant inventions. What do you see?"

"The trail goes into the center of the island but seems to stop. It looks like an empty field."

"I believe it's his control center. A few of your centuries ago, he deduced how to create strongholds one can't enter save through the dreamscape. I've examined a couple. I believe he controls the chitin and the planetary force field from here."

Liam spared Jarek a glance. "How does he control a living organism?"

"He started out with a small hive insect he found on the planet Beta Gemini Three," Jarek explained. "The result of his tampering is what you see today. Azurius can control them telepathically to some extent, but that type of control has limits. With his mind, he can give simple mass commands or somewhat more complex commands to individuals. Also, he can take control of an individual chitin if he wants to use its eyes. For more nuanced things, he needs these controls."

"How would that technique work?"

"He uses ultrasonic frequency commands. The chitin and their tiny forebears communicate through subsonic vibrations. The device I believe is here makes use of that ability. I suspect he used the same means to put up the planetwide force field. As a point of fact, the force field would make subsonic vibrations easier to transmit."

"How would subsonic commands make it easier to nuance commands to individual groups of chitin?"

"It's not that difficult," Jarek told him. "You condition the chitin to broadcast individual identifiers as each individual hatches. The computer records and keeps track of them so you can select an individual or group for a specific task, using the force field to carry those vibrations across the entire planet. However, the tricky part is their enormous size."

"Why?"

"Insects usually have a size limit. To get huge insects requires an atmosphere with a great deal of oxygen. On Old Terra, they had insects one meter in size hundreds of millions of years ago. However, the oxygen levels at the time were at thirty-five percent, according to oxygen isotopes found in paleosols. After sixty million years, that oxygen level dropped, and the insects shrank with it."

"Here it's only twenty-two percent," Liam noted.

"Azurius figured out how to change their physiology so they could make use of atmospheres with a more limited oxygen supply," Jarek explained. "Otherwise, they'd only be useful on planets with oxygen levels around seventy percent. Considering the drawbacks of that kind of atmosphere, breathing would be the least of their worries."

Jarek turned. "Liam, we are only scouting. Touch nothing, for any reason. You can't do any lasting good. If we try anything, Azurius will be aware and able to undo what we try before we can exploit it. Even if we're lucky enough to escape, he'll put defenses on this compound that we will never breach."

Liam nodded. "I am puzzled why he hasn't."

"Because those types of defenses require a lot of energy and attention. Both of which he feels are better spent elsewhere. However, if he does get them up, we'll never get them down, even if he's dead."

Jarek looked down at the island. "When your parents contacted me, I assembled a squadron of star cruisers and a team. We're on our way to you, but we can't do anything until you bring down the force field. Also, you will eventually have to confront and stop Azurius. Now remember, if he dies, the chitin will have no control. Your people will have to kill them in detail, and there will be huge casualties. Unless I miss my guess, Azurius programed in a recall command that will make all of them return to their hives. Once activated, I can use the cruisers to sterilize the hives."

"So, do nothing until he's dead."

"Except look," Jarek replied. "Let's go."

Liam found himself beside Jarek in a corridor.

"This way." Jarek walked normally.

"We aren't floating?"

"Easier this way."

Liam caught up with him and realized he was right.

The corridor opened into a control room.

"The ability to control reality in a dream." Jarek shook his head with a sigh. "Such a pity he couldn't use this knowledge for constructive purposes."

They had taken a few steps into the room when Jarek stopped and caught Liam's attention.

"Notice the panel there?"

Liam nodded.

"That panel controls the hives. It works like a touchscreen drawing program. Draw a circle around a group and type a command, in this case, *recall*. Type that command in on the touch pad below."

"I don't recognize those symbols," Liam pointed out.

"Oh right, Old Gothowan script. We spoke it before we contacted other species of sentient beings. I'll give you the symbols you need to spell it once we're back at your body."

Jarek walked around the console. "Ah, here it is."

Liam followed.

"That green light there is the indicator. When it turns to amber, the force field is down. You see the five covered breakers down there?" Jarek pointed out the five toggles. "You must lift the cover, throw the breaker, then close the cover to kill the power. You must do all five in order, and the force field drops."

Liam nodded and looked around the compound.

"Let's get out of here before we run out of luck."

Liam followed him down the corridor. Soon, they headed out of the lab and off the island.

"When the time comes, will you be able to get back here?"

Liam nodded. "If I don't have to worry about Azurius."

"Let's get back to your body," Jarek advised. "This scouting trip has taken a lot out of you. I'll give you the symbols next time. Let yourself enter a deep sleep. Your brain is producing fatigue toxins. You need to purge them from your system, or you'll wake up with a headache."

.   .   .   .   .

Randolf listened to reports from the battle in the city. He had been thinking about the intercity portals. The chitin had now driven a wedge between the Temple compound and the portals. Randolf sighed. The chitin spread out into an arc that, if completed, would encircle the inner city. Then the chitin could press inward until they reached the Temple.

Teresina and Celinia listened with him, a comforting presence and liaison with the Temple.

"Still no word on Kia?" Teresina asked Captain Simon.

Captain Simon shook his head. "We haven't had time to look. We have many people missing."

Teresina started to retort but thought better of it. A single person was not a priority.

"Wouldn't you be able to sense your friend?" someone asked.

Celinia shook her head. "The barrier inside the Temple blocks us. I tried to contact Priestess Kia outside the compound. I'm not getting anything."

Randolf nodded and turned to Captain Simon who continued his briefing.

"We looked over the assassin and his gear. I can't say I know him, but one councilor says he has seen him with Licinious, not that this information tells us something we don't already know. He had a communicator similar to our military comm but on a different protocol. Our tech thinks he can break the code. It may be possible to use it to locate his companions. Also, we have set up a monitor within the Temple. We can intercept any calls they make."

Randolf perked up. "Excellent. One less thing to worry about. Get on with trying to locate the spies outside the Temple. It may be important and help us find Licinious."

"Yes, sir."

"How about our communications?" Randolf asked.

"We have a comm expert monitoring our channels," Captain Simon explained. "He took the precaution of developing a new cypher for our comms. Our communications are secure."

"What about food and water?"

"We have supplies for a couple of weeks," a councilor told him. "We have chitin between us and the hydroponic farms and the livestock pens. However, they aren't moving to destroy them. I think a hungry chitin may go in and grab something, but it isn't the mass destruction like we've observed elsewhere."

"Curious."

"They're also between us and the automated mines," the councilor continued. "Since they aren't being monitored because of the power outage, we don't know their condition. The reports I have indicate the chitin don't seem to go into the mines."

"Why would they?" Randolf asked. "They're between us and our factories as well. Azurius needs his troops here."

The door opened. The sergeant entered and approached Randolf. He whispered, "Sir, Lieutenant Janus is back and wishes to report. It's about Devon and the missing priestess."

Randolf stiffened and chanced a glance at Teresina and Celinia. He nodded to the sergeant. The sergeant motioned to the lieutenant.

Lieutenant Janus entered. From his grim expression, Randolf knew his news was not good.

"Sir," the lieutenant announced. "We've found Priestess Kia and Private Devon."

Teresina and Celinia's faces showed a mixture of bleak hope and dread.

The lieutenant took a deep breath. "I regret I must inform you they're both dead."

Teresina and Celinia stifled sobs but mastered themselves.

The lieutenant glanced at them, then turned back to Randolf. "Sir, they may not wish to hear the rest of my report."

Randolf looked at them. Celinia shook her head slightly.

"High Priestess Celinia, Priestess Teresina," Lieutenant Janus said with quiet respect, "I fear my report will cause you more pain."

They looked at each other.

"Thank you, Lieutenant, but she was our friend and fellow priestess," Celinia told him. "She and Devon had become close. We will bear the pain for their sake and report what we hear to Arch Priestess Arria. Then we shall mourn."

The lieutenant nodded. "We found them outside the perimeter. Chitin didn't kill them. We found them tied up, and their throats cut. However, before Kia and Devon died, these people assaulted Priestess Kia. It is likely they forced Private Devon to watch. His face was beaten and bloody. We collected evidence and brought the bodies back. A priestess trained in forensics is collecting genetic material. I pray we will bring the murderers to justice."

"Thank you, Lieutenant." Randolf's voice broke. "I know this experience can't have been easy. I think we should take a break while the priestesses give their report. We will reconvene in one hour."

Celinia nodded stiffly and guided Teresina toward the door.

Randolf got up and followed them. They were waiting for him as he left.

"I can make the report myself," Celinia told them.

"We'll be in my room," Randolf promised.

"I'll knock," Celinia replied. "I think I'm going to need a shoulder, too."

She hurried away.

Randolf put his arm around Teresina as they walked to his room. Tears streamed down her face. Once they entered his room, she fell apart. He guided her to the bed and removed the top of his armor. Then he took her in his arms and held her as great, tearing sobs wracked her body. She'd been there for him. Now it was his turn. A short time later, they heard a knock on the door, and Celinia entered. When she closed the door behind her, a sob escaped. Randolf held out his free arm, and she fell into it. She buried her face in his shoulder and wept bitterly.

Randolf mused at how envious other men might be to see such beautiful women hanging on him. All he felt was grief. He wondered if there would be anyone left to grieve for them.

.   .   .   .   .

The hour ticked by as the tears burned themselves out. Someone knocked.

"Sir, they're waiting," the sergeant called through the door.

"I'll be right there," Randolf answered.

Slowly, he disentangled himself from the two women.

"I have to go." He donned his armor. "If you want, you can stay here."

Celinia shook her head.

"As you said before," she replied, "they wouldn't thank us for neglecting our duties."

They looked at Teresina.

"I'll go too," she said. "I need to be doing something."

"We should stop by our rooms and freshen up," Celinia advised. "We look like we've been crying our eyes out."

Randolf threw her a puzzled looked.

She gave him a forced smile. "It's a woman's thing, my friend. We'll meet you."

He nodded and left.

.   .   .   .   .

When Randolf walked into the ready room, Captain Simon and the others looked up.

"We got the tests back." Captain Simon had a deadly look in his eyes. "You're going to hit the roof."

He handed a list to Randolf. Randolf saw the first name on the list and felt his blood boil.

"Licinious, you filthy animal. Shooting is too good for him. Pity, it's all I have time for. Circulate these names to our troops. Every one of them, except for Licinious, is to be shot on sight. He's mine."

He slammed the list on the table just as Teresina and Celinia entered.

"They completed the genetic testing," Randolf told them. "We know who's responsible for what was done to Kia and Devon."

Celinia picked up the list. Both she and Teresina went white when they read it.

"We don't have time to hunt them down," Randolf continued, his voice hard, "but if the opportunity presents itself—"

"Begging the captain's pardon," the sergeant replied, "I respectfully disagree. We now have a partial list of the people who betrayed us. I respectfully suggest we neutralize them."

"Thank you, Sergeant." Randolf felt gratitude going through him. "Lieutenant Janus, I want you to handpick a platoon of men and organize them into hunting teams. I'll forward information to you if the assassin's communicator gives us any more names."

"As you wish, sir," the lieutenant replied. "Thank you for the opportunity."

He saluted and left the room.

Celinia spoke up, "Can we afford to put the resources into a hunt for vengeance?"

"It's tactical, milady," the sergeant informed her. "Our enemy relies on them. If they're dead, they can't help him anymore."

Celinia put the paper back on the table and stood erect.

"Be sure 'tactical' is all there is to it," she commanded in a soft but firm voice. "Vengeance belongs to the Creator alone. If we start hunting for vengeance, it could destroy us as easily as Azurius. Now excuse me. I must remind the lieutenant of this principle before he starts."

She nodded to Teresina and left the room.

•   •   •   •   •

Liam and Swift Hunter spent the next morning scouting the area around Boulder sector. It appeared the chitin were too busy at Archer to bother with the other sectors. Making their return trip along the edge of the forest, a bradnock, a meter-long wild herbivore with two straight horns, broke cover. Swift Hunter pounced before it realized it made a mistake. The great predator's jaws closed around the creature's throat. It was all over in seconds. Liam let out the breath he'd sucked in when the bradnock startled him.

Lunch, Swift Hunter declared offhandedly. *Need change.*

Liam gasped. "Now I know why they call you *Swift Hunter*."

Swift Hunter carried their prize back to camp. Liam could help a little as Swift Hunter expertly showed him how to clean and dress wild game. He pursued his curiosity about his friend as they roasted meat over the rekindled fire.

"You mentioned some things about your people, Swift Hunter," Liam ventured as he cut a piece of meat off a bone. "I'm curious. How do they live? Are they organized into tribes or something?"

Swift Hunter stabbed a piece of meat with his claw and stared thoughtfully at it for a moment.

Mostly loose bands, in hills. He gestured with his paw. *Shaman walk dreams and speak for Maker. Live in families, in caves. Mother, father, children. Children find mate, move new cave, go make more children. Big hope, mother, father. Children go before death.* He flashed Liam a wry look.

"My parents said something similar." Liam laughed. "They wanted Randolf and me out of the house before they died."

Maker, sense of humor, Swift Hunter noted with a throaty chuckle.

"I think we'd all be in trouble if she didn't," Liam agreed as he savored the fresh meat after a diet of rations.

Your people? Swift Hunter asked.

"We're organized around the city's Council and the Temple of the Creator," Liam replied. "I don't know what it's like to have an extended family. Marcus, my father, told me that when the chitin drove us from our other cities, his parents and my foster mother's parents died. I know nothing of my mother's and father's families. My brother, Randolf, always looked out for me when we were young. Once I grew older and learned to protect myself, we looked out for each other. Do you have siblings?"

Five. Three hatch with me. Two, older hatching. Parents dead now. See brothers and sisters at gatherings. Occasionally other times. Spread out. Difficult visit, he finished regretfully.

"You said you had children," Liam coaxed.

Four, Swift Hunter replied. *Two hatchlings. Closest, two days walk from den. Great Heart visiting youngest. New parents, give advice. Spoil hatchlings. Usual,* he finished with a shrug.

Liam smiled. "In other words, some things are universal."

Swift Hunter nodded in agreement.

After enjoying lunch, Swift Hunter preserved the remaining meat. Liam lay back and allowed himself to drop into a dreamwalking trance.

•　　•　　•　　•　　•

Liam met Jarek again by the fountain in Liam's dreamscape.

"Feeling rested?" Jarek asked.

"Yes," Liam confirmed, "and well fed for a change."

"First, let me go over the chitin's console," Jarek began.

A copy of what they saw in Azurius's lab appeared. Liam came and looked over Jarek's shoulder.

"I can't guarantee what I'm showing you is precisely what you'll see," Jarek told him, "but it's what I've seen in his other labs."

He touched the screen, and a rotating image of a planet appeared. Liam saw some large, colored circles on the map, with individual dots in corresponding colors.

"The big circles represent the hives," Jarek told him. "Each hive's color corresponds to the hive's members. To control a group, Azurius will draw a box around the group and give his instructions."

Jarek demonstrated, using galactic standard commands.

"So, he can type in complete phrases," Liam observed.

"Yes," Jarek replied. "You will give a hive a command. In your case, tap each hive and type *recall*."

"Except he isn't using galactic standard," Liam pointed out.

"Right," Jarek agreed. "Azurius likes Old High Gothowan. Those symbols look like this."

Jarek typed the command. Liam nodded, seeing the symbols, and committing them to memory.

"He could also use Modern Gothowan," Jarek told him, "which looks like this. If you type it wrong, you'll see this standard error message. If you get that message for Old High Gothowan, type it again in Modern Gothowan."

Jarek typed in some somewhat different symbols. Again, Liam committed them to memory.

"How do you make things like this console in the dreamscape?" Liam asked.

"You have to know what it is you're creating," Jarek explained. "The more you know about it, the easier it is to create."

Liam closed his hand and created a plasma blade.

"Very good." Jarek smiled in approval. "It's a pity I don't have more time to train you. If we had ten years, you just might be able to turn off the force field when we arrive and keep Azurius back while we land. Then I could come and help directly."

"You're able to work through me, though."

Jarek shook his head. "I can scout with you as a relay. To fight, I have to do it directly."

Liam sighed. "I suppose being easy would be too much to ask."

Jarek smiled and patted his shoulder.

"I want to give you some pointers on stepping out of time," Jarek said. "You may have figured out that there is a relationship between walking in the dreamscape and stepping out of time."

"I suspected they were," Liam replied. "They both seemed a bit...unreal?"

Jarek nodded. "Not a bad choice of words. If you want to be more accurate, their connections with reality, as we understand it, are tenuous. However, stepping out of time usually involves the movement of your body into a narrow part of this other space. Walking the dreamscape requires only your consciousness, but you can move to a deeper level. Dreamwalking requires a certain degree of telepathy. Some people can move their physical body into the dreamscape. I hasten to mention, such people are normally close to the end of their lives anyway and aren't seen again."

Liam suppressed a shudder.

Jarek graced him with a grin. "Next great adventure. Now, how have you used this ability?"

"In battles with the chitin," Liam told him. "I find myself pulled back into regular time within a minute or two."

"Not enough." Jarek frowned. "Not nearly enough to face Azurius. We must work on your endurance."

"How long can he step out of time?"

Jarek shrugged. "No one has ever measured him flat out. I can manage five minutes. Ten if I want to spend the rest of the day in bed. He's at least at my level of endurance."

Liam frowned.

"Fortunately, in a fight with Azurius, you will step in and out of time," Jarek told him. "You will because he will. It's an excellent way to throw off your opponent's *timing*."

Liam nodded, grasping the basics of the principal.

"The other bit of good news is that sparring with me will help boost your endurance," Jarek went on, "and I can teach you exercises that will help as well. Best of all, we can do them in the dreamscape."

Jarek produced two play swords. Liam gave him an odd look.

"We're using these for a good reason, Liam. Do you remember what I told you yesterday about belief in the dreamscape?"

Liam nodded.

"It applies here too," Jarek continued. "You don't believe these *toys* will hurt you, so they won't. It will also give you some practice in case you're caught by an enemy in the dreamscape before you're ready. It will buy you a few seconds to escape."

Jarek tossed him a sword. "Let me watch you do a basic sword form, like when you practice with a plasma blade."

Liam began and took the sword form through to the end.

"Not bad for never having practiced in the dreamscape."

Jarek gave him a challenging grin. "Now, care to test your skill against me, child?"

Liam faced him, practice blade in hand. They circled each other. Liam let Jarek make the first move. He did not have to wait long. Liam found Jarek on him in less than a second, giving him a love tap on the head.

"First round to me."

"Now I know how the chitin must have felt." Liam shook his head, bewildered. "I didn't even see you move."

"Let me jump back and forth," Jarek suggested. "See if you can pick the moment I leave time and respond. Don't just stick out your sword for me to run into. That trick won't work. Let me do it three times, then try to respond."

Liam nodded, and Jarek did the maneuver three times. By the third, Liam thought he saw the prep.

Jarek attacked a fourth time, and Liam stepped out of time at the same instant, sidestepped, and pivoted to deliver a spinning blow. Jarek caught the blow and countered. Liam blocked, and as he countered, Jarek dropped into time. It looked as if he'd moved in slow motion. Liam's blade cut just before Jarek came in range. Then Jarek stepped back out of time, and Liam was completely wrong-footed. He threw himself out of the way of Jarek's blade before it reached him, falling back into normal time, feinting, and cutting upward. He pulled the blow before accidentally striking Jarek in the groin.

"Wow," Jarek gaped. "You learn fast. Thank you for pulling that strike. Even toy swords would have hurt."

Liam saluted him. "It was like I knew where you'd be."

Jarek beamed at him. "I was hoping you'd master that skill. I didn't realize you would master it so quickly. You seem to have an affinity for this type of fighting. I am honored to be your teacher."

"My fighting arts instructor said the same thing when he found I could step out of time," Liam replied. "I've always been good at it."

Jarek nodded with approval. "Let me explain the exercises I want you to do. Take your sword forms, and do three steps in regular time, three stepping out of time. Once you've done that routine with all your forms, practice two steps and four, five steps and one. Just keep varying it."

The swords vanished.

"Also, practice with something similar to your own plasma blade," Jarek instructed. "I think you should rest now. We'll meet tonight and figure out how to get you into the city."

•   •   •   •   •

When Liam woke up, he found Swift Hunter had cleaned up the mess of butchering the kill and was resting himself. He had the cut remaining meat into strips and had it drying over the fire. They spent the rest of the afternoon relaxing and discovering more about each other.

With the shadows lengthening, Liam looked at his friend.

"I have to meet with Jarek again," he told him. "We're going to figure out how to get me into the city."

Luck.

"See you when I wake up."

Liam made himself comfortable and tranced down.

•   •   •   •   •

He found Jarek waiting for him by the fountain.

"Ready?" Jarek asked.

"Let's do this."

Liam followed Jarek out of his personal dreamscape.

He looked at Jarek. "Any ideas?"

"Where does the water supply go into the city?" Jarek asked.

"I've never been there, but there are pipes coming from underground springs in the hills and running into the cisterns for the city's fresh water supply."

"Do you know approximately where the pipes are?" Jarek asked.

"I think they run between the four sectors of the city's outposts," Liam replied. "They must be deep enough to run under the force field."

"Let's try to find one," Jarek drifted toward Grizzly sector.

Liam followed him as Jarek kept close to the ground.

"Historically," Jarek told him as they moved, "a fortification's weakest point is the water supply."

Jarek stopped. "Wait here."

He sank into the ground for a moment, then came back almost immediately.

"Found it."

"How?" Liam asked.

"Heard the water running. The water delivery system also solves the problem of getting past the city's force field. The pipes do run deep enough to clear it."

Liam followed Jarek until they came to the defensive barrier. He saw a shallow depression in the ground.

"Is that depression there an entrance?"

Jarek sank down for a moment and returned.

"It is," he confirmed. "You're going to need to remove forty-millimeter bolts. You'll also need a pry bar. The pipe is large, and the current goes in the direction you want to go. We should scout to the cistern. It's underground. So, I don't think we'll draw Azurius's attention. Follow me."

Liam followed Jarek into the pipe. The current went in the right direction. It was also fast. Liam traveled at the pace of the water to identify the dangerous parts where he would need to hold his breath. Then he caught up to Jarek in the cistern.

"What kept you?" Jarek asked.

"I wanted to know what I'll run into and where I'd have to hold my breath," Liam replied. "When I'm in and can only go forward is a bit late to figure out where the problems are."

"Good thought," Jarek agreed before looking up. "I see a problem. No way to climb out."

Liam stayed at neck level in the water and looked around the cistern. The catwalks had no facilities for people swimming into the city.

"I think I've got an idea," Liam offered. "Let's travel the pipe one more time, so I remember all the places I need to hold my breath."

They retraced their steps.

"It's mostly straight with a slight grade toward the city," Jarek told him. "My compliments to your engineers. The flow is swift, but it gets fast toward the end. Not too many places to duck until you get close to the city."

"How long do you think it will take?" Liam asked.

"Maybe an hour," Jarek replied. "The war cut short my engineering training. I never got the chance to finish. So, understand what I tell you is an educated guess."

"I think I can rig my rifle to fire a heavier bolt and have it carry a rope for me to climb out with," Liam said. "The problem is, I'll probably burn out the coil."

"Rest for the remainder of the night and tackle this problem in the morning."

"Agreed," Liam replied. "I'll contact you when I'm in the city."

They returned to Liam's body. Jarek nodded and vanished. Liam fell into a deeper sleep.

•　　•　　•　　•　　•

The next morning, as Liam and Swift Hunter ate breakfast, Liam explained what he intended to do.

Difficult. More so with ribs.

114 KURT D. SPRINGS

"A calculated risk, my friend. Azurius won't expect it. What worries me is getting out of the cistern."

Need rope to climb out.

"I can rig a grappling hook, but without something to stand on, I'd never be able to throw it high enough."

Liam took out his assault rifle. "I'm afraid it means sacrificing the one weapon that gave me an edge."

Swift Hunter nodded. *More in city?*

"If I can get to them," Liam replied. "I know how to modify this one to fire a projectile which carries a line, but I'll only get one shot."

Hope only need one.

Liam nodded in agreement. "It means modifying the barrel and increasing the energy output. That surge of energy will burn out the electromagnetic coil. Well, no in point putting it off."

Swift Hunter watched curiously as Liam first took out the case he had scavenged from a diagnostic kit, emptied it, and waterproofed it with all-purpose tape.

What do?

"I'm waterproofing it," Liam replied. "I have to carry some things that don't enjoy getting wet."

Liam took a waterproof medical blanket and made it into a carrying bag. Then he began gathering his gear. The utility rope was lightweight and thin. He put some drinking water, some rations, and a med kit into the case. Then he took a metal bar and, using his plasma blade, shaped it into a makeshift crowbar.

Lever, the bear-lizard observed shrewdly.

Now came the part Liam wished he could avoid. He disassembled the rifle and separated out the barrel. Normally, it would fire needle thin projectiles. He found a round piece of metal, adjusted his plasma blade to a fine point, and shaped the end of the rod into a dart to carry the line, fashioning two barbs at the tip.

"That modified rod should do for my grapnel dart. Now I've got to widen the barrel. Can you hold the plasma blade upright for me?"

Swift Hunter braced the hilt in his paws while Liam worked the barrel until he'd widened the hole enough to hold the dart.

"There." Liam nodded with satisfaction.

Liam put a hole in the dart, threaded a sturdy piece of cable into it, used pliers to twist it into a ring, and used his soldering iron to secure it.

Why use that metal rope?

Liam attached the line to the loop he had made. "I don't want the rope cut when the dart penetrates the rock wall of the cistern. The metal loop will keep the rope away from the wall."

Liam rummaged through the supplies and found a power pack for a sniper rifle.

"Excellent," Liam said. "This power pack will deliver the extra charge."

He stripped away the stock of the rifle so the larger power pack would fit. Then he wrapped the electronics in pieces of another waterproof blanket and taped them down.

Swift Hunter gave him a quizzical look.

"I'm taking extra precautions," Liam explained. "I need to travel quite a way in the water."

He wrapped the rifle in another blanket and taped it down as a carrying case.

"It only needs to work once," Liam noted, "but it needs to work."

Then he gathered everything together.

Part ways soon. Swift Hunter gave him a sad look.

"We'll meet again, if I'm successful," Liam promised as he stood up.

He took the rifle and bags and climbed onto Swift Hunter's back. They left their makeshift camp and made their way toward the access hatch to the pipe. Once they had passed the ridgeline, the route was mostly flat.

"When they first built the outposts," Liam explained, "they set up a force field fence around the city to keep the chitin away from New Olympia. With the force field behind the outposts, when they attacked the barrier, we could turn the weapons inward and destroy them as they wasted their energy on it."

Remember. Young then. Like watch bugs pop.

"Most of the burn marks from previous attempts by the chitin are overgrown now," Liam noted. "After wasting chitin, Azurius must have realized the best way into the city was through the portals."

They came to the depression Liam had seen in the dreamscape. He slid off Swift Hunter's back and laid his gear down. Then he stripped off his armor and put it in the watertight bag he'd created from the blanket.

"Care to help dig?" Liam asked.

Yes, Swift Hunter replied.

Liam took his digging tool and, with the bear-lizard's considerable aid, cleared the hatch. Liam tried to ignore his complaining ribs. The hatch to the pipe was not too deep, and Swift Hunter's claws made quick work of the sandy soil. Soon, they'd exposed the hatch.

"As I thought. They welded the bolts in place."

Swift Hunter moved back as Liam took out his plasma blade. The plasma blade made quick work of the bolts. He deactivated the blade and stowed it in the package.

Liam wedged the lever he'd prepared between the hatch and lip. With his great strength, Swift Hunter pried the hatch off, and they wrestled it to the side. Liam was breathing hard and felt his sore ribs complaining again. He had to lie back and rest awhile.

Once Liam had rested, he rolled and leaned over the opening, sticking his head into the pipe. He measured a ten-foot drop. It had not looked that deep in the dreamscape.

"Thank the Creator, this thing has a ladder, but climbing out on the other end will hurt."

Liam stripped down and put everything into the waterproof bag except for the modified rifle. The rifle he strapped onto the outside using his utility belt.

"I've made sure I tied down everything. That way, if something comes loose, it won't drift away."

Wise precaution, Swift Hunter agreed. *That?* he asked, pointing to the pistol.

"Our weapons are waterproof under normal circumstances," Liam said, "but I exposed the electronics on the rifle when I altered it. Everything else on the belt is waterproof."

Liam took one more look at his friend and smiled. "Okay. Now I'm ready. Thanks for all your help."

He reached out and touched the bear-lizard on the shoulder. Swift Hunter returned the gesture.

"The current will sweep me away once I'm in," Liam said. "I will tell my people about you if I can. Would you move the cover back over this hole after I go? I don't want anyone to fall in."

Yes, Swift Hunter replied. *Wish success.*

"Until next time, my friend."

Swift Hunter wrapped him in a bearhug, then backed away.

Clutching the watertight bundle, Liam climbed down to the last rung. After taking several deep breaths, he slid feet first into the water.

.   .   .   .   .

The current took hold of Liam and pulled him along. At once, he realized a flaw in his plan. He could not see. The pipe had no light. Fishing around the utility belt, he found his torch. Once he activated the chemical cell, and it bathed the pipe in a white light. Liam adjusted the cover, so it became more of a lantern.

"That's better."

He laid back and tried to relax, holding his bundle to his chest like a life preserver. He floated easily through most of the journey. The current got faster as he got nearer to the city, as Jarek had predicted. He reached the first downward bend in the pipe and ducked his head as the flow neared the top.

The flow became faster as he got to within a few minutes from his goal. Reaching the next bend, the level of the water reached the top of the pipe. He ducked but got too close to the edge of the pipe, and the hand holding the torch hit the wall, knocking the torch free. It fell into the water, and Liam tried to reach its lanyard without letting go of his pack. Trying to maneuver his body, the pack almost got swept out of his arms.

Liam swore as his head broke the surface. His head struck the pipe, leaving him dazed. He clung to the pack like a shield, trying to keep it between his head and the pipe. The pack pushed his head underwater. He did not have to swim, but he had to hold his breath. The icy water alone made his ribs ache. The ache became worse as his lungs began demanding air. Liam fought panic as he felt his pack take impact after impact on the pipe. His lungs now burned.

The downward slope of the pipe got sharper. Without warning, Liam plunged down. He held tight to the pack, straightened his body, and shot into the cistern like a bullet.

Liam's head broke the surface of the water. He felt relief as his lungs filled with air. He held on to the pack and rested a few moments, using the pack as a pillow. The torch surfaced and bobbed there, as if asking what took him so long. Liam frowned at the errant torch, then grabbed the lanyard and retrieved it. The catwalk was three meters above him and illuminated by chemical light cells.

After he had rested, Liam took the assault rifle from its waterproof case and propped it on the pack. Knowing he would only have one shot from this modified weapon, he looked carefully through the scope at the wall above the catwalk. His floating in the water made for a tricky shot.

Finally, he saw a point he hoped would hold the dart. Praying this plan would work as he anticipated, he squeezed the trigger. He noticed a faint ozone smell as the shaft sped toward its target. Wisps of blue smoke wafted from the barrel as the metal arrow struck home, carrying the thin rope. Liam released the useless weapon, allowing the lanyard he'd rigged to prevent it from sinking into the city's drinking supply. He tested the line. It held. He tied the end of the rope to the bundle to anchor it and climbed. Liam's arms ached, and his ribs were in agony as he climbed. He gritted his teeth and felt the world darken. Willing himself not to faint, he reached the bottom of the railing. He was tempted to rest, but if he did, he would end up back in the water. Grimacing with effort, he swung a leg up and grabbed the top of the railing.

Then he lay naked and dripping on the catwalk. Liam curled up and forced himself to relax until his ribs were tolerable, and he had caught his breath. After fifteen minutes, he could force himself up. Breathing hard, he pulled up his bundle and took the projectile from the wall. Then, still panting and clutching his aching ribs, he had to climb two flights of stairs before reaching the entrance to the corridor. Here he rested a few minutes and then unpacked his gear. He looked around and spotted a door marked "Utility Closet."

Liam opened the door and found a ragged old towel, which he used to dry himself. He removed the wet tape from his ribs and re-taped them with fresh tape. Then he dressed and put on his armor. Without the diagnostic kit, he could not tighten the armor to compensate for his injuries.

Resting, he opened a rations packet and water and had a quick lunch.

He looked at the assault rifle he'd taken from Archer sector. The coil had become charred and blackened. After all the work he'd put in, he felt wistful at its loss. He put it aside with the remaining rations and continued down the corridor.

The corridor twisted and turned. With pistol drawn, Liam passed several abandoned offices. He checked for anything he could use but found nothing. Finally, he reached a door in the rear of the building. Keeping to the shadows of the entryway, he visually scanned the area. No chitin. He slipped into the yard and made his way around to the front and saw signs of a fierce battle. Some soldiers fought their last stand here. He found a decapitated body trampled and shoved up against the wall.

"Forgive me, Corporal," he told the body. "I need to link to your suit for a moment."

He took a cable, plugged it into the corpse's armor, and used the console to bring up the diagnostics. It worked. His ribs were no worse. He typed treat and felt his own armor tighten again.

"Thanks," Liam said as he disconnected the cable.

He searched for a working comm, but the chitin destroyed all the ones he found.

Liam checked the assault weapons and found them all ruined. He inspected the remains in case he could salvage the coils, but the chitin had destroyed them. He gathered the ammunition belts and moved them inside the building.

Liam sighed in disappointment. *If I could have salvaged a coil and a barrel, I could have fixed the rifle I left below.*

Liam did not know if he would make it back here, but if he did, he would reclaim the ammunition. He worked his way to the front entry of the yard and checked an alley. So far, the coast was clear. He moved into the alley, toward the street, and glanced up at the gate. The sign said Water Station Three. Peering into the street, it looked empty. He saw a few abandoned transports. He made his way to one and realized it had no power. Azurius must have had the main power to the city cut.

The fighting had already driven people out of this area. He moved into the street, remaining alert for movement. He did not notice the insectoid eyes tracking him.

*   *   *   *   *

Azurius moved quickly. He did not need the chitin. In fact, they would be a hindrance. A chitin scout had spotted Liam near this part of the city. Azurius just had to keep ahead of him until he was ready to confront him.

Azurius remembered a battle where he tried to make his way through a city. Cut off from his command and alone, he had used the tallest building he could find. He figured Liam would do the same. Azurius chuckled as he looked upon the perfect building. It was the tallest in the city.

From Licinious's intelligence, they make armor and weapons here. He entered and did a quick reconnoiter of a storage area and assembly line.

The chitin had done their work well. Everything was in ruins. Now he had to get to the roof.

*   *   *   *   *

Liam made his way through the streets of the industrial section. While he found a few pieces of bodies, there were no sign of anyone living. What he needed was a bird's-eye view. Liam thought of the perfect place. Tower 99 was one of the taller buildings. He could get a commanding view from the top and, perchance, find the parts to fix his armor.

He moved to the building and checked the door. It opened with no trouble. He slipped in and let it close behind him. In the lobby, behind the now vacated security desk, he saw the automated lifts. He knew without power they would be useless but tried one anyway. Nothing. With a sigh, he headed to the stairs and began his climb.

After climbing twelve flights of stairs, he felt winded. Liam stepped onto the roof and scanned the city. Now he understood. It looked like the chitin were herding the people toward the Temple compound. It was the most defensible area in the city. Good—for a last stand.

"Quite a view," came a familiar voice.

Liam froze, shifting enough to look behind him. Azurius leaned against the outer rim of the flat roof. Liam dropped out of time and whirled, drawing his pistol. Azurius, eyes glowing black, struck faster. Liam felt himself lifted and slammed against the ledge. His hand reflexively opened, allowing the pistol to bounce free and over the edge.

Liam gasped for breath as his armor released his ribs. Azurius, his eyes still glowing black, held him pinned without touching him.

"A useful ability," Azurius commented, smiling as his eyes turned green. "Licinious thinks all I do with it is tear things apart. It keeps him guessing."

Liam felt himself released, but it was still a struggle to move.

"I see your injuries bother you." Azurius tried to sound sympathetic.

"Why don't you just kill me?" Liam gasped as he struggled to his feet.

Azurius smiled. "Like I said before, you intrigue me. I knew you would try to get into the city, but the city's water supply didn't even occur to me. I fear I must deny it to you as a base of operation now. Chitin now patrol it."

Liam ignored the taunt. He had not expected to return.

"So, are you planning to take me prisoner?" Liam asked. "You know I'm prepared to go down fighting."

Azurius's eyes returned to neutral red. "I told you before, I am thinking of grooming you as my second in command, but I want you to perform a labor for me."

Liam laughed, though it hurt his ribs. "What makes you think I want the job?"

"Oh, you don't, just yet, but think of the benefits. The people will be beholden to you. You drove out the chitin. I can teach you the finer points of command and power. How to use the abilities you are just beginning to understand. Imagine, fleets of state-of-the-art starships jumping to your orders. Legions of soldiers, trained by you personally, loyal to only you. Who knows? You just might replace me, eventually."

For a moment, Liam could see himself leading troops in a pitched battle or commanding a vast empire. He pushed those thoughts firmly aside.

Azurius smiled. His eyes were green again. "Of course, you don't know what you could do with that kind of power."

"I don't know why I'd want the bother." Liam tried to clutch his ribs through his armor.

"In time," Azurius replied. "I am sure ideas will occur to you. My test is not anything you wouldn't want to do, anyway. Simply kill Licinious."

Liam wanted to laugh but became wary. "I won't deny, I would love to put a bullet in his head but, since it's something you want, maybe I should just let the city courts deal with him."

Azurius's smile dropped, and his face turned serious, his eyes dull red. "I understand why you may think that way, but I have something I need to tell you. Then I will leave you to make up your own mind."

Liam did not move.

"Licinious had your foster family killed," Azurius told him. "High Councilor Marcus died, opening his front door. The assassin shot the Lady Lidia in the back."

Liam's mouth dropped open in shock. His legs became unstable, and he slid down against the wall.

"I thought you should know." Azurius turned and climbed down the fire escape to the ground and disappeared into the maze of streets, leaving Liam feeling numb.

Liam sat there, staring after Azurius.

"Mother," he whispered. "Father."

Tears came to his eyes, but he pushed them aside. He had work to do. Slowly, painfully, Liam got to his feet and limped back into the building. He knew the location of the production lines and storage areas. Clutching his ribs, he went to the storage areas. He did not think he would find parts to replace his damaged armor, but nothing could prepare him for the destruction he saw. The chitin had pulled apart all the armor in storage. The chitin destroyed any electronics in the armor. He searched the facility, but everything was in fragments. Next, he went to the production area. The chitin had been thorough. Still, he went through the pieces, but nothing remained.

Then Liam investigated the repair section in the basement. Again, the chitin had been thorough. They had destroyed all the diagnostic equipment. Heading back upstairs, he searched the offices, one by one, looking for anything useful. After several hours, he admitted defeat, abandoning the fruitless search. Now that Azurius knew where he was, he could not stay here any longer.

Liam staggered to the front door. After looking around and seeing no chitin, he walked to the part of the building he thought his pistol landed. He found it, smashed. The plasma blade and daggers were all he had left.

Liam sighed and slipped into the side streets leading away from the armory. After going several blocks, he realized he had come to the front of a tavern he'd been to many times—the Green Griffin. Needing something to eat and a place to rest, he went inside. Going to the bar, he found a bottle of New Olympia whiskey. He did not want to get drunk, but he needed an antiseptic, and a sip might help with his spirits. He went to the kitchen.

As he had hoped, Liam found the freezer still cold, even without power. He hoped no one would notice him making a hot meal. Rations could do with a change. He knew the chitin could not pick out thermal signatures. So, he went to the freezer, picked up a rack of charodont ribs and prepared them. The restaurant had its own gas source, so he used his plasma blade to ignite the oven and a burner. Reaching the right temperature, he lowered the gas and basted the ribs with some sauce he had found. He also found some vegetables to cook.

While the food cooked, Liam climbed the back stairs and entered a hallway to the apartments. He climbed the stairs to the top floor and entered one apartment. It looked like people had evacuated successfully. He could rest here. Returning to the kitchen, he retrieved his meal and turned off the stove. Then he brought his dinner upstairs and took off his armor and tunic. His ribs looked more bruised now, but the break did not seem much worse. He re-taped them.

Then he sat down to his meal. The barbecued charodont ribs tasted like ambrosia in his mouth. It reminded him of the open-air feast he had shared with Swift Hunter.

Did I really spend three days with a creature everyone thinks is a dangerous predator?

The water still ran but, without power, it was cold. He rinsed off the sticky sauce, then he took a sip of the whiskey.

Right now, Liam needed to contact Jarek and sleep. He considered the bedroom, but he felt it would be disrespectful to the owner. So, he borrowed a blanket and laid back in a recliner. When he considered his ribs, it seemed the wiser choice.

His mind turned toward Celinia. With what he had learned, he wanted to talk to her, to let them know he was alive, but he knew he could not penetrate the dreamscape barrier surrounding the Temple.

CHAPTER 5

Liam waited by the fountain again. Jarek came a few minutes later. "You got into the city?"

"After a fashion," Liam replied. "Once I dropped into the pipe, I couldn't see. Can you see in the dark in the dreamscape?"

Jarek looked embarrassed. "Uh, yes. I'm sorry, Liam. I do it so much that I took it for granted. My oversight could have been a fatal mistake on my part."

"Is there a way to tell if you will need a light in the real world?"

"Many little things," Jarek explained. "The way shadows fall. Seeing a light source. It's kind of knack you pick up. It seems light and dark mean little in dreamwalking. So, seeing is not a problem."

"Still, getting in was the straightforward part. Just after I got into the city, I met Azurius. My ribs took a beating, but the pieces are still connected. I guess that's something."

Jarek winced.

"His eyes change colors," Liam continued. "I didn't know black could glow. I've seen near black glow, though it looks purple."

Jarek's embarrassment deepened. "I should have told you, Liam. I am sorry. It was very important. We just had so much else to cover."

"Tell me about it, and I may forgive you." Liam tried to sound lighthearted.

"Azurius conducted experiments on living subjects," Jarek explained. "My people have some telekinetic ability which he sought to improve. These events happened before the Rebellion. When some of his test subjects went mad and broke loose, the Ministry of Public Safety ordered him to shut down the experiments. Before he did, he injected one last serum into himself. His eyes now glow with his mood. Red is a neutral mood. Green is happy or amused. Blue is fear. Yellow is anger. Black is him accessing his abilities."

"My foster parents are dead," Liam whispered.

Jarek bowed his head. "I'm sorry. I can sense how close you were to them."

Liam looked at him, eyes blazing with wrath. "Azurius told me Licinious had them assassinated. I'm guessing he's interested in me replacing Licinious as his stooge."

"Azurius senses you're becoming stronger," Jarek surmised. "Strength is something he admires. I guess your Licinious isn't strong enough for him. If you joined him, you would be a magnificent prize in his ambitions."

"He also suggested I could replace him."

"Azurius is trying to tempt you," Jarek confirmed. "He wants the thought of taking his place to eat at your mind. You just have to join him and do his will until you are powerful enough. I suspect he believes he can cross that bridge when the time comes. However, in your case, it is very possible you could seize power from him."

"I just shouldn't be too attached to my soul," Liam replied sardonically.

"True," Jarek agreed. "I suspect Azurius doesn't put a great store in souls."

"He wants me to kill Licinious," Liam added. "The problem is, I want to kill Licinious."

Jarek nodded. "Azurius loves those games. To pit an old servant against the new and see who comes out on top."

He sat down next to Liam and put a hand on his shoulder.

"You have two ways to think about the situation. First, killing Licinious is what Azurius wants, so you should leave Licinious alone. However, Licinious is a threat. Unless I miss my guess, he controls other humans under Azurius's sway. Chitin are useful servants, but they can't think creatively. Skilled warriors are something Azurius needs to be successful."

"So, eliminating Licinious is a good thing."

"That depends on how well you handle the elimination," Jarek cautioned him.

"I have another problem."

"What do you need?" Jarek asked.

"I want to set up a defense in case Azurius tries to scout my position in the dreamscape. I also need enough warning to get my armor back on if chitin start nosing around, especially if I'm asleep."

"That type of defense is doable," Jarek told him. "You can *mine* your location in the dreamscape. I can show you how."

"I would appreciate that," Liam replied.

Jarek smiled at him. "Remember how I said that battles in the dreamscape are based on belief?"

Liam nodded.

"Same principle." Jarek opened his hand and produced a strange-looking device. "What I'm holding is a dreamscape representation of a mine from Old Terra. It's called a *claymore*."

"What does that lettering say?" Liam pointed to the words on the front.

Jarek turned the mine back toward himself. "Oops. I forgot language and lettering have changed since then."

The words re-shifted until it read "Front toward enemy."

"Absentmindedness." Jarek sighed. "Something you can look forward to when you're seven hundred years old."

Liam smiled and gave him a sympathetic pat.

"Now, soldiers used a remote detonator with the original claymore mine. However, they found ways to give them a proximity fuse. Now let's see what it does."

Jarek set the mine up, facing away from them.

"Can you conjure a couple of chitin?"

Liam focused a bit, and some chitin came out of the bush. Jarek detonated the mine, and the chitin went down, their carapaces shattered. Liam dismissed any that still lived.

"With real ones, we wouldn't have been so cavalier with our safety. I can control my belief, and you were well behind me and out of the danger zone."

"How do they work?" Liam asked.

"You know what a shotgun is?"

Liam nodded again.

"Small pellets are strategically placed in the explosive," Jarek explained. "These spread out in front of the mine and kill or injure the enemy."

Liam considered the benefits of this ability.

"Now," Jarek continued, "seeing this device explode will affect Azurius because he ran up against similar devices when he tangled with your ancestors. However, as I said before, he has experience with this game. Chances are, it will startle him when he sees them, and he'll forget, for a moment, they aren't real. He will remember soon enough, but the explosions will force him to retreat, and you will have warning he's around."

"What about things in the real world?"

"Similar principle, with a hidden *trip line* in the real world," Jarek replied. "Have that trip line act as a trigger to detonate a mine. It won't hurt whatever's out there, but it will make a noise which will alert you."

"How will that type of system work?" Liam asked, confused. "The mines are in the dreamscape. How can you wire them to detonate from the real world?"

"When we scout outside our bodies," Jarek explained, "we move in a border area between the dreamscape and actual world. Few can influence the real world from the dreamscape in a major way. However, most of us can do very minor, seemingly insignificant things across the border. The hidden trip line for example."

Liam whistled. "I can create these things?"

"In time," Jarek promised. "For now, I'll set it up with your help and help you tie yourself into it. Shall we start?"

They went outside the building. Being a dream, clusters of claymores soon lined the outside of the building with the trip lines set along the approaches to the building. Jarek tossed something across a trip line, detonating the mines. When Liam looked, the mines remained.

"A pleasant benefit of the dreamscape," Jarek explained. "With this place as your base of operations, no need to reset."

"If I move?"

"Once we tie you in, you can set the system up easily anywhere you go," Jarek told him. "Now, you saw everything I did?"

"Yes."

"I want you to feel every device, every wire, every part of the trap," Jarek spoke with a calming voice.

Liam closed his eyes, fumbled for a moment, then willed himself to relax and sense all the parts of the trap. He felt something like a snap.

"Very good," Jarek said. "Now place a similar system on the adjacent buildings."

Liam obeyed and soon, he had placed an extensive minefield on the surfaces of all the nearby buildings.

"Excellent. No one will sneak up on you while you sleep."

"I thought you said this type of thing would take time." Liam looked at Jarek.

"To create something new, yes," Jarek replied. "Here, you're just copying from a template. Still, a good night's work. Now it's time for you to get some proper sleep."

"Okay. I just want to do my exercises first, then I'll shift to deep sleep."

"Very good," Jarek agreed. "I'll take my leave then. Have a good rest."

Jarek vanished, and Liam produced a practice blade and went through his exercises a few times. Then the dreamscape looked foggy. He decided it was time to stop. Liam returned to his body and soon entered a deep sleep.

• • • • •

Randolf opened his eyes, wondering when his mother would call him and Liam to breakfast. Then he remembered. *She wouldn't. No more breakfasts from Mother. No more seeing Liam at the stove, helping.* Randolf thrust away the grief and sat up.

The last couple of days had passed in a blur. He was desperately trying to keep his people alive as the city disintegrated around him. A way of turning the tide still eluded him. Every day, they lost more ground, and more soldiers they could not replace. It was maddening. Azurius's offensive had only one point of failure he could see—Azurius himself. Yet they had come no closer to figuring out how to kill him.

When the ebb and flow of battle allowed him a moment to think, grief and despair stared him in the face. Liam was gone when he needed him the most. Licinious had ripped his parents from him. The ring of chitin continued to tighten around them. The Creator, Herself, seemed to have abandoned them.

Teresina. In those all too brief, stolen moments they had shared since the battle began, she had comforted him. She had drawn his mind into hers in a way he could never have imagined. He could only dream of what life with her would be like. That thought made him want to live. It gave him something to fight for. He would continue to fight until his last breath.

Someone knocked on the door.

"Yes?"

The sergeant entered with a tray of food and some coffee.

"Thank you, Sergeant. Anything new?"

"No change from yesterday, except a little less space to defend."

The sergeant put the tray on the desk.

Randolf rolled out of bed and sat there for a moment. "Sergeant, I need to know your name."

"Yes, sir," the sergeant replied. "Call me *Sergeant*."

"You are a stickler for military custom." Randolf took a bite of toast.

"It's important, sir," the sergeant told him. "You need a bit of separation between the commander and the soldiers. They know you're human. They need you to be a bit more. It could mean the difference between survival and extinction. After the battle is over, I promise to tell you my name."

"We have several sergeants," Randolf said. "If I have to pick you out of a group, it'll be Sergeant Hey You."

The sergeant graced him with a slight chuckle. "Works."

"If something happens," Randolf asked, "who do I write the letter to? You know, it starts with 'I regret to inform you...'"

The sergeant thought a moment. "I'll leave a note with the arch priestess. She'll release it to you if anything happens."

Randolf put his fork down, his mind drifting back to those lazy days in his mother's kitchen.

"Thinking about your brother, sir?" the sergeant asked, taking a seat on the edge of a small desk.

Randolf nodded.

"I met him a few times," the sergeant informed him. "I was friends with Jorge."

"What did you think of him?" Randolf asked.

The sergeant paused. "As a soldier, lone wolf."

"Do you mean 'lone wolf' in a good way or a bad way?"

"Neither really." The sergeant fell silent for a moment. "You must understand the term. The wolf was a Terran animal. They were pack hunters. So, I define a lone wolf as someone who should be part of a team but prefers to operate independently."

"My brother worked with the team," Randolf protested. "He led Third Squad in when the chitin almost overran Devon's position. When the portals fell, he..." Randolf almost choked up, reliving that horrible moment.

"Yes, sir," the sergeant conceded. "It's not that he didn't like people or couldn't work with a team. When he had to, he worked well with his comrades. Most of the men who worked with him I've talked to thought highly of him. That being said, he was quite skilled. More so than most people. When he used those skills in a fight, he had to be careful he didn't endanger a teammate. Moreover, he had a hard time opening up to people. When he did, he formed strong attachments, and he hated to bury friends."

Randolf nodded. "True."

"So, to best use all his abilities," the sergeant continued, "without putting a friend at risk, he found it more comfortable to work alone."

Randolf finished his meal. "Thank you, Sergeant. Tell everyone I'll be there shortly."

"Very good, sir."

•   •   •   •   •

After waking, Liam went to the kitchen for breakfast. Searching through the pantry area, he found some melie eggs, charodont bacon, and a starchy root vegetable they called *spuds*. After putting them on the counter, he put a kettle on to heat some water.

First, Liam sliced the spuds and began frying them along with the bacon. Once he had finished the home fried spuds, he slid them onto a plate and cooked his eggs. He used another burner to toast some bread. The kettle boiled, and he added the eggs to his plate. Then he made a pot of tea. Liam grabbed a mug from the bar and picked a table out of view of the windows, which still gave him a commanding view of the street. He realized he rather enjoyed cooking. For a moment, he allowed himself to remember how he had enjoyed helping his mother in the kitchen. He poured tea into his mug and tucked into his breakfast.

Liam considered his next steps as he ate.

I need more equipment. I also need to shut down the portals. Equipment, I might find at various depots or by scavenging the dead. I have to shut down the portals from the Center, and it has the armory in one wing.

I need to know what's happening. He took a sip of tea. *I need a route to the Center. The easiest way is the dreamscape.*

However, I risk running into Azurius. Jarek's warning about fighting him in the dreamscape came back to him. *The alternative is to trust to blind luck.*

His eyes drifted to the street. *Troops probably raided the depots once they knew they would have to set up in the Temple, especially if they didn't have a chance to clear the Center's armory. Would Azurius have had the chitin destroy the armory as they had destroyed Tower 99?*

Liam shook his head. *I can only hope Azurius missed the armory. He is trying to move things quickly. He also expects me to go after Licinious. My first duty is to even the odds for the city's defenders. Evening the odds means throwing what wrench I can into Azurius's plans. Taking down the portals will hopefully force Azurius to readjust those plans, and changing plans will take time.*

Liam finished eating and used the remaining hot water to clean his plates. He went back upstairs and prepared himself to enter the dreamscape.

•   •   •   •   •

Liam watched as the city flew past. The chitin ranks thinned as he moved away from the perimeter and toward the Military Center. Small groups headed to the line, but other than those chitin, Azurius had not set patrols to guard the area outside the ring. Liam dropped low as he got closer to the Center, paying attention to the placement of things.

I'd better check an underground route when I go back, assuming I don't have to snap back to my body to avoid a confrontation with Azurius.

The only chitin at the entrance of the Military Center quickly departed. He waited for the next group to pass. Then he waited some more. Another group passed short time later.

There appears to be a short time lag between groups.

He entered, checking the Archer portal room. He saw two chitin on guard here. The flow had reduced to a trickle. He checked the locker room and saw the chitin broke open all the lockers with their contents destroyed. Then he checked HQ.

Making it to the stairs, he saw the debris scattered along the entire flight. When he reached the shattered doorway, Liam could only gape at the destruction he saw. HQ was no more. Chitin could not have created this kind of destruction. The faces of all the HQ staff flashed through his mind. Liam's lips curled in anger.

Another debt for Licinious to pay.

He headed down the hall to a closed door. He passed through and saw the armory remained intact. Liam grinned.

Azurius was in such a hurry to get chitin to the lines he missed the armory. Liam reconsidered. *Azurius is no idiot. If I consider his plans, he must want it intact. He didn't think anyone could get this far past the chitin. So, he thought it was safe to ignore it.*

He slipped out the door and headed to the adjacent building. The building looked like it had taken some kind of hit. Cracks ran through the outer walls, and it looked like the Civil Corps would have to condemn it, assuming anyone survived to condemn it. Down one corridor, he found the stairs to the basement. After some searching, he found an entry hatch to the sewers. Following the sewers, Liam periodically drifting to the surface to check his position, and found the engineers had laid the sewers out in a neat grid. Along the way, he noticed a few blind alleys and dead ends, but for the most part, it was logical.

Finding a hatch in the back alley near the Griffin, he returned to where his body rested. Liam felt certain he could use the sewers to navigate the city.

The sun had reached its noon position.

●　　●　　●　　●　　●

Liam stood and had a quick lunch. He re-taped his ribs, put on his armor, and holstered his plasma blade. Then he headed into the back alley.

Heading for the sewer entrance, Liam grasped the recessed handle, opened the hatch, and slid onto the ladder inside. Closing the hatch behind him, he climbed down and followed the route he had scouted in the dreamscape. Light filtered through the occasional storm grates, creating a gloomy atmosphere. The dreamscape had not prepared him for two elements of his route—the smell and the ankle deep, mucky water. The latter made for slow going. He made it under the damaged building in an hour and a half and left the hatch open for a quick getaway. Azurius would probably come running when the fun started. He shook the muck and water off his boots, climbed the stairs, and followed the corridor to the front entrance.

Liam paused by the door and waited. After five minutes, a group of chitin exited the Military Center. Liam continued to wait, counting to himself. The next group exited seven minutes later. Liam waited until they had passed, then made his move. Checking to see the door opened with little trouble, he exited the building. Upon checking to his right, he saw the back of the chitin. He sprinted across the street to the planter beside the entrance, then stopped and ducked behind the shrubs. Wanting to give himself maximum probability of getting to the armory without the chitin seeing him, he let one more group pass him. Keeping a running count in his head, he waited. In just over seven minutes, another group of chitin went past.

Liam stepped out of time and dashed behind the chitin. He knew the Military Center well. He also knew chitin did not explore. They just followed Azurius's commands. He commanded them to get to the line. Liam hoped he had guessed right, and Azurius expected him elsewhere. He moved around the perimeter hallway to the armory and found the door locked.

He took his plasma blade and activated it, wincing at the slight noise it made. Liam adjusted the blade to a fine point and cut into the lock. Its charge was almost gone.

He went inside, making sure the door closed without a sound behind him. The light came on. HQ would normally have a red alarm light, but there was no HQ now. First, he grabbed a pistol, inserted a magazine and a power pack, then holstered it. Then he found a diagnostic kit, which he plugged into his armor and checked his status. His ribs were a little worse. He punched in treat and felt the armor tighten on his ribs. Then he took an assault rifle from the rack, armed it, and leaned it against a table. He considered a sniper rifle but decided against it. He had enough to carry. Liam gathered together several high explosive bayonet grenades, and several hand grenades, attaching four of the grenades to his belt and armor. He pulled a helmet off the rack, adjusted it to fit, and then checked the night-vision visor to make sure it worked. Unfortunately, the Military Center kept the comms in another wing, where he suspected Azurius had set up camp. Not worth the risk.

Liam grabbed a rucksack. He collected the diagnostic kit and as many of the grenades as would fit into it. Three bayonet grenades he attached to the rucksack's frame and put more in the rucksack. Then he replaced the power supply on his plasma blade. He took two more power supplies and put them in his pack, then grabbed extra ammunition and power supplies for the guns. He filled the empty pouches on his belt. Almost as an afterthought, he grabbed four trip mines and a roll of wire. With the rucksack now as heavy as he could manage, he slung the pack onto his left shoulder and picked up the rifle. He took one more bayonet grenade from off the shelf and snapped it onto the end of the rifle.

Now he was ready. He opened the door and slipped out, again making sure it closed without a sound.

Liam made his way along the corridor until he approached the T-junction, which led to the Archer portals. He heard chitin and crouched, ready to fight. A group of chitin crossed the junction

without seeing him. After they passed, he crept forward. ~~Leaning~~
He leaned the rifle against the wall, careful that it did not fall over, *and* he
took two hand grenades, pulled one pin, and threw it into the portal
room. Then, he pulled the second pin and tossed it after the chitin
that had just passed. Then he grabbed the rifle and turned away,
crouching. The grenade exploded in the portal room, followed by
another explosion in the corridor.

Liam leaped to his feet and charged into the Archer sector portal
room. No chitin survived to challenge him. He fired the bayonet
grenade into the controls of one portal and ducked. Once he heard
the third explosion, he grabbed another bayonet grenade from the
frame. Fitting it to his rifle, Liam aimed for the second portal control
as he heard the skittering of chitin in the distance. He ducked as the
grenade put the last portal out of action.

Liam got to his feet and dashed to the corridor. Chitin were
coming back to investigate the explosions. He opened fire and
charged. The chitin went down. He kept firing until his chamber
registered empty, then slapped home a new magazine and kept
pressing forward. The chitin backed away, then tried to push
forward again.

Liam stepped out of time. His withering fire caused the chitin to
fall back. Entering normal time, he grabbed a grenade, pulled the
pin, and tossed it into the middle of the remaining chitin. He
stepped out of time again and dove for the T-junction corridor,
dropping a trip mine as he reentered normal time. The grenade
exploded. Liam ran until he reached the armory door. He stopped,
grabbed another bayonet grenade, and loaded it onto the rifle. Liam
began moving again just as he heard the trip mine go off. He hoped
the explosion would discourage and confuse the chitin as he ran for
the exit. Coming back into the lobby, he saw Azurius entering from
the north wing where the offices were. Their eyes locked. Liam
stepped out of time once more. He aimed and fired straight at
Azurius. Azurius's eyes opened wide, and he stepped out of time just
in time to throw himself back the way he'd come. Liam dashed out

the exit and smacked another trip mine onto the doorframe. He ran across the street and into the damaged building where he had exited the sewers.

The chitin in the street followed as Liam returned to normal time. He waited to see what would happen. He tossed the rucksack onto his back as Azurius came through the door in a blur. The mine exploded as Azurius reached the bottom of the steps, throwing him forward. The chitin stopped their pursuit, confused. Liam wondered if he had gotten lucky. Azurius moved and picked himself up painfully. The chitin charged the building again, obscuring his view of Azurius. Liam dashed down the stairs and into the open entry to the sewers, grabbed the cover, and pulled it closed after him. Taking wire and a grenade, he wedged the grenade above the top rung of the ladder. After tying the pin to the cover handle, he jumped down and ran.

Just as he rounded a corner, he heard the cover open. Using the last of his reserves, he stepped out of time once more and put distance between the explosion and himself. The explosion came just as exhaustion forced him back into normal time. Then came the unmistakable sound of the tunnel caving in. Liam grinned and continued on his way back to the Industrial District.

•   •   •   •   •

After an hour and a half, Liam exited the sewer and entered the alley behind the Green Griffin. He found the janitor's room and stripped off his dirty armor and cleaned it. Then he took his pack and armor upstairs, collapsed on the recliner, and rested for a few minutes.

Liam had worked up an appetite. He could not decide if he needed rest or food more. Food won. He grabbed his utility belt and looked for something to eat. The melie wings looked good. He found a spicy sauce to cover them. Going into the bar, he got himself a glass of strong cider. The wings would be ready in about a half hour. So, he made his way upstairs and put his glass on the table. A shower would be nice. Unfortunately, it would have to be with cold water. He hoped the owner would not mind his using a towel. Once as clean as conditions permitted, he got dressed and went to get his dinner. Liam went into the kitchen and put his wings on a plate with some stalks and a chunky cheese sauce, then returned to the apartment.

When he finished, he returned the dishes to the kitchen, boiled some water on the stove, and washed everything he'd used. If Stuart, the owner of the Green Griffin, survived, Liam planned to reimburse him and the apartment's owner.

Upon returning to the room, he lay back on the recliner. With Azurius licking his wounds, perhaps the time had come to do some more hunting.

•   •   •   •   •

Randolf poured over a ground plan of the Temple compound and a floor plan of the Temple itself, trying to plan for the last defense. People still trickled in, and he had soldiers fighting holding actions across the city. They had slowed the chitin down and, in some cases, pushed them back. In the end, however, they faced a last stand with Azurius throwing almost limitless numbers of chitin at them.

Randolf heard a knock at the door, and the sergeant and Captain Simon entered. Celinia came in as well—the arch priestess's liaison.

The sergeant glanced down at the spread-out maps. "How's the battle plan coming, sir?"

"Depressing," Randolf replied. "It's going to be a last stand against a limitless horde of chitin. So far, all I can come up with are ways of delaying the inevitable."

"We have some good news for a change." Captain Simon smiled.

"Azurius and the chitin have dropped dead?" Randolf asked sourly.

The sergeant gave a grim laugh. "Not quite that good. We don't have chitin entering the city. Someone attacked the Military Center and shut down the last portals."

Randolf started out of his mood, and Celinia's eyes opened wide. "What happened? Who did it?"

Captain Simon shrugged. "We just got the report. As you know, we set up a makeshift observation post deep in Azurius's area of the city on a building overlooking the Center. A steady stream of chitin had been coming through. Our scout said that, without warning, all hell broke loose. He heard several explosions, some gunfire, and more explosions. The scout admits he looked away a few times. After all, he didn't think he'd see much except more chitin. He observed Azurius come out of the building like a shot. The door exploded a second later. It looked like Azurius was eating pavement for a change. He sent the chitin into the closest building. Our scout heard one last explosion and a rumble that sounded like a cave in. The center of the building sagged. Azurius stared at the building before limping into the Military Center, a little worse for wear."

Randolf wondered why his eyes had not fallen out of his head.

"The scout says no more chitin have come out of the Center since," the sergeant finished. "The chitin have stopped their advance and seem to be consolidating."

Randolf straightened from the table. "You mean Azurius is now uncertain of our capabilities and doesn't want his main force to fall into a trap. He's stopped to rethink his plan."

Captain Simon shrugged. "More or less."

Randolf pulled out a map of the city. "We may have a chance. Not an all-out attack. A defensive strategy will keep our forces intact longer. How much ammunition do we have?"

"A fair bit," Captain Simon replied. "We had other supplies in the city, and we grabbed most of it, but it's not limitless."

"Get some sharpshooters, with any weapons they can find, into the buildings within range of the chitin lines," Randolf ordered. "They are to kill as many chitin as come into range. One shot, one kill, if they can. Now, he doesn't quite have the limitless numbers we feared. If we can thin his ranks, we might just win by attrition."

"Sir," the sergeant replied. "If attrition is our goal, I suggest we make bayonet grenades available for targets of opportunity. Say, ten or more chitin clustered together."

"We may want to lob a few at the Military Center," Captain Simon suggested. "Just to keep Azurius off balance."

Celinia spoke up for the first time. "Azurius could destroy the barrier and bring the chitin in overland."

Captain Simon nodded. "It's possible, but it will take time."

"We need to pressure him into thinking he doesn't have the time he wants," Randolf decided. "Gentlemen, Lady High Priestess, these are all excellent points. It's a long shot, and we still need a lot of luck. Let's go with the plan we've just outlined. Keep looking for Licinious and his men. Also, detail people to watch the borders of the city. We need to know if Azurius brings in more reinforcements overland."

Captain Simon and the sergeant saluted and left.

Randolf heaved a sigh and let his shoulders slump.

"You should rest," Celinia advised.

"Always a hundred details to figure out." Randolf looked up at her and smiled. "Thank you for being concerned."

"Who do you think the brave warrior is who has bloodied Azurius's nose?" Celinia asked.

Randolf shrugged. "No way of knowing. He must have the luck of the Creator with him. Perhaps She hasn't abandoned us."

Then he blushed. "Forgive me."

Celinia smiled, walked around the table, and hugged him.

"All these setbacks have left even the arch priestess's faith shaken," she told him. "The Creator gave all of us, Azurius and Licinious included, choices, and those choices have consequences. We don't know all the choices Azurius and Licinious have made in their lives. We must believe that the good choices we've made count for something, if not in this world, then the next. All we can do is our duty."

Randolf sighed and put his hand over hers. "I wish you could have gotten to know Liam. If I could have had one wish, it would have been to see him happy."

Celinia squeezed his shoulder. "I wish he could be at your side now."

She released his shoulder and walked to the door, then paused. She turned to face him again. "However, since he is not here to look out for you, I can send Teresina in to nag you into resting."

She left him with that mischievous grin of hers.

•　　•　　•　　•　　•

Azurius yelped as the chitin pulled the last bit of shrapnel from his back. It was fortunate he had gained some distance in his pursuit of Liam before the mine exploded. Using the chitin's eyes and claws, he tended his wounds, then dismissed the creature. Under his orders, chitin now patrolled the building and dismantled the armory.

I wish I could leave it intact. It would be useful later, but I want no more surprises.

He sat up and grimaced. *I underestimated Liam. I must applaud the human's audacity, ingenuity, and skill. However, he can become a liability. Apparently, I haven't won him over yet.* Azurius calmed himself. *I must admit, this raid on my stronghold highlights the reasons I want his skills at my disposal.*

Azurius put Liam aside for the moment. He had more immediate concerns. *First, Liam destroyed the portals into the city. My technical skills are in chemical biology. I might be able to work out how to reopen the portals. However, it will take time. I have a good size horde of chitin in the city. Will they be enough? I'd planned to keep bringing them through and overwhelm the inhabitants with sheer numbers. I also can't be sure if Liam has contacted the Temple.*

He considered having the chitin disable the barrier, which should be possible to do from the inside, so additional chitin could come in overland.

Then I can go back to my original plan.

However, he was not sure how to do it. *Maybe I should attack the Temple with Licinious's forces. They might kill some important people before the security inside the Temple neutralize them. Then again, the security forces might capture them. They're best used to keep my enemies looking over their shoulders.*

A series of explosions rocked the Center. Azurius flung himself flat. The barrage lasted a few minutes, then stopped. Azurius raised his head and picked himself up. Debris that landed on him fell to the floor.

He growled. *More than one person launched that attack. Randolf has a way to get troops past the chitin.*

He went out into the hall to check the damage. The roof over part of the hall had collapsed.

They hadn't built this building with a direct assault in mind. Licinious told me that fact specifically.

He entered the central mezzanine and examined the extent of the damage.

They're trying to keep me guessing and will probably attack at random. I need to get directions to the chitin. However, he did not dare trance down here. *Trancing down would leave me too vulnerable if they attacked again while I traversed the dreamscape.*

Azurius reconsidered the plan he had just abandoned. He picked up his communicator and called Licinious.

"Yes, Azurius?" Licinious answered his comm.

"I want you to detail five people to get into the Temple," Azurius ordered. "They're to kill the leadership. It doesn't matter if they escape."

He closed the communicator before Licinious could respond. If the humans intercepted that message, they would pull forces back to the Temple.

•   •   •   •   •

Randolf reviewed reports from the hunter groups. The chitin moved about without direction, making them easy to pick off. A *target-rich environment,* one man called it.

Someone knocked, and the sergeant entered and came to Randolf.

"Sir, we've broken Licinious's code, and we've just intercepted a message," he reported. "Shall I send the tech in?"

Randolf nodded.

A moment later, the tech to whom they had given the dead assassin's communicator to entered.

"Azurius just sent a message to Licinious," the tech reported. "Azurius told him, and I quote, 'I want you to detail five people to get into the Temple. They're to kill the leadership. It doesn't matter if they escape.'"

"How long ago did you intercept this communication?" Captain Simon asked.

"Minutes ago," the tech replied. "I tried to lock onto the locations before I came, but the message was too short."

"So, we still don't know where Licinious has holed up," Randolf stated.

"I have someone waiting to see if he uses his communicator again," the tech promised. "We can get a rough triangulation from this information. However, it will take time."

"Just do your best," Randolf told him. "If there's nothing else, you may go."

The tech saluted and left the room.

Randolf started to say something, then cursed.

"I'm an idiot," he muttered. "Captain, is anyone watching Licinious's house?"

"Sir, that location's on the other side of the Theater District," Captain Simon objected.

"It's also the perfect place for him to hide," Randolf countered. "He'd assume his house would be obvious, and difficult to get to under the current circumstances. Therefore, not worth wasting the time. We've got people past the chitin. Let's see if anyone is home."

"Covertly, of course," the sergeant added.

Randolf nodded.

"We've got to rattle Azurius," Randolf declared. "It may be the only chance we have."

•   •   •   •   •

Liam decided to use the dreamscape to his advantage. The first place he looked was Licinious's house. He moved away from the Green Griffin and headed past the Theater District. He seemed to have hit pay dirt. Guards patrolled around Licinious's house— human guards. He drifted down through the roof and heard voices.

"I don't like this, Councilor," one voice was saying. "The security technicians at the temple probably intercepted the communication."

"Perhaps you'd like to take it up with Azurius," Licinious snapped. "I'll give you what chances I can, but he gave a direct order. No arguments."

Seven people stood around a map of the sewers.

"Now, if no one has any more objections..." Licinious looked around at the assembled men dressed in black uniforms.

"Take the sewer hatch in the alley in back," Licinious ordered. "Follow this route through the Industrial District. Once you get past the park, you can come up unseen. You will have standard armor, so you will look like their soldiers. We will modify the armor to look battle worn. Find whoever's conducting the debriefings and tell them you've seen me. I should be very popular about now."

Someone stifled a laugh, but Licinious ignored it.

"With luck, they will bring you to Captain Randolf and his emergency council," Licinious finished.

Liam's heart almost stopped. *Randolf's emergency council? Randolf is in charge? That means no one senior to him has survived.*

"I'll bet it's because someone got too close for comfort at the Military Center."

Licinious threw the man a withering look. "Keep those observations to yourself, Jom. It will increase your chances of survival."

"Who else is on this council?" someone asked.

"I don't know," Licinious growled in frustration. "We have no intelligence inside the Temple. I can give you a few guesses, though. Another captain and a high priestess should be on the council. That redhead, more than likely."

Liam gasped. *Celinia as well.* He forced himself to stay, rather than rush off. He had to get this right.

"You know those abilities the priestesses have," the man called Jom pointed out. "They're going to have some skilled ones checking everyone they don't know."

Licinious laughed. "I am way ahead of them there. I had the helmets fitted with a device that will block telepathic penetration."

"They'll get suspicious if they see a blank spot instead of a mind," Jom countered.

"Your news is urgent," Licinious stated. "Tell them where I am if necessary. If you do this right, it won't matter. I'm going to give you some weapons Azurius gave me. They're a type of *sticky grenade*. Once made active and thrown, they emit a residue. It will stick to whatever it touches. Then it will release hot plasma, incinerating anything within three meters of it. Kill by whatever means necessary. If the opportunity presents itself, Captain Randolf and the high priestess should be prime targets."

Liam seethed. He swore he would destroy Licinious and his band. Meanwhile, he had to intercept this group before it got to the Temple. He had to protect Celinia and his brother.

Unseen, he moved around the table and looked at the map, examining the route. He knew where he could intercept the assassins.

"When do we leave?" Jom asked.

"We need to alter the armor." Another man looked at Licinious. "Half hour maybe. Shouldn't take long."

"Very well," Licinious said. "Get moving."

The five assassins broke up to get ready. They took out the armor and scored it. Liam did not need to watch. He had to get ready.

In moments, his body jerked awake on its recliner. He leaped to his feet and began pulling on his armor. He tightened his chest with the diagnostic kit, then grabbed his rucksack and his rifle and headed for the door.

•   •   •   •   •

Liam went down into the sewer and dropped the visor on his helmet, switching it to thermal mode. He headed for the point where he planned to intercept the assassins. They would start out soon. He prayed they would not alter their plans. He considered setting out the trip mines, but he did not want to waste them. Arriving at the intercept point at the tunnel junction, he saw nothing with which he could wedge some grenades as a makeshift trap. Passing the junction, Liam saw a bend he could hide behind and decided to use his last two trip mines.

Backtracking, he paced out a spot he thought the entire group would be in the tunnel and placed the two trip mines just under the water, hidden by muck. He left enough space for someone to get between them. Once he set the proximity fuses to sandwich the lead person between the two explosions, Liam retreated to the bend to wait.

The wait was interminable. His mind kept inventing scenarios where they would alter their plans; perhaps take a different route at the last minute. Liam crouched down and tried to still his mind and push aside his anxieties. He had deliberately fought and killed mindless chitin—but never humans. He had to wrestle with his emotions until he heard the splashes of booted feet in the tunnel. Getting to the junction, he risked a glance. He saw the one named Jom stop at the junction. Liam pulled back, terrified they might hear his heartbeat. He thought of what they planned for his brother and Celinia, and his fears turned to fury. His trembling faded, replaced with resolve. He heard the assassins continue down the tunnel toward his trap. He counted the paces.

The explosion in the confined space of the sewer left Liam's head ringing. He shook his head to clear it and dashed around the bend. Two surviving assassins tried to pick themselves up. He opened fire. Both fell dead. Then he relieved them of what ammunition survived and found four strange grenades. He stuck these in his rucksack and dragged what remains he could back to the bend.

Liam took a deep breath as he walked back to the junction. He had done it. Now he just felt numb.

He made his way back to the industrial sector of the city. Once out of the sewer, he headed to the Green Griffin. Soon he would have to move against Licinious himself.

Liam stripped down and washed his gear and body again. Once he had finished, he picked up the bottle of whiskey and poured a shot. Aware he was pushing his luck, Liam hoped it would take some time before Azurius and Licinious realized their assassins were dead.

Liam drifted off to sleep.

•   •   •   •   •

Liam stood by his parents' house. Jarek arrived shortly afterward.

"You look tired," Jarek noted.

"I used the dreamscape," Liam told him, "to scout the Center and spy on Licinious."

"Scouting enemy positions in the dreamscape could have been risky. Azurius might have protected Licinious's house from dreamscape incursions. I guess he didn't consider him that important. The Center could have been suicidal. He must have thought no one would attempt it."

"Or he doesn't realize I am getting additional training in the dreamscape," Liam suggested. "Licinious sent out assassins to kill the leaders at the Temple, including my brother and some friends. I intercepted and killed them."

Jarek sighed. "I won't say eliminating them isn't a good thing, but I wonder if it might not have been better to have faith in your friends' ability to deal with them. The priestesses are skilled telepaths and will be on high alert for such an attempt."

Liam felt defensive. "Licinious gave them helmets that would block the priestesses' telepathy. He also gave them grenades which stick to and incinerate their targets. I wasn't going to let them unleash that type of weapon on my brother."

Jarek put a hand on Liam's shoulder. "I understand. I would also be a moral fraud for saying that I wouldn't have acted the same. Just be mindful. You are the one wild card Azurius can't predict. Speaking of which, are you planning a raid on his stronghold?"

"I raided his stronghold," Liam replied. "In the process, I destroyed the last portals, and Azurius needed clean underwear. I also got some weapons and equipment."

Jarek looked concerned, then relieved. "Very good. While Azurius is good at adapting, he doesn't like surprises. Your success might give him pause. Also, it will make him more interested in getting you to change sides. Again, be mindful, my friend. That raid will also make him aware that you are a highly skilled opponent. He may decide you aren't worth the risk. Still, I'm impressed, and knowing Azurius as I do, so is he."

Liam smiled at the praise.

"Oh, and I need to tell you we have reached the halfway point," Jarek informed him. "We will arrive in system soon. However, we can't do anything with the planetary force field up."

"Therefore, I have to deal with Azurius before we can drop it." Liam sighed in frustration.

Jarek nodded sympathetically.

"Now," Jarek directed, "these activities have cost you energy which you need to replenish. I suggest you get some deep sleep."

Liam nodded and sighed. "I don't know what time it is where you are, but good night."

"You as well," Jarek replied.

•   •   •   •   •

Randolf met the sergeant and Celinia.

"No sign of assassins yet," the sergeant reported.

"The arch priestess has instructed the priestesses to be careful of people they can't read," Celinia told them.

"I wish they'd get here and get it over with," Randolf growled in irritation. "We've got enough to deal with."

"At least we've breached their communications," the sergeant offered. "If they communicate again, we can triangulate on Licinious, and we've got scout teams looking for him."

Celinia gave the sergeant a cross look. "Remember the Creator's commands on vengeance."

The sergeant nodded, and Celinia turned to report to the arch priestess.

•   •   •   •   •

Azurius settled into a comfortable chair. It had not been easy, but he had gotten out of the Military Center. He entered a nearby building, went to the basement, and located a hatch into the sewers.

An unpleasant experience, but if Liam can do it, so can I.

He found another hatch a short distance away, and it led into another building where he'd found a nicely furnished office on the basement level.

Now the Neo-Etruscans dropping bombs on the Center can do it as long as they wish.

Azurius tranced down and went to his lab. He first checked the chitin's status. He grimaced. *I stopped their advance after Liam's raid to prevent them from being led into a trap. Now it appears the trap has sprung up around them. Snipers are picking them off in numbers. I possess a considerable force, but the Neo-Etruscans have whittled their numbers down to two-thirds of what I had.*

He ordered the chitin to attack the attackers and to clear the buildings that snipers used as platforms to launch attacks.

The chitin's blind obedience has its uses, but I wish they could take more initiative. I also wish I could overcome their natural tendency to be less active at night. Continuous attacks would deny the humans the opportunity to rest.

Once they pushed the snipers back, he could regain the initiative. Now he needed reinforcements.

He went to his computer console and pulled up a schematic of the city's force field. *A weak point exists somewhere. The Neo-Etruscans built four reactors early in the conflict, one behind each defensive sector. With chitin already inside the barrier, I can take one down. However, the Neo-Etruscans protected the reactors well.*

He brought up a more detailed view of a reactor. *Where could a chitin penetrate to deactivate it?* He rotated the view. Then he laughed. *The chitin don't have to penetrate the reactor. Just expose and cut the power lead to a section of the force field. They should succeed, given time.*

He selected a small group of chitin and ordered them to travel overland to the reactor behind Archer sector. He gave them directions on how to dig up one conduit and cut it. They would probably fry, but he had more chitin where they came from.

He then sent orders to the three hives on the central continent to send a surge of chitin to that section of the barrier. Chitin breed quickly, and about twenty thousand per hive should have emerged from their chrysalises by now. He set up an alarm to inform him when they had deactivated the force field and returned to his body.

Now he had time to consider Liam.

I have to admit the raid on the Military Center was pure audacity. Liam possesses superb skills at infiltration. His timing—flawless. He took down the chitin that could have stopped him and destroyed the portals.

Azurius winced at the pain in his shoulder. *I also must admit my own carelessness. I came out personally to investigate the commotion and almost gave Liam a perfect opportunity to finish me. Then I let my anger get the better of me—to my cost. Even after stepping out of time, that mine proved uncomfortably close. I underestimated Liam's skill at stepping out of time and using the dreamscape. Liam must have observed how thin the chitin were in the Center and decide the benefits outweighed the risks.*

Azurius chuckled. *The boy has the guts to get things done. For now, I'll continue to try to recruit him, but first I need to find Liam.*

He tranced down again and entered the dreamscape.

.   .   .   .   .

Azurius started where he had seen Liam before. From the top of Tower 99, he looked out over the city. *Where would Liam go from here? His raid was an act of desperation. If Liam got to the Temple, he wouldn't need to stage such a raid alone—or would he? Liam is one of a handful of people on Etrusci capable of stepping out of time. He may have felt it easier to stage the raid alone.*

Azurius shifted his eyes to the infrared spectrum. *Perhaps Liam has come by recently.*

Azurius laughed at his good fortune. Not only did he see fading footsteps, but he could also see faint traces of heat coming from one building. The sign read Green Griffin Inn.

So, unless they're still doing business, someone is using the inn as a place of refuge. Moreover, in a place I might not have thought to look.

Azurius floated off Tower 99 and moved in for a closer look. Getting close to the building, he saw something vaguely familiar. He remembered what it was just as it, and several others like it, exploded.

Azurius sped backward, forcing himself to remember he was dreamwalking. More detonated behind him and his back exploded in pain. Faster than thought, he sped back to his body.

.   .   .   .   .

On his recliner, Liam snapped awake at hearing an explosion and Azurius's cry. He suppressed a grim chuckle of triumph. Jarek had warned him it would not be easy to kill Azurius in the dreamscape, but Azurius had underestimated him again. Liam got up and strapped on his armor. He needed to leave the safety of this building. Azurius would have chitin after him.

•   •   •   •   •

Azurius shot up, clutching his head. The pain in his back faded, but his head pounded like a hammer.

Where did Liam learn that technique? Azurius needed to get to the lab, but he dared not risk it with this headache. He rifled into a rucksack and found some pain medication. He swallowed a pill and sat back down and tried to relax.

Liam's skills have grown. I can't let the whelp have it all his own way. I need to knock him off balance again. Soon, the headache faded. He could not spend much time in the dreamscape. He would not need much.

Azurius went to the chitin controls in his lab and detached a swarm of fifty to raid the Green Griffin. He ordered chitin to attack Liam and pursue him wherever he went.

Liam might shake them, but they will keep looking until either they kill him, or he destroys them. If the latter, then I'll consider extending another offer to him. Once done, Azurius went into deep sleep to rest.

CHAPTER 6

In the Green Griffin's kitchen, Liam gathered any food he could use in the field and stuffed it into his rucksack. The early morning light filtering through a window fell on the bottle of New Olympia whiskey. It might be useful—for medicinal purposes. It went into the rucksack.

Liam's head snapped up when he sensed explosions in the dreamscape. He suspected chitin had tripped the dreamscape mines. They would not notice the explosions. Upon slinging the rucksack on his back and grabbing his rifle, Liam opened the gas and rigged two grenades at the door between the kitchen and the bar. He sprinted for the back stairs and raced up, past the apartment, and headed for the roof. The sound of the Griffin's main door splintering and crashing echoed up the stairs.

If Stuart survives, perhaps he can charge Azurius for the cost of repairs.

The grenades detonated, the concussion throwing him to the floor as the gas exploded, and the entire building shook. He wondered how many chitin he had destroyed. He scrambled to his feet and ran up the stairs to the rooftop door.

Locked.

He took his plasma blade and sliced away the lock. Once on the roof, Liam stepped out of time and ran. He leaped to the next building, just catching the edge of the roof. He stumbled a little, but his momentum carried him forward as he reentered ordinary time.

Liam headed toward the access hatch but needed to know what he was up against. He ran back to the edge. Flames engulfed the

Green Griffin, and the fire rapidly spread to the rest of the building. He raised the rifle until he could peer through the gunsight. With a trained eye, he swept the building and saw chitin through the windows. The fire spread fast, and the electronic fire suppression system did not have power. The spreading fire trapped any chitin still in the building.

Did the entire group Azurius send go in? He glanced down and grimaced. *The smoke at ground level is making it hard to see anything in the street.*

Liam turned away and dashed to the rooftop door, forced it open, and ran down the stairs.

I have to get out before the fire spreads to adjacent buildings.

By the time he made it to the street, flames engulfed the whole structure. He also realized the entire swarm had not gone into the building. At least fifteen chitin raced toward him.

Liam stepped out of time and started shooting. Four fell, but the rest pushed after him. He unslung his rucksack and grabbed a sticky grenade. He pulled the pin and threw it with all his might. Then he grabbed his rucksack by the strap and backpedaled. The grenade hit the center chitin. Seconds later, it detonated. The explosion thinned the numbers. Now only six singed bugs remained to stagger to their feet. Liam opened fire and took down three more, then ran to gain distance. He skidded to a stop when he saw another group rearing up to attack. Five more had come up behind him. He slung his rucksack over his shoulder and opened fire. Three went down in this group. A chitin struck him from behind, throwing him into normal time. He heard the shriek of tearing metal as the bug threw him forward. Another slammed Liam into the ground, tore his rucksack from his back, and threw it aside. He grabbed his plasma blade and twisted as it ignited, cutting into the chitin's thorax. Rolling to his feet, he slashed the head off another. One chitin kicked the rifle out of his reach. Liam stepped out of time and charged the remaining three. He decapitated one as the last two recovered. Spinning, his cut uncoiled like a spring, cutting a chitin in half, leaving only one.

Liam pulled out his pistol and fired at the back of its head. The last chitin went down.

Gasping for breath, Liam slid into normal time. The fight had depleted his reserves. He checked his rifle

Thank the Creator it's still intact.

He found his rucksack. It had a tear in it, but he thought he could patch it. The battle had left the diagnostic kit a mass of smashed electronics. Unable to reset his armor after taking it off, he would have to sleep in it. One hand grenade plus three of the sticky grenades survived. His last bayonet grenade was also unusable. He found the magazines for his rifle and pistol intact, and he still had the power pack for the plasma blade and extra power packs for the pistol. Of the two power packs he had for the rifle, the chitin destroyed one. His food was a little mashed but edible. By some miracle, the bottle of whiskey remained intact.

Liam discarded the ruined equipment and attached the remaining grenades, magazines, and power packs to his armor and utility belt. Holding the rucksack to him to protect his food, he headed for the sewer. After climbing down, he moved toward the Theater District, near Licinious's house. Liam wanted to strike soon.

•   •   •   •   •

The sun rose as the scout team climbed out onto the roof high atop a building at the edge of the Theater District. With precision that came from practice, they set up and scanned the area with high-powered binoculars. They scanned the one building they came to observe.

"Something is going on at ex-Councilor Licinious's house." Lieutenant Janus adjusted the focus. "I see armed people on the grounds."

One soldier followed his gaze through his own binoculars. "Should we call it in?"

The lieutenant lowered his binoculars and nodded. He reached for the controls of his scrambled communicator.

"Sir!" another soldier called. "Chitin are moving. It looks like they're attacking sniper positions."

Lieutenant Janus turned his binoculars to where his soldier directed him. The chitin charged up the outside of buildings to get at the snipers.

"Get down!" the lieutenant ordered.

Lieutenant Janus activated his communicator. "This is Watcher Leader; we have activity at subject's house."

"Any sign of the subject himself?" came the call back.

"Negative," the lieutenant replied. "Also, the chitin are on the move again and heading this way."

He heard a curse.

"Sir," the lieutenant ventured. "I think we can stay hidden and keep watching."

"Negative, Lieutenant," came the response. "Take one more look, then get your people out of there before you're spotted. We're getting word from other units. The chitin are climbing up buildings to attack our snipers."

"Understood." The lieutenant swung his binoculars back to Licinious's house. "I've just made a last look. No change. We're on our way out."

Lieutenant Janus led his men to the stairs.

"With our luck," one man grumbled, "he'll step out to stretch his legs two seconds after we're off the roof."

•   •   •   •   •

Randolf looked up as Captain Simon entered the room. "I've got good news and bad news."

Randolf sighed and nodded.

"The good news is our scout team reports activity at Licinious's house, though they haven't seen Licinious himself."

"Have them keep watching," Randolf ordered.

Captain Simon shook his head. "That leads to the bad news. The chitin are moving again. Now they're climbing up the outsides of the buildings and attacking the snipers. The scout team just escaped."

Randolf slammed his fist on the table. "Are we able to maintain contact?"

The captain nodded. "We're executing a fighting withdrawal. I think we can slow them down with the damage we did during their hiatus. There are scout teams watching the borders of the city. Nothing yet."

Randolf sat down hard. "Unless Azurius makes a mistake, it's just a matter of time."

Captain Simon said nothing.

"We need to plan a course to Licinious's house, which avoids the chitin," Randolf decided.

"We know he's sending assassins," the captain countered. "Chasing Licinious just might save them the trouble."

Randolf closed his eyes and rubbed them. "I'll wait till I get confirmation he's there. He may be elsewhere, and it would be a wasted trip."

Captain Simon looked relieved.

Randolf raised his head and look Captain Simon in the eyes. "If we're going to die in a last-stand battle, I want to make sure Licinious, at least, isn't around to pick up the pieces."

"I understand, sir," the captain replied.

•　　•　　•　　•　　•

Liam exited the sewer into the Theater District. He remembered coming here as a child. *I enjoyed the shows and the beautiful, bright lights. I could forget how I didn't belong.*

He remembered a bistro his parents liked to take them. In fact, he had eaten there himself many times since then. Peter was the owner. Liam made his way through the deserted streets until he found Peter's Bistro. He slipped to the rear and checked the door. He found it unlocked.

Apparently, the staff left in a hurry.

He stepped inside and checked the building was clear. Then he went to the kitchen.

Great! he thought. *The stoves use gas.*

Liam emptied his rations onto a shelf in the cold room and took out his tool kit. Rummaging through it, he found a needle and thread to repair the tear in his rucksack as best he could. Upon investigating the dining area, he found some pastries still in the display case.

Probably stale, but beggars can't be choosers. The coffeemaker and other hot drink machines need power. No coffee.

He took some food out of the cold room and cooked himself a quick meal of a warm tarpier sandwich. Looking up from the table, he noticed a wine-rack.

Why not?

Liam wasn't familiar with wine. So, he picked the first one he came to, grabbed a glass, and brought it to the table. Examining the label, he read NeoConnacht 2950. Unsure what that name meant, he shrugged and poured a dark red liquid into a glass and took a sip. It had a tart flavor he found enjoyable.

I better keep a mental tally in case Peter survived. I hoped I haven't picked the most expensive wine in the place.

After his second glass, he re-corked the bottle and returned it to the rack.

Liam made his way to Peter's office and found a comfortable chair. Collapsing into it, he rocked back and let himself slip into the dreamscape.

•   •   •   •   •

Liam found himself back in the garden. A few moments later, Jarek appeared.

"You look tired," Jarek observed. "Didn't get much rest?"

"Azurius came nosing around," Liam told him. "The defenses worked, but I had to make a break for it. He put chitin on my trail. I killed them, but I needed a new place to set up shop."

Jarek nodded. "Not surprising, considering his interest in you. He is clever. I should warn you I suspect his mind and yours work almost the same way, except you're a good person."

"It's a pity," Liam wistfully mused. "The building I just left came with apartments and a nice kitchen. I rather like cooking."

Jarek laughed. "It's a family trait. Your mother's people, the O'Connors, pride themselves on their cooking. They like to say, 'Not even a mortal enemy leaves an O'Connor table hungry.' Your aunt, that is your mother's sister, once conceded one almost did, but your great-grandmother, Bayvin, caught him before he could make good his escape."

Liam gave a slight laugh.

"A whole part of myself I never knew existed." He brooded for a moment. "After I've had some rest, I plan to settle things with Licinious. He's a danger as long as he's alive."

Jarek closed his eyes and sighed. "I won't say that you aren't taking a necessary step. Be careful. I don't just mean of what our enemy can do to us."

Liam sensed Jarek wanted to say more, and he prepared to defend his actions.

Instead, Jarek changed the subject. "You best reset your defenses before you rest. Also, practice those exercises I gave you. It will be important. Azurius isn't as clumsy as the chitin."

Liam nodded, disappointed in himself for forgetting to reset the defenses when he got to Peter's.

"Do you want to spar?" Liam asked. "I doubt Azurius will wait until I'm rested."

Jarek considered the request for a moment. "A brief bout only. I want you to have the energy to reset the defenses."

Jarek produced two toy swords again and tossed one to Liam.

They circled each other. Jarek struck. Liam deflected the sword and pushed his hand into Jarek's chest.

"Whoa!"

Liam jumped back, horrified.

Jarek looked down at his chest. "That was startling."

He looked at Liam with a mixture of pleased surprise and accusation. "That move was also dangerous, Liam. Did you intend to attack that way?"

"Forgive me, no," Liam replied contritely. "I thought of it as I parried. I should have considered the consequences. That's why I pulled back so fast."

Jarek straightened. "If you get into a dreamscape battle with Azurius, that kind of attack could prove an effective technique. As I said before, he and I are nearly equal at dreamscape combat. If it startles him as much as it did me, it would have an effect. Anyone less skillful, it could kill. Azurius, I doubt it. Though it would concern him enough that he might break off."

Liam still looked worried.

"I'm fine, Liam," Jarek assured him. "In the future, let me know before you try a new technique."

Liam nodded.

"I think we've done enough for tonight. I am pleased with your progress. Reset your defenses and call it a night."

Jarek left, and Liam set about his task.

Slipping back to his body, he went outside. Remembering how Jarek showed him to reset the claymores, he imagined them on the Bistro and the surrounding buildings. Azurius would be wary of approaching him now. The dream explosives would at least give him warning if chitin entered the area. He removed the old system of traps from around the Griffin. Satisfied, Liam returned to his body and drifted into a deep sleep.

•   •   •   •   •

Azurius paced around the room. He had had no word of activity at the Temple from a chitin scout he had sent to a high vantage point overlooking the Temple. Something should have happened by now, which would indicate a major shakeup.

Tired of waiting, Azurius grabbed his communicator and called Licinious.

"Yes?" Licinious answered.

"Did you send out the assassins?"

"Yesterday," Licinious replied. "We've heard nothing back."

"I have chitin watching the Temple," Azurius told him. "It has shown no activity suggesting an assassination attempt, successful or not."

"They should have been there by now." Licinious sounded unnerved. "Could your chitin have attacked them, thinking they were soldiers?"

Azurius closed his eyes. "What route did they take?"

"They went through the sewers until they found the hatch just inside the perimeter," Licinious explained. "Their best chance was to pretend to just be coming in from the field to report."

Azurius nodded. "If they took that route, they shouldn't have crossed paths with any chitin. I'll give them more time."

Azurius closed the communicator and brooded.

•   •   •   •   •

Randolf also brooded over reports when he heard a knock at the door. His sergeant and the tech entered. The latter looked exultant. The former looked worried.

"We've got him," the tech announced. "Azurius just communicated with Licinious. Licinious is at his house."

"Where our last report suggested," the sergeant added in even tones.

"Azurius is in a building near the Center," the tech went on, "and they haven't heard from their assassins."

"However, the chitin are between us and both of them," the sergeant pointed out.

Randolf had already pulled out a map and began looking over possible routes.

"We can do this." Randolf placed his finger on a point in the Temple. "That's all, Lieutenant."

The tech saluted and left.

The sergeant came around and followed Randolf's finger.

"We have a hatch under the Temple which we can use," Randolf explained, "in the subbasement. We leave through the hatch and follow the sewers through to the Theater District—right to Licinious's backyard."

"I suppose it's pointless to tell you that your place is here," the sergeant countered.

"Sergeant," Randolf replied. "In another day, we may die under a mass of chitin. Do you want the traitors to outlive us?"

The sergeant shook his head. "It's a good plan. We head down out of view. We're only exposed when we strike. Azurius won't know you've left. I wish I could persuade you to stay here and let us do it."

Randolf looked up at him. His eyes were hard. "It has to be me."

"I understand," the sergeant replied. "Even if I don't like it."

•   •   •   •   •

While Azurius could do some directing telepathically, the lab provided his best control. He heard a signal from his console. He sat back, closed his eyes, and fell into a trance.

When he got to the controls, he saw the chitin had breached the force field fence at Archer sector. The three hives had marshaled their contingent of new warriors.

I have ample reinforcements on the way. Another day or two and the city's defenses will start to fray if not collapse.

He gave the order for the fresh chitin to head for the breach and join the fight. Then he returned to his body, well pleased with this turn.

•   •   •   •   •

Liam woke from his nap. Feeling hungry, he investigated the pastry case in the dining area and picked up a pastry that did not feel too stale and a couple of pieces of fruit. After eating his snack, he grabbed one of Peter's monogrammed bar napkins, wiped his hands and, without thinking, tucked it into a belt pouch. Liam's anger had not abated, but his mind seemed clear. He decided to travel light. His rucksack and assault rifle would only slow him down. So, he tucked them behind the bar. After a quick glance, he stepped outside and stayed in the shadows until he got to the sewer hatch. Lifting it, he slid onto the ladder.

Following the sewers, Liam kept a steady pace, covering the distance of five kilometers until he reached the hatch behind Licinious's house. He decided to see what he faced.

Liam tranced down and stepped out of his body. The house was a single-story structure of ten meters by ten meters. He spotted three guards in the backyard and two in front. He slipped inside. Licinious sat in his living room with one man. Three others moved about the house. Liam grinned and returned to his body.

Making his way up the ladder, he felt the pain in his side. His ribs were making their displeasure felt.

Liam crept out of the hatch and slithered on the ground, ignoring his ribs. Looking into Licinious's backyard, he saw the three guards. Rising to a crouch, he pulled his two knives and weighed the heavier of the two for a longer throw. Everything seemed to merge—the hand, the knife, the enemy, the heart. Liam released the first knife, not having to look to know his aim was true. The other knife left his hand less than a second later. Stepping out of time, Liam hit the third man. The two knives struck home as Liam broke the third's neck.

Liam retrieved his knives, cleaned them with a cloth from his belt pouch, and slid them back into their sheaths. Without looking, he returned the cloth to its pouch. He drew his pistol and crept around the house. Two men guarded the door. He stepped out of time and gunned them down. A third rounded the corner of the house and stopped short before he, too, died. Liam fell back into time as he approached the front door.

The door shattered as Liam's foot connected. Time slowed as he leaped, killing a guard with a burst from the pistol. His blade ignited, and he tore into the second as he turned. The third fell where he stood.

Liam charged into the living room, gunning down the last guard. Licinious came to his feet but could not reach a weapon.

Remembering the third man in the front he had missed when dreamwalking, Liam scanned for further threats. The kitchen was clear. The bedroom door was open, and a glance told him the bathroom was empty. He noticed pottery, bookcases, and an ornamental spear which hung over the fireplace.

Liam holstered his pistol, his mind in flames. "Nice place you have here, Councilor."

Licinious backed away from him. Liam held his plasma blade between them, preparing to strike.

"Lieutenant, please." Licinious's voice trembled with fear.

Liam's steel-gray eyes became hard, pitiless, without mercy. "Brave warriors and innocent people have died because of you. Your treachery caused the deaths of my friends. You murdered my parents and my foster parents."

Liam's rage stole his voice.

"I can help you." Licinious raised his right hand, trying to calm him. "I know his plans."

Liam slashed. Licinious screamed as his right hand fell away. "Please, no!"

Liam stayed his hand as the traitor caught his breath, clutching his stump. "People are rallying at the Temple. Azurius plans to attack. I was supposed to reason with them after he destroyed the warriors."

"Treacherous to the end," Liam sneered. "How does it feel, knowing no one will trust you? Not Azurius, not the soldiers, not the people."

Liam cut away a leg. Licinious fell to the ground, shrieking.

"And not me."

His blade fell a third time, slicing across the traitor's abdomen.

The plasma blade cauterized the wound. Death would not be quick. Liam took the ceremonial spear from the wall and jammed it into the traitor's shoulder. Then he lifted him off the floor and rammed the spear into the wall.

"If Azurius bothers to look for you here," Liam snarled. "Tell him I'll be waiting for him."

He turned away and walked out of the councilor's house without a backward glance.

He walked outside and looked around, suddenly choking back his bile. Other enemies could arrive at any moment. He ran past the bodies, into the alley, and found the hatch he had come up.

Creator! I butchered the old man!

He climbed down into the sewer and pulled the cover over his head.

Dear Creator! How can I call myself better?

He had exalted over his foe, his mind flaming, savoring his vengeance.

Liam took a few more steps, fell to his knees, and threw up. Soon, it was just dry heaves as tears poured down his face. He stood and went a little further. Then he stopped and leaned against the filthy wall and wept.

"Creator, what have I become?" he cried aloud.

Liam stumbled forward, trying to get control of himself.

Liam!

Marcus stood in front of him. Liam stopped, confused.

What have you done? Marcus demanded.

Liam's control faltered. "I'm sorry!" he wept.

You know our teachings on revenge, Marcus reproached him. *Licinious will die in agony.*

Suddenly, irrationally angry, Liam straightened. "How can you defend him after what he did? To you, to Mom, to my birth parents, to everyone we cared about?"

I'm not defending him, Marcus responded quietly, *but how do his misdeeds make yours right?*

With a howl of despair and emotional agony, Liam dashed forward through the shade of his father, blindly running into the sewers.

Liam! Wait! Marcus watched him go with a stricken look on his face.

•   •   •   •   •

Randolf checked his weapons and turned to meet his squad in the subbasement. Celinia stood in the doorway. "So, you located Licinious and are going to kill him."

Randolf kept his expression neutral. "He's a threat, Celinia, and a traitor."

"You know our teachings on vengeance," she countered. "Vengeance is one of evil's greatest traps."

"This is about justice." Anger crept into his voice.

"Is it?" Celinia asked coldly. "Or is it about taking revenge for the deaths of your brother, parents, and friends?"

"Like Kia and Devon?" he shot back.

Celinia did not flinch. "If you execute him in cold blood, how does that make you any better? He isn't even the most dangerous. We need you here, Randolf. Azurius is still in the city, and it's only a matter of time before they converge on us."

"Celinia, move," Randolf ordered angrily.

Equally angry but defeated, Celinia stepped aside.

•   •   •   •   •

Randolf found the sergeant with the handpicked squad waiting by the hatch. He nodded. A soldier lifted the hatch, and they began their descent. Soon, they all entered the tunnel. They moved through the shallow water. After about thirty minutes, they heard the skittering of chitin above them and the sounds of battle. On occasion, they heard the screams of men dying. They continued, and soon the battle sounds faded. They pressed forward, following a miniature map of the sewer. Approaching a T-junction, the point man held up a hand.

"Sir," the corporal reported, "someone set off an explosion here."

The sergeant and Randolf looked at the large, burned holes blasted into the wall.

"It looks like trip mines," the sergeant commented. "About a day old."

His two lead soldiers scouted ahead. The corporal entered the main tunnel and scouted a little way. The private continued around a bend into a dead end.

"Sir!" He motioned them over.

Randolf and the sergeant went to him. They saw the remains of five bodies. Five bodies dressed in regulation armor.

"I've seen that one with Councilor Licinious." Randolf looked at one body that was still recognizable. "I think we've found the assassins Licinious sent."

"Who did this?" the sergeant asked. "We didn't have anyone in the Theater District."

"Someone cut off in the early stages of the fight," the private suggested.

Randolf continued to look. "Maybe, but how did this person know they were traitors?"

"One of Licinious's men turned on him?" the sergeant ventured.

"Maybe we can ask Licinious when we find him," Randolf decided, signaling the end of speculation for the moment.

They returned to the junction, regrouped, and continued, more alert for danger or clues.

They approached another junction as they neared the exit point. The corporal raised his hand. He examined something on the wall.

"Someone leaned here," he observed. "Not just a brush, and it's recent."

Randolf filed that information away to consider later and signaled for them to continue. The point man scrambled up ladder and cracked opened the hatch. He scanned the area and signaled them to follow. Soon, they all gathered in the alley outside the back of Licinious's house.

Creeping into the yard, they saw three men lying on the ground, all dead. The sergeant stopped Randolf and motioned three soldiers to check the rest of the grounds. One soldier investigated the front of the house. Soon, they all returned.

"Sir," the corporal reported. "Outside the house, we've counted six bodies. Someone broke open the front door. Back here, two knife wounds and one broken neck. In the front, someone shot all three. The knife wounds seem to be from thrown knives. They were a little more elongated from the blade spinning into the body rather than a knife thrust. We didn't enter the house."

Randolf wondered who had beaten them here. *Is Licinious dead, or is he still on the loose, causing trouble?*

Randolf looked around the neighborhood. "Let's check the house."

They formed a row and went around the house, keeping in physical contact with each other. They saw the broken door and approached on high alert.

Randolf and his men entered Licinious's house. They led with assault weapons, ready for an ambush. More dead bodies littered the floor.

"What the...?"

A whimper came from the next room. A soldier went in, leading with his weapon.

"Captain," the soldier called in an emotionless voice. "I found him."

Randolf stopped short when he saw the traitor. He seemed to just cling to life. A detached part of his mind noted the plasma blade wounds.

"So," Randolf stated, "Azurius decided he couldn't trust you."

Licinious looked up and managed a coughing laugh.

"No," he wheezed. "Liam..."

Randolf jerked back in shock. "Liam?"

"...has a cruel streak I didn't suspect."

Randolf struggled to get himself back under control. "Further than I would have gone. My brother never did things by halves."

"You..." Licinious coughed again, and his eyes rolled back into his head. His body slumped on the spear holding him pinned to the wall.

A soldier felt his neck. "Dead."

"Let's get out of here."

Randolf let the soldiers pass as he contemplated his family's old enemy. He did not know how he felt. He should feel a thrill of joy and hope his brother was alive. Yet, this evidence of his brother's ruthlessness shocked him.

"Sir?"

"I'm trying to get my head around what I'm seeing, Sergeant," Randolf admitted. "He was a traitor, but he must have hung there for some time. What's happening to my brother?"

The sergeant looked at the traitor.

"Sir, we need to go."

Randolf and the squad returned the way they had come and reentered the sewers. They paused at the first intersection. Randolf wondered if his brother had stopped here. The corporal traveled a short distance in the opposite direction.

"Sir," the man reported. "I see signs someone went this way. Do you want to follow him?"

Randolf wanted to. Liam went that way, and Randolf wanted to find his brother and bring him back to safety.

He looked to the sergeant who gave a brief negative shake. He would not allow Randolf any more indulgences.

"We have no time," Randolf replied. "We're needed back at the Temple. Liam is highly skilled. He'll catch up when he's ready."

"Sir," the corporal persisted, "one or two more people won't matter. Private Dillon and I can track him from here. Even if he isn't ready to come in, some extra hands may help."

"Furthermore," Private Dillon added, "we can open communications with you."

Randolf glanced at the sergeant. The sergeant gave a slight nod.

"Very well," Randolf commanded. "Find my brother and do what you can, Corporal...?"

"Ephram, sir. Thank you for your confidence."

Corporal Ephram hit Dillon on the shoulder, and they continued to follow the trail.

The others continued back toward the Temple. The sergeant put his hand on Randolf's shoulder, and the look in his eyes showed he empathized.

"Liam must have neutralized the assassins and then went after Licinious," Randolf surmised.

"I would say he attacked the assassins over a day ago," the sergeant observed. "He beat us to Licinious by no more than an hour. I must say, I appreciate your brother's creativity."

Randolf cracked a slight smile. It was a feeble attempt at humor, and they both knew it.

"I'm worried about him, Sergeant," Randolf confided. "Not about the challenges he faces, but what this means is happening to him. I never knew my brother to be vicious. An opportunity to settle old scores?"

The sergeant shrugged. "We can't know until your brother decides to tell us. We have other things to do. Ephram and Dillon can find him. They may also give him someone to unburden himself to."

Randolf fell into step with him. "Once we're back, I want a guard at the entrance to the subbasement. Let them know about Ephram, Dillon, and my brother."

"Understood, sir."

•   •   •   •   •

They got back within an hour. Randolf entered the Temple's subbasement and made his way back to the main Temple as the squad dispersed to other duties. He cleaned up and returned to the ready room. Randolf slumped into a chair and buried his head in his hands. He heard a knock. Teresina and Celinia entered.

"Randolf?" Teresina asked. "Did you find him?"

Randolf lifted his head and nodded.

"So, you didn't enjoy exacting vengeance on him?" Celinia asked coldly.

Teresina threw her a warning look.

"I never got the chance," Randolf answered. "He was dying when I got there."

He remembered Celinia's warning about vengeance.

How do I tell her what happened?

"He displeased Azurius," Teresina reasoned incorrectly.

Randolf shook his head. "Liam got to him first."

Celinia's face radiated joy. "Liam's alive, how...where...?"

"I don't know," Randolf replied. "He was gone before I arrived."

Randolf paused to consider how much he should tell them. "Liam cut off a hand and a leg and disemboweled him. Then he pinned him to the wall with a spear for good measure. Licinious hung there for an hour. He lived long enough to tell us Liam is alive."

Celinia's face fell in shock. Teresina put an arm around her shoulder.

"Creator, have pity," Celinia whispered.

"Don't judge him," Teresina counseled. "We knew there were scars on his soul. He needs us more than ever if they're going to heal."

Celinia reached up and grasped her friend's hand. "You speak wisely. Reason and judgment won't help him." She looked at Randolf. "Love is the answer to the darkness surrounding him. Love and time are best to heal a soul.

"I ask your forgiveness, Randolf," she continued contritely. "I was wrong to judge you."

She reached out to Randolf, who took her and Teresina's hands. "Thank you." He smiled at them. "You comfort me, but I wonder if we may defeat Azurius only to find my brother lost to us."

"No," Celinia replied. "We have to believe we can reach him."

•   •   •   •   •

Liam sat in the burned-out remains of his parents' house. He did not want anyone around him. Not chitin, not his parents. Was he any better than Licinious or indeed, Azurius?

A black-scaled hand rested gently on his shoulder. "Want to talk about it?"

Liam wanted to shout "no" but decided he needed to talk.

"I killed Licinious."

"Ah." Jarek sat next to him without lifting his hand. "I take it that in the process, you found an ugly little part of yourself you didn't realize was there. I know it made me a little off-color when I discovered it in me."

Liam looked up at him. "I cut him into pieces and left him to die an agonizing death."

"Just," Jarek offered. "At least in the manner of rough justice. I won't ask for details."

Liam buried his face in his hands.

"Believe me, Liam," Jarek said kindly. "I understand the significance of what you're feeling. You have some noble standards. Yet, in anger—righteous anger, I might add—you gave in to your darkness. It happened to me. When I still fought against the Rebellion, I visited a similar punishment on a person whom I had thought a friend and a fellow champion against Azurius. He'd betrayed a family that..." Jarek sighed. "The details don't matter. After I'd finished killing him, I felt like I'd betrayed everything I held dear. The shadow lives in us all. Our feeling this way, while it pains us, is a sign of hope. It is the big difference between beings like Azurius or Licinious and us. When we let the shadow loose on our enemies, we feel remorse. For them, it's just business as usual."

"Somehow, that doesn't make it any better."

Jarek squeezed his shoulder. "It isn't supposed to. We learn from it. We must never forget the price we pay for vengeance or putting aside our morals. After all, what did we gain from our cruelty? Vengeance? Yes. A sense of evening the score? Maybe. But not what we truly sought."

"Which is?"

"Peace," Jarek told him. "In the future, we leave the Azuriuses and Liciniouses of the universe to those charged with passing judgment. If it isn't possible and nothing else will serve, we kill them. Quickly and with no more pain than we can help, to prevent them from hurting anyone else. We don't try to be judge, jury, and executioner. They just aren't worth twisting yourself into a knot."

Liam nodded. "What do I do now?"

"If you are asking about life," Jarek replied, "you learn to live with it. If you mean the current battle, this wretched situation ends when Azurius is no longer a threat. While it may seem foolish and a little melodramatic, you should try to reason with him. Try to neutralize him without bloodshed. If he refuses"—Jarek paused—"then you do what you must, taking no pleasure in it. It will go a long way toward healing your soul and bringing peace."

Liam nodded. He felt Jarek depart, leaving him to his thoughts.

Then Liam felt another presence. He looked up and saw his foster father.

Marcus hesitated. "I'll go, if you wish."

Liam shook his head.

"I hope you don't mind, but I overheard your conversation with Jarek. It was more helpful that he'd been there before, I suppose. I didn't mean to sound so judgmental. You are the one I was worried about, not Licinious."

Liam stood, and amid the ruins where Marcus found him as a child, he embraced his father. Marcus put his arms around him as Liam wept again.

• • • • •

Corporal Ephram called a halt as they came under the Theater District. They leaned against the wall and broke out canteens.

"The captain's worried about his brother." Dillon took a long drink from his canteen.

The corporal nodded. "He attacked in anger and tortured Licinious. What will the aftermath of his actions do to him inside?"

Dillon shrugged. "Small loss, you ask me. I can't think of anyone who wouldn't have found it very tempting."

The corporal shook his head. "If an animal goes mad, you put a bullet in its head. You don't torture it. I'm not saying I don't understand or don't sympathize, but it will have an effect, especially on someone like the captain's brother."

Dillon just grunted and put his canteen away. They moved out when they heard an explosion. It sounded like a grenade.

They looked at each other, then raced toward the sound.

• • • • •

Liam woke with a start at the sound of dreamscape explosions. Someone approached. He picked up his assault rifle and kept low, moving from Peter's office to the kitchen. The back door to the Bistro opened, and someone tossed a grenade inside. Liam stepped out of time, leaped into the restaurant area, and dove for cover. He came back to normal time as the grenade detonated, throwing open the swinging door.

The main door of the Bistro crashed inward as three armored men burst through. Liam stepped out of time. One tried to track him with his rifle. Liam sidestepped and struck him with the butt of his own rifle. He delivered a kick to the second, stunning him, and punched the third in the head. The man fell backward, his helmet flying off, as time resumed its normal course. Liam spun and covered the door to the kitchen as another entered.

"Hold it!" Liam commanded.

"We saw what you did to Councilor Licinious, misborn," the man snarled contemptuously as he opened fire.

Liam jumped out of time and returned fire. The man went down. Another man burst through, his gun spitting metal before Liam's bullets found their mark.

One man he had downed grabbed his leg. Unbalanced, Liam returned to normal time. Another man hit him from the side, shoving Liam's rifle into his cracked ribs. Liam cried out as the third hit him from the front. Instead of knocking him down, the blow threw Liam backward, out of the others' grip, and into the pastry case. The glass shattered on impact. Liam's head was ringing, and he could not focus to step out of time. For some reason, Celinia's face appeared for a second. Liam grabbed a sticky grenade from his belt and pulled the pin.

His assailants froze. Liam threw the grenade at the central one, pushed through the case, and rolled behind the counter. The assassins panicked and tried to back away from their comrade. The grenade flashed with white hot heat. Liam felt more focused. The grenade left the corpses of two traitors burned. The third had lost his helmet and received severe burns over his body. Liam drew his pistol and stepped around the counter, pointing it at the man. He pulled the trigger, and the man collapsed, dead.

Liam re-holstered his pistol and checked his assault rifle. The explosion had damaged it beyond repair. He walked to the entrance of the kitchen. The leader had a different assault rifle. It looked more compact, with a barrel the same length as a normal rifle but set deeper into the stock, making it effective for close quarters fighting. Liam took the leader's ammunition belt and found it held five magazines and a power pack. He checked the ammunition and power pack. It was the same type as they used in the standard assault rifle. Liam collected several more magazines and put them into his rucksack. The leader and his second still had three hand grenades between them. Searching the bodies, he found a bloody cloth. Upon scrutinizing it, he saw it had Peter's monogram.

Liam closed his eyes. *Idiot!* he cursed himself. *I used it to clean my knives and must have dropped it at Licinious's house.*

The explosion ruined the equipment of the traitors caught in the blast. Liam found nothing else of use. Now that the enemy knew where he was, he needed to move, and quickly. He gathered up some cold meat and some rolls and refilled his canteens. These would have to do for food unless he found another restaurant where he could hide. He looked at the bottle of whiskey. It had survived this long. Hating to leave it behind, he slipped it into the rucksack.

Liam stepped outside the front door and just missed being hit by a bullet. He swore and ducked back inside, trying to find the source of the attack. The window next to him shattered, forcing him to crouch. He examined the pattern of the shattered glass, then tracked the direction from where he guessed the shot had come. He saw a shape pop out and take aim. Liam crouched lower as a bullet buzzed overhead. He rolled across the doorway, but by the time he had an angle, the shape vanished.

Liam stepped out of time and dashed into the street. He heard bullets impact behind him as he sped toward where he had seen the shape. The shape stepped out to shoot just as Liam made it to the corner. He slammed his shoulder into the assailant's chest, carrying the man back into the alley. Liam fell back into time as they crashed to the ground. Pain exploded from his ribs as Liam drove the butt of the rifle into the man's throat. The man gurgled and struggled for breath. Liam rolled to his feet and looked back out into the street. Four more assassins charged out of the side streets. Liam fired a burst from his rifle, downing one. The others took cover and returned fire.

Liam ducked back. He tried to step out of time. He fell back in just as he pulled the trigger. One man took a shot to the shoulder and fell screaming. Liam just managed to get back under cover. Then he heard more bursts of gunfire. Glancing out, he saw all his opponents were dead.

Liam looked back at the man whose throat he had crushed. He no longer moved, and his face had turned blue.

"Sir!" Two men emerged into the street. "Lieutenant Liam?"

Liam leveled his rifle.

"That's far enough."

Both men stopped.

"If you're on my side, I apologize, but I was just ambushed. Please put the guns on the ground and step back. Keep your hands where I can see them."

The two men obeyed and stayed still. Liam approached, stepping over their rifles.

He examined both men. "I recognize both of you from Archer group. Corporal Ephram and Private Dillon."

He stepped back and motioned them to pick up their weapons.

"Well, we're all still alive," Dillon gave him a lopsided grin. "I guess that means we got them all."

"Let's get to cover before more show up," the corporal advised.

"Collect weapons and ammo from the dead," Liam ordered. "I left one in the alley."

Soon, they had five more rifles, pistols, ammunition, and grenades. The three dashed into the Bistro and raced out the back and headed for the sewer.

"Let me patch into you, Corporal," Liam requested. "I cracked my ribs awhile back, and an explosion back at Taho fried my armor's diagnostics."

"Of course, sir," the corporal replied.

They connected the ports on the armor. The corporal saw the damage to the ribs and punched *treat.*

"How did you find me?" Liam asked, feeling relief in his ribs.

"We tracked you, sir," Corporal Ephram explained as he disconnected their armor. "The two of us volunteered to go with Captain Randolf to kill or capture Licinious and found you beat us to him."

"My brother..." Liam looked around.

"I'm afraid he couldn't stay with us," Dillon told him. "He's taken charge of the defenses at the Temple. We volunteered to find you."

"How did you know it was me?"

"The late councilor told us before he died," Corporal Ephram explained.

Liam felt sick again.

"Not that any of us blame you." Dillon reached out and put a hand on his shoulder. "The captain was prepared to settle for just blowing his head off."

"He killed my parents," Liam stated in a flat voice. "My biological parents and my adoptive parents."

Ephram and Dillon stared at him with shocked understanding.

"He was also responsible for the murder of Devon and Priestess Kia," Dillon told him. "He did more than just kill Kia."

Liam stiffened and nodded, feeling a little better.

"How did you find out about your foster parents?" the corporal asked.

"Azurius told me," Liam replied.

Both men looked at each other.

"It's a long story," Liam told them, "and I think we want better accommodations before I tell that tale."

"Agreed, sir," the corporal replied.

"The smell down here is getting to me," quipped Dillon.

"These rifles are a different design," Corporal Ephram noted. "Barrels deeper into the stock."

"Takes the same ammo as ours, though," Liam replied. "I tested one out just now. Seems to be designed for close quarters fighting but doesn't sacrifice range."

"Do you want us to take you to the Temple, sir?" Corporal Ephram asked.

Liam shook his head. "Not just yet, Corporal. I think I can still help my brother from out here. Once I'm back, all I can do is wait for the end with him."

"Where to then, sir?" Dillon asked.

Liam thought for a moment. "Tower 99," he decided. "It'll give us a good view, and we can find comfortable lodgings there."

"How often do you get to stay in an executive suite?" Dillon asked with a grin.

*   *   *   *   *

Celinia knocked on the door of the arch priestess's chamber. "Enter," the voice called from within.

Celinia opened the door and approached her superior, head bowed. "Randolf has returned, milady."

"Well, Celinia?" the arch priestess asked. "Randolf was successful?"

Celinia sighed. "Someone attacked Licinious before Randolf got there. He died from his wounds within moments of Randolf's arrival."

The arch priestess sat back. "This turn of events has left you troubled. My guess is the killer is known."

"Randolf's brother, Liam," Celinia told her.

The arch priestess's eyes opened in surprise. "Liam is alive?" Then she motioned Celinia to sit.

Celinia took a seat next to the woman who had been her mentor since entering the service of the Creator.

"Now, what happened?"

"When Randolf arrived at Licinious's house," Celinia explained, "he found the guards dead. Licinious still clung to life, pinned to the wall by a spear. Liam cut off his right hand and left leg, then disemboweled him. Randolf guessed he'd hung that way for at least an hour. He lived just long enough to tell Randolf about Liam."

"Liam must have deduced who had betrayed us," the arch priestess mused. "He may have also discovered the fate of his parents."

"Teresina advised us not to judge him," Celinia ventured.

"Teresina is right," Arch Priestess Arria replied.

"She gave me hope we haven't lost him, but I'm worried." She looked up into the arch priestess's eyes.

"What you feel is more than a simple concern for his soul," the arch priestess noted shrewdly. "You harbor feelings for him."

"I think I'm falling in love with him," Celinia whispered.

"Hmm."

"Randolf told Kia, Teresina, and me about him," she continued. "After hearing his tale, I chose Liam as my escort this year. I thought he needed to be drawn out of his shell."

"You weren't expecting the assault or betrayal," the arch priestess noted. "None of us were."

"I met him after the first attack," Celinia went on. "Randolf went to the Military Center, and we went with him. We wanted to help with the wounded. Soldiers brought Liam back on a stretcher. He had a serious head wound and a claw wound on his shoulder. Teresina took care of the shoulder, and I dealt with the concussion."

"Requiring you to probe his mind," the arch priestess guessed.

"I found he was very remarkable. Skilled, brave, loyal, but also vulnerable."

"I know about his birth parents," the arch priestess noted. "That experience would leave deep emotional wounds."

"I talked with him while he recovered," Celinia continued. "He still had trouble with nightmares. I think I helped him with those. During that time, in one of his dreams, I kissed him, and our spirits touched...in an intimate way. We met several times after I discharged him. You know what happened on Festival Day. I thought a part of me had died when we lost contact with his outpost."

The arch priestess reached forward and took Celinia's hand. "For your sake and his, I hope you both survive this battle. Perhaps you and he can still explore these feelings. Does he return them?"

"I think he was starting to," Celinia told her. "Once resigned to the fact he wasn't going to the outposts this Festival, he seemed to look forward to it."

Celinia smiled. "A friend of his brought his family to the Temple hospital. The children had adopted Liam as an uncle. When I came in, they'd cuddle up to him. He looked so natural. The little girl asked if I was going to be their aunt."

The arch priestess smiled. "'Out of the mouths of babes.' Did they make it?"

"Jorge died fighting beside Liam," Celinia replied. "The wife and children arrived safely here."

"But," the arch priestess noted, "Liam's executing Licinious and the manner in which he did it disturbs you."

Celinia nodded.

"You'll know nothing for sure until you meet him again," the arch priestess told her. "Remember, love is a two-edged sword. You are seeing the other edge of love. You know about the caring and romance. This other edge of love is more violent. Here, Licinious murdered someone beloved. Liam felt Licinious needed to be punished. He didn't think he would feel whole if he left it to another. It is likely he now realizes he still isn't whole. The fact it provides no true closure is what makes the hunt for revenge so treacherous. Will Liam realize it was a mistake, or will he feel he needs to hunt down others to slake his thirst for vengeance? We can't know until we see him again."

The two women rose and embraced.

"Keep me posted on the situation," the arch priestess instructed.

"Of course, Milady."

CHAPTER 7

Liam, Ephram, and Dillon came out of the hatch near the Green Griffin.

"Creator," Dillon gasped. "What happened to the Griffin? It was my favorite pub."

"Mine too." Liam gave them a rueful look. "I'm afraid it's my fault. I holed up here for a while. Then the chitin caught up with me. Stu may have me working as a short-order cook to pay for damages."

Ephram and Dillon looked at him in surprise.

They navigated the side streets to a back entrance of Tower 99. Liam had them search a few locations he had not had time to check before, but they found no more diagnostic kits. The three located an executive office, and Liam divided what food he had to make into a light meal.

After they had eaten, Liam stood. "I need an overview of the situation."

"We'd better stick together, Lieutenant," the corporal suggested.

Ephram and Dillon followed Liam up to the roof.

"Looks like the chitin are tightening the ring," Corporal Ephram observed. "Azurius must have found time to give them new orders."

Liam studied the city in other directions and saw nothing else of interest.

He turned to the others. "Let's make camp in the penthouse office."

They removed their boots and armor, and cleaned them in one of the service centers in the tower. Once they had neutralized the odoriferous residue from the sewer, they brought their equipment to their camp and settled in for the night.

"So, sir," Corporal Ephram began, "what happened to you after the fall of Taho sector?"

Liam made himself comfortable in the chair behind the desk. Ephram pressed a button on his wrist console.

"The explosion of the heavy weapon tossed me through a breach in the dead portal's partition. I woke up in the machinery room with cracked ribs."

Dillon winced.

Liam nodded. "I went to Grizzly base, where I finally found a usable diagnostic kit. With my canteens ruptured, I had no water."

Corporal Ephram whistled. "You must have been in sorry shape when you dragged your butt in there. I'm surprised a bear-lizard didn't decide you'd make an easy meal."

Liam snorted. "I did meet a bear-lizard. His name is Swift Hunter."

Liam grinned when he caught Ephram and Dillon exchanging worried looks. They saw the grin.

"You're pulling our leg, sir," Dillon said, feeling relieved.

"Actually, no," Liam told them. "He likes the faux beef stew rations. They're highly intelligent telepaths. Swift Hunter carried me to Grizzly sector after I passed out between Taho and Grizzly. He probably saved my life."

The worried expressions returned.

"Okay." Liam paused, then sighed. "If I am crazy, however, I suggest you behave in a manner conducive to your safety and humor me. It will seem like the sanest thing I'm going to tell you."

"Could you have imagined it?" Corporal Ephram ventured.

Liam shrugged. "I won't discount the possibility, but I don't think so. We were together for several days. For now, we have work to do. So, trying to prove or disprove it until we've dealt with Azurius is irrelevant."

"How did you re-enter the city?" Dillon asked.

"I floated through the city's water supply pipes between Boulder and Grizzly sectors," Liam replied. "It was quite a ride."

"I've been to the cisterns once," the corporal noted. "How did you get out? They don't have any provisions for people to climb out, save if someone throws you a safety line."

"Moreover," Dillon added, "how did you know where to find the access hatch?"

Liam smiled. "It's time to convince you I'm completely insane. You know about dreamwalking."

"Yeah," Dillon answered. "Priestesses use it to help people with some, er...mental problems."

"Usually, it is limited to a person's own subconscious mind." Liam squirmed to ease the discomfort in his ribs. "It can be much more. I found I can use it to explore the real world and use it to speak to a friend of my biological parents. His name is Jarek. He has been teaching me to expand my abilities."

Again, the worried glances.

"It's handy for scouting." Liam watched their expressions with amusement. Then he became serious again. "First, I used it before I raided the Military Center. Then I spied on Licinious, which is how I learned his plans to assassinate my brother and other council members. I took care of the assassins. Then dealt with Licinious."

"Okay, sir," Corporal Ephram said. "Now you are scaring me because it sounds like you did what you said you were doing. We found the assassins where you left them in the sewer. I'd figured you'd done it, but I didn't know how you knew to be there. You appeared to have set an effective trap for them. That requires advanced knowledge of their plans to succeed."

"You believe him?" Dillon asked, then blushed when he realized he had said it out loud.

"It's okay, Private," Liam replied. "If someone had claimed what I just told you about to me, I'd find it hard to swallow too."

Corporal Ephram sat on the desk. "If what you're saying is true, you must have learned things. Tell us about Azurius first."

"I still want to know how you climbed out of the cistern," Dillon interrupted.

"Here's the short answer," Liam told Dillon. "I modified an assault rifle to act as a grapnel gun. It burned out the coil, but I could climb a utility line to the catwalk."

"With those ribs!" the corporal exclaimed. "You are crazy. That climb must have hurt like the blazes. I'm surprised you didn't pass out and fall back into the cistern."

"I almost did," Liam conceded. "Sometimes I find something that helps me adjust the armor for the injury, but it is a nuisance. It's easier to rest without the armor.

"I met Azurius in the dreamscape first. He wants the city and its population as intact as possible. I gather he wants to use us as fodder for his attempt at domination of the galaxy. He claimed to be impressed with me. Wanted me to change sides. I threw him out."

Liam fell silent.

"Which explains why the chitin are only blocking us from the hydroponic farms and livestock pens," Ephram mused, "rather than destroying them. Azurius doesn't want to exterminate us. So, he needs our food supply. He also needs our mineral resources."

"You met him again," Dillon coaxed.

"In the real world, when I re-entered the city. Before, he had told me Licinious had killed my biological parents. This time, he told me Licinious ordered the assassination of my foster parents. Then he set me a test. Kill Licinious."

"Which is something you wanted to do anyway," Corporal Ephram noted. "Obviously, you did it for your own reasons."

Liam gave them a nasty grin. "The last time I saw Azurius, he'd just missed getting flattened by a trip mine."

"So, you orchestrated that incident as well." Dillon chuckled. "All right, I'm starting to believe you, and I know you're crazy."

"Desperate." Liam corrected. "I'd lost most of my equipment. The chitin hadn't destroyed the armory, so I figured the Center was the best place to start. Afterward, I guess Azurius sent the chitin after me."

"What about this Jarek?" Corporal Ephram asked.

Liam struggled to his feet, trying to get relief for his ribs. "Same species as Azurius. The same culture but a different kind of person. He's on our side. He's been teaching me to use the dreamscape and step out of time more efficiently."

Liam walked to a window. "Jarek is coming with a fleet, but they can't get to us because of the force field. I learned Azurius put it around the planet."

"It makes sense," Dillon agreed.

"So, you're thinking it's going to come down to you and Azurius?"

Liam did not answer. Ephram and Dillon did not press him.

"I need to rest," Liam told them. "Let's take three watches."

"I'll take first watch," the corporal offered.

"Wake me up after three hours, Corporal," Dillon told him. "Then I'll wake you up, sir."

"I'm going to talk to Jarek," Liam told them. "Then I'm going to need to go into deep sleep until my watch. I'll talk to you in the morning."

"Sir," Corporal Ephram ventured. "I've recorded our conversation. I want to pass it on to your brother. He should have this information and will be glad you're no more insane than usual."

Liam smiled but shook his head. "Thanks, Corporal, but let me finish talking to Jarek first. Besides, I don't know what kind of eavesdropping Azurius has at his disposal."

"We're on scramble," the corporal assured him.

Liam nodded. "Let me get back to you. Good news can usually wait."

Liam returned to his chair and leaned back.

•   •   •   •   •

Liam hovered outside the tower. He had left out this part of his dreamscape activity. Ephram and Dillion already questioned his sanity. Besides, it would not take long. Soon, he had taken down the minefield from near the Bistro and placed it around Tower 99. They did not need to know what he was doing, anyway. Once done, he slipped back into his personal dreamscape.

Liam stood looking at the burned-out hulk of his parents' house and peered inside. Then Jarek stood beside him.

"Try to concentrate on how it was before," Jarek coaxed.

Liam closed his eyes and tried to pick out forgotten childhood memories. He opened his eyes and saw it as a living, breathing home.

Jarek peered in a window. "The sitting room looks inviting."

Liam led Jarek through the front door. They sat down on two comfortable chairs. Liam chose a rocking chair.

"I barely remember this place," Liam whispered.

"I believe your mother used to rock you in that rocking chair."

Liam took a few experimental rocks in the chair.

"When I was young and innocent," Liam mused.

Jarek shook his head. "Liam, innocence is never truly lost. It's just covered over."

Liam chuckled. "I suppose I'll understand that concept in a few hundred years."

"Then again, you won't look as good as I do." Jarek laughed, then became serious. "I take it you've suffered a minor setback."

"A group of Licinious's men found me," he told him. "After I dealt with them, I decided I couldn't stay in the Bistro. I'm in a building near the place I was before."

"From what I am reading from you, you did something which shocked you," Jarek observed.

"I shot a man in cold blood, and I don't even feel remorse."

"Oh?"

Liam got up and paced. "I killed the first two. Then three more attacked me. I used a sticky grenade. The blast killed two, but only injured the third."

"Leading you to put the third out of your misery," Jarek guessed.

Liam nodded. "When I intercepted Licinious's assassins, I had to shoot two that the trip mines didn't kill. I felt numb then. Now, I feel nothing."

Jarek let out a sigh. "Liam, you are a soldier at war. War isn't just killing mindless monsters like the chitin. War involves killing people who never did you any harm. They were just on the opposite side. In addition, you are acting in the role of a single commando behind enemy lines. That role involves a certain amount of ruthlessness. He would have killed you if he could. So, it would have been too dangerous to leave him alive."

"I know. It's the lack of remorse that's got me worried. You remember what I did to Licinious?"

"Liam, I was a soldier for centuries," Jarek told him. "Azurius wasn't always limited to chitin and a few traitors. Once, he commanded a potent military force. I did my share of black ops against the Rebellion. If I'm ever given permission, I may even tell you a few stories. The big problem with killing is, once you start, it gets easier. The most moral of people find themselves amazed at how easy it is."

Liam stopped and looked out the window. Jarek stood and put a hand on his shoulder.

"You aren't becoming a bad person," Jarek told him. "You're a good person, taking part in a huge bad thing—war. If you want my assessment, you didn't feel remorse because you are in full survival mode. Because you tortured him, you felt remorse for killing Licinious. You may have had to kill him to survive, but you didn't have to torture him."

"It must seem strange," Liam mused. "Finnian heritage, and I'm having a crisis of conscience."

Jarek smiled. "I don't think it's strange at all. During their conflict with the old Earth government, your forebears had a similar crisis of conscience."

Liam looked up, suddenly curious.

"The people who created the Finnian made a fundamental mistake," Jarek told him. "Finnian males, originally, could only produce a few Y chromosomes. So, they had a birth rate of twenty-five percent men versus seventy-five percent very frustrated women. The Finnian had the advantage when they began the war with Old Terra. Over time, the number of men dwindled. Two things then happened. The Finnian discovered human soldiers weren't as inferior as their creators had led them to believe. Second, the Finnian woman began looking to human prisoners of war to, shall we say, fill the void."

Liam laughed.

Jarek's black scales turned purple when he realized what he had said. "It wasn't like I made it sound. I don't mean to imply that these desperate ladies grabbed prisoners against their will, dragged them into the woods, and had their way with them. An ancestor of yours, one Brigadier Aisling O'Connor, wouldn't stand for it. She improvised appropriate ways for them to get to know each other. These relationships led to the Finnian guards and human POWs comparing notes. The Finnian were not happy about what they discovered. Your great, great, great, probably many greats, grandmother and her troops staged a coup and took their founders into custody. Then she made a deal with the Earth government. She would turn the founders over to them for legal action, cease all hostilities, and align the Finnian with Old Terra."

"What did the Finnian get in return?" Liam asked.

"Earth government recognized their right to exist, and they got to keep those single, male POWs who didn't have sweethearts waiting for them. In addition, they announced they needed men. The men and marriages came, of course. They found the union of Finnian and Terran produced a more balanced population but kept almost all their original advantages. Aisling snatched up her opposite number among the humans. The story sounds quite romantic, though the legend has grown up that she carried him off. If true, he wasn't unwilling."

Liam stared ahead.

"I think Aisling would be proud of you," Jarek whispered.

Liam decided to change the subject. "Tell me something. Like you, I don't need details, but when you killed that person you told me about, did you have someone to talk you through it?"

Jarek shook his head. "I had to muddle through it myself. I'm just giving you the benefit of centuries of agonizing over it."

"My brother sent two people to look for me." Liam gazed out the window. "They found Licinious. He lived long enough to tell them I was the one who attacked him."

"You have two companions." Jarek perked up. "This is wonderful news."

"They want to contact my brother."

"Why haven't they?" Jarek asked in surprise. "He would be glad to hear from you. Hope is a powerful weapon against despair."

"I'm not sure what kind of listening devices Azurius has in place, especially if he wants to find me."

Jarek thought for a moment. "I suspect he relied on Licinious for comm specialists. Azurius has many faults, but he knows his technical limitations. Ask your new companions if there's any sign of Licinious's men responding to your military's communications. If not, I'd say your secure channels are still secure."

"I think it's almost time to rejoin the people in the Temple, anyway. I don't know if we can accomplish anything else on the outside."

Jarek nodded in agreement. "You're probably right."

●   ●   ●   ●   ●

Liam opened his eyes just as Dillon nodded off.

"Corporal?" Liam asked. "Has the comm-tech noticed any sign of Licinious moving to counter your movements, which might have been given away by your communications?"

"No, Lieutenant," Corporal Ephram replied.

"Then Jarek thinks the channel is probably still secure." Liam got up, wincing as his ribs complained.

The corporal switched on his comm systems and dialed in Central Communications Command.

"Corporal Ephram from the Hunter Squad," he called. "I need to speak with Captain Randolf. It's about his brother. Also, I am sending a conversation I recorded. He may want to listen to it."

He touched the send button on his wrist display.

Liam sat back down and waited.

Corporal Ephram flinched. "No, sir! He's right here! Give me a moment."

He took his earpiece and handed it to Liam.

"I think he'll be happy to hear from you." The corporal grimaced. "My ear is still ringing."

Liam laughed and put the earpiece in his ear.

"Hi, big brother." Liam felt happier than he had in days.

"Liam!" his brother exclaimed. "Dear Creator, we thought you were dead. I'm having someone find Celinia. Are you all right?"

"Apart from some cracked ribs," Liam replied. "You?"

"Liam, Mom and Dad—"

"I know." Liam's smile faded. "I guess you saw... I paid him back."

He heard silence at the other end. Liam decided not to fill it.

"Yes, I did."

"It's a long story," Liam told him. "The file Corporal Ephram sent you will bring you up to speed on what I've been doing. What's the situation there?"

"We're just barely holding our own," Randolf told him. "Someone knocked out the portals at the Military Center Azurius was using to bring in the chitin."

"That was me." Liam smiled.

"I should have known." Randolf almost sounded giddy with relief.

"A Festival present. From me to you."

"And all I got you was a pair of socks." Then Randolf's tone got serious. "It bought us time. Azurius may figure out how to breach the force field and bring the chitin in overland. Do you know about Azurius?"

"It's on the recording," Liam informed him. "I met him. A nasty piece of work."

"Celinia's here," Randolf warned. "Brace yourself."

"Liam!"

He could not answer around the lump in his throat.

"Liam?"

"Uh, sorry I missed Festival Day," Liam replied.

"Oh, Liam." Celinia sounded as if she was giggling around tears. "I thought I'd lost you."

"Ephram and Dillon told me about Devon and Kia. I..."

"Don't, Liam," Celinia whispered. "No unhappy thoughts, just for a few moments, please."

"Okay."

"Liam." Celinia sounded on the verge of tears. "I want you back here."

Liam sucked in his breath. "I want to come back, Celinia. You said no unhappy thoughts, but it's going to depend on conditions on the ground."

"I know," she replied.

"If it helps," Liam whispered, "I was looking forward to Festival Day for the first time in years."

"Oh, Liam," Celinia murmured.

Liam tried to touch Celinia through the comm.

"Liam, your brother wants to talk to you again," Celinia told him. "Good night and sleep well."

"Little brother," Randolf's voice came on a few moments later. "Where are you now?"

"Penthouse of Tower 99," Liam replied. "Despite what I told Celinia, I considered making my way back to the Temple."

"Contact me again in the morning. If things seem stable, come on in."

"Okay," Liam replied. "Good night, big brother."

"You too, Liam."

Liam handed the earpiece back to Ephram.

"Wake me if you need me."

• • • • •

Randolf took off his earpiece and handed it to the lieutenant in charge of communications. The lieutenant handed him the chip with the recording, saluted, and returned to his post. Celinia and Teresina threw their arms around him.

"Sergeant!" Randolf called. "Get Captain Simon and have him meet me here in the ready room."

Randolf detached the two women. "Can one of you get the arch priestess, please? I want to review this recording with her as well."

Teresina nodded and dashed off.

"He's all right." Celinia laughed with relief as she took a seat.

"Except for cracked ribs."

"What?" Celinia exclaimed. "He's fighting with cracked ribs?"

"Let's review the recording," Randolf suggested. "We'll get a better idea of what's going on and can talk about it with him tomorrow."

Randolf and Celinia waited until the sergeant, Captain Simon, Teresina, and the arch priestess arrived. Randolf turned on the recording, and they listened in grim silence to his brother's tale. They all felt shaken when it had ended.

"I have to wonder about your brother's mental state," Captain Simon began.

"I've touched Liam's mind," Celinia reported. "If he were female, the priestesses would have snapped him up. When I touched his mind, I found he has more potential than I'd ever seen."

"First," Randolf asked. "How possible is it that the bear-lizards are as Liam says? Even he admits he might have imagined it."

After a moment's hesitation, the arch priestess shook her head. "There, I can't be sure. He admitted to the possibility. So, he knows the difference between fantasy and reality. He's also right. Dealing with Azurius is a more pressing need than proving or disproving the bear-lizards are intelligent telepaths."

"But the rest?" Captain Simon persisted. "His scouting outside his body, meeting this Jarek, who sounds more like an imaginary friend."

"Corporal Ephram and Private Dillon believed him," the sergeant countered. "They're both intelligent. If, in their judgment, he's sane, then he's sane."

"They could be humoring him," Teresina pointed out.

"Talk to Corporal Ephram first," Arch Priestess Arria suggested.

"If what he's telling us is true," Randolf asked, "what does it mean?"

"Just physically," Celinia told them, "I'll be worried until he is back in our care. Especially with him trying to field treat his ribs for this long."

"I hate to keep beating on about this," Captain Simon persisted, "but could his condition cause hallucinations?"

Celinia shook her head. "Dehydration might. Once hydrated, the hallucinations would stop. If you want to worry about his sanity, then worry about his attacking the Center, ambushing the assassins, and going after Licinious by himself, with cracked ribs."

"We designed the armor to compensate," the sergeant informed her. "Especially when a soldier can't get back to base at once."

"All right." Randolf leaned back. "What does this information tell us about Azurius?"

"I'd like more details," the arch priestess replied, "but it sounds like he wants the population intact. He doesn't want to exterminate us down to the last child. Your brother also seems to have impressed him. Whether he's still impressed enough to want to recruit him remains to be seen."

"What about this Jarek?"

"Help would be welcome," Teresina agreed. "What about the planetary force field?"

"I remember Father telling me that around forty years ago, our aircraft started crashing on takeoff," Randolf told them. "It makes sense. If Liam's expanding his abilities, it could mean he is getting help, but this Jarek must be some distance away. Is there any known precedent for such long-range dreamscape travel?"

"Under certain, limited circumstances," the arch priestess informed them. "You must be very familiar with the person or someone closely related. You'd also need a very strong telepathic ability."

Randolf turned to Celinia. "You've touched his mind. Can you contact him that way?"

Celinia shook her head unhappily. "I would need more than just one or two sojourns into his dreams, Captain. Jarek had some familiarity with Liam's biological parents. Liam's mental patterns would be very similar. Somehow, he knew Liam needed him and homed in on that mental pattern. We won't know until we ask him."

"So," Captain Simon asked, "we're taking what he said at face value?"

"What Liam says explains much, Captain," the arch priestess replied. "He went directly to where he needed to go—in the Center, intercepting the assassins in the sewers, and to Licinious's house. If we need to worry about his mental state, we just need to look at his treatment of Licinious."

Captain Simon looked at the table. "If what he says about his parents is true..." He paused, "I can't imagine his rage upon discovering Licinious murdered his parents and adoptive parents. I think he had cause."

"Might I suggest," Teresina put forward, "we all be here when we contact him tomorrow? We have more questions than answers. On many issues."

"I agree." The arch priestess looked around the table. "I suggest we take it as a given that he can do what he says he can and confine our questions to Azurius, Jarek, and how best to make use of this knowledge."

"Agreed," Randolf replied.

Captain Simon and the others nodded.

"Now, it is very late, and we all need sleep." The arch priestess rose. "I'm happy for you, Captain Randolf, son of Marcus. I will take your brother's survival as a sign of hope."

•   •   •   •   •

The star of the Etrusci system was peaking over the horizon. Azurius heard the alarm alerting him that his reinforcements had reached the breach at Archer sector.

He tranced down and checked his lab. He gave the new chitin commands to march to the city and merge with the existing force. When each combined group reached a size of one hundred, he ordered ten of each hundred to enter the sewers to block key junctions throughout the city.

He decided to scout the dreamscape to minimize surprises.

•   •   •   •   •

Randolf sat in the ready room early the next morning, eager to talk to his brother again. He heard a knock on the door, and Captain Simon entered.

"We've got a problem," the captain announced.

The rest of the emergency council filed in to hear the worst. The captain waited for everyone to seat themselves.

"Scouts have sighted a sizeable group of new chitin marching toward the outskirts of the city," Captain Simon reported. "Azurius must have breached the force field. The scouts say it looks like they're coming from near Archer sector and heading for the lines. By nightfall, they will be fully engaged."

One councilor slumped back in his seat. "It was a matter of time before Azurius circumvented the downed portals. Can we do something to stop them before they reach the city?"

Randolf shook his head. "Mounting that kind of operation takes time, especially in the numbers of men we'd need."

"What now?" another asked.

"The sewers?" The sergeant looked at Randolf. "We know Azurius hasn't been sending chitin down there yet. We can come up behind them and abandon the city."

"That idea is okay as far as it goes," Captain Simon countered. "It begs the question of 'What then?' We don't have a means of mass transport at our disposal. So, we can't take everyone to a new position."

"If we got power back," Celinia asked, "could we use the old intercity portals to head to another city? Azurius will need time to locate us and muster the chitin."

"Moving the population to a new city would buy us time," a councilor agreed. "It wouldn't be a permanent solution, obviously."

The sergeant shook his head. "We checked on the portals when the chitin broke into the city. The late Licinious's men were thorough. It will take weeks to get power back up to run even one portal. Before then, Azurius would know what we were doing and stop us."

"Can we scatter into the sewers and try to use them as a maze to fight the chitin on our terms?" Captain Simon asked.

"If everyone was a trained soldier," Randolf replied, "maybe. They aren't. Many aren't used to such close quarters. Close quarters fighting requires a great deal of discipline. Moreover, it won't take long for Azurius to know where we've gone. Even not knowing the tunnels as well as we do, all he has to do is flood them with chitin. They don't worry about falling in battle. They'd just keep swarming until we're all dead."

"We keep talking about what we can't do," Celinia snapped. "What can we do?"

"Who knows the portals?" Randolf asked.

"We have some dimensional engineers," the sergeant offered.

"Get them," Randolf ordered.

The sergeant left the room.

"One problem with plans is they rarely come to you all at once," Randolf leaned on the table, "or from one source. Before we give up on the portals, let's see if the engineers know something we don't. Meanwhile, instruct everyone to get ready to go into the sewers. Get the small arms to anyone capable of using them. It will give people a fighting chance."

The sergeant returned with three engineers.

"Gentlemen," Randolf began, "milady. We're short of time. I need you to do the impossible and get the intercity portals active and opened to a defensible city."

The engineers looked at each other. "Those haven't been in wide-scale use since the last cities fell some thirty years ago. Scout teams have gone through to a couple of the abandoned cities since then. The last was about twenty years ago."

"Power will be the hardest part," the oldest added. "The next will be getting there and getting people through before Azurius figures out our plan."

"If you can do it," Randolf told them, "we'll all be getting there the same way, through the sewers. I have some ideas for keeping the chitin off. Do you have any ideas for getting the portals working?"

"A few," the engineers' spokesman replied. "Again, the problem is we haven't used those portals in over twenty years."

"They've independent power supplies," the woman put in. "Getting it kick-started would be the hardest part. However, it should be viable."

"Those old power supplies could be temperamental," the spokesman warned, "but she's right. Without the city's power, they'd be the best hope. We can get them running, but we must leave the logistics to you."

Randolf dropped back into the seat. "I'm just at the beginnings of my plan, mind you, but I suggest we break the military into several forces. We'll send a squad with you to keep watch. Be as inconspicuous as possible. Once the portals are working, a larger force heads through and sets up a defensive perimeter. Then we can start evacuating while another group provides cover. Azurius will realize what we're doing eventually, but we need to keep his attention on the Temple for as long as possible. Once we get everyone through, the rest of the military goes through, and we'll shut the portals from the other side. Then we figure out how to defend those positions."

"What about your brother?" the sergeant asked. "Perhaps he can find a way to get Azurius's attention."

Inwardly, Randolf cringed. He wanted his brother with him.

"Your brother's alive?" one councilor asked.

The councilors exchanged stunned looks.

"We found out last night," Captain Simon told them.

"He's been out there with cracked ribs for many days," Celinia warned. "He needs to return here for treatment. If he over-strains his ribs, he could collapse and would be helpless."

The sergeant countered, "We have little chance now, but Liam might create an opportunity for us."

"At the cost of his life." Celinia's green eyes flashed.

"A fate that awaits us, anyway." Randolf looked at the engineers. "I'll get you destinations before you go. Get ready. You leave within the hour."

The engineers departed, and Randolf pulled planet-wide maps from the shelves and spread them on the table.

"We need some destinations."

•   •   •   •   •

Liam watched the sunrise out of the office window. He looked up with a start. Something felt wrong. He shook Ephram and Dillon awake.

"What is it, sir?" Dillon asked.

"Something's happening."

They went out onto the roof of Tower 99.

"Binoculars," Liam ordered.

Ephram handed him a pair of high-powered binoculars. When Liam raised them to his eyes, he saw columns of chitin marching toward the city.

"Not good," Liam muttered. "They must have broken through the force field. Now we have hordes of bugs making their way to the ring encircling our people."

Corporal Ephram swore. "What now?"

"If Randolf has a plan," Liam replied, "maybe we can buy him some time."

"A direct assault on Azurius?" Dillon asked.

"I need to talk to Jarek."

Liam led them back to the penthouse.

"I'm going to trance down," he told them.

"What if we need you?" Ephram asked.

"Call me," Liam told him. "I can hear. I don't think you should try shaking me."

The communicator on Ephram's belt chirped. "Yes? No. Okay, sir."

He looked up at Liam. "Can you hold off, sir? Your brother wants a word."

Liam took the earpiece and put it in his ear. "Yes, Randolf?"

"Liam," Randolf began. "The chitin broke through the perimeter."

"I saw," Liam reported. "Did you listen to the recording Corporal Ephram made?"

"We did."

Liam smiled. "You think I'm crazy."

"Little brother"—Randolf forced a laugh—"I've known you were crazy since we were kids. You didn't seem much crazier."

"That's debatable," Celinia's voice came on the comm. "Considering how you're treating your ribs."

"We're on conference," Randolf warned him.

"Liam, from what we've heard," Celinia told him, "your ribs need treatment. I'm surprised you haven't killed yourself yet."

"With Corporal Ephram and Private Dillon here," Liam said, "I have a consistent means of bracing them now."

"If you take another hard hit," Celinia warned, "the armor could let go and actually break your ribs."

"Liam," Teresina suggested, "just so we know what we're arguing about, can you have Corporal Ephram plug into your armor?"

"I'm putting the earpiece down for a few minutes," Liam motioned to Ephram. "I need to put on my armor."

"We'll be here," Randolf replied.

Liam got his armor and strapped it on.

"Corporal, patch my armor in so they can get a diagnosis," he ordered.

Ephram grabbed a cable and attached it to his armor's port, then patched into Liam's armor. He typed in the code to send Liam's status to Captain Randolf as Liam picked up the earpiece.

"You should see it coming through," Liam told them, "for what it's worth."

He heard a pause on the other end.

"Liam," Teresina said, "your ribs aren't good. You have a nasty crack across three of them. You can stabilize them with your armor and taping, but if you exert them, you run a risk of breaking them."

"Why are we even discussing this?" Celinia was becoming angry. "He is in no condition to be going into battle!"

"Randolf," Liam asked. "Could you give me and Celinia a private moment?"

"I'll give her an earpiece and move everyone outside," he promised.

Liam motioned Ephram and Dillon to go outside for a moment.

"Celinia?"

"I'm here."

"Celinia, I'm a soldier. When I became a soldier, I knew I might have to do things that will hurt, even kill me."

"Liam—"

"Let me finish. I knew my ribs were bad when I woke up after that explosion. Believe me, I want to get them looked after. You wouldn't believe how much they hurt when I exert myself, but I swore to protect the city and those who live in it. There are some things worth dying for."

"Liam." Celinia's voice had softened. "We never had time together. I want that time. I don't want to lose you. I love you."

"I don't want to die," Liam told her, "but that fate awaits us all. We must confront what's happening. Now, if you have any suggestions to keep my ribs together until I can get proper treatment, please tell me."

Celinia fell silent for a moment. "You're still in Tower 99?"

"Yes."

"Find the infirmary," she advised. "They may have a rib vest. A rib vest will stabilize the ribs better. How have you been breathing?"

"It hurt at first," Liam informed her. "It isn't too bad now. Just don't make me laugh."

"Okay. If you find the vest, lose the tape. Tape could make breathing more difficult. Your armor should readjust. The vest has its own internal computer. How are you sleeping? In other words, do you feel rested when you wake up?"

"I found it difficult to get comfortable at first," Liam replied. "I find recliners and chairs easier than lying down."

"If you have to lie down, lie on your injured side. It may hurt a little more, but you'll breathe better. Are you taking anything for the pain?"

"No," Liam conceded, "I've had nothing to take."

"A standard pain med will help. Just be careful using the dreamscape. Pain medicine can make dreamscape travel dangerous."

"Anything else?"

"Only be careful and come back to us as soon as you can," she told him. "I'll bring the others back."

Liam signaled Ephram and Dillon to enter the room.

"Liam," Randolf began, "we're back on conference."

"Understood."

"Okay," Randolf began. "What more can you tell us about your encounters with Azurius?"

"He can step out of time and has a lot more practice at it than I do, so he has more endurance. Also, he has some kind of telekinetic ability."

"I've seen his eyes change," Randolf said. "It's like he's unleashed hell itself."

"That's at full power," Liam reported. "He can regulate it. He gave me a good slam when I met him the second time. Jarek has told me about other things."

"Okay," Randolf ventured. "Some people wonder if Jarek is an imaginary friend."

Liam sighed. "And?"

"The knowledge you gleaned from your travels is too accurate," Randolf replied. "I'm prepared to take it on faith."

Liam smiled. "Thank you, big brother. I admit. It would sound mad to me, too."

"I agree," came another voice.

"Liam." Randolf sounded impatient. "Captain Simon feels he would like a little more confirmation."

"The captain from Grizzly sector?"

"The same," Randolf confirmed.

"Lieutenant," the captain began, "describe the process you went through to raid the Military Center."

Liam reviewed the actions he took the day he raided the Center. Captain Simon frequently stopped him to ask for more details or clarify certain points.

"All right, Lieutenant," Captain Simon finished. "I'm satisfied."

"Lieutenant," came a new female voice. "I am Arch Priestess Arria."

"Milady."

"We need to know what you talked about with Jarek," she began. "What has he told you that might help us?"

"Jarek and Azurius are of the same race," Liam reported. "However, they're on opposite sides, and Jarek's eyes don't glow. He told me his race has a limited telekinetic ability. Azurius was trying to expand that ability. He succeeded, as you saw for yourselves, but his eyes glowed. Red is neutral, green pleasure or happy. Yellow means anger, and blue is fear. Black means he's accessing his abilities."

"He isn't invincible," Randolf put in. "I saw him after he damaged that building. He looked like he needed to rest. Have you found information on the planetary force field?"

"Azurius has a base," Liam reported. "I've been there. I can only access it through the dreamscape. His base controls the planetary force field and the chitin. Jarek said he can give some mass commands telepathically or control individual bugs. To nuance the commands, he uses his base. It uses a type of subsonic signal that only chitin can hear."

"Can you drop the force field from there?" Randolf asked.

"Yes," Liam replied, "but if Azurius is still alive, he can undo whatever I do and make it so no one can get into it, even if he is dead. Once he's gone, the chitin won't have anyone controlling them. We must eradicate them, or they'll destroy us."

"Could you keep him out of the base long enough for help to arrive?" the arch priestess asked.

"Azurius is more experienced than I am at that type of combat, milady," Liam replied. "Jarek made a point of warning me. Azurius could kill me on that battlefield unless I was very, very lucky. We must neutralize Azurius first, then I can turn off the force field and send a recall to the chitin."

"When we get to that point, Lieutenant," the arch priestess warned, "be very careful. If you are physically exhausted, it can be like being drugged or drunk. You might not find your way back."

"I understand, milady," Liam promised.

"Liam," Randolf broke in. "We are trying to get the intercity portals back up. If we can, we're going to evacuate. Can you cause a distraction?"

"Disrupt things from behind?" Liam suggested. "I have no more trip mines or bayonet grenades. They got ruined in a fight with some chitin. I've got two new grenades, though. Azurius gave them to Licinious. They stick to their targets and incinerate them. Does

PRICE OF VENGEANCE 207

anyone have information on a new assault rifle? Some of Licinious's men used them. They seem to be made for close quarters. The barrel is further into the stock. You get the same range but a shorter weapon."

A pause followed.

"Those aren't familiar to me or Captain Simon," Randolf responded. "However, all of the senior officers are dead."

"The rifles take our magazines and power packs," Liam told him. "We're good for those."

"Lieutenant," Captain Simon replied, "at the moment, we can't spare anyone to get you more grenades. We're running short ourselves."

"I understand, sir," Liam replied. "Now I'd like to talk to Jarek and do some scouting. I'll be in touch."

"Okay," Randolf said. "Take care of yourself, little brother."

"You too."

Liam returned the earpiece to Ephram. He removed his armor again.

"I'm going to talk to Jarek. Dillon, find the infirmary."

"Yes, sir."

"Please see if you can find some standard pain meds and a rib vest," Liam ordered. "It could make my life easier."

"Of course, sir," Dillon turned to go.

Liam looked at Corporal Ephram. "I may be out awhile. Call me if you need me. If it can wait, let me finish."

"Yes, sir."

Liam sat back in the chair and tranced down.

•　　•　　•　　•　　•

Liam sat in the rocking chair. Jarek came in and sat in the easy chair.

"You know. If you ever have a family, I suggest you have a room like this one in your house. You look comfortable there."

Liam skipped the small talk. "Azurius has reinforcements. It looks like at least three hives are converging on us."

Jarek nodded. "So, the final crisis begins. Ideas?"

"My brother has a plan," Liam told him. "He wants to reactivate the intercity portals but needs time. I'm thinking I can try to find Azurius and keep his attention focused on me. If I can blind him to everything else, it may give Randolf time to do what he needs to do."

"You will be three men against the entire horde—tactically, very challenging. The three of you would end up surrounded by chitin."

Liam slumped.

"The only tactical advice I can give is an old human adage." Jarek paused. "Are you familiar with an ancient Terran animal called an elephant?"

Liam shrugged. "Vaguely."

"The elephant was the largest land animal on Old Terra from one hundred thirty centuries ago until some five centuries ago," Jarek explained, "weighing in at close to eleven metric tons. It wasn't the biggest animal that ever lived on Old Terra, mind you."

Liam whistled through his teeth, trying to imagine a creature that large.

"How do you eat an elephant?" Jarek asked.

Liam shook his head at the puzzle.

"'One bite at a time.'"

Liam looked thoughtful at the answer to the riddle. "In other words, take the problem in bite-size pieces."

Jarek smiled in approval as he rose. "The fleet is in system now. We can't break through the force field without doing this planet irreparable harm. Once you neutralize Azurius, you need to shut it down for us and recall the chitin. Not necessarily in that order."

"I will." Ideas began to form in Liam's head as Jarek vanished.

•   •   •   •   •

Randolf approached the assembled squad and the three engineers.

"Keep to the sewers until you get to the portals," Randolf ordered sergeant in charge. "The comms have a secure channel. Let us know when you're there and keep us apprised of your progress and the situation."

"Yes, sir," the sergeant replied.

Randolf turned to the lead engineer. "Set the destination for either South Corinth or New Santorini. South Corinth is on a peninsula off the southern continent. New Santorini is an island city. Those would be the easiest to defend."

"We'll do our best," the lead engineer replied.

"Good luck," Randolf said.

"You too."

CHAPTER 8

Liam sat, thinking about what Jarek had told him. *One bite at a time. I need more information to take that first bite.*

He went back to where he left his body. Dillon had returned. It looked like he had found the vest and a med kit. He sat with Ephram, keeping watch.

In the dreamscape, Liam moved into the city. He watched the hordes of chitin entering and observed how they combined with the first groups. Liam worked his way back toward the Military Center, scouting for anything useful.

Several buildings had signs of battles on the rooftops. Liam skimmed close. One building looked as though the group on it had not gotten away. Blood covered the roof. Then he saw it.

The chitin missed a sniper rifle. Long range shooting could come in handy.

He also noticed at least one spare power pack and a few magazines of ammunition. Noting the location, he continued to the Center.

I hope Azurius didn't destroy everything at the Military Center armory. The building certainly took a pounding.

Soldiers must have harassed Azurius. Liam went to the wing where he had seen Azurius emerge from during his last raid. The attack had smashed that part of the building. He moved through the building, seeing evidence of the destruction. At least he detected no chitin.

He rechecked the locker room, glancing in each locker, in case he'd missed something last time. He tried the armory. After his last foray, Azurius must have had the chitin destroy it. The chitin had smashed everything. He looked closer and realized a few bayonet grenades and hand grenades had escaped the chitin's notice.

A trip to the Center could be useful.

He left the building and considered some more scouting. Without warning, Liam felt himself seized by the back of the neck.

"I thought I sensed someone snooping around," crowed a familiar voice. "You had a splendid idea, establishing an alarm. I thought it wise to follow your example. My alarm, however, is more subtle than explosives."

Azurius struck with an open hand, throwing Liam backward. With his head still ringing, Azurius grabbed him again.

Lieutenant! came a panicked call.

"You need more experience in dream combat if you intend to sneak around like this." Azurius laughed in triumph.

Liam's hand shot out and went into Azurius's skull. He almost felt brain material as Azurius cried out, threw him back, and vanished. Liam snapped back to his own body.

•   •   •   •   •

Liam jerked awake.

Corporal Ephram and Private Dillon grabbed him to keep him from hurting himself.

"Ouch."

"Sir!" Ephram stared at him in shock.

He touched the side of Liam's head. His hand came away bloody.

"Sir!" Dillon sounded shaken. "You seemed to jerk and cry out. We actually saw the wound appear."

Liam winced in pain. "You were right, Jarek." He almost heard an "of course."

Dillon grabbed the med kit to clean and treat the wound.

"I guess it looks worse than it is." Dillon sounded relieved.

"I bet it still stings." Ephram wiped the blood from his hand.

"Sir," Dillon asked, "what happened?"

"After talking to Jarek, I went scouting. Azurius ambushed me." He sat back to let Dillon work. "Well, Jarek warned me."

Liam had wanted to move out today, but this battle had drained him. His head felt like someone had driven a spike into it. He felt exhausted to the point of falling over.

"Sir," Corporal Ephram advised. "I suggest we contact your brother and have a priestess check out your condition."

Liam nodded. Ephram and Dillon helped Liam into his breastplate and helmet. Corporal Ephram plugged Liam's armor into his own.

"This is Corporal Ephram," he called. "We need to report to Captain Randolf. Lieutenant Liam is hurt."

"You make it sound worse than it is," Liam grumbled.

"Yes, sir," Ephram spoke into the comm. "Yes, sir, er...ma'am." He turned to hand Liam the earpiece. "It's your brother and High Priestess Celinia."

Liam took the earpiece and braced himself for a scolding from Celinia. "I'm here."

"Liam! What, in the Creator's name happened?" Randolf exclaimed.

"I went scouting and ran into Azurius." Liam winced again. "Do you think you could lower your voice? The fight left me with a blazing headache."

"Liam," Celinia cried with concern, "your body is full of fatigue toxins. We see things like what you have in younger priestesses who overexert themselves. Your toxin levels are a lot higher. Where did you get that gash?"

"Courtesy of Azurius," Liam replied. "He struck me in the dreamscape. Private Dillon says he saw the wound appear."

Celinia paused. "Liam, can you have Private Dillon patch his comm into this conversation?"

Liam looked at Dillon. "Private, they want you to patch in."

"Yes, sir," Dillon replied.

He put his helmet on and joined the conversion.

"Private," Celinia commanded, "please describe what you observed while Liam was in his trance."

"Wasn't much to tell at first," Dillon reported. "He seemed to mumble every so often. Suddenly, he convulsed. The corporal and I called to him. He shuddered and his head jerked. The gash appeared like someone struck him. Then he jerked forward and woke up. We restrained him in case of more convulsions, but he was awake with a headache."

"Liam," Celinia began, "I've heard about things like this—wounds received in a dream manifesting themselves in the waking world. However, the priestesses haven't documented such an incident for hundreds of years. I've certainly experienced nothing like this."

"Jarek has," Liam replied. "He warned me I could be putting myself in danger. I gave as good as I got. I pushed my hand into Azurius's head in the dreamscape and almost felt his brain. He broke off afterward."

"Did Jarek have anything to say?" Randolf asked.

"The fleet has arrived in system," Liam informed them. "I just need an opportunity to bring down the planetary force field, which means an opportunity to eliminate Azurius."

"Not today," Celinia ordered. "No arguments, Liam. In this condition, you won't be doing anyone any good."

"I don't plan to." Liam sighed. "I wanted to get going, but my head hurts too much, and I feel like I'm about to fall on my nose."

"Anything else?" Randolf asked.

"I observed the new chitin merging with the existing force," Liam told them. "I am thinking of heading to the Center. Azurius has abandoned it, and it looks like I can salvage some grenades and a sniper rifle. Then I'm planning to look for Azurius—if only to distract him."

"Okay, Liam," Randolf told him. "Try to get some rest and start out tomorrow. Call us if there's any change."

"Any chance of getting another comm?" Liam asked. "I have to keep borrowing the corporal's earpiece."

"I'll see what we can arrange," Randolf replied. "Have a good rest, little brother."

"Please take care, Liam," Celinia's voice softened.

"Talk to you soon," Liam replied. Then he whispered, almost to himself, "I love you."

The link closed, and Liam handed the earpiece back to Ephram.

•   •   •   •   •

Azurius groaned as he sat up. He almost felt the human's fingers on his brain. If he had not remembered that what was happening wasn't real...

He sent a brief signal for the chitin to start. With the plan already programmed, he did not need to go to the lab.

Liam is proving a cunning foe. Again, two impulses warred with each other. *The Finnian is a danger. I should destroy him. Yet, the Finnian is good. I should recruit him. I need someone with nerve.*

He sighed and laid back. *The former looks more likely. However, I'll hold out hope for the latter. Perhaps I can find some kind of leverage. At least I put Liam out of action for the rest of the day.*

"Just like me." Azurius laughed without humor. He closed his eyes and rested.

•   •   •   •   •

While their commander rested, the line of chitin reached the preset critical mass Azurius had programmed. Ten in every hundred started breaking off and headed for an entry to the sewers. They congregated at choke points in the sewers and moved with the line above them, closing the ring in the sewers and the city.

At the outer perimeter of the city's defenses, the soldiers had waged a steady fighting withdrawal. The chitin lines continued to swell. When one chitin fell, five seemed to replace it. Without warning, the chitin surged forward. The gap between the human soldiers and the insects collapsed. The humans fought a desperate close quarters battle to keep open a gap. A gap the chitin were determined to deny them. The ring began to shrink.

•   •   •   •   •

Azurius woke with a groan. His head did not hurt anymore, but he still remembered the feel of Liam's fingers on his brain.

An unnerving feeling.

He noticed an alarm sounding in his lab. It took a moment to recognize the signal. Then it hit him: his subspace communicator. He had adjusted it to bypass the subspace barrier. Since his falling out with his comrades in the Rebellion, there was no one he cared to communicate with, and no one he could think of who would want to talk to him. He had not used it in decades.

He tranced down and soon sat at the control panel.

Marisa. What a surprise. I thought she was dead. What does she want?

He hesitated to answer it, but curiosity got the better of him.

He activated the tridimensional transceiver, and soon the female appeared. She belonged to the same race as Azurius. Her scales were much finer, and she had long brown hair with slight purple highlights.

"Ah, there you are, Azurius," she greeted him with a cheerfulness Azurius found annoying. "Did I wake you up?"

"I've had a rough day," Azurius snapped and regretted it at once. "What do you want?"

"Let me guess, you underestimated the humans on the planet." She did not bother to hide her amusement.

He did not dignify her statement with an answer.

"I'm contacting you because the Rebellion is falling apart." Her tone turned serious. "Too many factions are attempting to win the war on their own or have decided if they go to ground, the Alliance will forget about them."

"Not surprising after the battle at Tau Ceti Three," Azurius replied. "You know the one, just after you all betrayed me."

"We weren't interested in a more expansive government." Irritation crept into her voice. "You are so narcissistic. You think we joined you in this whole sorry mess to make you the emperor of the galaxy. We didn't like being treated like chitin."

"Speaking of which,"—Azurius smirked—"I hear your experiments with intelligent chitin turned out better than you could have hoped. They became so intelligent they kicked you out of the hive and off the asteroid."

Marisa glared at him. "At least they didn't kill me. They even take my calls."

"Though they still refuse to take sides," Azurius pointed out.

"You don't seem to be doing much better," she countered. "None of us are, to be honest. If you're willing to accept that we will not make you emperor, we're willing to take you back as a military commander. You can be very good when you stick to purely military goals. Also, you held us together for almost five hundred years."

Surprised by this admission, Azurius sat back and thought.

"Where are you now?" she asked. "Perhaps I can help."

He hesitated a moment. "The Artemisian Plains of the Central Continent on the planet. I've pushed Neo-Etruscans into one last city and am in the process of taking it now. When they surrender, we can add new blood to the Rebellion."

"So," she asked, "where are you having trouble?"

Azurius paused, wondering if she could use this information against him.

"Resistance is stiffer than expected," he admitted. "Nothing I can't handle by piling on more chitin. One human is proving troublesome. I just caught him in the dreamscape. He almost ripped my brain out of my head."

Marisa looked impressed. "I'm only just at your level in dreamscape combat. Humans rarely use the dreamscape. I've heard the Neo-Etruscans have a limited capability in dealing with it. The only humans with any true proficiency would be Finnian."

"He is Finnian," Azurius told her. "The Neo-Etruscans adopted him after his parents died."

"Interesting," Marisa mused. "Even the Finnian aren't so powerful. Any chance of taking him alive?"

"I'm trying to convince him to join me."

"Let me guess. You started the conversation with the glories of following you, and he wasn't interested," she countered scornfully. "You could have listed the Rebellion's grievances with the Alliance. He might have at least been willing to listen. Perhaps I can convince him."

"How?" Azurius sneered. "On your back?"

She snarled. "Just because we were once lovers doesn't give you the right, Azurius. I'm a week away."

"It will be all over before then."

"If you can't keep him alive," she offered, "his genetic material might still be useful."

"I'll see what I can do." Azurius turned off the subspace transceiver.

I must admit she is right. She might be useful during negotiations. He paused to consider it. *No, I won't wait. It will be resolved soon.*

·   ·   ·   ·   ·

Randolf finished strapping on his armor. Stepping out of the room, he saw the sergeant and Captain Simon hurrying down the hall toward him.

"The chitin have stepped up their attack," Captain Simon told him. "We're losing ground and soldiers."

They raced to the ready room while Randolf wracked his brain for a solution.

"According to the reports," the sergeant added, "they made a sudden charge. They're trying to wage a close-quarters battle, denying us the distance to use our guns. Also, people patrolling the sewers say that chitin have moved into the system and established choke points. They're moving with the line, but not as aggressively. We've got to do something soon, or the whole line will collapse."

Randolf stopped. "Do we have any explosives with remote detonators?"

Captain Simon and the sergeant glanced at each other.

"The only real stores we have left are construction explosives at the Building Ministry," the sergeant informed him. "The chitin are dangerously close though."

"Get anyone who knows anything about munitions," Randolf ordered. "Direct them to get the explosives. Assign as many troopers as we can spare."

Once in the ready room, Randolf pulled a map from the pile. "Where is the line now? How fast is it closing?"

Captain Simon traced a line on the map. "It will be there within the hour if it isn't already. Another hour, it will move here"—he pointed to another point—"assuming the chitin don't speed up their charge."

Randolf nodded. "Order the sappers to place a line of explosives one hundred meters back from that line. Once we have everything ready, we send the signal and have our troops withdraw past the line as fast as they can, and reform here." He pointed to the rally point. "When the chitin cross the line of explosives, we set it off. Then try to regain ground."

"One more concern about the explosives," the sergeant advised. "They're pretty old. They may blow up if you look at them wrong."

"You have a better idea?" Randolf asked.

The sergeant shook his head. "No, sir."

"Then do it," Randolf ordered.

The sergeant and captain ran to organize the trap. Randolf slumped into his chair.

"Please, let this work," he prayed.

•   •   •   •   •

Azurius opened his eyes and rolled to his feet. The chitin had stepped up the assault.

It's time to get Licinious and his people doing something useful. Maybe a chitin will accidentally eat the traitor.

Azurius picked up his communicator and called Licinious. The *sending* tone kept ringing. Azurius waited a few minutes, then turned it off.

Interesting. He considered checking by the dreamscape but decided against it.

The humans are being pushed into an ever-shrinking ring, anyway. Azurius grabbed his plasma blade and entered the hallway. *I can bypass the battle zone and go myself.*

He followed the corridor to the stairs leading from the basement where he had camped. Emerging into the morning light, Azurius winced.

I've never quite gotten used to the brightness of this planet's sun. He put some sunshades over his eyes. Then he headed for Licinious's house. With the streets empty, he had time to admire the classical lines of the Neo-Etruscan architects.

While the Neo-Etruscans wisely abandoned their Founder's concept of Utopia, I've always found the Greco-Roman designs of Old Terra's classic and neoclassic period pleasing to the eyes.

He considered a chitin guard, but that would take chitin from the battle. *Besides, if the humans noticed the chitin, they might try to follow.*

I wondered where Liam might have hidden himself, Azurius mused. *I drove him from one base, but except for the last encounter, I've lost track of him.* He still felt the dual pull. *Liam is dangerous. I should have the chitin kill him on sight. Still, I must admire the human's ingenuity. Few humans can face me in the dreamscape, take it on the chin, and give it back with interest. Then again, Liam has learned a great deal about the dreamscape. How? What else has Liam learned?*

Liam's dangerous for precisely the reasons I need him. Perhaps I can lure Liam into joining the Rebellion. Chitin are useful tools, but they can't think creatively or independently. Traitors, like Licinious, are a liability. People like him obsess over insignificant matters when the best tactic would be to take a few precautions, then ignore them. While they want power, they wouldn't know how to use it. They want things done, but only if someone else does it for them. Traitors will also switch their allegiance, if so blows the prevailing wind.

People like Liam lead from the front. *They think outside of the box, can prioritize, and deal with problems in the field.* Azurius remembered many Rebel soldiers with similar attributes. *At the Rebellion's height, the Galactic Alliance trembled.*

Azurius shook his head. *All gone now. Over the centuries, some ran out of luck. Some went down fighting against overwhelming odds. The Alliance captured some. Others died. The rest turned on me. I started alone. I might as well end alone.*

·   ·   ·   ·   ·

Azurius slowed as he approached the house and discovered the bodies of Licinious's private troops littered about the yard. He walked around the house, carefully noting how each had died—thrown knives, broken neck, magnetic bullets. Azurius prided himself on his ability at reading the signs.

One warrior wrought this mayhem, a warrior who moved with speed and ruthlessness. He did not have to guess. He went inside the house. The odor of death hung heavy. He found Licinious's body and shuddered. He lay on the floor, a bloody spear nearby and a hole with a large smear of blood on the wall.

Someone hung him like a slab of meat. Liam, obviously. Could this destruction mean Liam had crossed the line?

He lifted his treacherous ally's head by the hair and looked into the glazed eyes. He had been dead a couple of days.

"By the way, Licinious," Azurius said pleasantly, "I think I forgot to mention that Liam is still alive. I guess you already know. You've been here, what? A day—maybe two? I guess he was really upset about his family."

Azurius let Licinious's head fall. *Liam lashed out in vengeance. He tortured and killed his enemy without mercy. Reading these signs, things have become very touchy. Still, perhaps he'd stepped over enough lines to shake off his old morality. I'll have the chitin keep an eye out for him. One more test and perhaps Liam would see reason.*

It was time to return to the front. *Liam's brother is also full of surprises. With luck, perhaps I'll get the set.*

•   •   •   •   •

Randolf's communicator chirped.

"Yes," he answered.

"Sir, this is Sergeant Collins."

"Yes, Sergeant?" Randolf straightened, hoping for good news.

"The engineers have started," Sergeant Collins reported. "The intercity portals are in good shape. Power supplies have proved temperamental, as expected. However, they know what the problem is and are chasing it. They just need some time."

Randolf nodded. "Remind them that time is in short supply. Once they get the power supply working, call me."

"Understood, sir," Collins replied. "The chitin haven't noticed us yet."

"Good," Randolf said. "Let us know when everything is about ready, and I'll get you troops."

"Yes, sir. Collins out."

Randolf felt a surge of hope. He picked up his weapons and headed to the door.

The sergeant met him as he came out of the ready room. "Sir?"

"Get your squad, Sergeant," Randolf ordered. "We're counterattacking."

"Sir," the sergeant objected, "we need—"

"They're making progress on our project, Sergeant," Randolf told him, "but they need time. We need the chitin to focus their attention on us. Azurius doesn't have sharpshooters. If we can push out and create a bulge away from the true area of interest, we can pull it off. Are the sappers almost ready?"

"They're just finishing now."

"Have our reserves ready to attack to the north when ordered," Randolf commanded.

"Yes, sir."

Leaving the Temple, Captain Simon fell in beside them with his men.

"You aren't going to the front, are you?" Captain Simon demanded.

"No," Randolf replied, "but I need to know what's going on. We're playing for time."

"Have you thought about how we're going to get our troops disengaged?" the sergeant asked.

"Do we have any leftover explosives?" Randolf asked.

"We should have plenty," Captain Simon assured him. "I used to be an explosives expert. We didn't use more than we needed. We had twice as much as we needed to do the job."

"Then the same way we're doing it now," Randolf responded. "Have the sappers move forward two hundred meters from the last line and set up there once we're past. We'll let the bulge collapse like we just couldn't do it. Then try to hold until we get the signal. We'll retreat past the new line. When the explosives force the chitin to hesitate, we send our forces into the Temple and down into the sewers."

"Yes, sir," the sergeant replied.

"Captain, you'll push the bulge northward," Randolf said. "Make it convincing but don't break out, or you could find yourself trapped."

"Understood, sir."

"Let's do this."

•   •   •   •   •

Liam put the rib vest on and touched the button to set it against his ribs. It felt much more comfortable than the tape or armor.

"Okay." Liam looked over the vest and nodded in satisfaction. "Armor."

Dillon and Ephram helped him put the breastplate on around the vest. Then Dillon connected a cable to Liam's armor.

"The medical scanner still shows the cracked ribs, but it saw the vest and compensated for it." Dillion looked up at Liam. "I guess the people here knew what they were doing."

Corporal Ephram's comm chirped.

"Yes, Captain." The corporal handed the earpiece to Liam.

"Yes?"

"Liam," Randolf began. "We've got a plan in place. We're going to fall back to a rally point and detonate a line of explosives when the bugs cross. Then we counterattack. The main thrust will go to the north, keeping Azurius's attention away from the intercity portals."

"I'm getting ready to start," Liam reported. "I know where I can get a sniper rifle. A long-range weapon should help."

"If you mean against Azurius, good luck," Randolf replied. "You'll have to get lucky and catch him distracted, if he comes out of his hole at all."

"He must." Liam motioned for Ephram and Dillon to get ready. "He can't use the chitin to deliver ultimatums. How are the portals coming?"

"They're getting started," Randolf told him. "They're chasing a problem with the power supply, but they say it will take time. I'll give them what I can, but—"

"Time is a precious commodity at the moment," Liam finished for him. "A quick trip to the Center and we'll be as ready as we're going to be."

"Understood," Randolf replied. "I can't spare anyone to bring you a comm. Can you still borrow one?"

"I can make do."

"Good luck."

"You too, big brother." Liam closed the link and handed the earpiece to Ephram. "I'd like to pick up another one of those. I hate to keep borrowing yours."

"If we can't, I'm okay with it, Lieutenant."

"Take the newer assault rifles and all the ammo and power packs we can carry," Liam ordered.

Once the belts and armor had all they could take, Liam put the rest in his rucksack. He smiled to see the whiskey bottle still intact, tucked into an inside pocket.

"Do you want one of us to take your rucksack, sir?" Ephram asked.

Liam started to decline but thought better of it. He handed the pack to the corporal.

·   ·   ·   ·   ·

Randolf, the sergeant, and the squad made it to a secure observation post outside the Temple compound. Randolf watched as the lines got closer.

"Sappers report ready," a voice came over the comm.

"All troops," Randolf ordered. "On my mark, those engaged will disengage and retreat to the rally point. Be clear of the 'surprise' in thirty seconds. Sappers, you will detonate thirty seconds from my mark."

Randolf received confirmation from all commanders. He felt his heart pounding.

He looked at the sergeant. "When I call 'mark,' give the countdown over the comm."

The sergeant nodded.

Randolf watched until the circle of battle reached the predetermined distance. The sergeant kept his eyes on his wrist console.

"Mark!"

"Twenty-nine, twenty-eight, twenty-seven..."

Randolf held his breath as the soldiers disengaged and ran to get past the explosives and to the rally point. Surprised by the sudden retreat, the chitin hesitated for a few precious seconds. Then they were on the humans' heels.

"Fifteen, fourteen, thirteen, twelve…"

The troopers at the rally point waited with weapons ready. Randolf saw some soldiers had fallen dangerously behind. Most of them overran the rally point.

"Five, four, three, two, one."

A string of explosions detonated in a ring, catching a sizeable portion of chitin in the blast. Humans who were not fast enough got thrown forward by the blast. Chitin, who had not made the line of explosives or had passed them, got thrown backward or forward.

Everyone at the rally point opened fire. The fresh troops cut to pieces all the chitin picking themselves up or trying to push forward. Soldiers who'd survived being thrown, laid flat and waited. The soldiers at the rally point and those who had made it past the rally point advanced, driving the chitin back.

The chitin wavered and retreated.

"Captain Simon," Randolf ordered over the comm. "As we discussed."

The surge in the north had more troops than the rest of the ring.

The counterattack proved particularly fierce. Once more, Randolf wished he was down with the troops. He watched as the counterattack picked up speed. The initial success of a desperate gambit before it ran out of steam. At least, that illusion was what they were trying to project.

"Sappers!" he called. "Forward two hundred meters and set the next line of explosives. First group! Disengage and set up at new rally point."

Randolf watched as his soldiers carried out his orders. He wanted to move to a better observation post, but he dared not take his eyes off the battle. He prayed to the Creator his plan would work.

•　　•　　•　　•　　•

Liam, Ephram, and Dillon made their way down to street level, where empty streets waited.

"Street or sewer?" Dillon asked.

Liam did a quick mental review. "Street. We need speed more than stealth. We want to attract attention."

"You're the boss, sir," Dillon replied.

Liam, assault rifle at the ready, led the way.

They heard the explosions. Randolf must have started his distraction. Ephram and Dillon cast concerned looks over their shoulders.

"Let's pick up the pace," Liam ordered.

The two men fell in with him.

"Where are we going, Lieutenant?" Dillon asked.

"I saw a sniper rifle on one building," Liam told them. "I want to see what's happening, anyway."

"You think you can take him down?" Ephram asked. "Our snipers couldn't get him to sit still long enough."

"I'm not holding my breath, Corporal," Liam replied. "Maybe if he gets careless. I'm thinking more of long-range shots against chitin."

•   •   •   •   •

Azurius had left Licinious's house and headed to a previously arranged meeting with one of Licinious's men. He heard the explosions as he approached, then fierce weapons fire.

I need to know what is happening.

Azurius stepped out of time and sprinted to the nearest tall building and climbed the stairs. He burst onto the roof and came into ordinary time as he reached the edge. He watched as the chitin fell back in confusion. The humans pushed out in all directions. The force in the Temple must have set a trap with explosives.

I should have given Randolf more credit.

Azurius gave a mental order to get the chitin to rally. The bugs fell back to their own rally point where they could turn and fight. He scanned the battle zone. A bulge in the line formed to the north.

They must be trying to break out. Of course, I can hunt them down, but if I want to use these people as a new group of soldiers, I need them in one place.

He returned to the stairwell, sat down, and went into a trance.

I'll use the chitin's eyes before going to the lab. Azurius let his mind drift through the various chitin, his mind capturing images of the battle. He noticed sappers setting a fresh line of explosives. *Curious. What are they planning?*

Azurius selected some chitin to climb up the nearest buildings. He then did a quick scan through their eyes.

With the second line of explosives, the bulge makes little sense.

Snipers shot down the chitin before they got to their vantage points. Azurius sent another group. A few more made it this time. He would have left it, but something did not make sense. He sent another group up, and, in a quick scan, saw it. For a split second, he saw a form going into the old intercity portal building.

Azurius released the chitin, laughed, went deeper into the trance, and headed for his lab.

Randolf is trying to get the portals up, using this attack as a diversion. When they retreat to the Temple, they'll send people through the portals and use that new line of explosives to buy their rear-guard time to make it into the sewers. Brilliant. Except now I see what they are doing.

Once in the lab, he selected five hundred chitin and sent them to the intercity portals. The rest, once they reached his rally point would turn and attack.

Just not the way Randolf expects.

He ordered the chitin to attack in relays, so relatively small pockets made it to the explosives at any one time. The chitin pushed back at the bulge, which would be what his enemies expected him to do. Chitin would break through the line and exploit the breach. The chitin who reached the line would be a waste of explosives. These groups would hunt the sappers and eliminate them. Then the main body would advance.

Azurius came out of his trance. He found a man in black coming up the stairs.

"Ah," Azurius said, "good, I don't have to go looking for you. I have new instructions for the rest of your people."

•　　•　　•　　•　　•

The building came into view.

"Over there. Let's move!"

They ran to the door, which hung by one hinge. They pushed the door aside and dashed in, taking the stairs two at a time. Liam's ribs complained at the exertion.

"There," Liam gasped, panting for breath as he made it to the rooftop exit and pointed to the mess on the roof.

"Sir?" Ephram looked worried. "Ribs?"

Liam nodded and went forward, the other two following.

"Well," Dillon muttered, "I'll be—"

They saw the rifle where it had fallen. Liam picked it up and saw it was serviceable. Dillon handed him the extra power pack out of the remains of the sniper team. Ephram retrieved the two remaining magazines. Liam checked the magazine on the rifle.

"It's half full," he noted.

"It's in good shape?" Ephram asked.

Liam checked the scope. "Sights are a bit off. It must have taken a jar when the sniper dropped it."

"You going to adjust them?" Dillon asked.

"If I do line up Azurius," Liam replied, "it won't do us any good to hit a chitin standing next to him, will it?"

He opened the bipod and sighted on a small black spot on a white brick in a building at one hundred meters. He did a rough adjustment, then fired five shots. The shot was off by a meter. After readjusting, he fired again. Having dialed in the windage, he needed to adjust elevation a few minutes of angle.

"Sir." Ephram looked across the city. "They are pushing the chitin back."

Liam fired again, and the spot disappeared.

"Okay," he said. "If the scope is off, it's by less than one MOA. It'll have to do."

He swung his prize across his back.

"Next stop, the Military Center." Liam stood next to Ephram and Dillon as they looked toward the temple.

"First, I want to check in with my brother."

Ephram called in to the Temple. "This is Corporal Ephram. The lieutenant needs to talk to Captain Randolf."

After a pause, he nodded as he listened to the answer.

"Okay," Ephram replied. "Patch us through."

He removed his helmet and handed Liam the earpiece.

"Liam," Randolf's called over the comm.

"You've begun your distraction?" Liam asked.

"That's affirmative," Randolf replied. "We led the chitin into an ambush and are pushing them back. I'm having Captain Simon create a bulge to the north. I want Azurius to think we're breaking out in that direction. It'll look like we've stalled. We have a second line of explosives waiting. When we're ready, we'll slip down into the sewers and make for the portals."

Liam nodded. "I hope it works."

He glanced toward the intercity portals.

"Don't wait for me," Liam went on. "This battle ends when we neutralize Azurius. I've got to get to him."

"What about Corporal Ephram and Private Dillon?" Randolf asked.

Liam looked at the two men. Even hearing only half the conversation, they knew what was being discussed.

"I'll stay with you, sir," Ephram promised.

Dillon nodded. "I'm in too, sir. Someone has to look after the officers."

Liam smiled. "They've volunteered to stay with me."

"Okay," Randolf replied. "Try to stay in contact."

"Count on it," Liam promised.

He closed the link and handed the earpiece to Ephram. "Let's head to the Center."

The three soldiers descended the stairs and exited into the street.

•   •   •   •   •

By circling around the battle zone, they got to the Military Center undetected.

Liam and his companions slowed as they went into the damaged building. They saw no chitin this time. Azurius had abandoned the building as being useless.

"No guards," Dillon noted.

They went straight to the armory. Its door lay across the hall where the chitin had flung it since Liam's last visit.

"Azurius had the chitin destroy anything he thought useful before abandoning the Center," Liam told them. "They made an enormous mess, but they didn't get everything."

Ephram groaned as he surveyed the carnage. "We just have to find it."

They began a quick, methodical search.

"Sir." Dillon grinned, holding up a bayonet grenade.

"Good." Liam returned the grin. "I found a hand grenade. What else we can find?"

They found five bayonet grenades and two hand grenades. Liam passed the hand grenades to Ephram and Dillon. The bayonet grenades he slipped into his rucksack. Ephram took it again. They checked the rest of the armory and found one more magazine for an assault rifle.

"That's it," Liam told them. "Anything else will be a waste of time."

Suddenly, Ephram raised his hand. "Sir," he whispered. "Company!"

Liam used hand signals and signed they should creep into the corridor. Soon, they could make out the voices.

"So Azurius wants us to stand by until called for." They heard one man saying.

"When did you make contact?"

"A short time ago. He said he sent chitin into the sewers, blocking movement to and from the Temple."

"Finally!" another voice exclaimed. "Maybe Councilor Licinious would still be alive if he'd sent the bugs into the sewers to begin with."

"Wouldn't have helped," countered the second voice. "The late high councilor's adopted, misborn brat got to him first."

"How do you know?"

The second voice replied, "Martius overheard them. He saw a squad going into the councilor's house and crept close. He heard the conversation. Captain Randolf missed his chance by about an hour. Martius had to get out before they spotted him. When they left, he went back. He found Licinious hanging from the wall. That misborn brat cut off an arm and a leg and cut him open. Then he left him hanging there, still alive."

"So, if someone had gotten back sooner..."

"Not without more medical attention than Azurius has available. Then Martius tried to track down the misborn with his people. We lost contact with them. When we found them, they were all dead."

"So how do we reclaim the population with Licinious dead? He was our ticket past the chitin. We're as cut off from the Temple as they are from escape."

"Azurius says he has a plan," replied the first voice. "He'll call us when he's ready. He's just sent some chitin to eliminate a group at the intercity portals."

Liam looked back at Ephram and Dillon. Their faces mirrored the horror on his.

He used hand signals. *Eliminate this group.* He risked a quick peak. *Ten men.* He signaled again, *No explosives.* He sent Dillon back to the T-junction. They'd start in one minute.

"How many of us are still alive?"

"We're it," replied the first. "The rest of the pro-Founder's group doesn't trust Azurius. I'm not sure I do either."

Liam and Ephram waited, counting down the seconds. A minute later, they came around the corner and opened fire. Dillon attacked at the same time.

A hale of electromagnetic bullets cut four people to pieces as the other six dove for cover. Liam and Ephram pulled back as their enemy returned fire. Liam signaled Ephram to get to the front so the traitors could not escape. Ephram nodded, and Liam counted down to mark. Then Liam laid down a suppressing fire, taking down one man who rose. Ephram dashed to the front door and got through as another person rose and fired, hitting the doorjamb. A burst from Dillon's gun took that assassin down before he could duck.

Liam saw Ephram was just out of their enemies' sight. He signaled, *Relay to Dillon—charge in five seconds.*

They attacked. A round hit Ephram as he leaped through the door. The bullet spun him by his hip, and he landed hard. Liam and Dillon fired as they advanced. Two rose to attack. They died immediately. Soon Liam and Dillon advanced close enough to their enemies' cover to see them. The traitors died before they could further defend themselves.

"Clear!" Dillon shouted.

Liam turned and saw Ephram struggling to his feet. "Corporal!"

"I'm okay, sir," Ephram replied in disgust. "My comm deflected the shot. Comm's destroyed."

Liam swore. "Private, we need to contact my brother."

Dillon took the comm from his belt and the earpiece from his helmet.

"Why don't you take it, sir?" He handed the unit to Liam. "They'll want to talk to you, anyway."

Liam attached the comm to his belt and put the earpiece in his ear. Then he signaled the Temple.

"Communications."

"Lieutenant Liam," he called. "I need to communicate with Captain Randolf."

•   •   •   •   •

Meanwhile, Randolf's comm signaled another urgent message. "Captain Randolf."

"Sergeant Collins!" came the frantic call. "We're under attack. A mass of chitin attacked us from out of nowhere. We're trying to hold them at the doors, but we're badly outnumbered."

Randolf swore. "Can you get out of there?"

"Negative," Collins replied, "we're..."

Randolf heard a burst of static, then he heard screams, gunfire—then silence.

The sergeant turned to look at him.

"The chitin have taken the portals," Randolf stated.

The sergeant slammed his fist on the side of the observation post.

Randolf heard another chirp from his comm.

"Captain Randolf." He spoke evenly, trying to sound in control.

"Communications, sir," replied the comm officer, "Lieutenant Liam."

"Patch him through," Randolf ordered. "Liam?"

"Randolf," Liam called urgently. "Azurius is on to your plan. He's sending chitin—"

"Great timing, little brother," Randolf replied. "I just got their last message. The chitin own the portals."

Liam fell silent for a moment.

"We just overheard it from more of Licinious's people," Liam informed him. "We had to kill them before we could warn you. I'm sorry, Randolf."

"It's not your fault," Randolf replied.

"Also, chitin are in the sewers," Liam told him. "They've formed a ring around the Temple to prevent escape."

"Lovely!" Randolf exclaimed. "I got that information this morning. Azurius must have figured out we'd use the sewers."

"Gun fire destroyed Corporal Ephram's comm," Liam went on. "Private Dillon turned his over to me. I'm going to try to make my way back to you. I'll keep you posted. We're not done yet."

Randolf smiled, despite the situation. "Take care, Liam."

"You too, big brother."

Randolf killed the link and looked back over the battlefield.

•   •   •   •   •

Liam looked at his two companions. "We're too late."

Ephram looked stricken. Dillon swore.

"Come on!" Liam ordered.

"Their stuff?" Dillon asked.

"Leave it!"

The three raced out of the ruined Military Center with Liam in the lead. Liam, Ephram, and Dillon jogged through the Military District and entered a residential district just outside the military zone.

Spotting a sizeable group of chitin making its way to the front, they checked their ammo. Liam looked at his men. He pulled a hand grenade from his belt and nodded. Ephram and Dillon did the same. Liam indicated their target zones. They pulled the pins and threw.

Two grenades landed at the sides and one in the middle. The three explosions tore many chitin apart and tossed others off their feet, creating confusion.

The three men raised their weapons and opened fire, pressing forward. Chitin staggered to their feet and charged. They fell as the men pressed forward. Then the surviving chitin reached them.

Liam dropped his rifle and drew his plasma blade. The blade decapitated the lead bug. He considered stepping out of time, but he had to protect his team and save his strength for Azurius.

Ephram drew his own plasma blade, and in a spinning move took down two. Dillon kept firing, trying to pick off those coming up on Liam and Ephram. He saw the chitin too late to switch weapons. The chitin lifted him in its mandibles and threw him through the air, onto a house porch. The sound of boards cracking was explosive. Liam cut through another and tried to make his way to Dillon. Ephram drew his pistol and fired at one coming up, then cut down the one next to it. A chitin kicked Liam in the side. It tossed him back, causing him to lose his grip on the plasma blade. With it bearing down on him, Liam pulled his larger dagger off his thigh and struck into the neck joint. He rolled to his feet, and another picked him up in its mandibles. Liam cried out at the pressure and drove the dagger into the creature's skull. The blade snapped as the bug collapsed. Liam drew his pistol and started firing. In seconds, the last one fell.

"Dillon!"

Both men ran to the porch. Dillon groaned in pain and opened his eyes as they kneeled beside him.

Corporal Ephram checked his diagnostic. "Cracked fibula and tibia." He ordered his friend's armor to treat. "Mild concussion too. He was lucky."

"Define lucky," Dillon gasped.

Liam went to activate his comm. Nothing. He looked at his belt. During the fight, chitin had smashed the communicator. He swore.

"We're down two comms now."

"Three if you count the one you lost at the start," Dillon put in. "Can you pry me out of this porch?"

Liam and Ephram lifted him out of the hole he had made when he landed.

"Two restaurants and a porch." Liam sighed. "We definitely owe people money."

"Hey," Dillon laughed through his pain. "I'm just in for the porch. Blame Azurius for the restaurants. I didn't think the Bistro was too bad."

They sat down and gave him some water.

"So," Ephram observed. "We can't talk to the Temple now."

Liam looked out over the deserted city. "So much for trying to distract him. I think we'd better get to the Temple. Azurius must get there, eventually. Dillon is of limited use in a fight, and we still have to break through."

Ephram nodded. "We can't do much good out here, anyway."

Dillon staggered to his feet. Ephram adjusted the rucksack so he could support his friend.

"I can't put a lot of weight on it for long," Dillon said.

Liam got on his other side. "We're going to have to pick our battles more carefully."

CHAPTER 9

The situation had become desperate. The chitin did not press back evenly.

Azurius must have figured out what we're doing. Randolf could only stare. *What do I do now? Chitin have the portals. They'll ruined the work the engineers did, even if we retake them.*

"Okay," Randolf called, trying to sound confident. "Everyone, back to the new rally point."

His troops disengaged. Azurius held the bulk of the chitin back. In only one sector did the chitin attempt to overtake his troops. In the sector to the north, Captain Simon's group executed a fighting withdrawal.

"Sappers," Randolf called. "Is it possible to detonate only part of the line?"

"Not without resetting," one sapper answered. "We set up quickly, so we have it set to go with one push of the button."

"Is there any other way to detonate?"

A pause followed. "Which sector, sir?"

"Northern sector," Randolf replied. "Captain Simon's got chitin on his heels."

"Consider it done, sir."

"Keep watching the rest of the chitin," Randolf told his squad.

Keeping his binoculars turned to the north, he watched the northern group racing toward the relative safety of the rally point. Then two figures dashed past the rally point and stopped at the ends of the string he wanted to detonate. They waved to the retreating troops to hurry, and they took out grenades. Then he understood.

They intend to use hand grenades with ten-second timers as detonating devices, by-passing the electronics.

They pulled the pins as the last of the troopers raced past and drove the grenades into the terminal points of the explosives. Then the sappers ran for their lives. The chitin crossed the line five seconds later. Grenades detonated that section of the line. In a flash of fire, the explosion vaporized the chitin on the explosives. The explosion threw any who were too close. The rally guard fired into any chitin still alive. Soon, they received support from Captain Simon's company.

"Captain Simon," Randolf called. "Join me at the observation post. Are the sappers all right?"

"A little shaken, but okay," he heard Captain Simon say. "I'll be there as soon as I can."

By now, the rest of the force waited at the rally line. The problem was the chitin also waited a safe distance from the explosives. The only place they pressed forward was to the north.

A few minutes later, Captain Simon joined him.

"The chitin took the portals," Randolf told him, still observing through the binoculars.

Captain Simon swore. "What now?"

"I don't know yet." Randolf looked at him. "If you have any ideas, now's the time."

Captain Simon looked around the observation post. "The Temple."

"Excuse me?"

"I think we need a better view of what's happening," Captain Simon suggested. "The Temple tower has a better view."

"But that's..." Randolf started, then dropped it.

The clergy reserved the Temple's tower for special ceremonies for the priestesses and was not open to the public.

Randolf sighed. *It's that desperate.* "Let's go."

They abandoned the observation post and made their way back to the Temple.

Randolf called communications as they went.

"Communications," came the voice.

"Captain Randolf," he ordered. "Get me Lieutenant Liam."

There was a pause.

"Sir," the communications officer reported. "Lieutenant Liam is not responding. We aren't getting a return signal from his comm."

Randolf stopped in mid-stride.

"I'm sorry, sir."

"Understood," Randolf replied. "Out."

The sergeant tugged on his shoulder. "It may just be something with his comm."

Randolf held to that hope.

They dashed through the front doors just as Celinia came into the main hall.

"Randolf, what's wrong?"

"We need to get into the Creator's Tower," he told her. "It's got the most commanding view of the city. We need to know what's happening."

"The portals?"

"The chitin took them," he told her, "and we've lost contact with Liam."

Celinia looked horrified. She did not argue the point the tower was forbidden. She turned and led them through the Temple and into the private quarters. Soon, she stood outside the door of the arch priestess's apartment. Celinia knocked, heard a soft voice, and entered. Randolf stepped up and heard a brief conversation.

Celinia opened the door. "Follow me."

They entered as the arch priestess retrieved the key. Her quarters were elegant but simple. The arch priestess unlocked the door and led them up the stairs. The stairs were steep and long. Despite her age, the arch priestess moved nimbly up the stairs. Celinia followed right behind her.

"You are the first non-clergy to enter the Creator's Tower since its construction," the arch priestess told them. "May She provide you the wisdom to use what you see."

Randolf inclined his head as he passed her. He dashed out to the balustrade around the balcony with his binoculars, followed by the squad, the sergeant, and Captain Simon.

"North is still holding," the sergeant informed them. "How much longer? I don't know."

"The chitin are still holding back elsewhere," Captain Simon reported.

Randolf looked toward the intercity portals. The chitin feasted on the bodies of those people he had sent.

"Captain?" the arch priestess asked, seeing his stricken expression.

He handed her the binoculars. She raised them to her eyes and gasped. She almost dropped them, but Celinia took them from her. The arch priestess looked back at Randolf, tears streaming down her white face.

"I sent them into that trap," Randolf whispered.

Captain Simon put a hand on his shoulder. "We all knew it was a gamble."

"This plan was the last throw of the dice." Randolf's shoulders slumped in defeat. "I realized the chitin had taken the portals, but I needed to see for myself. I owed it to them."

The arch priestess reached out and put her hand on Randolf's cheek. "Don't despair. Until the last of us falls, we have hope... while even one of us draws breath."

On impulse, the arch priestess embraced him as a mother might embrace her child. "We were not wrong to put our faith in you, Captain Randolf, son of Marcus and Lidia. Courage is our best defense now."

She tipped his head and kissed him on the forehead.

"Thank you, milady," he replied. "With your permission, I will guide the battle from here while I still can."

She nodded and stood beside him as he tried to work out the puzzle of the battle. He wondered where, in all this mayhem, Liam was.

Is he even still alive?

•   •   •   •   •

Liam and Ephram helped Dillon into the next residential district before ducking out of sight. Chitin controlled this district to the northwest of the Temple compound. They heard sounds of fighting ahead. Liam looked around for an overwatch in this upscale section of the city close to where he had grown up.

"This way." He nodded toward a back alley.

They made their way into it. The alley ended just as they drew level to the fighting.

He nodded to a house on the corner. "Over there."

They moved forward and tried the back door—locked. Ephram took his plasma blade and cut the lock.

"You realize we're breaking and entering," Dillon joked feebly. They entered the house and found the stairs.

"Sorry to do this to you," Liam told Dillon, leading them toward the stairway.

Dillon just nodded.

They helped him upstairs and found a child's room in the house's corner, facing the battle. Liam picked a window on the cross street and opened it.

"That way," Liam pointed to some soldiers in need of help. "Bayonet grenades?"

"It will give them some cover to fall back," Ephram agreed.

"You can land those things on a pinhead anyway, Ephram," Dillon said. "I'll take the pack and hand them to you."

"We'll take the other window, sir." Ephram helped his friend over to where they would set up.

He helped Dillon down and handed him the pack.

The chitin pressed in with the soldiers trying to hold their ground. Liam unslung the sniper rifle and opened the bipod. He scanned the area first, picking and prioritizing his targets. Then he fired. Chitin, in key spots of the battle line, began falling. Shots coming from different directions confused the chitin as they tried to locate the new threat. The soldiers sensed the chitin's distraction and intensified their attack.

"Wait for my signal, Corporal."

"By your order, sir." Ephram snapped a bayonet grenade in place.

Liam used up the partial magazine and loaded a fresh one. No one in the battle below them could figure out which chitin died at the hands of the hidden snipers, and which fell to the soldiers blocking the chitin's way.

Then Liam identified a threat the soldiers did not.

"Left and right!" Liam called. "Chitin are trying to flank them."

Ephram let fly. The grenade exploded on the left flank.

Liam aimed and fired right. When the first chitin fell, the soldiers realized the threat. They fell back. Liam swung the gun to cover their escape.

Ephram dropped another grenade on the right flank. The soldiers executed a fighting withdrawal. Liam swung back to the primary group of chitin, which again looked for its hidden foe. Liam continued to pick them off. It seemed he took them out just as they sensed where he was. Ephram fired his third grenade into the main body, thinning it further.

Liam loaded his last magazine and continued to take chitin down. Soon the battle had moved beyond the cross street, and the last chitin looking for them fell.

Liam looked at his two soldiers. "It's time to go to underground. We need to get to the Temple."

He crept back from the window and folded the sniper rifle's bipod, gathering the empty magazines and checking his last magazine. Two-thirds of the magazine remained.

"Two bayonet grenades left," Dillon reported. "Should we find bugs to use them on?"

Liam slung his sniper rifle and picked up his assault rifle.

"If the opportunity presents itself. We don't have time to create one."

Liam and Ephram assisted Dillon and returned downstairs and out the back door.

"I noticed a sewer hatch at the cross street," Liam told them.

"It may be one with chitin under it," Dillon warned.

Liam pulled out a sticky grenade, throwing them a nasty grin.

"Then I have a surprise for them."

He returned the grenade to his belt, and they continued to the cross street.

•　　•　　•　　•　　•

Azurius had watched as the humans detonated part of the line of explosives.

A rather clever way of changing plans since they had rigged the explosives to go together.

The chitin pressed from the north, but the north resisted.

Azurius slipped into the dreamscape and found the sappers. He used his telekinesis to push the button on the detonator and snapped back to his body.

The explosion roared across the distance between him and the temple. He sent the chitin forward. The chitin hit the lines just as the defenders picked themselves up. They recovered quickly, but with the chitin on top of them, the Neo-Etruscans had to pull back.

"'Once more unto the breach, dear friends,'" Azurius quoted his favorite ancient human playwright with a chuckle.

Azurius enjoyed Shakespeare. His universal themes had survived down through the ages and spoke between civilizations.

•   •   •   •   •

Randolf watched the line all but collapse.

"What happened to the explosives?" he called into the comm.

"I don't understand, sir." The sapper sounded confused. "I was looking at the detonating button. It looked like some invisible finger pressed it. I—"

"I understand," Randolf replied. "Get back to the Temple. You can't do anymore good there."

Randolf looked around and grimaced. "All troops retreat to the Temple compound."

He turned to the arch priestess. "If it weren't for people who couldn't navigate the sewers, I'd take everyone out that way and try to fight past the chitin."

The arch priestess nodded. "No one wants to leave the helpless to the mercy of the chitin."

"I'm going downstairs," Randolf told her. "I'll lead the last battle."

"The Creator give you strength."

Randolf turned toward the stairs. "I have need of it. Pray for a miracle."

•   •   •   •   •

Liam lay on top of the sewer hatch and listened.

"Well, sir?" Corporal Ephram prodded.

"I don't hear anything. Well, here goes nothing."

Liam stood back and took Dillon's arm while Ephram heaved open the hatch and looked down.

"No chitin," he declared.

"They must be ahead," Liam surmised. "I'll go down, and you can lower the private to me."

"Once I'm on the ladder," Dillon said, "I think I can hobble down."

"Okay."

Liam dropped into the sewer. Ephram helped Dillon onto the ladder. Dillon managed the ladder rungs with one leg until Liam caught him and helped him the rest of the way. Ephram came down last and pulled the hatch closed.

They heard an explosion. It sounded like it came from the sewers ahead, and a rumble suggested a possibility of them collapsing.

"We'd better move," Liam advised. "If that part of the tunnel falls, I don't want to be on the wrong side of it."

"With you there, sir," Dillon agreed.

The trio moved forward toward the Temple.

Helping Dillon along, they heard the telltale sounds of chitin ahead. The sewers grew narrow. Liam caught his teammates' attention and signaled what he wanted to do. *Stay quiet. Stagger the fire line—I'm in front left, Ephram second middle, Dillon third right.*

They moved, making minimal noise. Soon, they approached an intersection. The chitin directed their attention toward the Temple. Once they got within range, the chitin sensed them and turned.

Dillon pulled away from Liam and Ephram and lay prone to the right, just out of the water and muck so he could still shoot. Ephram and Liam took their positions just as the chitin attacked. Liam began firing, followed by Ephram. Dillon waited for any chitin to move into his field of fire. Ten chitin tried to cram their way into the tunnel, tangling up and getting in each other's way, making it relatively easy to pick them off.

When the last one got too close, Liam reached for his plasma blade, only to remember he had lost it. He reflexively threw himself to the side, and two shots rang out. The chitin collapsed at his feet.

Liam released his breath. "Thanks."

Ephram helped Dillon up and moved forward.

"Sir," Dillon handed him his own plasma blade, "in my condition, it isn't likely to be of much use to me. Why don't you take it?"

Liam smiled in gratitude. "Thank you, Private. I appreciate this."

Liam holstered the plasma blade and helped support Dillon.

"You know, sir," Dillon said with mock cheerfulness, "it's really a pity the chitin aren't more intelligent."

Liam cocked an eyebrow.

"Well," Dillon explained, "assuming it comes down to a fight between you and Azurius, I could canvas the crowd taking bets. At just ten percent, I could make a huge profit."

Ephram laughed. "I wonder how many chitin would put money on you, sir?"

Liam laughed, too.

They moved forward. The next intersection contained a much larger group of chitin. Liam signaled Ephram and Dillon to get in place on their own. He would throw a sticky grenade into the middle of the group. Then they would deal with survivors. The two men nodded. Liam separated from them. Grabbing the grenade from his belt, he approached until he got an unobstructed view of the center of the throng.

They noticed him as he pulled the pin and began to move. He threw the grenade into the midst of the group and dropped, covering his head. The chitin recognized the threat, freezing in confusion as it stuck to a bug in the center. The others started hitting it to drive it away. Ten seconds later came a white-hot flash of plasma, leaving more than half cooked.

Dillon and Ephram opened fire. The bewildered chitin tried to regroup, and Liam came up firing as well. Chitin staggered and fell. Liam held up his hand to cease fire as the last one dropped. Ephram put his arm around Dillon, and they went toward him. Liam moved to the center of the junction and waited until they caught up with him. The path forward was clear but slow going, with the intersection thickly littered with chitin remains.

Then they perceived the chattering and clicking of bugs coming from both sides of the cross tunnel. Liam swore. More chitin were coming to investigate.

"Bayonet grenades," he ordered.

"We've just got two left." Ephram unslung the pack. He handed Liam one grenade and took the other.

"Try to bring down that tunnel as they come into view." Liam pointed out one tunnel as he snapped the grenade onto the end of his assault rifle. He looked at Dillon. "How are you with a sniper rifle?"

"Not as good as you, sir," Dillon conceded, "but I can do the job."

Liam unslung the sniper rifled and handed it to Dillon. "Can you use it without the bipod?"

Dillon nodded, taking up the sniper rifle. He kneeled, wincing as he put down the knee of his bad leg. Then he checked his field of fire in both directions.

The sounds got closer. Liam and Ephram got into position. Liam looked through the assault rifle's scope, looking for a weak point in the roof. Ephram did the same on his side as the chitin came into view. Liam and Ephram waited. When the first one made it to the point he had picked, Liam pulled the trigger. The bayonet grenade struck home. Liam covered his head as the explosion reflected down, crushing the chitin immediately below. The roof collapsed an instant later, burying the remaining chitin and blocking the tunnel.

Ephram fired just after Liam. The explosion crushed the chitin immediately underneath. The roof held for several critical seconds longer, allowing six chitin to pass before the ceiling collapsed.

Dillon fired the sniper rifle in rapid succession but dropped only two before the remaining four bowled into Ephram. Liam opened fire as a chitin threw Ephram aside. Two more chitin fell. Dillon took the fifth. With a burst of speed, the last one bore down on Liam, who pulled his last dagger and struck. The creature hit him and threw him aside just as Dillon's last round took it in the head.

Liam picked himself up and felt a stab of pain.

Ephram jumped up and ran to him. "Sir, you all right?"

"Rib vest loosened a little." Liam winced. "Okay, the computer readjusted it. I'm fine. Get Private Dillon. I'll be right with you."

Ephram hastened to obey while Liam went to retrieve his shoulder dagger. He lifted the creature's head and found Dillon's bullet had struck the blade. The blade had snapped at the haft. Liam swore and took up his assault rifle. He checked it. It still seemed okay. He shook it to clear the water. Then he rejoined his men.

"Good shooting, Private," Liam praised Dillion.

"Fair, sir," Dillon replied as he slung the rifle across his own back. "'Good' would have meant none got past."

Liam supported Dillon on the other side.

"I'd call your shooting superb, sir," Ephram chimed in, "from what we saw back at that house."

"Practice, gentlemen." Liam grinned as they headed for the Temple. "Talent only gets you to good. Practice gets you to superb."

"We'll try to remember that, sir," Dillon replied.

They shuffled on as fast as they could. He made light of it, but Dillon grew more fatigued. It took another fifteen minutes to make it to the hatch into the Temple's subbasement. Liam supported Dillon as Ephram went forward to wrestle the hatch open.

"Halt!" came a voice. "Identify yourself."

"Corporal Ephram, Private Dillon, and Lieutenant Liam," Ephram called back. "Dillon's hurt and needs to see a priestess. The lieutenant wants to see Captain Randolf."

"Ephram, Dillon!" the voice cried with relief. "You're back! Come ahead!"

Liam and Ephram assisted Dillon up the ladder and through the hatch. Fresh hands relieved them of their burden and began helping Dillon to the Temple infirmary.

The man in charge of the guard saluted Liam. "I'll take you up to the main Temple, sir."

Liam and Ephram followed the people helping Dillon until they got to the Temple proper.

"Lieutenant!" an unfamiliar voice called.

Liam turned to see a sergeant he recognized from Archer sector approaching.

"Get back to the basement. Corporal Ephram, you may rejoin your unit."

The guards obeyed immediately. Ephram nodded and turned to Liam.

"Good luck, sir." He saluted and went to find his unit.

The sergeant approached and looked Liam over. "Lieutenant, I have been acting as Captain Randolf's aide. Will you please follow me?"

Liam fell in beside the sergeant.

•   •   •   •   •

Azurius watched the humans retreating. He decided the time had come to issue his ultimatum. Passing the humans' last defensive line, he kept his awareness open in case snipers tried to take him.

He opened a case he had brought with him and took out a voice projector.

"Citizens of New Olympia!" Azurius called, his voice echoing. "Well met. You have fought bravely and proved yourselves stimulating opponents. I especially applaud your leader, Captain Randolf, son of Marcus, who gave me some exciting moments. Captain Randolf, please come to where we can speak."

A few minutes later, Randolf appeared at the main gate to the Temple compound, with other soldiers at his side.

"What do you want?" Randolf shouted.

"Your surrender, of course." Azurius smirked. "Chitin have the Temple compound surrounded. As we speak, chitin I have sent into the sewers are closing in. You won't escape that way. However, I am prepared to be magnanimous. I need skilled warriors and leaders. I don't want to massacre your people."

"Did you give the people working at the portals a chance to surrender?" Randolf asked.

"I am sorry, Captain," Azurius countered. "I only have chitin troops. Your brother saw to that. While they are useful in battle, I still haven't taught them to offer terms."

"Do you think you can manage to teach them in the next few minutes?" Randolf asked.

"I am here, Captain," Azurius replied. "While I hold them, they will not attack until ordered. By the way, if you have a sniper drawing a bead on me, you'd best tell him to stand down. It is likely he won't succeed, but if he does, the chitin won't be under my control anymore. They will simply attack and feed."

"Your point is well taken," Randolf conceded.

"I make you the same offer I made your brother," Azurius told him. "I can make you a commander in my army with human warriors at your command."

"Did my brother accept?" Randolf asked.

"He will, if you do." Azurius gestured back to the city. "He's out there, somewhere. If you want to save him, perhaps you can make him see reason. Your people can be part of a new empire that will span the galaxy and beyond, or they can become extinct. I give you fifteen minutes to decide."

Randolf and his entourage backed from the gate and closed it.

•   •   •   •   •

Randolf turned to look at those next to him—Captain Simon, Arch Priestess Arria, Celinia, and Teresina. Others from his council gathered around him.

"Well?" he asked.

The arch priestess looked around at the terrified faces. "Everyone in the compound heard him. Some of those with families will consider his offer, if only to save them."

"After the things I've seen come from his commands, I choose death in battle."

"I agree, Captain Randolf," the arch priestess told him, "but can we expect everyone to behave as a soldier? Do we even have the right to?"

Randolf leaned against the wall.

"I suggest we have the priestesses go among the people and ask what they will do," the arch priestess offered. "Then we can make our decision."

Knowing of no other options, Randolf nodded his agreement.

Celinia and Teresina left to carry the order to the other priestesses.

"I wish Liam were here."

The arch priestess squeezed Randolf's arm. "I don't believe the Creator has deserted us completely. Have faith."

Then she left to take charge of her priestesses.

"Sir!"

Randolf looked up, and his heart leaped. The sergeant escorted his brother toward him. Forgetting protocol, Randolf rushed forward and threw his arms around him.

"Liam!"

Liam let out a gasp of pain, and Randolf quickly released him.

"Creator, Liam," Randolf apologized. "I'm sorry."

His brother managed a weak smile.

"It's okay, big brother." He put down his rifles. "I've learned to live with it."

"How did you get in?" Randolf asked.

"The sewers." He took his remaining grenades and pistol and putting them with his rifles. "Sorry not to stay in touch, but we lost our last comm in a fight with some chitin."

"Liam!"

Randolf looked up to see Celinia and Teresina approaching. Celinia looked as if she could not believe her eyes and could not find the words. Liam's expression was almost comical. Liam's expression vanished, however, as if a mask fell in place. He turned to face his brother.

"Azurius is outside?"

Randolf nodded.

Liam turned to the door.

"Liam!"

Randolf leaped forward and grabbed his brother's arm.

"Liam," Randolf began. "You're in no shape—"

Liam shook off the hold. "I'm sorry, big brother. It has to be this way. I'm the only one who can end this."

"Then let me…"

Liam placed his hand on his brother's chest.

"In other circumstances, I would have no one else at my side. The sons of Marcus and Lidia, shoulder to shoulder." Liam shook his head. "You can't protect me this time. It has to be me."

Liam turned and headed toward the door.

"You do realize that if you kill him, the chitin will not be under his control," Randolf called after him.

Liam looked over his shoulder. "Yes. I know how to deal with the chitin. You'll just need to give me time to get to Azurius's lab."

Randolf turned to the sergeant, pulled him close, giving him orders.

•   •   •   •   •

Azurius had waited long enough.

"I am waiting," he called. "Shall I send in the chitin?"

A figure emerged from the gate. Azurius stood still. Undaunted, Liam approached him until he was only ten feet away. Azurius met the young warrior's gaze and saw something different, almost a calmness.

"You've come," Azurius said.

Liam nodded but otherwise remained silent, regarding him.

"My offer still stands," Azurius told him. "Join me and become my lieutenant and heir."

They heard gasps of disbelief from the onlookers.

"Azurius," Liam began, "I'm glad I have earned your respect, but my answer remains the same."

Azurius stared at him. "Think, Liam, of what you would throw away. On my word, the chitin will kill everyone in the compound."

"You need them to defeat me?" Liam asked. "I think in the end, it comes down to you and me."

Azurius looked over his shoulders and gave a general mental command. The chitin line backed up several paces. Azurius turned back to the human.

"I agree," he replied.

•   •   •   •   •

Liam stood between Azurius and the gate of the Temple compound.

"I will give you one last chance, Finnian," Azurius pressed. "Join me and end the bloodshed."

Liam took a deep breath. When he spoke, his voice remained calm yet firm. "You speak of bloodshed. You've caused a great deal of harm, Azurius. Not just here, but across the stars. Over the centuries, our ancestors and even your own people tried to stop you. Haven't you done enough? No one, not even your long-lived race, lives forever. In the end, you must face the Ultimate Judge, but it's not too late. You can stop now and try to atone for what you've done."

Azurius's eyes widened, stunned by this speech. "I saw what you left of Licinious. I confess, you did save me the bother. However, your treatment of him doesn't sort well with these convictions."

Liam glanced over his shoulder to see his brother, Teresina, and Celinia watching. He turned back to Azurius.

"I'm not proud of what I did," he said at last. "What I did was unworthy of the ideals I'm supposed to uphold. I can only ask forgiveness from my Creator, my friends, those who had a right to expect better of me and do my best to atone for what I did. What of you, Azurius? Your debt is much greater than mine. Shouldn't you pay it back now while you still have time?"

"I see you're no better than the weaklings in the Temple." Azurius's eyes turned yellow, his lips curled in anger.

Liam shook his head. "I will do what I must, though I take no pleasure in it."

He ignited the plasma blade which Dillon had given him. Azurius did the same with his own blade. Slowly, they circled each other.

"I was wrong to think such a fool would see reason," Azurius snarled.

Liam shook his head. "You were wrong not to put your trust in something greater than yourself."

A slight smile appeared on Azurius's face. "'Lay on, MacDuff, and damn'd be him that first cries, Hold, enough.'"

Liam returned the smile despite himself. "Macbeth, act five, scene eight."

Still smiling, Azurius shook his head in regret. "Such a pity."

He stepped out of time and attacked. Liam followed and parried the first flurry of blows. To those watching, it seemed a blur. The combatants had no time to think. Strike followed parry and counterstrike. They slipped in and out of time, trying to throw off each other's timing. The burning blades of hot plasma clashed, sending out showers of sparks. The strength and extensive experience of Azurius pitted against the agility and raw skill of the young Finnian warrior.

Liam's blade grazed Azurius's sword arm. Azurius gave no sign he had even felt it bite. Liam rolled away from a decapitation strike and countered, trying to cut Azurius's legs from under him. Azurius leaped over the strike and brought his blade down with both hands. Liam caught the full force on his blade. The blow drove him to his knees. He grabbed a handful of dirt and threw it at his foe. Azurius spun aside as Liam tumbled backward and rolled to his feet. He gasped in pain as his ribs complained.

Both stepped into normal time.

"Exhilarating!" Azurius exclaimed. "Isn't it?"

Liam did not answer. Glancing about him, he realized the chitin surrounded them. He looked back at Azurius.

"You didn't really expect me to fight fair." Azurius grinned evilly.

Two chitin leaped forward. Shots rang out from the Creator's Tower. The chitin crashed to the ground.

"Actually," Liam replied, trying not to show his relief, "I didn't."

•   •   •   •   •

On top of the Creator's Tower, the sergeant watched in satisfaction as the chitin closest to the lieutenant collapsed. His two handpicked snipers continued shooting.

"Remember," he told them. "Any bug moving into that ring is a target."

"What about Azurius?"

The sergeant shook his head. "Negative. Too much of a chance of hitting the lieutenant, especially if they start moving fast."

"Understood," replied one sniper, who lined up another shot as a soldier swapped magazines for him.

Corporal Ephram and three other soldiers locked bayonet grenades onto their assault rifles.

"Start thinning the ranks further back," the sergeant ordered.

Ephram looked at the three with him. "Concentrate on the sectors I gave you. Aim for tight bunches."

They took their positions as the sergeant directed them all with a spotter's scope. Grenades began falling into the chitin, blowing apart clusters. They only had a few bayonet grenades left, and each one had to count. The sergeant hoped it would be enough.

•   •   •   •   •

Liam leaped forward, jumping out of time then back in as his blade whirled and struck in a long arc. Azurius leaped out of time, losing track of Liam's blade until the last second and only just missed getting cut in half. The blade flashed across his ribs. He howled in pain while Liam scrambled to follow through as he leaped out of time again. Azurius caught the next stroke on his blade. Liam spun his sword again, driving Azurius back. Azurius charged, ramming his shoulder into Liam's injured ribs, throwing both into normal time and disabling the rib vest.

Liam felt his ribs move as he landed on the ground. Azurius's eyes glowed black. All at once, two Azuriuses moved forward. Liam came to his feet, ignoring the pain. He caught the first's sword, but the second's blade passed through his defenses, and Liam desperately bent over backward to avoid it. He screamed in agony and almost collapsed but recovered enough to catch the first's blade solidly.

"A useful ability," Azurius commented.

Liam realized he wasn't fighting two Azuriuses, but the same one. Somehow, he fought both in reality and in the dreamscape. Liam continued to fight, trying to figure out how to fight on both battlefields.

The two parts of Azurius merged and separated. The doubling confused him as to which was the physical. Liam tried to trance down while still fighting and nearly succeeded in getting himself skewered.

He backpedaled.

"Liam! Behind you!" He heard his brother cry.

Liam just caught the swipe of a chitin's claw on his blade, severing the limb. He followed through and dispatched the insect. Then he caught the severed claw out of the air and spun, throwing it at the two images as they crossed again. As one, they threw themselves aside to avoid being hit.

That distraction gave Liam his chance. He stepped away from the chitin and tranced down. He stepped out of his body while maintaining the connection with consciousness. The doubling images felt like when he had a concussion. He froze in confusion.

Azurius and his dreamscape self had regained their balance.

"Not bad," he commented. "Unfortunately, it takes years of practice to learn how to use that ability."

Liam heard the sounds of battle around them. Randolf and the soldiers fought their way through the chitin. Again, Azurius had to allow his attention to waver, to direct the battle.

Liam grasped for a solution.

"Actually," he countered with more confidence than he felt, "I don't have to."

Liam went deeper into his trance and sped to Azurius's lab.

•   •   •   •   •

He found himself in the corridor, knowing Azurius would soon be close behind. Liam rolled around the door as he entered. Azurius came through and parried Liam's downward cut.

"How did you know?" Azurius cried.

Liam laughed. "It was obvious!"

Azurius swung at him and drove Liam back in his fury and fear. Liam stepped out of time and tried to push his empty hand into Azurius. Azurius grabbed his wrist and grappled with him.

"You won't get me with that technique a second time," he snarled, trying to bring the plasma blade around. Suddenly, some force dragged Liam and Azurius from the lab and out of the dreamscape.

•   •   •   •   •

Liam opened his eyes. Randolf had tackled Azurius. Azurius, caught off guard, went down under Randolf. Randolf forced his rifle into Azurius's neck.

"Surrender!" Randolf shouted.

Azurius's eyes glowed black, throwing Randolf backward.

"No!" Liam cried, trying to get to his feet.

Randolf rolled a way as a chitin tried to bring both claws down on him. He fired at the bug, shattering its carapace.

Liam looked around and saw only his brother had broken through the ring. The chitin had driven the other soldiers back or killed them. Liam lunged at Azurius as the chitin converged on Randolf. Randolf lost his rifle and drew his own plasma blade. He cut his way back into the ring, desperately keeping the bugs at bay.

The snipers fired as fast as they could. Too many chitin closed in.

Azurius caught Liam's sword with his blade and kicked him in the ribs. Liam felt them give as he went backward and landed, gasping in a heap, his plasma blade flying from his grasp. He tried to get to his feet and jump after it, but Azurius hit him again in the ribs and seized him by the throat.

The grip choked off Liam's cry as they both staggered into regular time.

Azurius lifted Liam by his neck and squeezed, denying him breath.

"A good fight," Azurius commented, "but I'm running out of patience. I won't make this offer again. Join me, and you can save your brother, your friends, and yourself. Otherwise, I will unleash a massacre."

Liam feebly clawed at his hand, seeing his brother, plasma blade and pistol out, trying to stay alive. Liam shook his head.

"So be it," Azurius hissed.

Liam saw stars and felt final darkness closing in on him. Celinia's face flashed before his eyes.

Then his instincts took over. He struck up with two open palms despite the pain it cost him. Azurius's grip loosened. Liam jammed both arms between his opponent's, breaking the grip. He summoned the last of his strength and brought both fists down on Azurius's collarbone. Azurius screamed as his collarbone cracked. He backhanded Liam. Liam felt a rib stick into his lung as he landed. Oddly, he felt little pain.

Azurius came forward in obvious agony. Liam tried to come to his feet to continue the fight. His strength had finally deserted him. Azurius stood over him, his plasma blade in his hand. He raised it but hesitated. Then a cry startled him. Azurius turned, and Randolf crashed into him. Azurius absorbed the blow, staying on his feet but staggering back. Randolf's hand came away, a bloody dagger in it. Liam saw shock on his brother's face, which he quickly mastered and replaced with an impassive mask. Azurius staggered and fell onto Liam, driving the rib in farther.

Liam gasped, finding it hard to breathe.

Azurius rolled back in Liam's arms. His eyes had lost their glow, and Liam found himself looking into normal eyes with violet irises. Azurius's eyes found his, and he tried to speak.

"'No,'" Randolf quoted, "''tis not so deep as a well, nor so wide as a church door; but 'tis enough...'"

"'...'twill serve,'" Azurius finished for him. "Romeo and Juliet, act three, scene one."

Azurius gasped and his eyes lost focus. Then he chuckled as if laughing at himself.

"A pity," Azurius whispered at last, a smile on his lips. "People who know Shakespeare are worth knowing."

Liam felt a deep sense of sorrow as the life left Azurius's eyes. What's more, he got a sense that Azurius had not thought himself slain by enemies but dying among friends. His eyes found his brother's face. Randolf's expression mirrored his.

The skittering of the chitin alerted him to the danger. Azurius no longer controlled them.

•   •   •   •   •

Liam sank into a trance and found himself back at the lab as Jarek taught him. He wasted no time racing down the corridor. His mind fogged with pain, but he needed to send the recall, or fate would decide whether the last to fall was chitin or human. He also had to drop the force field that kept Jarek and his fleet from landing.

Without warning, he felt himself jerked to a stop and hauled back into his body.

•   •   •   •   •

Randolf and the sergeant had lifted him and tried to carry him to safety. Other soldiers dashed past them, firing as they went. It would be a hopeless fight. Liam tried to force himself back into the trance. At last, they reached the gate to the compound. Randolf and the sergeant pivoted and fired as Celinia and Teresina came down the steps to him.

•   •   •   •   •

Liam slipped back into the trance and began following the corridor to the lab, which filled with a thickening fog. Again, he jerked to a stop.

He turned and found Celinia holding him back.

"Celinia! No!"

"Liam, please!" The fear and pain in her voice made his heart ache.

"Celinia, if I don't get down this hall, you'll all get torn to pieces," he argued. "Azurius no longer controls the chitin."

"You may not be able to return!"

"If I don't, there'll be nothing to come back to."

"Then I'll be your anchor," she insisted stubbornly.

No longer impeded, Liam raced down the corridor, Celinia at his side. They came into the lab. To Liam, it seemed full of a dense fog. Celinia's presence seemed to drive it back a little.

"We've got to lower the force field," Liam told her.

"How?"

He staggered forward, and Celinia came to his side and helped him. Then he found the breaker panel.

"Over here!" Liam staggered to the panel and opened each cover, tossed the breaker, and snapped the cover back into place. Once he threw the last one and closed the cover, the light switched from green to amber.

Liam then went to the chitin control console and touched the display. Nothing happened.

"Jarek! I have a problem!"

"We're busy, Liam." Jarek sounded like he was far away. "We've begun the landing procedure."

"The console lost power," Liam reported. "I can't recall the chitin!"

"Start throwing breakers until you get power back," Jarek replied. "I'll abort the landing."

"Celinia!" Liam ordered. "Start throwing the breakers back on!"

Celinia ran to the panel, opened the covers, and began closing the breakers.

"Nothing." Liam turned to look. "You need to close the covers to complete the circuit!" Liam told her. "One at a time!"

Celinia nodded and closed the first cover, then the second, then the third.

"Liam, Celinia!" came Randolf's voice. "The chitin are pushing us back!"

"Don't jiggle us!" Liam called. "I'm trying to send the recall."

"We may not have a choice!"

The panel lit up. It showed three hives and almost every chitin on the continent converging in one area. Liam touched each of the three hives and typed *recall* in Old Gothowan. He got an error sign. Cursing, he did it in Modern Gothowan. The dots moved back toward the hives.

"Done!" Liam called. Pain and exhaustion had almost overwhelmed him. "Celinia! Kill the breakers."

While Celinia worked, Liam felt the fog closing in. He slumped over the console. Celinia grabbed him around the shoulders and pulled. He felt like he was being jerked back by a hydraulic winch. Exhausted, he slipped into unconsciousness.

•   •   •   •   •

Liam opened his eyes to see Celinia and Teresina in healing trances. He could feel his ribs move back in place and stabilize. The wound in his lung was closed, but he still found it hard to breathe.

Celinia rocked back. "That's all we can do here."

"We have a stretcher coming!" someone called.

Liam tried to rise. "I can walk," he whispered.

Celinia gently but firmly pushed him back down.

"Not while I'm here, you can't," she told him.

"We—" he started.

"Later," she commanded.

"But—"

"I said later," she repeated.

He felt his brother and another soldier pick him up and lay him on a stretcher.

"What's that?" Someone pointed into the sky.

Three ships broke through the clouds.

"Help," Liam managed.

"Liam, we'll be in the Temple soon," Teresina promised him.

"They're here to help," he gasped. "I was trying to tell you they were coming. I should show them where to set up."

"Absolutely not," Celinia snapped. "You're in no condition. Randolf can take care of it."

Randolf shook off his shock.

"Sergeant," he called to his aide, "get the emergency council members and a squad of troops. Find out what they'll need. Tell their leader I'll be with them shortly."

"By the way, sir." The sergeant grinned at him. "It's Josephus, son of Titus and Drusilla."

Sergeant Josephus turned to obey his orders.

Randolf saw his brother motioning him to come closer. He could see a mischievous twinkle in his eye. He leaned close so Liam did not have to shout.

Liam grinned at his brother. "I think Jarek wants to find a mountain where he can set up as a wise guru. He's already mastered the part about tormenting his students."

Liam collapsed back on the stretcher, still grinning.

Randolf shook his head and headed for the landing zone.

•   •   •   •   •

Randolf entered the landing area as a flustered Sergeant Josephus spoke with a being who appeared to be of the same race as their former foe. He saw other strange creatures, as well as several people who appeared human.

"Thank you, Sergeant." Randolf patted the man's shoulder. "That will be all."

Relieved, Sergeant Josephus saluted and rejoined his men.

"Jarek, I presume." Randolf extended his hand.

"You presume correctly." Jarek took the hand. "You must be Randolf, Liam's brother."

"Liam warned me of your arrival just as you were setting down," Randolf told him. "Over the objection of his attending physician, I might add. She put her foot down when he tried to come himself."

Jarek threw back his head and laughed. Then his smiled faded, and he looked a little embarrassed and very concerned. "Forgive me. How badly was he hurt?"

Randolf shook his head. "No need to apologize. It was rather amusing to watch. I might have laughed too, had recent events not made laughing seem out of place. He needs to put the soldier aside occasionally, even to be a patient. His cracked ribs broke in the fight, puncturing a lung, and Azurius bruised his throat, trying to strangle him. His physician says he will recover."

"Physically, at least." Jarek nodded. "Emotionally, some wounds may be too deep to heal—at least quickly."

Randolf turned to face the setting sun as shadows lengthened.

"Save with love and time," Randolf said. "I've started to put faith in those recently."

Jarek stepped up beside him, watching the sunset as well. "His attending physician. Forgive my curiosity, but judging from your tone, and the fact you indicated she is female, I gather she also places a lot of faith in the healing properties of love and time, especially where Liam is concerned."

Randolf turned and smiled back at this strange creature. Despite his similarity to Azurius, Randolf felt himself warming to him.

"When we get to his bedside," Randolf told him, "we might actually hear a harp in the background."

"Ah."

•   •   •   •   •

Liam sensed the swelling around his throat fade as Celinia held her hands against the bruises.

"The bruises will fade in a few days," she told him. "I've healed the damage, but you are going to be on soft foods until tomorrow evening. I also removed the fluid from your lung. We need to monitor the seal in your lung for a few days."

He reached up and took one of her hands in his. She brought a hand around to close over it.

"After I killed Licinious, I didn't think I could face you again."

Her expression softened. "Are you asking me to be your judge?"

"I don't know." He shook his head. "Jarek spoke with me afterward. Something about him helps me to see things in a clearer light."

He looked up at her. Her green eyes held his. He felt he could lose himself forever in those eyes.

"I know now Licinious had tried to hurt me and my adoptive family since I was a baby. Then I found out he helped murder my parents—both sets. He sent out assassins to kill the emergency council, including you and Randolf."

Celinia regarded him.

"I eliminated the threat," Liam said. "I wanted to hurt him. It felt like my soul was on fire. I wanted to watch as he slowly died in agony. I..."

Liam did not finish. He wanted none of those thoughts.

"After I cut him up and pinned him to the wall, I felt a moment of triumph," he continued. "Then I felt sick. I turned, walked from the house, and returned to the sewers. Then I became ill. I hated myself. I'd just betrayed everything I'd ever believed in."

"Oh, Liam," Celinia whispered, putting her arms around him.

Liam leaned his head into hers. She gave him an encouraging squeeze.

"Jarek found me," he went on. "I guess he knew something had happened. Got me to talk. He told me the difference between Licinious and me is Licinious wouldn't feel guilty, but I would have to learn to live with what I'd done. At least, that was the general idea."

Celinia kissed him on the cheek. "I agree. You possess integrity and honor, and you have a good heart. Otherwise, you wouldn't have been in such pain. I will have you. I want to be part of your life. When I thought you had died, it felt as if something in me died, too."

Liam regarded her for a long moment.

"After the explosion of the heavy weapon, there were times it would have been easier to die. To fall in a blaze of glory. To lay aside the burden. My comrades, my family, everything the city stands for. It was all something worth dying for. Thinking of you kept me stubbornly clinging to life. You are something worth living for."

"Oh, my love," she whispered as her lips found his. Liam closed his eyes and put his arms around her, pulling her close. When they separated, she cradled his head. Comforted, the tears came.

"Celinia," he whispered, "Jorge's family. How can I face them?"

She continued to rock him gently.

"I know intellectually there was no choice," he continued. "He did his duty. I just can't help—"

"Feeling responsible," she finished for him. "Tell them he died bravely, and he loved them very much."

They heard a knock. The door opened.

"Yes," a familiar voice chuckled. "I think I hear a harp playing in the background."

Celinia disentangled herself from Liam and stood up.

Liam saw Jarek standing in the doorway, his brother behind him. Both grinned from ear to ear.

"It is a pleasure to see you in the waking world at last, Liam." Jarek reached out with both hands to grasp Liam's hand.

"Likewise," Liam replied.

"Sorry about the breakers," Jarek apologized. "I think Azurius was being economical with his resources when he built his lab this time."

Jarek turned to Celinia and offered her his hand.

"High Priestess," he greeted her with an approving look. "I am Ambassador Jarek of the Galactic Alliance."

"Celinia," she replied graciously. "So, you are the one who supported Liam during this trial?"

"It was mostly moral and intelligence support," Jarek replied. "The rest was his skill and ingenuity. You helping him at the end may have made all the difference."

Jarek turned to Liam. "I understand you did very well."

"I couldn't have done it without your help," Liam said, "and Randolf's."

Randolf laughed. "You did all the hard work. I just tidied up the loose ends."

"Azurius was a large loose end, big brother," Liam told him fondly.

Jarek took Liam's hand again and glanced back at the fiery-haired priestess. "You have found something to live for. It's time for you to live."

Liam smiled back at the strange being.

"Now, I have to meet with your arch priestess and temporary council," Jarek told him. "Thousands of little details need seeing to. If you need something to help you sleep, you might want to sit in. Otherwise—"

Liam laughed. "I'll be all right."

Jarek smiled at them and let himself out. Captain Simon waited to escort him to the meeting. Teresina slipped in the door.

"It's good to have you back, little brother."

Randof walked around the bed and took a chair next to his brother. Teresina claimed the other chair, and Celinia sat on the edge of the bed.

"Your Jarek is an interesting fellow," Randolf noted. "I rather like him."

"He's lived."

"You seem to have survived rather well, all things considered," Randolf went on. "I was wondering—"

"The details can wait," Celinia scolded. "This ordeal exhausted him physically, mentally, and emotionally."

Randolf nodded. "I'd wondered about Licinious. Forgive me, little brother. I should have had more faith in you."

Liam took his brother's hand. "I already told Celinia some of what happened. I found out Licinious had killed my birth parents and our mom and dad."

Randolf understood. He gave his brother's hand a squeeze.

"I found out from Azurius," Liam told them. "He first approached me in the dreamscape and told me how Licinious helped the chitin kill my mother and father. However, he made the mistake of mentioning it was under his orders. So, I rejected his offer to join him."

"I understand, little brother," Randolf replied. "Only too well."

"I found out about our mom and dad from him as well," Liam continued. "He confronted me after I re-entered the city. Tried to sound like he wanted to be my friend. I couldn't understand why he would think I would join him. It was obvious the traitors followed his orders."

"I saw what you did to Licinious," Randolf told him. "Personally, I'd planned to just put a bullet in his head. You didn't even know what he did to Devon and Kia. It was...bad."

"When I learned about our mother and father's murder," Liam remembered, "it felt like I was filled with flames. That feeling lasted until I cut him up. Then it felt like someone threw cold water on the fire. I felt horrible."

"We know," Teresina soothed. "We heard what you told Azurius."

"Jarek helped me," Liam finished, "and I realized something. That I would always consider him a mortal enemy seemed to escape Azurius. He didn't understand love. His nearest reference was desire. I think Councilor Licinious was the same. I hated them before, but now I pity them."

Celinia beamed at him.

Liam changed the subject. "What do we have to do to get married? I'm tired of spending time in the company of death. I'd rather spend it in the company of a beautiful woman."

Celinia put her hand to her mouth, happy tears coming to her eyes. Teresina whooped and seized her friend in a hug.

"You took the words out of my mouth, little brother," Randolf seconded.

Teresina turned to look at him, her shocked expression becoming a smile of joy.

"It's time to live, beloved," Randolf reached over the bed to take her hand.

CHAPTER 10

They heard a knock on the door. Before Liam could respond, it opened, and a young woman wearing a strange uniform entered. Long, dark, curly hair coiled into an official bun and gray eyes were the first thing he noticed. The woman was slim and a head shorter than everyone in the room save Liam, and she wore a side arm similar to their own pistols.

"Oh." She paused, noticing Liam was not alone. "Excuse me, but I would be looking for Liam, foster son of Marcus and Lidia."

"That's me," Liam replied, intrigued by the accent, so similar to the accent of his birth parents.

Her face lit up with a smile of delight. *"Dia dhuit*, Liam! I'm your cousin Gráinne."

Liam gave a start. "Cousin?"

"Aye."

"What was that?" Teresina asked. "That greeting?"

"Dia dhuit?" Gráinne repeated with a smile. "It means 'God Be With You' in our language."

Celinia scrambled out of the way so Gráinne could throw her arms around her cousin. She pulled back and looked at him.

"My mum and yours were sisters," she told him. "When Jarek made a call for volunteers, I raised my hand. Especially when I heard a cousin was in trouble."

She suddenly remembered they were not alone. "I'm sorry. I've interrupted. Captain Gráinne O'Connor, Alpha Company, First Battalion of the Thirty-Third Finnian Shock Regiment."

Liam found his voice at last. "This is Captain Randolf, son of Marcus and Lidia. He's been in charge since our leadership was all but decimated, and my foster brother. I usually call him *big brother*. The lady next to him is Priestess Teresina, his fiancée."

"Congrats to ye both." Gráinne gave both a hug and a peck on the cheek.

"This is High Priestess Celinia," Liam told her as Celinia reclaimed her seat on the bed. "My fiancée."

Gráinne froze in surprise for a moment, then her smile returned. She embraced the embarrassed Celinia like she'd found a new cousin. "Oh, fair play to you. Welcome to the family."

Randolf broke out of his shock and ran to grab another chair.

"I must say," Randolf stammered, "I'm happy to meet a member of Liam's family."

"More would have come," Gráinne replied with a twinkle in her eyes, "but we felt we should start slowly, and get ye use to one of us first, before unleashing the entire clan on ye."

Liam blinked. "Clan?"

"You are part of two enormous families, cousin." She took her seat. "The O'Connors and the McGregors, your *daidi's* family."

Liam sighed. "I didn't know. My mom and dad died when I was barely two years old."

Gráinne's smile softened. "Well, it's two whole families who will want to be seeing you, Liam. Especially when they hear you killed Azurius. I had hoped for that pleasure myself. Ah well, at least it was someone with O'Connor blood."

"Actually, Randolf killed Azurius," Liam corrected. "I just got in the way of his body blow."

"You're too modest, little brother," Randolf scolded. "Without Liam, I would never have had the chance."

"Adoptive family then." Gráinne laughed. "Mum, however, is going to be furious with you."

Liam gave a start. "Oh?"

"Here you are," Gráinne scolded, "marrying this lovely lass, and Mum can't plan the wedding. It's a tradition. Your mum would usually plan it, but since she can't, it would have fallen to her sister. I think the only way she's going to forgive you is if ye have yer honeymoon on our home planet, *Éire Nua*, which the rest of the Milky Way calls 'New Ireland.'"

Liam glanced at Celinia, who looked overwhelmed.

"If my cousin is any example," Liam advised, "I don't think we want two whole Finnian clans mad at us."

Celinia shook her head and smiled. "We would be delighted and honored."

Gráinne cocked her head at Randolf. "The invitation goes for you as well, Foster Cousin. We'd be happy to have the four of ye."

Randolf looked at Teresina. She smiled and nodded.

"Count us in," Randolf agreed.

"Jarek didn't say one of my cousins was with him."

Gráinne laughed. "That one likes to surprise people."

She looked back at Randolf with a more official tone. "I do need to tell you the chitin are within twenty-four hours of completing the recall to their hives. Then we will start sterilizing the hives. Afterward, we'll track down any other hives on the planet. The chitin will finally be extinct."

"That's good news, Captain," Randolf agreed, "and good riddance. Over time, we can expand to the other cities."

"Also, after talking to your sergeant," she told him, "I put your Military Center under guard. My company's going to discourage looters or the curious until you can put a team together to sort through it. We will refer any of your soldiers to you until we get your decision. You may have things there ye'll want, and we don't want them damaged or ruined. I can take you to my colonel when you're ready. After what your people have gone through, ye need a rest. We're putting people in place to maintain order and help with the cleanup until ye're back on yer feet."

"Thank you," Randolf told her. "When I'm done here, I'll talk to him. I don't want our citizens to think it's an invasion."

Gráinne laughed again. "I promise we'll be gentle. Ye folk have been through enough. Our technical people are looking into yer power supply. We're using one of our ship's reactors to replace it until it's fixed."

"We couldn't have hoped for more," Randolf said. "I just had a thought. It occurs to me we need guards around the intercity portals. We had some people trying to restore them when the chitin attacked. It will take time to collect their remains." His voice broke, and Liam touched his hand.

Gráinne saw the flash of pain and became serious. "I'll take care of that."

She took out an earpiece and called her company. She spoke in a strange language, in crisp commands. Then she gave a curt nod and closed her link.

"Done," she announced.

"Well," Gráinne regained her cheerful demeanor. "I think I've dominated the conversation long enough. I want to hear what's been happening here."

Randolf and Liam gave her a brief account of the struggle to defend the city and their roles in it. Gráinne listened with rapt attention, nodding grimly. She smiled as Randolf tried to give her a blow-by-blow description of his brother's final battle with Azurius.

When they finished, she placed her hand on Randolf's shoulder. "Since you've become another sad, wee orphan in this war, Captain," she told him, "I want you to remember that to both the O'Connor and McGregor clans, your family. Finnian clans look after their own," she finished fiercely.

"Liam has had a rough time, and it is getting late," Celinia warned. "Now, I want him to rest."

"Call me if you need anything, Liam," Gráinne called as Celinia ushered everyone out of the room.

Celinia closed the door and returned to the bed. She pulled the blankets around Liam, kissed him, then placed a finger between his eyes.

"Sleep, my love," she whispered, and he felt himself drift off.

• • • • •

The next day, still recovering in the infirmary, Liam dozed on and off. His eyes opened. Someone had knocked on the door.

"Come in," he called as he pulled himself into a sitting position.

Sharina came in with Justin and Sylvia, who looked far too subdued. He wanted to weep on seeing them.

"Sharina," he whispered. "I'm so sorry."

Tears came to Sharina's eyes. She took a seat and lifted her children onto her lap. They clung to her as if they feared to lose her too. He was certain they hated him.

After a long, uncomfortable silence, she asked, "How did he die?"

"The traitors sabotaged our heavy weapon so it would explode," Liam explained. "Jorge discovered the tampering. When the chitin overran us, he detonated it intentionally."

Sharina closed her eyes, fought back her tears, and regained control.

"How did you survive?" she asked, her voice cracking.

Liam closed his eyes. "If you are asking what saved me, the blast threw me into the dead portal service room, knocking me out and cracking my ribs. If you're asking why I survived the battle when he died, I've been asking myself that question ever since."

He opened his eyes and looked at Sharina.

Little Sylvia slid off her mother's lap, climbed onto his bed, and took his hand.

"I know you didn't want Daddy to die, Uncle Liam," she whispered. "Before he left, Daddy told us if he couldn't come back anymore, you'd look after us."

Justin looked at him. "Will you teach me to be a soldier, just like Daddy?"

"I would be honored," Liam told him.

"Justin," Sharina whispered as she lifted him off her lap. She stood, came, sat on the end of the bed, and took Liam's hand.

"Oh, Liam," she cried. "I wanted to blame you because he died, and you came back. I even guessed you had to give him an order you knew he wouldn't survive. No! Don't tell me. I don't want to know. He told me it was the price a leader paid." She let the tears flow freely now. "I know it wasn't your fault. I've stopped blaming you, and the children never blamed you. Please, stop blaming yourself."

He reached out and put his arms around her, his own tears flowing. "I promised I would do what I could for you. If you need anything, just ask."

"An aunt?" Sylvia asked hopefully.

Liam managed a smile. "For you, love, of course. She's already said yes. Further, I've just met someone else you can call aunt."

It was worth it to watch the little girl's face brighten.

•   •   •   •   •

A few days later, Liam sat on the edge of the bed with Celinia's hands over his ribs. At last, she stood back.

"Okay, Liam, I know you've been eager to get out of here. You're ready to go."

Liam smiled, stood up, and pulled on the tunic of his field uniform. Then he caught her up in a hug and kissed her. Her arms went around him and held him tight. Liam heard the door and opened his eyes. Randolf stood in the doorway, grinning at him. With a sigh, he broke the kiss.

"I love you," he whispered.

She smiled and caressed his cheek. "You're going into the city?"

Liam looked around and saw someone had brought his long-suffering rucksack.

"Some people I want to visit." Liam shouldered the beat-up rucksack. "I also want to show my cousin the sights, such as they are."

"Smashed buildings and ruins." Celinia shook her head. "Something to tell the folks about."

"Hey!" Randolf countered with a laugh. "Which makes it historic. He can show her where he was and tell her what he did."

"I wish I could go with you," Celinia told them, "but I have patients. Your cousin is certainly interesting. When I told her about the insane things you did with those broken ribs, she laughed and said, 'He's not mad. He's an O'Connor. Though some folks say it amounts to the same thing.'"

"We better go find her," Liam advised.

Celinia walked down the corridor with them.

"I'll bet she's with Jorge's family," Celinia guessed.

Randolf looked up.

"Sharina is having trouble coping," Celinia explained. "I'm trying to help her. The children are a big support to her."

"I told Gráinne about them," Liam put in. "You know her. When I suggested that, since I'm their adopted uncle, maybe she would be their aunt, there was no stopping her."

"She shocked Sharina at first," Celinia added, "but she has been a big help with Justin and Sylvia. They took to her immediately."

They found them in the lounge area. Gráinne sat in a chair with the children at her feet. The children sat in rapt attention as Gráinne spun a fantastic tale for them. They heard a rhythm and cadence to the telling. Even Sharina listened attentively. "'Cú Chulainn shall be your name, the Hound of Culann,' said the druid Cathbad."

Gráinne's voice changed as she voiced another character. "'I like that name!' replied young Setanta."

"I feel bad for the hound," Justin said.

"Aye," replied Gráinne. "So did Setanta. Now, I think yer turn has come with yon high priestess."

The children's faces lit up. "Uncle Liam!" They raced to him and threw their arms around him.

Sharina sighed. "I lost a husband and have gained a family." Tears came to her eyes, and she tried to stop them.

Gráinne put an arm around her shoulder. "It isn't an easy thing, even for the likes of the Finnian. Time, my dear, will be what it takes. It won't lessen the burden, but you'll find it becomes easier to carry."

Sharina nodded and gathered the children. Celinia touched her shoulder. Then she looked back at the Finnian woman and mouthed, "Thank you."

Gráinne stepped between Liam and Randolf. "The wee ones are being strong for their mum, and she's trying to be strong for them."

"Love and time," Randolf mused. "Something we all need."

They watched until Celinia took them into a private room.

"So," Gráinne asked, "will the two of ye be showing me around?"

"I'd like to stop at the house first," Randolf requested. "Neither of us has been back there since Mother and Father died. At first, there was the battle. With Liam confined to the Temple, and I didn't want to face it without him."

"Lead on then," Gráinne said.

•   •   •   •   •

Approaching their house, Liam saw his brother pause, a look of pain on his face. He was the one who had found their parents. He put a hand on Randolf's shoulder. Then Liam went ahead of them and opened the door for them.

Liam stopped short upon seeing the blood on the floor of the foyer.

Randolf and Gráinne came up behind him. "The assassin killed him here, opening the door. I found Mom in the hall."

Liam felt the lump in his throat. Now, they had time to grieve.

Gráinne looked around, quiet for a change. She stopped at a family picture taken when Randolf and Liam were still boys. She studied the faces of Marcus and Lidia.

Liam and Randolf came to stand beside her.

"I was just thanking them on behalf of the O'Connor clan," she explained. "I promised them we'd return the favor."

She turned and hugged them both. The three stood quietly.

Gráinne pushed back a little. "I know the wounds are still raw. Do ye want me to have a crew come and clean this mess up for ye?"

Liam and Randolf exchanged sad smiles and nodded. Then they left the house and walked into the city.

"The battle damaged a lot of the transports," Randolf observed. "Some came back online when you hooked into our power."

"We brought some military transports," Gráinne informed them, "and some atmospheric craft."

"We can show you more if we walk," Liam suggested.

Walking through one residential district, they noticed signs the city was coming back to life. Children played outside, under watchful eyes. Those who had not made it to the Temple emerged from hiding.

"It must have been quite the city," Gráinne observed. "Amazing that chitin have hemmed ye in for nearly thirty years."

"With them gone," Randolf said, "we can bring the other cities and towns to life."

"Well," Gráinne informed them, "there is one thing we can do for ye."

They looked at her.

"Someone's got to teach ye how to throw a party."

"Have you been in many battles, Gráinne?" Liam asked.

"Over ten different engagements across the galaxy," she told him. "I know it sounds boastful, but the Thirty-Third is usually the spearhead with Alpha Company the tip of the spear. We drop from orbit, behind enemy lines, usually ahead of a major invasion."

"An entire race used as shock troops?" Randolf asked incredulously.

Gráinne laughed. "Hardly. We provide two other shock regiments and six regular corps. The Old Terran people have several special operations forces they provide, including their marines. Almost up to our standards, but they weren't bred for it. Jarek's folk, the Gothowans, have similar forces, as do other species in the Alliance. The only way they match our fame is by being more venerable."

They entered the Industrial District. Liam pointed to the tall building across the way.

"It's the tallest building in the city, aside from the Temple," Liam told her. "Tower 99. When I got back to the city, I met Azurius up there. I found out about his telekinesis—the hard way."

"Where were you?" Gráinne asked.

"The roof," Liam replied. "I had to get my bearings."

"I'm glad he didn't throw you off the top," Gráinne said.

"Likewise," Liam answered.

Then they came to the burned-out Green Griffin.

"Used to love that place," Liam told her sadly. "I hid out there after my first physical encounter with Azurius."

The owner peered into the doorway of the burned-out building as they approached.

Liam came up behind him. "Stu?"

"Oh, hi. I wish I had something to offer you, but well..." Stuart waved his hand at the burned-out structure.

"I'm afraid this mess was my fault, Stu," Liam apologized. "I used the Green Griffin as a base when I first came into the city. Azurius and the chitin found me. What you see is the result."

Stuart's eyes went wide, and he glanced back into the building. "That fight must have been a battle to behold. I wish I could have seen it."

Gráinne gave Liam a playful poke. "Shame on you, Cousin. Wrecking a bar that way."

"The chitin weren't stopping by for a drink."

He looked back at Stuart. "I don't have much to tell. I opened the gas and rigged a couple of grenades to explode when the chitin entered the kitchen. Then I ran."

"We can rebuild buildings. I'd rather lose the building than lose a customer. When I rebuild, I'll name a drink after you."

"I wanted to make amends," Liam persisted, "to you and your tenants."

"The Temple and the Galactic Alliance will compensate ye," Gráinne added. "You and the tenants. Get us a list of what ye lost, and we'll do the rest."

"I'll spread the word to my tenants," Stuart promised. "Thank you. To be honest, now that the Alliance has gotten rid of the chitin, I've heard rumors of plans to open the abandoned cities again. I'm thinking of relocating to South Corinth."

"Let me know," Liam said. "Maybe I can talk my fiancée into relocating there."

Then Liam reached into his beat-up rucksack. "I saved something, though."

He pulled out the bottle of New Olympia whiskey. It had survived with him through hell and back.

Stuart laughed. "Keep it. Consider it a wedding present. I'm looking forward to some new liquors and brews from across the galaxy."

They all laughed.

"I'll see what we can do for you," Gráinne said, "and if any glasses survived this conflagration, I'd like to sample this local brew."

Stuart grinned and reached for a small box at his feet.

"My portable bar," he explained. "The only other thing that survived."

He opened the box and pulled out four small glasses. He took the bottle and poured some into each glass.

"To victory," Stuart declared.

"Victory!"

They downed their glasses.

"Not bad." Gráinne handed her glass back to Stuart.

"You know," Randolf mused, "we still need a cook and bartender for our wedding reception."

Stuart beamed. "It would be an honor."

"Great," Randolf replied. "That's one thing ticked off the list."

"We've got other people to talk to, Stu," Liam told him.

"I'll be in touch," Stuart promised.

After stepping back into the street, Randolf turned to his two companions.

"You're going farther?" he asked.

"I want to talk to Peter," Liam told him. "Another mess to apologize for."

Randolf smiled. "The interim council is meeting shortly, and I've been told to be there."

"I understand." Liam put the bottle back into the rucksack and handed it to Randolf. "Do me a favor. Drop my rucksack off at the house. We may want another toast."

"Sure, little brother." Randolf smiled. "Check and see if Peter will be open tonight. If he is, we'll have dinner there."

Liam placed a hand on his brother's shoulder. Randolf returned the gesture.

"Okay, Liam," Randolf said. "See you soon."

Liam felt his cousin step up beside him.

"Seeing the two of ye together," Gráinne observed, "I understand what you mean about really being brothers."

Liam glanced at her. "He's always been there for me when I needed him."

"As it should be."

Liam and Gráinne walked back across the city. Passing the Military Center, he saw Ephram and Dillon going in and waved to them. The two smiled and waved back but did not have time to talk.

"They found me at the place where we're going," Liam told her, "and stood beside me until the time came to face Azurius. I guessed I should fight him on my own."

"Aye." She looked at them. "Perhaps you'd be introducing me to them later."

Liam laughed. "Deciding if you want to carry one off?"

"Only one?" Gráinne laughed. "Seriously though, your soldiers don't seem to be used to girls who are soldiers."

"I noticed," Liam agreed. "I'd been wondering."

"Blame the Utopian Founders," Gráinne told him. "They didn't hold with girls doing certain things like fighting in wars. Rather than merely forbid it, they bred their girls so it would hold no interest for them."

"The Finnian's founders thought differently?"

"Aye." Gráinne's face darkened. "However, they also thought we'd attack Terra for them and kill a bunch of innocent people. They thought wrong."

Liam realized there was more to the story but decided not to press it.

"This is the Theater District," he announced as they crossed out of the Military District. "Mom and Dad used to take us here as boys. Puppet shows, art, street performers. I used to love watching the shows. I could forget how different I was."

"It canna've been easy," Gráinne observed, "but you had a family who loved you and have since earned your place. Not only here, but any place in the galaxy you care to call home."

Liam smiled at her.

"We're going to a bistro my family often went to," Liam told her. "I hid there after the chitin drove me from the Griffin."

"Well, I hope you left this one standing."

"Yes," Liam replied, "but I didn't have time to get rid of the bodies."

"Ah. We have a group working on that problem."

Rounding the corner, Liam and Gráinne saw the owner, Peter, sweeping up out front. Other members of his staff were visible through the newly replaced windows.

"Hi, Peter," Liam called.

"Liam," Peter greeted him. "How's the life of a hero treating you?"

Liam shrugged. "I still feel like me. I want to introduce you to my cousin, Gráinne."

"Wow!" Peter exclaimed, extending one hand from his broom. Gráinne gave him a hearty handshake. "Pleased to meet you."

"Likewise," Gráinne replied.

"I wanted to apologize for the mess and the bodies," Liam said.

Peter's eyes widened. "Wow! I guess those guys were Licinious's men. The traitors in the kitchen weren't too bad. I wish you hadn't incinerated two of them. Getting the smell of charred flesh out of the place was wretched."

"I truly apologize," Liam told him. "I'll try to come up with something else next time I'm outnumbered ten to one in here."

Peter shook his head. "You're developing a sense of humor. At least, I hope you are. I'll have to charge you extra if you're going to have running battles in my place."

"Perhaps I can direct some foreign coin your way," Gráinne offered.

"Can't hurt," Peter replied.

"At least you don't have to rebuild from the ground up like Stu," Liam pointed out.

"That was you too?" Peter asked. "In all seriousness, it sounds like you were in the thick of it. How are your ribs?"

"Much better," Liam replied. "You have a bottle of NeoConnacht 2950 in the cold room. I opened it when I was hiding here. I found it quite enjoyable, and I wondered if I could buy it."

"You were taking liberties, weren't you?" Peter accused with a laugh. "I think I can part with it. After all you went through, you've earned it. I'm glad you took the time to develop a palate."

"I'll say!" Gráinne exclaimed. "You picked a venerable one. The 2950 was a vintage year. It's an O'Connor-clan wine. Likely the last to arrive before the force field appeared. I can have someone bring you some more, Peter, when they're in the neighborhood."

"That would be great." Peter smiled in gratitude.

"Randolf wanted to know if you'd be open for business soon," Liam probed.

"Tonight, I hope." Peter crossed his fingers.

"Can you fit five more, then?"

"Certainly." Peter took his hand. "No more hiding at the outposts."

"No more need," Liam replied. "Though, I'm thinking about relocating to South Corinth."

"Well, visit us—now and again."

Liam smiled, realizing he had always had friends. "Count on it. We'll be seeing you tonight, then."

"We'll have a table ready and the bottle of wine." Peter waved as they left.

They left the Bistro and began walking back toward the Temple.

"How long will you be on planet?" Liam asked.

"For as long as we're needed," Gráinne replied. "Though, when you take your honeymoon, I'd like to tag along and introduce you."

"Two families. Life is going to get interesting."

"Aye, that," she replied.

They reentered the Military District. On a whim, Liam veered toward the Center.

"Lieutenant!" someone called. A man Liam recognized from Grizzly sector, snapped to attention, and gave a salute which Liam returned.

"I wanted to see Corporal Ephram and Private Dillon."

"They're inside, sir." The man glanced at a captain.

The captain nodded.

Liam entered, his cousin in tow.

"Lieutenant," Captain Simon greeted him warmly.

"It's good to see you, Captain. This is my cousin, Captain Gráinne O'Connor."

Gráinne smiled at him.

"I saw Corporal Ephram and Private Dillon coming in earlier," Liam went on. "I haven't seen them since we first got back to the Temple."

He spotted his teammates in the reception area, directing the removal of the debris.

"It's Sergeant Ephram and Corporal Dillon now," Captain Simon informed him. "I think we can spare them for a few minutes."

"Thank you, sir."

Liam and his cousin picked their way over to the two men.

"Lieutenant!" Corporal Dillon called, giving them one of his comic grins.

The two men came over to Liam.

"Well," Liam beamed, "look at you two. Promotions."

"I suspect there'll be one for you as well, sir," Ephram replied.

"When you figure out what you're doing next, we'd like to join you."

"We did work well together." Liam smiled as he turned to his cousin. "Gentlemen, let me introduce my cousin, Captain Gráinne O'Connor, commander of Alpha Company, First Battalion, Thirty-Third Finnian Shock Regiment."

"I'm pleased to meet ye both," Gráinne said. "The way my cousin tells it, ye two are heroes in yer own right."

Dillon smiled at her. "The lieutenant exaggerates."

Ephram looked a little tongue-tied. Gráinne cocked an eyebrow at him.

"Forgive me, ma'am," he stammered, trying to recover. "I'm just not used to seeing ladies in uniform."

She graced him with her most infectious smile. Dillon looked at Liam and winked.

"We're having dinner at Peter's Bistro," Liam offered. "Would you like to join us?"

"Oh," Dillon replied, waving his hand, "my wife is still complaining about how long I was gone. I promised her a quiet night at home. Ephram's free though."

Ephram blinked. "I am?"

"You are," Dillon replied.

"I look forward to it," Gráinne said.

Liam hid a smile, and Ephram blushed.

·　　·　　·　　·　　·

Just before midnight, they approached the front door of their house. Liam produced a key and opened the door.

"Great night."

Liam smiled at Randolf. They'd just seen their fiancées back to the Temple.

"I thought giving Teresina Mom's pendant was nice," Liam observed. "Thanks for remembering Dad recovered some of my mom's things. That gold knot-work necklace nearly stole the show."

"I had a vague memory of Dad bringing it home, and Mom putting it away," Randolf explained. "When I planned to give the pendant to Teresina tonight, I felt bad you had nothing to give Celinia. It just popped into my head. I found it in Mom's jewelry box."

"The smiles on their faces were worth it."

Randolf laughed. "Ephram floated through the evening. Your cousin had him completely entranced. Out of uniform, she is surprisingly feminine and quite pretty."

"Maybe Aunt Máire can plan a wedding after all."

"Except," Randolf pointed out, "the tradition is for the male's mother to do it."

"Ephram's mom would just leave it to the priestesses." Liam shrugged. "They would have to compromise."

Then he laughed to himself.

"What's so funny?" Randolf asked.

"More ironic than funny. I'm just thinking of how this all started. A typical detail to guard the outposts, and you dating a new girlfriend."

Randolf caught the irony of it. "Me trying to lure you into having fun, too."

"Tragedy," Liam mused as his smile faded, "grief, and joy." He looked up at his big brother. "Randolf, if you have nothing pressing tomorrow, I'd like to visit the sectors, the ruins, anyway."

"Want to find your sniper rifle?"

Liam shook his head. "I found it—what the explosion left of it. I wanted to see them, and see if I can find Swift Hunter."

Randolf fell silent, still not sure he believed that part of the story.

"It may be a chance to try out one of those atmospheric craft our friends brought," Liam suggested, trying to tempt him.

"Okay," Randolf replied with a laugh. "I'm itching to try one of those things, too."

•   •   •   •   •

Liam and Randolf got off to an early start the next morning and made their way to the air station in the city's south near the mining district. Gráinne, ever curious to explore this new chapter in family history, flew with them. The atmospheric craft they planned to use, the *Boobrie*, proved to be a tilt and transverse rotor utility vehicle.

Gráinne wore armor this time. Two soldiers waited with her. When they got closer, Liam noticed their weapons.

"I've seen those before."

Randolf looked at him quizzically.

"It's the same kind of assault rifle we took off of Licinious's assassins," Liam explained.

Gráinne held her rifle up. "Finnian developed these over four decades ago. They're more flexible than what we used before.

Though, we've made some modifications since. Finnian now favor the bullpup style rifle."

Liam took it and examined it. "I see some subtle differences. Azurius must have gotten hold of a prototype and had the traitors revise the design to use our type of ammunition and power packs."

Gráinne nodded as she took her weapon back. "Makes sense. Humans favor the projectile weapons over energy weapons for ground combat. I suspect he wanted something he could get ammunition for."

"I also found something called sticky grenades."

"Standard for both sides," Gráinne told them. "Azurius wanted what human troops he did have to have an edge."

Liam nodded.

"So where to first?" Gráinne asked.

"Taho sector is to the west," Randolf directed. "Thirty-two kilometers."

Gráinne spoke into her comm as they climbed aboard. The pilot gave a general response as the *Boobrie* lifted off and turned gracefully westward.

•   •   •   •   •

The flight proved a lot faster than walking but not as fast as using the now dead portals. Still, both Liam and Randolf acted like excited children on their first carnival ride. Soon, they reached Taho sector. Liam stared into the crater where his outpost had been.

Randolf sucked in his breath. "It's one thing to hear about it, little brother, but to see it..."

Liam nodded. Gráinne's "gift of the gab" failed her. She spoke briefly into her comm, and the *Boobrie* circled and landed on the flat plain in front of the crater.

"*Cruthaitheoir*, Liam," Gráinne whispered as she climbed out. "You survived in the center of that destruction?"

"When the weapon blew," he explained, "I was up against the portal. The explosion shoved me into the maintenance room. I got knocked out. When I woke up, I had three cracked ribs."

Liam remembered the men who'd died when he'd somehow lived. Tears came to his eyes.

"Liam?" Randolf put a hand on his shoulder. "I think they'd be proud of you."

"*Síochán agat*, Liam." Gráinne put her arm around him. "You lived so you could avenge them."

Liam looked quizzically at her.

"It means 'be at peace' in our native tongue."

Liam briefly leaned his head against hers.

"What was that you said before?" Randolf asked.

"*Cruthaitheoir?*" Gráinne replied. "It's 'Creator' in Finnian."

"We need a guard here to keep the scavengers away until we can recover what remains we can."

"Archer as well," Randolf added.

"Can we go to Boulder sector?" Liam asked.

"Of course, Cousin."

"It's on the other side of the city," Randolf told her.

Gráinne smiled. "For my cousin, I don't mind."

They climbed aboard as Gráinne ordered the pilot to lift off and gave him his vector.

•   •   •   •   •

Within a half hour, the *Boobrie* circled the last sector Liam had stayed at before returning to the city. After disembarking, Liam led them to the locker room where he'd sheltered.

"Looks cozy," Gráinne commented.

Liam looked out over the plains toward the forest, searching. He wondered if Swift Hunter knew he wanted to see him. He concentrated for a few moments, trying to contact his friend telepathically.

Randolf looked at him. "Are you sure you weren't imagining it?"

Gráinne gave Randolf a puzzled look.

"He claims he spoke to a creature we call a bear-lizard."

"Everything else I told you was right," Liam countered.

"Even you admitted you may have been a little out of it," Randolf reminded him.

Liam sighed. "Look, if we find him, and he eats us, we'll know I was imagining things."

He looked back out over the plains. A large bear-lizard ambled out of the bush. Liam sent a quick mind touch and knew this was Swift Hunter.

He raised a hand in greeting. Swift Hunter reared onto his hind feet and raised a paw. Then he dropped to all fours and came forward. Liam ran out to meet him.

"*Cruthaitheoir*," Gráinne whispered under her breath, amazed at the size of the creature.

"Liam, wait!" Randolf strode after him, Gráinne right behind him, freeing her rifle.

Greetings, Liam. The bear-lizard enfolded his friend in a bear hug that Liam happily returned.

Randolf and Gráinne stopped, having heard the greeting as well. Randolf's mouth fell open in shock.

You brought friends?

"Swift Hunter. This is my brother, Randolf, and my cousin Gráinne. Randolf, Gráinne, this is Swift Hunter."

Randolf extended his hand, then wondered what he was doing.

Greetings, Liam's brother in all save blood, Swift Hunter said in an amused tone. He lifted a paw and took Randolf's hand in a firm but not crushing handshake. *It is wise to be cautious.*

He then turned to Gráinne. *Greetings to you as well, sister's daughter of Liam's mother.*

"*Dia dhuit*, Swift Hunter," she replied, having recovered from her shock, and lowered her weapon.

"Good to meet you, Swift Hunter," Randolf began, still trying to recover his wits. "Liam wanted me to confirm bear-lizards are more than animals and are potential friends."

Then Randolf looked embarrassed. "That didn't come out the way I wanted, did it?"

Swift Hunter threw back his head and let out a roar that sounded like a belly laugh.

As the Great Shaman, Storm Cloud, once told me, new situations require new thinking. Missteps are to be expected.

"Is it just me," Liam asked, "or are your speech patterns getting less awkward?"

Swift Hunter shrugged. *This kind of speech can be evolutionary. With time, I may even pick up your idioms. Whether I will understand them is another matter.*

"So, talking this way will get easier with time," Randolf returned sheepishly.

Most things do.

Randolf looked gravely at his brother's friend. "Also, I want to thank you, Swift Hunter. You saved my brother's life."

It was fortunate opportunity. Chance to make friend.

"We have to introduce you to Jarek." Gráinne chuckled. "You sound just like him."

I look forward to it, Swift Hunter replied. *You won the fight in the city? Big bugs gone, and that is good.*

"We killed the bugs' master," Liam informed him, now serious. "I also killed several traitors. Jarek and the Alliance have removed the hives. However, that wasn't before many people and friends died. Our mother and father among them."

Swift Hunter bowed his head. *I grieve with you both. At least it's done.*

"Swift Hunter," Liam pressed on, "we're both getting married soon. I wondered if you and your mate would honor us by being guests at our wedding."

Randolf cast Liam a sharp look. Swift Hunter shook his head.

I believe that would be unwise. Those kinds of ceremonies are full of customs. Both our people would be uncomfortable. I am honored at your request, Liam, but considering the differences between us, I think your people would agree we proceed with less haste.

"I'm afraid I must agree with Swift Hunter, Liam," Gráinne put in. "It is a wonderful gesture, but humans and bear-lizards need to get better acquainted with each other before they mix in large social occasions."

Swift Hunter nodded. *Well put.*

"I do have an idea, though," Liam persisted. "After the wedding, why don't we have a picnic out here with Teresina and Celinia? If you can get free, Gráinne, maybe you and Ephram can come. We can show Swift Hunter and his mate the trivideo of the wedding and explain the customs to him."

Swift Hunter nodded. *I would like that. Great Heart may understand things I do not or find words to explain things better.*

Randolf looked dubious, but Liam felt intrigued. "Teresina and Celinia may be uncomfortable at first, but I'm sure they'll overcome their unease quickly and get on with Great Heart."

Swift Hunter looked amused. *I suspect that's what concerns Randolf.*

Liam laughed as he patted his brother's shoulder. Gráinne chuckled, and Swift Hunter let loose a roaring belly laugh. Randolf laughed sheepishly. He realized their lives were about to get very interesting indeed.

Swift Hunter escorted them back to the *Boobrie.*

"Best get back, my friend," Gráinne warned him. "The fans kick up a windstorm when they take off. I don't want you hit by flying debris."

After hugging each, Swift Hunter retreated to a safe distance and raised his paw in farewell as the *Boobrie* took off. They circled the bear-lizard once and headed back to the city.

"I think that is enough for today," Randolf decided.

"Aye, that," Gráinne agreed. "Ye are getting married tomorrow. Yon priestesses may seem peaceful enough, but if ye fall on yer noses during the wedding, I'm fairly certain Celinia will have my hide off in one piece. I don't even want to think about yer fate."

Soon the city came into view, and the *Boobrie* turned to land in an elegant arc.

"I have a few things to do. I want ye two to discharge any duties ye need to see to, then rest."

Liam and Randolf looked at each other and snapped her a crisp salute.

Gráinne laughed and returned it. "Now go, off with ye."

Liam and Randolf gave her hugs and then returned home.

• • • • •

Liam pulled at his dress uniform as he looked in the mirror at his new captain's insignia. He, Randolf, and the best men waited in an ancillary room off the main sanctuary of the Temple.

"Stop fidgeting," Randolf snapped. Randolf's own uniform sported shiny new major's insignia.

"Ah," Jarek mused, "pre-wedding nerves. I remember them well. Getting married doesn't hurt all that much, gentlemen."

Randolf grimaced, glancing again at the script for the service for the hundredth time. "Stop trying to be funny."

Jarek only smiled. "I'm just remembering. My dear wife died in the Rebellion."

Randolf looked stricken. "I'm sorry, Jarek. I know I should be more gracious."

"There's nothing to forgive," Jarek assured him. "The young don't always appreciate the gift of experience, especially when they're on edge. Like I said, I can remember my own pre-joining jitters. It's one reason many sentient species created what you call *maids* or *matrons of honor* and best men. To keep the bride or groom from making a last-minute break for it."

Liam, Randolf, and Josephus laughed. Master Sergeant Josephus had agreed to be Randolf's best man. However, he had stubbornly refused promotion to officer status, even though many argued he had earned it. Jarek informed them many militaries had various grades of sergeant. In the end, he accepted promotion to the newly created rank of master sergeant, saying his real ability was looking after the officers.

"Well," Randolf teased, "at least for Teresina, all the eyes will be on her. People are going to be watching you dance with your eyes peeking over Celinia's shoulder." He poked Liam playfully.

"Gentlemen," Jarek spoke serenely. "Both brides are sufficiently beautiful. You could be chitin for all anyone cares."

"Try not to embarrass those who are watching in absence," Sergeant Josephus admonished.

Randolf and Liam paused, suddenly serious, thinking about those who had died.

Then the music in the Temple changed.

"Gentlemen," Jarek told them. "The time has come to bid the life of a footloose bachelor goodbye. Take it from one much older and wiser than you. Pain does await you, but so does great joy."

They formed up and slow marched into the Temple of the Creator—the brothers, side by side, the best men following. Entering the nave, they saw the brides at the altar as they entered the main aisle of the Temple.

•   •   •   •   •

Marisa had come to Etrusci in disguise. She smiled as she watched the happy couples from the back of the Temple. The brides were indeed lovely, even by her people's standards. She felt happy for them.

After the death and destruction I've watched both sides inflict on each other, it's good to see something which promotes life.

She smiled, knowing her disguise would last until well after the ceremony ended. Then she could return her to her ship.

My own project is coming along nicely. A careful search allowed me to find some of Liam's viable genetic material. The site of the battle between Liam and Azurius yielded some of Liam's cells, which contained the genetic material I need. Azurius's material is easy. It sits in a freezer back at my lab. It will take several years to extract what I need from Liam's cells, but I am patient. Then I will need to reformulate so it will combine with Azurius's DNA. The last part will require the most patience of all.

She would use the results to impregnate herself.

A little girl, she thought. *A little girl who will shake the Galactic Alliance to its foundations, given time.*

•   •   •   •   •

Jarek is right, Liam thought as he gazed at Celinia. *She is beautiful.*

Celinia stood at the Creator's altar with Teresina. Both wore flowing blue gowns with pure silver and gold trim, the Creator's colors. Teresina had a circlet of silver flowers in her hair. Celinia wore a tiara of gold flowers with silver trim, the mark of her rank in the Temple, and it set off her red hair beautifully.

Beside them stood two other priestesses. Friends he had not met yet. Kia should have been beside one of them.

The ceremony of marriage to a priestess differed from weddings of ordinary folks. He had only heard of it. Now he was living it.

Arch Priestess Arria stood behind the four. The older woman still looked quite attractive. She wore a similar gown but no crown. Instead, living flowers were woven into her silver-frosted dark hair. Behind her stood little Sylvia and Justin, awed by the ceremony.

Liam risked a glance at Gráinne, who stood next to Ephram, both in their respective dress uniforms. They smiled at him in encouragement.

They approached the altar, and Randolf fell to his knees before Teresina. Liam did likewise before Celinia. Both had eyes only for their intended. All other eyes focused on the brides. They looked radiant.

The arch priestess turned to Randolf. "Major Randolf, son of Marcus and Lidia, hero of the city. It pleases us to see you before us. What have you come for?"

"I come for the hand of your priestess, Teresina."

"Indeed," the arch priestess replied, "a great request. What do you offer her?"

Randolf looked up at Teresina. "The people considered my deeds great, but they pale compared to the prize I now ask. All I have of value is my heart, my life, my soul, myself."

"Teresina"—the arch priestess gestured to the girl—"you have heard his offer for your hand. Do you find his offer and him acceptable?"

"I do," Teresina replied. "What he offers is priceless. I gladly take his hand—forever and always." With that, she kneeled before him, took his hands in hers, and locked eyes with him.

"Master Sergeant Josephus, son of Titus and Drusilla, Priestess Xaviera, do you bear witness?"

Both said in unison, "We do."

"Captain Liam, son of Seámus and Deirdre, foster son of Marcus and Lidia," she began, turning to Liam, "hero and savior of the city through your valor and sacrifice. We are most pleased you have come before us. What do you seek from us?"

"I seek the hand of your high priestess, Celinia."

"Indeed, this is a great request," the arch priestess replied. "What do you offer her?"

"My deeds are not worth mentioning compared to the prize I ask. All I have to offer is my heart, my soul, my very existence. I tremble, for I fear it is still not enough."

"Celinia"—the arch priestess turned to her—"you have heard his offer. Do you find his offer and him acceptable?"

Celinia looked down at him. "He undervalues himself. I find his offer more than acceptable. It is precious. I take his hand with joy. Forever and always."

She kneeled before Liam. He felt as if he had wandered into a strange dream as she took both of his hands in hers, and once more, he lost himself in her eyes.

"Ambassador Jarek, son of Martek and Elandria, Priestess Sindee," the arch priestess asked, "do you bear witness?"

"We do."

Arch Priestess Arria took a large piece of blue-and-silver cloth from Justin and wrapped it around Randolf and Teresina. "The Creator wraps Her arms about you. May your union be blessed."

She took another piece of cloth from Sylvia, this one blue and gold, and wrapped it around Liam and Celinia. "The Creator sees into your heart Liam, foster child of Marcus and Lidia, child of Seámus and Deirdre. She knows your heart has been wounded since you were a child. Celinia's light will help you see through the darkness. The Creator wraps you both in Her arms. May your union be blessed."

The arch priestess was not done. She directed their eyes to the altar. Liam gasped. He saw his parents, Jorge, his foster parents, and the others who had died. He felt Celinia's hands squeeze his as the apparitions smiled. His birth mother actually winked at them. Then the vision faded.

"Stand now," the arch priestess directed. "Show yourselves to the assembled. Not as two, but as one."

The two couples turned to the congregation.

"Now, place a final seal on these unions with a kiss."

Celinia's kiss seemed to cause an explosion of joy in Liam's heart. At the same time, it brought peace. The throng erupted in thunderous cheers.

Celinia pulled back and whispered into his ear. "I will be with you, Liam. Forever and always."

"Forever and always," he repeated.

ABOUT THE AUTHOR

Kurt D. Springs is an adjunct professor of anthropology and archaeology in New Hampshire. He holds a PhD. in anthropology from the State University of New York at Buffalo, as well as a Master of Literature in archaeology from the National University of Ireland, Galway, and a Master of Liberal Arts in anthropology and archaeology from the Harvard University Extension School. His main area of interest is megalithic landscapes in prehistoric Ireland.

In his archaeological career, Kurt has done research in Western New York, New England, Ireland, Turkey, and Mauritius. In addition to his dissertation, he has published a number of articles and edited *Landscape and Identity: Archaeology and Human Geography* in the British Archaeological Report International Edition.

NOTE FROM KURT D. SPRINGS

Word-of-mouth is crucial for any author to succeed. If you enjoyed *Price of Vengeance*, please leave a review online—anywhere you are able. Even if it's just a sentence or two. It would make all the difference and would be very much appreciated.

Thanks!
Kurt D. Springs

We hope you enjoyed reading this title from:

www.blackrosewriting.com

Subscribe to our mailing list – *The Rosevine* – and receive **FREE** books, daily deals, and stay current with news about upcoming releases and our hottest authors.
Scan the QR code below to sign up.

Already a subscriber? Please accept a sincere thank you for being a fan of Black Rose Writing authors.

View other Black Rose Writing titles at
www.blackrosewriting.com/books and use promo code
PRINT to receive a **20% discount** when purchasing.

Printed in the USA
CPSIA information can be obtained
at www.ICGtesting.com
CBHW021647201223
2699CB00001B/3